WALL STREET WIVES

ANDE-ELLEN WINKLER

JOVE BOOKS, NEW YORK

WALL STREET WIVES

A Jove Book / published by arrangement with
Eakin Publications, Inc.

PRINTING HISTORY
Diamond Books edition published in 1989
Jove edition / October 1990

ISBN: 0-515-10439-6

Jove Books are published by The Berkley Publishing Group,
200 Madison Avenue, New York, New York 10016.
The name "JOVE" and the "J" logo
are trademarks belonging to Jove Publications, Inc.

PRINTED IN THE UNITED STATES OF AMERICA

10 9 8 7 6 5 4 3 2 1

For Steven
For living and breathing every paragraph,
every sentence, every word.
For everything.

Acknowledgment

My warmest thanks to Sonja Massie, my editor, my friend, for binding my wounds, for her generosity in bestowing happy faces, but most of all for seeing that tall, dark stranger on a sultry summer night.

Tell me not, in mournful numbers,
  Life is but an empty dream!
For the soul is dead that slumbers
  And things are not what they seem.

—H. W. Longfellow
  Voices of the Night

prologue

Chilling rain slashed through the dark afternoon sky, the downpour snarling the already impossible Washington traffic. Miserable pedestrians huddled on street corners in shivery knots. Their thin coats offered little protection from the wind and sheeting rain. At their feet water rushed through gutters clogged with soggy newspapers and mangled umbrellas. Thick clouds overhead obscured the Washington obelisk. From his marble throne Lincoln stared down on empty streets.

Across the Potomac in a locked, windowless room the air conditioning hummed at a steady sixty-eight degrees. The comfortable climate was lost on the three men who sat around the long rectangular table, studying the dossiers and photographs spread out on its surface. Some of the photos were taken from a great distance with a zoom lens; others were police mug shots or file shots from the morgue. Mixed in among them was a picture of an attractive couple, wearing formal clothes and smiling for the

1

camera, seemingly without a care in the world. Their happiness was jarringly out of place with the photographs of the dead, tortured women.

"Are you sure this is the best way to get him?" The operative was dressed impeccably, as always, in a custom-tailored suit. There was an aura of darkness about him that had nothing to do with his black clothing and dark hair, an air of violence. There was a hardness about him, a dangerous quality that the cold, hard glitter in his eyes did nothing to dispel.

"Yes. Besides, we've run out of choices. He eliminated our man, but that could work to our advantage here. He'd never suspect another infiltration into his organization and certainly not through this roundabout avenue." The superior had sharp features and calculating blue eyes behind horn-rimmed glasses. With his conservative tweed clothing and thin ascetic appearance, he looked more like a schoolteacher than the head of clandestine operations.

"Does he have to be here?" The dark-suited operative gestured to the silent man sitting at the end of the table.

"You know he does. It's agency policy." He nudged his glasses up, as was his habit when he was faced with something distasteful. "Everything's in place. Your first meeting has been arranged. If he doesn't make his move we have other means lined up. Some of those have already been set into motion, although I don't think we'll need them. From the aggressive stance the firm has been taking, I don't think they're likely to pass up an opportunity like you. You're almost too good to be true."

"Aren't I though," the man in black commented sarcastically.

"Are you positive he's the right man for the job?" The heavyset man broke his silence, his disapproval evident as he glanced at the operative. He tried for a show of authority by tugging on the vest that pulled across his bulging paunch, but the condition of his clothes, wrinkled, ill-fitting, and dotted with food stains, strained his credibility.

"We've been over this a hundred times. He's the best we have and he's been out of the agency long enough not to have a trail. The Arab is dangerous. I want someone who can handle him and stay one step ahead of him. My man also happens to have the business savvy to enter through the back door. And, by the way, I don't like having my judgment questioned." He gave his glasses a forceful shove and, taking a deep breath conceded, "No matter how good your intentions may be."

"You want me out, just say so." The operative leaned back in his chair and adopted a casual pose. Too casual. "This wasn't my idea."

"Take it easy. He didn't mean anything. Just remember what we're up against." The superior pointed to the photographs on the table.

The operative glanced down at the photographs. The victims, women. Long-haired beauties. Once they had been young and attractive. Alive. Now the camera's callous eye had captured their image as they would be remembered, as they had died: naked with bruises on their wrists and ankles, bruises from being bound and tied. Their beautiful, long hair wrapped around their slender necks—the killer's trademark.

"We want the Arab," the superior stressed needlessly.

The operative's jaw tightened, a muscle bunching, his darkness smoldering. "Don't worry," he said. "I'll get him."

chapter 1

Holding a glass of white wine in her hand, Ariane Wakefield wandered around the Atrium Club while her husband, Craig, and his partner, Russ Newman, were deep in conversation with two other men. She caught her reflection in the mirrored wall and absently smoothed her long, black hair which had been neatly swept back into a chignon. Her idle gaze swept the dimly lit room as she adjusted the gold chain on her black Chanel alligator purse. From where she stood on the balcony that overlooked the lower lounge, she recognized her friend, Jessica Cushing, coming up the mirrored staircase.

"Jess, what are you doing here?" As a divorced real estate agent with no ties to the securities business, Jessica's presence was distinctly out of place with the Wall Street crowd.

"Oh, good. I was hoping you'd be here. I have an appointment to show Colin and Hattie an apartment and he asked me to meet him here." Jessica glanced around the room. "Are these things always like this?"

Ariane's gaze followed Jessica's, surveying the buzzing crowd, trying to see it as an outsider would for the first time.

The wives, brought by their husbands, were quickly left by the wayside as the men gave up the pretense of polite small talk and gathered in tight cliques to discuss the business at hand. It was nothing new. After six years of marriage, Ariane was used to being ignored.

"Business as usual," Ariane said blithely.

"God, this is depressing."

"Why?"

"All these men and they're only interested in each other. I was hoping to get a date out of this, but they don't even look. I may as well be at one of our luncheons."

"God forbid," Ariane said. "What is it about one hundred women, all dressed to the teeth and locked in a hotel room, that seems so terribly lonely?"

"Probably because it's the highlight of their day, or their month. What else do they have?"

A wave of depression washed over Ariane, startling her with its force.

"What do you say we duck out and go for a drink?" Jessica suggested.

"Love to." Ariane knew Jessica was kidding, but for a moment she was sorely tempted, tempted to run out of that crowded, lonely room. "Uh-oh, too late now. We've been spotted." With a nod of her head she indicated the two women walking toward them.

Madelyn and Denise were on the entertainment committee for the upcoming charity dinner, and Ariane didn't particularly like either of them. Their idea of a hard-core decision was which lipstick to buy. How they managed to snag a committee for themselves was beyond her. Today the urgent topic of their conversation was what color stationery to use for the invitations to the dinner dance.

Ariane was nodding agreeably at whatever choice they made, her attention wandering, when Kristen Newman joined them.

"Excuse me, girls," Kristen interrupted, "but this can't wait. Have you heard about Joanna? Her husband is having an affair with her old college roommate."

"Oh? How do you know?" Ariane asked, hoping Kristen was wrong.

"Let's just say I have my sources." Kristen preened, grinning maliciously. "Anyway, it seems Joanna had been eager for Stuart to meet Diana for a long time. When Diana divorced her husband in Chicago and moved into the city, it was the perfect opportunity. Joanna introduced them, and they've been together ever since. Nothing like having a dumb little wife do your matchmaking for you."

"I don't believe it," Ariane said, ever the optimist. "It's probably just idle gossip."

Kristen squinted her blue eyes, obviously irritated at having her gossip questioned. "Well, Stuart told me himself. I'd hardly call that idle gossip, would you?" She spied a passing waiter and, grabbing his arm, fairly rubbed herself against him. "I'd love a glass of champagne," she breathed. "Of course, that's not what I really want but I guess it'll have to do for now."

She was at it again, Ariane observed. Kristen never ceased to amaze her. She seemed to feel it was her duty to flirt with every male in her path.

"And just what were you doing with Stuart?" Jessica interrupted, freeing the waiter.

"Why, talking, of course. What else? Actually, we've become quite close over the past few months." Kristen's smug answer left no doubt as to her meaning. "See you later," she called back over her shoulder as she left to join another group.

"Whew!" Jessica exclaimed when she left. "How, or rather *why*, do you put up with her, Ariane?"

"She's not that bad all the time," Ariane answered half-heartedly, feeling it her duty somehow to defend Kristen. "Anyway, I can't help but feel sorry for her."

Jessica's mood shifted immediately. "I know. Sometimes I forget. When I think about it I get the shakes." They all knew that Jessica was referring to Kristen's son, Teddy, who had died of leukemia two years before. Kristen had gone to pieces. "If anything ever happened to Kim or Lizzie I wouldn't want to live. I guess that's how she copes."

"Everybody has their own method of surviving," Ariane said. "I suppose that's hers." She was aware, however, that Kristen's actions had become more blatant, her remarks more cutting lately. "Besides, Craig and Russ are partners, so we're stuck with her."

In the bar across the room two men conversed, oblivious to the dramatic view of Fifty-seventh Street revealed by the wall of glass.

"I had an interesting visit with my doctor on Friday," Clayton remarked offhandedly.

Clayton Travers was the senior partner at Travers, Crawford, and Brooks, better known as T, C, and B on the Street. Clayton was in his early sixties, recently divorced from his faithful wife of thirty-five years, and recently married to blond, statuesque Lydia, some twenty years his junior. The hot romance between the president of T, C, and B and his former secretary had given Wall Street plenty to talk about.

"Oh? Good news about your cholesterol?" Craig said jokingly as his eyes roamed the crowd, registering the small cliques that had formed.

"Why yes, as a matter of fact, but something a little

more interesting.'' Clayton glanced around, then lowered his voice. ''Harley Pierson isn't well. Seems he needs by-pass surgery, and the prognosis isn't good.''

''How the hell did you find that out?'' Craig asked, his interest sharply piqued.

''We share the same doctor. His chart was on the doc-tor's desk and I happened to glance through it. So, what do you think?'' Clayton asked, feigning nonchalance.

''How bad is it?''

''Sounds bad. Definite retirement, if not worse.''

''Christ, I'd better start shorting the stock. Without Pierson in charge, Zendex isn't worth a damn. Anybody else know about this?'' Craig quickly calculated how much stock he could sell and how fast, without causing a col-lapse in the stock. Obviously, Clayton had already been protecting himself in the stock and that accounted for the stock's drop the last two days. Craig couldn't blame him for acting on the information first. He'd do the same thing and had several times.

''Not that I know of. This was a surprise to me. How long are you?''

''Long enough that when I start dumping it, there's go-ing to be a resounding thud on the Street.''

''You and me both. Let's just hope we can dump it fast enough before anyone else catches on and the price starts to fall.''

''Well, I guess this qualifies me for placing myself on the 'restricted list,' '' Craig quipped, adjusting the French cuff of his Turnbull and Asser custom shirt. ''Good thing I don't let the SEC or NASD's nit-picking interfere with my business, or they'd cost me plenty.''

The cocktail party ended early, allowing Ariane and Craig plenty of time to make their dinner reservation with Kris-ten and Russ at the Four Seasons. They followed the maître d' as he led them through the hallway that connected the Grill Room and the Pool Room, passing the huge Picasso tapestry on the wall.

"God, that was awful as usual. Did you see that ridiculous-looking woman in the short leather skirt? It was so tight she could barely move," Kristen announced once the four of them were seated at their table.

They were in the coveted Pool Room. The large, square pool in the middle dominated the softly lit, hushed atmosphere.

Ariane had to stifle a snicker. With Kristen's red silk dress slashed down to her waist, allowing anyone an unimpeded view of her large breasts, she was hardly the picture of decorum.

Craig and Russ nodded politely and then proceeded to discuss a new issue they were underwriting.

"Christ, I've heard enough business for one night," Kristen exclaimed. "Must I suffer through it over dinner too? It's so boring!"

Russ smiled sheepishly, a guilty look in his soft hazel eyes, his passiveness completely at odds with his wife's brazen behavior.

"All right, Kristen. There's just one thing we have to discuss and then I promise no more business."

Kristen flicked her mass of blond hair and stuck out her lower lip in an annoyed pout, the childish expression incongruous with the large, shiny red mouth.

Craig caught Ariane's eye and smiled at her. Ariane smiled back at her husband. Craig was a handsome man, his sapphire blue eyes and strong even features set off by wavy chestnut hair. He was approaching forty, his face wearing the years well except when he was overworked and the grooves on either side of his mouth became more pronounced.

Ariane was about to ask Craig about his day, but before

she could his attention was diverted by Russ—by business, as usual.

"There's a man I've been hearing mentioned a lot lately in reference to some very big money," Russ said, fidgeting with his fork, turning it over. "It seems he controls a wealthy syndicate and is always looking for new investments."

"What's his name? Where's he from?" Craig's interest was always stimulated at the possibility of a new investor.

Ariane undid the gold jacket buttons of her Chanel black suit and shrugged out of it. It was an awkward movement saved by the alert captain who hurried to her side to assist her. She smiled her appreciation and returned her attention to the fountains bubbling in the pool.

"All I know is his name, Alex Savage. I can't seem to get any concrete information on him, who he represents or anything else. I did learn that he owns one of the largest ranches in Texas. He raises cattle and horses, with a little oil business thrown in for diversification. He splits his time between his ranch and New York. Everyone seems to whisper his name in awe, but no one knows anything more about him."

"Well, if he manages that much money, I'm sure we can track him down and maybe entice him to give us his account. An account that size certainly couldn't hurt."

"I agree—"

"Gentlemen, your time is up," interrupted Kristen. "Ariane, that demure blouse is simply adorable. You look so sweet," she oozed.

"Thank you," Ariane returned, trying, as usual, to ignore Kristen's veiled barb.

Dinner ended and the captain wheeled over the double-tiered dessert cart. He waited for Craig and Russ to end their conversation before asking, "May I help you ladies choose a dessert?"

Kristen leaned forward, the deep vee of her dress falling open. "Why don't you try and tempt me?"

Ariane watched as the captain valiantly attempted to ignore Kristen's offering as he listed the desserts. *Some things never change*, Ariane thought.

After dinner Ariane and Craig climbed into their waiting black stretch limousine and started the drive home up Park Avenue. The April night had turned chilly and Ariane huddled against Craig, seeking his warmth, his closeness.

"Alone at last," she said, resting her hand on Craig's. It was the first time they'd touched all night. "How was your day?"

"Hectic, as usual. There doesn't seem to be enough hours in the day sometimes." His voice sounded tired.

"Anything in particular?" she asked, concerned about the faint lines she detected around his eyes.

"No. Just the usual. You wouldn't understand." Craig turned away to peer out the window.

Hurt clouded Ariane's eyes. She pulled her hand away, wishing Craig would notice, knowing he wouldn't.

Ten minutes later he unlocked the door to their spacious duplex on Park Avenue and motioned Ariane inside. She automatically reached for the light switch and tapped the appropriate plate. The computerized system turned on all the lights in the front half of the lower floor, dimming them for a nighttime setting.

Ariane's high-heeled pumps tapped loudly on the white and black marble floor as she passed the Régence giltwood mirror hanging above the George II console. She started up the wide, carpeted staircase when Craig's voice stopped her.

"I think I'll work in the study for a while. I'll be up later."

She turned, her hand poised on the well-polished mahogany banister. The light flashed off the flawless ten-carat emerald-cut diamond on her finger. "But it's late and you said you were tired. Why don't you leave it until tomorrow?"

"Because it can't wait until tomorrow." Craig's voice took on the familiar brusqueness he used when he was impatient. Ariane winced and his tone softened. "I'm not going to be very long. I just have a few things to take care of. Go on up to bed. Don't worry. I'll be fine."

"But I do worry about you. You've been working so hard lately. You must be exhausted."

"Unfortunately, I have no choice. If we're going to take over Compton Securities I've got to go through their books with a fine-tooth comb. Adding their network of international offices to ours will be a score for Newman Brothers. Don't wait up. Good night." Craig lightly brushed Ariane's lips before heading for his study.

"G'night." She was accustomed to going to bed alone. It didn't matter much.

Ariane passed through the peach bedroom, heading directly for her dressing room and bath. Sighing heavily, she leaned on the peach-gold marble vanity and stared intently at herself in the wall of mirror. Behind her was the immense marble shower, large enough for four with its custom rainfall showerhead and ten body sprays and the equally large Jacuzzi whirlpool tub with its eight jets. There was a pile of thick, white towels waiting for her on the antique Venetian stool. She had turned twenty-nine this winter and ever since had been looking for telltale signs of aging. Approaching thirty seemed like a milestone in her life.

Well, there was no sense in getting depressed over it, she decided. Her ivory skin was smooth and flawless, and her waist-length hair glistened like black satin as she brushed it out, the overhead lights bringing out its healthy shine. The dark eyes staring back at her from beneath finely arched brows were almond-shaped with a slight upward slant at the corners and fringed with thick black lashes. Her small nose tilted slightly upward at the end above a generous mouth.

She kept her body trim, working out in the apartment's gym, taking ballet lessons, and playing tennis. She wasn't tall. Standing at a petite five feet three inches, her long, slender lines made her appear taller. Her breasts were round and full and more than adequate, her waist narrow, her belly flat, her hips a soft curve. The endless sweating hours working with her personal trainer had paid off in shapely legs. She wasn't muscular by any stretch of the imagination, but her body was tight, with no hint of slack.

Maybe she didn't look thirty yet, but sometimes she felt ancient. There were times when she wondered why she bothered to get out of bed in the morning. It was the same routine every day: shopping, luncheons, parties, all tedious, meaningless chores.

In the beginning of their marriage, Ariane had wanted to go to work. She was a paralegal when she met Craig and had intended to return to her job after their honeymoon. But Craig simply wouldn't allow it: he was wealthy and his wife didn't have to work. They had argued briefly, but Craig was immovable on the subject and eventually she gave up the idea.

Ariane walked barefoot into the bedroom, her small feet nearly swallowed by the thickness of the plush peach carpeting. Dressed in an ivory-colored silk nightgown, she slipped between the Porthault monogrammed sheets of their king-sized bed. The linen was changed daily, a fresh scent wafting up from the perfectly pressed sheets. It had been so long, she thought, closing her eyes, so long since Craig had made love to her. Even if he wasn't going to make love to her she wished he would just hold her, touch her. It hadn't always been like this. In the beginning he seemed to have more time, more interest. She remembered their honeymoon.

It had been perfect. Two glorious sun-filled weeks in a private villa on Anguilla, with its pristine white beaches and the clear turquoise water of the Caribbean.

Ariane had been a virgin and terribly nervous. Dressed in a shimmering white silk nightgown, her anxiety clamped down tightly, she moved into her husband's arms. Craig was tender and gentle, his rising passion obvious as his kisses became insistent and heated.

Craig touched her between her thighs and she cringed, her mind suddenly flooding with unwanted memories of a certain afternoon long ago, an afternoon she had sought so hard to forget.

She saw the look on Craig's face, the hurt, the rejection, and she wanted to explain. She knew she should, but she couldn't. She didn't.

Sometimes, as Ariane lay alone in that king-sized bed, she wondered what would have happened if she had told him about that afternoon. Would he have understood? Would it have made a difference in their marriage? Would things have been different now? What was the use in going over it? It was her fault and it was too late now.

I ought to consider myself lucky, Ariane thought, trying to improve her mood. *Things could be worse. I have a wonderful husband, we're wealthy, and I have nothing to do but enjoy myself. So, what was wrong?*

When she woke in the morning, Craig had already left for the office. He had come to bed sometime in the middle of the night, barely disturbing her with his presence. She had been vaguely aware of his getting in and out of the bed, but she had learned through years of practice to force herself to sleep through it.

In the early morning light the room was aglow in a wash of pale peach. Everything was peach, from the plush carpeting to the raw silk fabric covering the walls.

Ariane had scouted the antique stores until she found two French commodes for nightstands, a stunning Louis XV desk, and a delicate French sewing table.

Craig had reluctantly allowed Ariane to furnish the bedroom but had insisted the rest of the apartment be decorated by one of the city's top designers, demanding a clear and obvious display of his wealth. The designer had turned it into a veritable showplace filled with overstuffed, downfilled, silk-covered sofas, priceless antiques, and an important art collection.

But the bedroom was hers and she took great pride in the fruits of her labor, especially pleased with the warm inviting glow the room seemed to give off even on the dreariest of days. Anyone who saw the room complimented her, surprised at her lack of formal training. But she had always had a knack with color and design and once had even entertained the thought of entering the fashion industry as a clothing designer. Now that was long forgotten.

Ariane donned a silk robe to match her gown, then opened the French doors to the terrace and stepped outside. The sky was blue and it looked like the beginning of a rare clear spring day. She sniffed the air and believed she could detect the scent of spring, though it was nearly masked by the car fumes. Being a country girl, she had always loved the arrival of spring. It marked the end of a long, dismal winter and the beginning of a reawakening. Everything around her seemed to come alive. The grass would turn a vibrant green, small pale green buds would appear like magic on dead-looking bare trees, and the pointed leaves of long forgotten bulbs would begin pushing their way through the soil, eager for the warming rays of the sun that would encourage their explosion of color. Spring was soft and sweet-smelling, a season of rebirth. Spring was the beginning of Ariane's year and winter the end.

She was sitting on the terrace, glancing through *Town and Country*, when the portable telephone rang.

"Hello."

"Hold on a minute, Ariane. What do you mean he doesn't know the trade? Tell the bastard if he doesn't know it I'll rip out the goddamn wire and wrap it around his neck. I'm not eating a $50,000 error." It was Craig. She was used to being put on hold or having their conversations end abruptly. It came with the territory. "You still there?"

"Of course. What's going on?"

"Just the usual disasters, nothing I can't handle. But I won't be able to make it home for dinner tonight. If I don't stay and fix the problem now, no one will."

"When do you think you'll be home? Should I have Hilda leave a late dinner for you?" She was accustomed to eating alone.

"No. Don't bother. I'll catch something here. I'll try not to be too late. Bye."

She shouldn't be surprised. Craig was hardly ever home these days. But it was bothering her more and she didn't know why. Maybe spring was just beginning, but there was nothing new or reborn about her marriage, her life.

Craig hung up the receiver and swiveled his gray leather chair around so that he faced out into the late afternoon sky above the dark caverns that made up the area known as Wall Street. He stood and, lacing his hands behind his back, looked down at the rush-hour traffic. Below him workers were dodging the steady stream of cars, weaving their way through the shadowed, narrow streets.

Yes, he had work to do all right, Craig thought to himself. But he allowed himself this short break to savor the prospects of the upcoming business deal. It was taking all his efforts and then some to work this one out, but it would be well worth it. He smiled with satisfaction and nearly rubbed his hands together in eager anticipation when he thought of the Arab, Hassan, and the money he would bring with him.

Craig turned toward his granite-topped desk and glanced at the conference area, remembering how it all began more than twenty years ago. Princeton. A new world. A new life. He learned, absorbed, changed, evolved. He became another person. He picked his friends carefully, surrounding himself with young men who could help him in his new life, choosing only those who could be of use. And then he met Russ Newman, heir apparent to Newman Brothers, and knew he had met his future.

Tapping his platinum Mont Blanc pen on the gray stone, he looked with satisfaction at the pair of gray leather sofas, the gray lacquer tables, the Lucite lamps with black shades. A plant of miniature white orchids brightened the room. Matching silver Buccellati bowls sat on each end table, and a Léger hung above one sofa.

Craig had met Hassan Bjerabi quite by accident some months before at a cocktail party given by a company that had recently gone public. After being introduced by his friend, Brad, who had done the initial public offering, Craig found he and Hassan had an interesting trait in common: they both loved making money.

Hassan represented a number of wealthy Arabs interested in investing in American companies anonymously. There were so many ways to make money in the stock market, both legally and otherwise, but there was no sense in calling undue attention to themselves. With the widespread insider-trading investigations continuing, it was just as well the public didn't get in an uproar over Arabs taking over the market. If Hassan and his group remained unknown, it would be much easier for Craig to wheel and deal freely. And Craig needed all the freedom and independence he could get if he was going to put his plans into motion. Between Hassan's millions, Craig's creativity, and their shared lack of scruples, nothing would stand in their way.

Craig's eyes strayed to the priceless Khorassan carpet that broke the deliberate monotony of the gray silk-covered walls and gray marble floor. The Rodin sculpture on his desk was slightly off and he moved it one inch to the right.

It was going to be simple to avoid the SEC's rules of disclosure by using Hassan's offshore accounts in various names and by parking stock with Brad and Clayton. It was going to be a piece of cake.

chapter 2

Even though Ariane and Craig arrived late for the gala at the Metropolitan Museum of Art, there was still an endless stream of black stretch limousines lining Fifth Avenue.

Ariane could see Craig's impatience growing as they sat in line, waiting their turn, barely moving at all. He had been late, as usual, in coming home and had rushed through the apartment in a frenzy of activity.

"We'll be there soon enough," she said.

"I can see that. I just don't understand why they can't figure these things out. Are they surprised that three hundred limos showed up?"

Craig's voice was ripe with annoyance. After years of experience, Ariane knew better than to try to coax him out of it. She smoothed the black silk chiffon of her Galanos gown, the movement sending sparkles of light off her diamond bracelets, and leaned back with a sigh, knowing it was going to be a long night.

Eventually, they entered the Temple of Dendur. The

softly lit room glowed golden in the flickering candlelight. The tables were covered with gold lamé, as were the chairs that were festooned with ribbons and bows. White flowers with gilded leaves spilled from golden bowls.

United Cancer Fund was one of the most prestigious charities in the city. Anyone who was anyone was here tonight, the invitation greatly sought after, the $1,000 per person ticket highly coveted. Unlike the usual Wall Street functions which catered only to that industry, this dinner attracted all the captains of industry—from the garment center, to real estate, to Wall Street. The capacity crowd of more than five hundred held the cream of Manhattan society, encompassing both the old money of the Astors, Dukes, and Vanderbilts and the new money of the Steinbergs, Tisches, and Trumps. If a bomb were dropped here tonight, all of New York City would grind to a halt.

The women, in their finest gowns, their hair perfectly coiffed, wearing priceless glittering jewels removed from vaults only hours before, came to be seen and admired. The men came to be seen, to see, and to deal. In the enormous room a current of excitement hummed beneath the laughing voices and clinking glasses, a relentless pulsing, a steady drumming. It was the beat of money. Big money.

"I need a drink. What do you want?" Craig asked Ariane as they made their way to one of the half-dozen bars flanking the room.

"White wine," Ariane answered, glancing around the crowded room, looking for a familiar face.

Craig returned, drinking heavily from his glass of scotch, and handed Ariane her wine goblet.

"I see Clayton. I have to talk to him. You don't mind, do you?"

Ariane knew that Craig's question was merely a formality and he had every intention of seeking Clayton out, regardless of her wishes. Why should this party be any different than any other?

"No, of course not. Go ahead."

"Clayton, have I got a deal for you." Craig pumped Clayton's hand enthusiastically.

"Oh? And what would that be, an insider in Obermaier's office?" Clayton referred to Otto Obermaier, the new United States attorney for the Southern District, better known as New York.

"No, but I'm working on it. In the meantime I've got a little private placement going. I'm going to bring in Brad, Stuart, and Eric. Want to play?"

"Sure. How much? Not that it matters. If you're running it, it's sure to be a winner."

"Twenty-five grand. We'll build up some PR and take it public around November. We should score a real home run with this one."

"Sounds good to me. What's the name?"

"Anatech. By the way, did you ever get around to the drug testing you were talking about?" Though some firms were worried about the rampant use of cocaine on the Street, Craig didn't care as long as his employees performed well and kept it out of the office.

Clayton smiled broadly. "You're going to love this. I told you I really didn't want to do the testing, too many repercussions. But Crawford insisted. He's real uptight about drugs. Anyway, he decided the best way to do it was to disguise it as part of a health examination for life insurance. It went pretty well except for one guy who failed. Guess who?"

"I'll bite."

"Crawford's son-in-law." Clayton burst out laughing.

• • •

Left alone by Craig, Ariane wandered aimlessly through the crowded room until she found Joanna Conway.

"How are your French lessons coming along?" Ariane asked.

"I gave them up."

"Why? I thought you were looking forward to conversing with the natives in their own tongue," Ariane said, referring to Joanna's upcoming trip to France.

"We're not going," Joanna answered tightly.

"Oh? Why?"

"It seems Stuart can't get away right now. He's tied up . . . or is it down? I forget."

"Maybe things will ease up and he'll take off," Ariane said, uncomfortable at Joanna's veiled reference.

"You know, Ariane, you're probably the only decent person here."

"Thank you . . . I think. But I'm sure I'm not the only one."

"No? Look around. They're sharks with the scent of blood in the air, circling, looking for the kill. And tonight they're in a feeding frenzy, crazed with the need to devour. But they're really cannibals, you know, because they eat their own."

"I think you're exaggerating." Ariane tried to lighten the mood, not liking how bitter and morose Joanna sounded.

"Am I?" Joanna asked, and then she suddenly switched moods. "What table are you at?"

"Thirty-seven. You?"

"Fourteen. I wonder who I'm paired with." The executive committee of UCF made the seating arrangements, preferring to split husbands and wives with the purpose of making the evening more interesting.

"Looks like we're about to find out," Ariane remarked as dinner was announced.

Ariane's dinner partner was Trenton Hadley-Smythe, or Trent, as he preferred to be called when he introduced himself. He was classically handsome, in his late thirties, tall, with a well-developed muscular body, dark blond hair, and pale blue eyes. On Ariane's other side was Gilbert Hoskins, a senior partner at Goldman Sachs, a gruff and brusque man with constantly darting, narrow brown eyes. Ariane was introduced to him at the same time as Trent.

"Wakefield?" Gilbert questioned shortly. "Newman Brothers."

So that was her identity. "Yes."

"I'm sure the lady has other attributes as well," Trent commented smoothly.

"Yeah," Gilbert answered before turning his attention away.

"I hope you're not going to make me a liar," Trent said, leaning toward Ariane.

"Absolutely not. I'm a world-famous brain surgeon," Ariane answered, finding Trent terribly attractive.

"Good. Maybe you could put one in Gilbert's head," Trent whispered.

"I don't have one small enough." They laughed together.

"Trent, how wonderful we're at the same table," an attractive woman said as she took the empty seat next to him.

"Hello, Hattie," Trent said politely and then introduced Ariane to Hattie Davis.

Hattie was tall and reed slim, her platinum blond hair pulled back severely, drawing her fixed white features into a tight mask. She resembled someone who had been in a devastating car accident and had her face put back together. Everything was perfect but it didn't look real. Her cold green eyes flicked over Ariane and turned back to Trent as she whispered in his ear.

Ariane's napkin slipped, and as she leaned toward Trent to retrieve it she couldn't help but notice Hattie's hand moving up the inside of Trent's thigh.

"Would you like to dance?" Trent asked, his invitation taking Ariane by surprise.

"Yes."

"So, do you come here often?" Trent said flirtatiously as he led Ariane to the dance floor and took her in his arms.

"Only when forced." Ariane couldn't remember when she'd danced with anyone except Craig. And dancing with Craig was a rarity in itself. Trent took her by surprise. Maybe it was the way he looked at her, his pale blue eyes intent, as if he were actually seeing her. She wasn't used to having a man notice her. At these affairs the men talked to each other over the women, around the women, as if they weren't there.

"Do I detect the voice of a rebel lurking in there?" Trent smiled easily, charming her, revealing becoming dimples.

"No. Just the voice of boredom." But she wasn't bored now. She was too conscious of Trent's muscular body, of his hand on her back, of the faint, woodsy scent of his cologne.

"Fear not, my lovely. You'll not be bored tonight," Trent promised, his voice seductive. "I'll see to it."

The ladies' room was large and crowded, filled with women repairing their make-up and gossiping. Ariane couldn't get near the mirror, so she took out the small mirror from her Harry Winston gold and diamond minaudière to check her lipstick.

Lydia and Kristen emerged from the same stall and, noticing Ariane, Lydia came toward her.

"Can I borrow that?" Lydia asked, taking the mirror

from Ariane. She wiped at her nose, checking her reflection carefully. "The only way to get through one of these parties. If I had known you were here I would have invited you to our little party. Want some?"

"Don't be ridiculous. She doesn't even know what you're talking about. She probably thinks you're offering to powder her nose." Kristen laughed at her double meaning.

"No thanks, I don't indulge in that kind of powder," Ariane replied. She self-consciously played with her diamond earring.

"Well, you ought to try it, at least with Craig," Lydia said. "I sprinkle some magic powder on Clayton and it's like we're in the middle of a bull market. He goes for hours. Ooh, I get hot just thinking about it. Speaking of which, who is that gorgeous thing you're paired with?"

Ariane tilted her head, patting her hair. "Wouldn't you like to know?"

"Mmm . . . sounds interesting. Care to switch?"

"No. Take mine," Kristen said. "He only talks in eighths."

"I think I'll find Clayton and persuade him to meet me for a little quickie," Lydia said.

"Here?" Ariane asked.

"Sure. This place is so huge there must be a million places. And let's face it, that's what he married me for," Lydia finished in her usual candid way.

"Really? I thought it was for your brain." Kristen snickered.

"It was," Lydia said. "Only he doesn't realize it."

"At least he wants you for something. Russ is home so rarely sometimes I wonder what he needs me for."

Ariane heard the loneliness and rejection in Kristen's voice and empathized with her only too well. "I know what you mean."

"Well, I for one am not going to sit around waiting. If he doesn't want me, I'll find someone who does."

Suddenly, Ariane understood Kristen's behavior. She didn't condone it, but she certainly identified with Kristen's need. How often had she sat home alone, waiting, wishing, wanting more?

"Things should calm a bit after the Compton take-over," Ariane said.

"What Compton thing? What are you talking about?" Kristen asked.

"Newman Brothers is buying Compton. Didn't you know?" Ariane was surprised at Kristen's ignorance. How could she not be concerned about her husband's business?

"No. Who cares what they do?"

"I do. Doesn't Russ tell you what's going on?" Actually, Ariane wanted to know more about Craig's affairs but he didn't think it was necessary. It was all she could do to pry this much out of him.

"No. And I couldn't care less."

"Besides," Lydia interjected, "who understands what they're talking about anyway? All I know is Clayton makes the money and I spend it. A very equitable arrangement."

They left the ladies' room together, and Ariane wandered off in the opposite direction. There were dozens of rooms, all dimly lit, all empty. Except one. Ariane froze, unable to move, her eyes fixed.

Hattie Davis sat on a table, her head tossed back, her arms leaning on the table, supporting her weight. The white crepe Yves St. Laurent dress was bunched up around her waist, her long white legs wrapped around her partner's hips, a partner who wasn't her husband but a young, attractive man who was thrusting wildly into her.

Ariane stood, mesmerized by the carnal scene. Hattie was panting, her white throat arched, the tendons in her neck taut. Her lover slowed his tempo, his movements taunting and teasing. Hattie's hand closed around him, stroking, fondling, urging him on. Her partner opened his eyes, pulled her hand away, and began plunging savagely.

Ariane backed away, unnoticed by the lovers. She strolled back to the party, shocked and embarrassed by what she had seen. But it was more than that. She was jealous.

"I was afraid you'd deserted me," Trent said teasingly when she sat down. "I was going to go and look for you, but I was afraid of what I'd do if I caught you alone."

Trent's words, coupled with the scene she had just witnessed, sent a hot blush to Ariane's pale features. Would he want to ravish her and take her on a table like Hattie's lover had? How could she think such a thing? It wasn't like her at all.

"It's late," Ariane said, aware that the party was winding down, and noticing Hattie's return.

"It's a shame you're leaving. Perhaps we could continue our conversation over lunch one day?" The look in Trent's pale blue eyes suggested something more.

"No. I don't think so," Ariane answered slowly. "I'm very busy." *So that's how it begins,* she thought. Meeting at a party, then a "casual" lunch. So simple. So easy.

"I see," he said with a well-placed sigh. "It's been a pleasure meeting you, and I can only hope our paths cross again. But I warn you, next time you won't get away so easily."

"I thought the party was particularly good, didn't you?" Craig asked on their way home.

"Yes."

"How was your table? Mine wasn't bad. Did you know that Clayton's ex-wife tried to commit suicide when he left? He told me tonight. They tried to keep it quiet and shipped her off to a sanitarium in Europe for a rest. Clayton says she's fine now and he's financing her so she can open a clothing boutique. I think that's very good of him."

"Oh yes . . . lucky Katharine." Ariane had known Katharine Travers for years before Clayton had left her. She was a kind, quiet woman who had been content to stay home and raise their three children. Ariane had liked her.

Craig shot her a sharp look in the darkened limousine. "And what's that supposed to mean?"

"Nothing. I'm glad Clayton's helping her."

It was nine o'clock the next morning, the market opening only a half hour away, when Craig entered Newman Brothers' large trading room. This was the aspect of the brokerage business he loved best—the actual buying and selling of stock. As a market maker, Newman Brothers could change the price of a stock, forcing it up or down by an eighth, a quarter, a half, enough to profit from its position.

The room was relatively quiet now, the thirty-odd traders reviewing their lists of stocks, getting ready for the opening, preparing themselves for the madness that would begin precisely at nine-thirty. They were thoroughbreds at the gate, trained and primed for the race, their adrenaline pumping as they waited anxiously for the starting bell.

No designer decor was evident in the room, no fine furniture indicative of the wealth being made. Only a staggering amount of electronics worth hundreds of thousands of dollars.

Each trader sat at his place surrounded by an array of computers with multiple screens constantly flashing the changing markets. Desks were actually telephone consoles that blinked continuously with incoming calls from over one hundred firms. Traders had assistants; assistants had assistants. A good trader could be responsible for as many as two hundred and fifty stocks.

"The market's going to scream," Craig announced to the room as he took his seat next to Louis. "Let's be ready."

Instantaneous decisions would be made on information, on the feel of the market, or on blind intuition.

Once the market opened there would be no coffee breaks, no free time. Lunches would be gulped down at the desk. Traders only left the room to answer an occasional call of nature.

The market opened. Voices began shouting numbers, names of stocks, bids, and offerings. Fingers moved swiftly over keyboards seeking information. Wire lights winked. Private telephones rang incessantly. The room was alive. The race was on.

Craig punched Brad's private number. He got right to the point. "Hey, buddy, I have to take a haircut. The auditors are here and I want to build up my capital. Can I park 100,000 shares of Oxtel with you for a couple of three days? I'll sell it to you at twenty and buy it back at twenty and a half. Deal? Done."

While he was on the phone, Craig had punched up Sanimere on the computer, one of the stocks Newman traded. "Who the hell are these guys that are bidding me in between the markets?"

Louis glanced at the screen. "I think it's Moreland. They've been doing it to us all week. No matter how low our price is, they come in lower."

Craig's eyes narrowed. "Raise the price of the stock. I'll call Clayton and have him do the same. Screw Moreland."

Louis punched in the price change and Sanimere immediately went from seventeen and a half to eighteen.

"Craig," Eddie shouted across the room, trying to be

heard above the screaming and yelling. "Stuart wants to know what you want him to do in Sani?"

"Tell him to go up a half," Craig yelled back. Maybe now Moreland will think twice before messing with his markets.

"Craig, I'm still trying to fill that 10,000 share order in Lextec," Frankie bellowed.

"Damnit. Call Peter over at Island and tell him to step up to the plate and fill or kill my order." Craig had no tolerance with indecisiveness, no patience with slowness. Craig had no patience.

The elevator in Lenox Hill Hospital was crowded, the passengers jostling for space. Doctors carelessly discussed their patients' conditions while anxious visitors chatted or silently stared straight ahead. The scent of a visitor's fresh bouquet of flowers was overwhelmed by the unpleasant odor from the tray of cafeteria food held by an aid.

Ariane got off on the fifth floor and walked toward PCU, the Progressive Care Unit. Across the hall was CCU, the Coronary Care Unit that served critically ill patients. She passed the nurses' station, its dozen television screens blinking the status of each cardiac patient through remote monitors attached to their chests.

Ariane greeted the nurses. After two years of volunteer work she was well acquainted with them.

"Ariane, I'm glad I caught you," Dr. Wallace said, looking up from a patient's chart. "I'd like to talk with you. Are you free?"

"Sure."

Dr. Edward Wallace was in his early thirties, the new boy wonder of LHH. He'd come directly from an impressive start at the Texas Heart Institute, complete with fellowship and honors. Now he had taken it upon himself to revamp the hospital's cardiology department that had been languishing under Dr. Spinoza. Tall and thin with wavy brown hair and kind blue eyes, he was filled with a youthful enthusiasm that was infectious.

He led Ariane into the doctors' lounge down the hall and offered her a chair.

"I think you're doing a great job here. We all do," he began immediately. "You have no idea how much your presence has meant to some of the patients. Attitude is important with a heart patient. Sometimes it's half the battle to getting them well again."

"Thank you. But I just talk to them," Ariane said with a shrug.

"No. We've had volunteers that have left the patients climbing the walls or in the depths of despair. You're something special. I've watched you and believe me, I know what I'm talking about, so don't argue with me. You know the doctor's always right." He winked at her and she smiled.

"So, I want to offer you a full-time job as patient/doctor liaison. You've been here long enough to pick up the medical terms, and with a little more training you'd be fine. Your role would be sort of chief hand holder."

"I don't know. It sounds a little scary."

"Look, they're even willing to pay you, and that's no small thing. Of course, I wouldn't count on getting rich on what they're offering, but you will be able to afford to eat in the cafeteria." He shuddered, then smiled.

Ariane returned his smile. "Can I let you know tomorrow?" She couldn't make a major decision like this without first discussing it with Craig. After all, he was her husband.

Craig was late coming home, but Ariane decided to wait and join him for dinner, eager to talk over her job offer with him. When he finally arrived, she met him at the door and, leading him into the living room, offered him a scotch.

"What did I do to deserve such a warm welcome?" he asked. "It's not my birthday, is it?"

"No. I just thought I'd have a late dinner with you."

"Great. Let's sit for a while first."

"Bad day?"

"No more than usual." He loosened his tie and opened his shirt collar. "By the way, leave Thursday open. Canfield and his wife are coming in and we're taking them out for dinner. Hmm, that's better," Craig said as he took a deep swallow of his drink and leaned back on the sofa.

"I went to the hospital today," Ariane began hesitantly.

"That's nice."

"They offered me a job."

"Doing what?"

"As a patient/doctor liaison," Ariane answered and proceeded to outline her job.

"Sounds awful. Why would you even contemplate such a thing? Hanging around sick people all day? Must be depressing."

"It is sometimes. But I like it. It makes me feel as if I'm doing something worthwhile with my life, as if I'm needed," Ariane answered honestly, realizing how empty her life was, how empty she felt.

"I thought being my wife was enough."

"Oh, Craig. This has nothing to do with you."

"Doesn't it? When are you going to have the time to attend to my needs? What about your charity committees? You know I need those contacts for my business. And it's almost summer. We entertain every weekend out at the house. How are you going to manage that if you're working every day in the city? And what about vacations? You won't be able to just up and leave whenever the mood strikes you, you know. You'll have people depending on you. You'll have responsibilities. Have you given that any thought?'' he asked quietly.

Ariane hadn't. She had been so proud and pleased to have been offered the job, she hadn't thought it through completely. Now Craig's reasoning made her see how foolish she had been to contemplate such an undertaking.

''No.'' She never realized how much she had been looking forward to accepting the job until she felt her enthusiasm evaporate in the face of Craig's logic. ''But I can still do it. My God, what's the big deal of entertaining? A trained monkey could do it.''

Craig looked at her oddly. ''Do you really think you're capable of such a job? Sounds awfully technical to me and much too demanding.''

Dr. Wallace had thought she was capable, and she wanted this, needed it. How dare Craig tell her she was unqualified. ''I can do it,'' Ariane repeated with determination, her anger making her dark eyes bright.

''I'd rather you didn't. You know how I feel about you working.''

''Fine.'' Bitter resignation made her voice clipped. ''I'll tell Dr. Wallace my husband thinks I'm incapable.'' The sarcasm couldn't alleviate her depression.

''Good. I know you're making the right decision.''

After her phone call to Dr. Wallace the next morning, Ariane drove out to the beach house in Southampton. Traffic was light and she made the trip quickly. In less than two hours the red Mercedes coupe pulled into the hidden circular drive of the old, white-shingled house on Gin Lane.

She needed a day at the beach. She naturally gravitated toward the beach when something was bothering her or she needed a change. Lately she'd been coming out more frequently.

When Craig had bought the house, the dark, handsomely polished, wood-paneled interior had been gutted and replaced with lacquered walls, marble floors, and a large expanse of sliding doors that overlooked the swimming pool and ocean. Ariane had opposed Craig's plans to modernize the interior, preferring to leave some of the old charm of wood paneling and molding, but she had long ago learned to give up her objections in the face of Craig's stubbornness.

She headed for the sliding doors and the beach. It was chilly, but she found the fresh salt air exhilarating. There were times when she wanted to stay at the beach and never return to the city.

The solitary walks on the windswept sand, with nothing but the roar of the ocean to fill her head, usually left her refreshed. But not this time. Something was gnawing at her, a vague feeling of uneasiness that defied description. She couldn't seem to remember the last time she felt truly happy. Something was eluding her grasp.

The sun was turning golden, casting long shadows on the beach. Checking the time on her gold and diamond Bulgari watch, she realized the lateness of the hour. She walked back to the house for her drive to the city, no less troubled than when she had come out.

When the doorbell rang early the next evening, Ariane flew to the door too eager to wait for Hilda, the housekeeper, to answer it. The moment she opened the door a tall woman with wild auburn hair and sparkling green eyes rushed into the apartment. The two young women fell into each other's arms, laughing as they embraced.

"Kingsley, you're a sight for sore eyes! You look great," Sloane exclaimed, reverting to calling Ariane by her maiden name as she had when they were younger.

"You don't look too bad yourself for a world-weary traveler. Come in and tell me everything."

They walked up the stairs, their arms linked around each other's waists, chatting like a couple of teenagers. Ariane led Sloane into the pale pink guest room filled with fresh flowers and they both sat on the queen-sized bed.

"So, what were you and Justin doing in London?" Ariane asked, her hand moving over the pink satin comforter.

Leaning forward intently, Sloane began, "Well, we have the most fabulous script. Really, it's the best we've ever read. It's an old-fashioned love story with pain and suffering and the works. But never mind, you can read it for yourself. I have a copy . . . Anyway, the only problem was in casting. Justin got Samantha Evans for the female lead and was going mad trying to cast the male lead when he saw a Carlo Orsini film. That's why we flew to London."

"Ooh, Carlo Orsini. He's wonderful."

"I know. Justin has him all but convinced, but there are a few minor details they have to work out. Justin was afraid to let Carlo out of his sight, so he invited himself to Carlo's villa in Italy. And that's how I got time off to visit you."

"Will you be working on the film?"

"You bet." Sloane's green eyes sparkled with pride. "Producer, right here in the flesh. As soon as Justin signs Carlo, we start shooting. We have all our backing with private investors and a hefty chunk from some rich Texan. Justin didn't want to go to a studio because he wants complete control and total secrecy. So, how's your job at the hospital?"

Ariane looked away, unable to meet Sloane's gaze. "I quit."

"You quit? Why? I thought you loved it."

"I did, but they wanted me to work full-time and I was afraid it would take away from my time with Craig. I do have responsibilities as his wife."

Annoyance flickered across Sloane's features. "Of course."

"I'm glad you're here," Ariane said as she reached over and patted her friend's hand affectionately. There was almost something desperate in the gesture.

"Me too." Sloane had a questioning tone in her voice. Her eyes searched Ariane's. "How is Craig?"

"Fine. But he's been working so hard lately that I don't know how he does it. He's so driven that it worries me," Ariane confessed, her dark eyes troubled.

"Why?"

"I don't know exactly. It's just that sometimes I get the feeling that he's obsessed with making money. He doesn't seem to enjoy anything else."

"Maybe the two of you need to get away. Why don't you go off someplace alone, to a deserted beach in the Caribbean? No telephones and no office."

"I suggested that all winter but something always came up and he couldn't get away. Eventually, I just stopped asking." Ariane's throat tightened, cutting off the rest of her words. But she didn't need to say any more. As Sloane's hand squeezed hers, Ariane knew that her best friend understood. Sloane had always understood.

The tall, dark-haired man entered the house, his well-worn western boots leaving a trail of Texas dust on the dark wood floors. On a working ranch the dust was something one learned to ignore.

He entered his study and sat at the large walnut desk. It was old and scarred, two generations of his family having left their marks on it. There was a document in front of him and he picked it up, flipping through the pages of the movie contract. He signed it and tossed it aside.

He glanced at the pictures scattered on his desk—the couple, the man, the woman. Ignoring all of them, he picked up the picture of the dark-haired woman and peered intently at her image.

"Tom said I'd find you in here." A man with tawny brown hair and a Texas tan to match entered the study and stood next to the desk. "She's a real beauty," he commented, looking down at the photo.

The man dropped the picture, not answering.

chapter 3

"I think an evening out with the two most beautiful women in New York requires champagne," Craig declared with a flourish at their table at Le Cirque the next night.

"Well, you're certainly chipper after a hard day at the office," Sloane said. "What did you do, buy up all of IBM?"

"No, not exactly. But I'm close to finalizing a very important deal."

"Is it the Mid-East deal?" Ariane asked.

"Yes. Just one more trip there ought to tie up any loose ends."

Ariane's heart sank. "Don't tell me you're going away again. It seems you just got back. And Sloane is here. I thought we'd all be able to spend some time together."

Craig patted Ariane's hand. "Now darling, I won't be gone long. Actually, I thought this would be a good time to go, not that I have a choice really, but Sloane will keep you company. You'll be able to stay, won't you, Sloane?"

Irritation flashed in Sloane's green eyes before she turned from Craig to Ariane.

"Sure I will," she replied evenly. "Come on, Kingsley. We'll have fun. Two beautiful women, alone, loose in New York. Hell, we'll have a ball."

Later that evening in their bedroom, Craig surprised Ariane by taking his Hermès suitcase from the closet.

"Craig, what are you doing?"

"Packing."

"Yes, I can see that. I mean when are you leaving?"

"Tomorrow." He walked back into his dressing room to gather more clothes.

Ariane waited for him to get into bed before pursuing the subject.

"When you announced your trip this evening, I didn't know you meant to leave tomorrow. Isn't this rather sudden?" she asked, not a little annoyed as he proceeded to read a prospectus.

"It's business, Ariane, and I can't arrange my schedule to suit you," Craig snapped in the condescending tone that Ariane had come to despise.

"I didn't ask you to schedule your business to suit me, but I think you could afford me the courtesy of letting me know your plans. I am your wife, you know." Anger caused her usually soft voice to sound sharp to her own ears.

"I know. And I'm your husband, the one who goes to work every day to keep you in the style you've grown accustomed to. So don't tell me how to run my business."

Ariane rolled over, turning away from him. Maybe she should be more like other bored, wealthy wives and rack up monstrous bills on Craig's credit cards while he was gone. Make him pay for ignoring her. Or maybe she could have an affair with a dark, gorgeous, mysterious man. Maybe then Craig would notice her.

"God, I'm exhausted," Sloane complained as she took her seat at the small table outside Bice. The tables were quickly being claimed by late shoppers too tired to go home and business people needing to relax at the end of a harrowing New York City day.

"Don't blame me. This wasn't my idea," Ariane said, placing her shopping bag of Fogal stockings on the floor beneath her chair. "You know how I feel about shopping. Honestly, I can't understand how some women make it their life's ambition. I'd rather be at the beach."

Sloane grinned. "Maybe. But that didn't stop you from picking up a Bill Blass and a Geoffrey Beene at Elizabeth Arden."

"No. I guess it didn't." In a perverse way Ariane was glad she had spent Craig's money frivolously. Maybe this would make him pay attention to her. If not, it served him right.

The choking smell of carbon monoxide from the barely crawling, crosstown traffic on Fifty-fourth Street didn't stop the customers from ordering their Bellinis and enjoying the passing crowds.

"Maybe this is all I was cut out to do," Ariane mused aloud.

"Don't be ridiculous. How could you think such a thing?"

"I realized the other night my claim to fame is being 'Wakefield's wife.' Sometimes I feel I'm just an appendage of Craig, and an unimportant one at that."

"Maybe you've taken your devotion to your husband too far." Sloane toyed with her champagne glass. "What about the charity work you do?"

Ariane let out a sigh of disgust. "Please . . . thirty

women sitting around, drinking Bloody Marys, having lunch in a hotel is not my idea of charity work. All they can talk about is which dress to buy. I find all that self-importance revolting.''

''You've got to find something to do instead of sitting in that mausoleum of yours surrounded by Braque, Kandinsky, and Rodin, waiting for His Highness to come home.''

''It's not like that!'' Ariane said, denying Sloane's accurate assessment of how she had been feeling lately.

Sloane glanced away, studying the crowd. ''What a great pickup place.''

Ariane idly followed Sloane's gaze, not really caring. *She should consider herself lucky,* she thought. *Things could be worse.*

''Don't look, but I think there's a man watching us,'' Sloane muttered. ''No, I think he's watching you.''

''Where? Who?''

''To your right. He's got black hair, and he's gorgeous.'' She paused. ''Yes, he's definitely watching you.''

Ariane pretended to casually scan the crowd. Instantly, she knew who Sloane meant. The man's light silver eyes held her gaze for a moment before glancing away. They were intense eyes that saw right through her, that touched something in her. Unaccountably, Ariane felt a rush of heat warm her cheeks.

The dark-haired man with the silver eyes waited until the women had gathered their packages and left. Then he threw several bills on the table and walked out onto the street.

I shouldn't have followed her, he thought, disgusted with himself. He reached into his jacket pocket and touched the photograph that was quickly becoming worn around the edges. He could have blown the whole thing. But he hadn't been able to stop himself.

• • •

Two days after Sloane left, a much exhausted Craig arrived home. Ariane was in the kitchen preparing a late-night snack when she heard his entrance. She went to meet him and, smiling softly, said, "Welcome home."

"Hi." Craig offered her his usual perfunctory kiss.

She raised her hand and rested it on his cheek. "You look exhausted. Was it a hard trip?"

"Bad enough. They keep you standing on ceremony half the day, and then they expect you to work through the night. Am I glad that's over. Have you got anything to eat in there? I'm starving."

Ariane led him into the kitchen, where she made him a snack of Scotch salmon on thinly sliced black bread with cream cheese. She brought it into the breakfast room, preferring the informality of the yellow and white room to the formal dining room with its red silk-covered walls.

She sat with him, nibbling on a brownie while he ate.

"Did you miss me?" she asked.

Craig continued eating. "You know I miss you when I'm away. I always do."

It was after midnight when she noticed the food was gone and the wine almost finished.

The lines on Craig's face were deep tonight. "Why don't you go upstairs and get into bed? I'll put these things away," she suggested.

"Good idea. But I think I'll take a shower first and get the desert out of my hair. That's all you notice there, the goddamn sand."

Ariane was already in bed when Craig slipped beneath the covers and moved toward her. She was pleasantly surprised to feel him gather her close.

She moved into his arms, embracing him, enjoying the intimacy. It had been so long since they had made love that Ariane had almost forgotten what it was like to be held. She returned his caress, waiting for the usual warmth to envelop her. But it didn't come.

They made love with the sameness and familiarity of two people who held no surprises for each other, whose lovemaking had become mechanical.

"Sorry about that. I guess it wasn't very good for you. I'll make it up to you the next time," Craig said as he settled himself beneath the covers. "Good-night."

Ariane moved closer to him, wanting more, desperately needing more, afraid of the way she felt.

Suddenly, inexplicably, she thought of the dark-haired man at Bice, the one who had been watching her. He wouldn't leave her like this, feeling this way. She didn't know how she knew, but somehow she just knew.

She turned her back to Craig and closed her eyes. She couldn't get the image of the man out of her head. She couldn't stop the intimate scenes that filled her mind, scenes that made her ache. His mouth sensuous, moving over hers gently, then passionately. His touch loving and skilled, knowing just what she wanted, sensitive to her every need.

He'd know her, know what she wanted, what she needed. He'd know everything. And he'd want her, want her so badly he wouldn't be able to stay away from her, wouldn't be able to keep his hands off of her.

She turned her face into the pillow. Why torment herself with a dream of a man she would never even see again, let alone touch?

Stretching lazily under the warmth of the covers, Ariane glanced at Craig's bedside Cartier clock. Nine o'clock.

Craig entered the bedroom, straightening his maroon silk tie. "You're finally awake. I thought you were going to sleep all day."

"Mmm, not a bad idea. I see you slept rather late this morning."

"Well, it was a long flight and nothing beats the comforts of home."

Ariane decided that this was as good a time as any to tell him of her decision.

"Craig, there is something I would like to discuss with you, if you have the time."

"Sure, what is it?" he asked, adjusting the gold and onyx cufflinks on his French cuff.

She brushed her hair back from her face and plunged in. "I'd like to go back to school. I've thought about it a lot and it's something I really want to do." There, she thought to herself, now let him try and talk me out of it.

Craig was silent for a long, thoughtful moment. Then much to her shock, he replied, "If that's what you want, it sounds fine with me."

At first she was dumfounded by his easy acceptance. Then her face broke into a dazzling smile, her dark eyes sparkled, and a faint blush covered her cheeks.

"I thought you'd give me a hard time."

"Don't be silly, Ariane. If going to school will make you happy, why would I disapprove?" He glanced at the Patek Philippe gold watch on his wrist. "I've got to be going. Oh, I nearly forgot. I brought you a little something." He tossed a black velvet box onto her lap.

Ariane opened the box and was speechless at the sight of a magnificent emerald and diamond necklace and matching earrings. "Craig, it's beautiful!" she exclaimed, staring at the strand of perfectly matched square-cut emeralds surrounded by glittering diamonds.

"Glad you like it. Well, I've got to run. See you later." He brushed her lips and hurried from the room, leaving her in a state of happy confusion.

• • •

Craig sat at his granite desk trying to sift through the mound of work that had piled up in his absence. Having made some order out of his desk, he left his office to visit the various departments of Newman Brothers and see if anything of importance had transpired while he was gone.

He was going through some trades when Matt Hendricks approached him. In his mid-twenties, Matt had his MBA but more importantly, a hunger that set him apart from the others.

"Excuse me, Craig, have you got a second?" Matt inquired.

"Sure. What is it?"

Matt led him off to the side, against the wall, away from any eavesdroppers. "I think there's something going on with Bank of Manhattan."

"Oh? Like what?" Newman Brothers represented Bank of Manhattan, and if something was going on he'd better damn well know about it. Aside from representing them, the firm had a large position in Bank of Manhattan stock.

"Well, I'm not sure and I could be wrong, but my hunch is they're getting ready to be taken over by International Bank," Matt said.

"Why? What did you find out?"

"A few things. Alone they don't mean much but combined I think they add up to something we ought to watch closely."

"Go on."

"First, the Rawley family has been quietly buying up Bank of Manhattan stock and not through Newman Brothers."

"Oh?" Rawley was chairman of Bank of Manhattan. Craig knew that if the Rawleys were increasing their holdings, there had to be a good reason. The fact that Rawley didn't want Newman Brothers to know about it was interesting. And the fact that Matt had found out was even more interesting.

"An order clerk at T, C, and B mentioned it. A friend of mine plays racquetball with Rawley's son-in-law at the Athletic Club. The son-in-law mentioned he had ordered the new Ferrari F40. Costs over a mil. He intimated to my friend he expects to come into a lot of money in the near future."

"That's all very interesting, but I'm not sure that the Rawley family buying up stock and the son-in-law buying an expensive sports car add up to a takeover."

"I saved the best part for last. Philip Rawley had dinner with Frank Cartwright. And it wasn't the first time."

"How do you know?" Craig asked as he began to plan his strategies. Frank Cartwright was chairman of International Bank.

Matt looked embarrassed as he said, "Well, I've been seeing this woman over at McCauley, and I heard her arranging a hotel suite for a Mr. Cartwright. It was for one night, and she seemed very nervous about taking care of the details. I asked her what it was about and she sloughed it off, saying some bigwig needed a room, probably to cheat on his wife, and that it had been going on for weeks. Usually McCauley's secretary took care of it but she was in the hospital. My friend had to arrange for the room, the bar, and dinner for two. Only . . ." Matt paused for effect, "she had to make sure there was no shellfish. Mr. Rawley was allergic."

"I presume you haven't mentioned this to anyone else, including any of your *friends*?" Craig asked, his emphasis on that word all too clear.

"Definitely not. I came to you first."

"Good. Let's keep this our little secret, shall we?"

"Yes, sir," Matt returned.

Craig turned to leave but not before saying, "By the way, Matt, good work. And you might want to keep in touch with your friend at McCauley."

Craig headed directly for the trading room, the newly discovered knowledge buzzing in his brain. He walked over to Louis, who traded Bank of Manhattan, and told him to acquire as much stock as he could as quickly as possible. He didn't want the Street to see so many purchase orders coming from him, so he told Louis to continue on his own and to "broker" the rest. Brokering masked the true buyer or seller. It was unethical, but almost everybody did it.

Of course, brokering was an insignificant aspect of the business compared to the fact that Craig just burst through the "Chinese Wall."

Craig nearly laughed aloud when he thought of how the SEC's "Chinese Wall" was supposed to prevent him from using the information his firm gathered to his own advantage. It was ludicrous to think that he would let the information glide past him and not act on it. Sometimes he thought the world was so incredibly naive that it deserved to be ripped off. He certainly didn't abide by the credo "the meek shall inherit the earth."

No, "To the victor go the spoils" was definitely more to his liking.

Ariane was standing at her bathroom mirror, putting a finishing touch on her rose-pink lipstick, when Craig tore into the bedroom, frantic about not being able to find his diamond cufflinks. She sighed and directed him to his top dresser drawer. They were attending the annual fund-raising dinner dance given by the Opera Association at the Pierre Hotel. As usual, Craig was late coming home, which explained his flurry of activity.

A few minutes later, Craig, immaculately attired in his black tuxedo, joined Ariane in their bedroom. As soon as she clipped on her diamond and platinum earrings, she lowered her arms and stood for Craig's inspection. He eyed her critically, beginning with her shiny black hair swept back into a French twist, which enhanced her large, almond-shaped eyes and high cheekbones. The long black gown, entirely covered in black sequins, had a high neck and long, tight sleeves. It molded every inch of her well-formed figure. Her full round breasts, narrow waist, slender hips, and long legs were displayed to perfection. But when Craig walked behind her to get another view, he saw the real interest of the gown. Her back was entirely naked from her neck to a little below her waist. The effect of pale, creamy skin against shiny black sequins was dazzling.

"If this is the new dress you bought, I hope you only paid half price for it because the back is missing."

Typical, Ariane thought. Then she wondered why his indifference no longer hurt. Five years ago it would have hurt, but no longer. Perhaps she had grown to be as indifferent as he.

Most of the guests had arrived when Ariane and Craig joined the party having cocktails in the Cotillion Room. The center of the room was taken up by tables of hors d'oeuvres, each table manned by a chef. The highly perfumed air was filled with the buzz of conversation and clinking glasses.

Craig and Ariane circulated, greeting the people they knew, until Craig spied Russ and Kristen across the room.

"Hello, Craig, Ariane." Russ nodded to the tall dark stranger standing next to him. "I'd like you to meet Alex Savage. Alex, this is my partner, Craig Wakefield, and his wife, Ariane."

Craig and Alex shook hands while Ariane stared at the man towering over Craig and Russ. Her heart skipped a beat and then began racing. It was him—the man with the silver eyes. He appeared to be around forty, just over six feet tall, with a powerful yet lean body. His very black, straight hair was long, skimming over the collar of his tuxedo; the deeply bronzed, angular planes of his face were sharp and well defined. But it was his eyes that demanded attention. Under straight black brows were a pair of startling silver eyes, fringed with thick black lashes that seemed to scrutinize and memorize everything they saw. His look was dark and almost satanic.

He shifted his gaze to Ariane and greeted her in a deep, smooth voice. "Hello. It's a pleasure to meet you." His polite smile softened the chiseled features, displaying white, even teeth in sharp contrast to the sun-bronzed skin.

Looking up into his eyes, Ariane was startled by the intensity of his penetrating gaze, a look that seemed intimate and knowing. She returned his unnerving stare with a polite smile and a small inclination of her head.

"Alex is from Texas, Craig, but comes to New York frequently on business. He represents a few groups of investors and plays the market for them. Maybe we could persuade him to do business with us," Russ said with a good-natured grin.

"Anything is possible," Alex remarked as his eyes skimmed the shiny black dress that molded Ariane's body.

"Now, Russ, don't pressure Alex so soon," Kristen said as she eyed Alex. "You'll have plenty of time to do that at dinner. Oh, darling, I need a refill. Would you mind?"

As usual, Kristen's overabundant breasts were fairly exposed and she took the opportunity to call attention to them as she sidled up against Alex. "Tell me, Alex, is it true what they say about Texas?"

"And just what is it that they say about Texas?"

"Why, that everything is so much bigger out there," Kristen returned without flinching.

"Well, I suppose. It must be all that clean living and fresh air."

Usually, Ariane would have been annoyed with Kristen's predictable and obvious flirting. But not tonight. She was too caught up with her own mixed emotions about Alex, emotions that threw her off balance, emotions that surprised her.

Russ returned just as dinner was announced. Craig took Ariane's arm and led her toward the Grand Ballroom, followed by Alex, Russ, and Kristen.

Suddenly, Ariane was uncomfortably aware of her exposed back. With Alex behind her she thought she could feel his eyes caressing her back. What would his touch feel like running down her naked back?

The Grand Ballroom was large, accommodating the five hundred guests. There was a wooden dance floor in the middle of the room and a separate seating area on a raised platform, divided by columns and railings, that ran the length of the room. That area was better known as Siberia. Only those unimportant and smaller contributors without sufficient social connections were relegated there. Craig had warned Ariane long ago that if they were ever seated there he would leave immediately and drop the charity from his list.

Craig introduced Alex to the other guests at his table and seated Ariane next to Alex. She adjusted the long slit on her gown and took her seat, her heart doing a quick flip-flop at the thought of being so close to Alex. Did he remember her? Or was she just another woman, any woman, to him?

Seated on the other side of Alex, Joanna stretched forward and asked, "How did you enjoy Sloane's visit?"

Ariane could barely hear her above the din of conversation and music, so she leaned across Alex to answer. "You know Sloane. You have to have a good time when she's around. We . . ."

Ariane knew she was talking but was hardly aware of

what she was saying. She was too conscious of the warmth emanating from Alex, of his fresh male scent. Should she say something to him? What if he didn't remember her? She would look like an idiot.

Suddenly, Ariane straightened. "Oh, I'm terribly sorry. I didn't mean to keep you from your dinner."

Alex gazed at her and smiled. "When someone as lovely as you keeps me from my dinner, I consider it my good fortune."

Much to her consternation, she felt the warmth rush to her face as she looked into those light eyes that peered at her so intently, eyes that sent a shiver through her. She was uncomfortable with his compliment so she ignored it. "Do you come to New York often?"

"Only when necessary which, unfortunately, is more than I would prefer. Have you ever been to Texas?"

"No, I'm afraid not, although I've always had a secret desire to go there. Have you lived there long?"

"I was born and raised in Texas. Perhaps you and Craig would like to visit sometime."

At the mention of his name, Craig turned his attention to Ariane and Alex.

Alex shifted his gaze to him and said, "I was just telling your wife that if you and she were interested, you could come down for a visit."

"Why, that's very gracious of you. I'd love it. I just hope Ariane won't be too bored. Will you, darling?" Craig asked in that tone which set her teeth on edge.

Her voice was overly pleasant. "Bored? Don't be silly. I find the idea quite stimulating." She turned to Alex. "I hope you don't feel obligated to invite us simply because of what I said."

"I'm sure Alex doesn't offer invitations he doesn't mean, Ariane," Craig cut in, as though afraid that Alex would withdraw the invitation. Ariane knew that a contact like

Alex could be worth a small fortune to Craig. He wasn't going to let anything stand in his way, certainly not his wife's courtesy.

"No, I don't offer invitations I don't mean. And having your wife . . ." Alex paused before continuing smoothly, "and having you visit the ranch is something I look forward to. Unfortunately, I expect to be in New York for quite a while this trip so I don't know when I'll be able to offer my hospitality to you. Shall we just leave it open for now, to be decided at a future date?"

Alex gave Ariane a lazy look that made her heart skip a beat. There was an air of insolence, of utter assurance about him.

"So what do you do for amusement?" Alex asked while dinner was being served. His leg brushed hers and she nearly jumped at the contact. Was it an accident? Somehow she didn't think he did anything by accident.

"Nothing." Ariane answered quickly without thinking.

"Oh? And how do you find it? Fascinating?"

"Boring. Very boring." Alex was a stranger. She'd probably never see him again, and maybe that was why she found it so easy to admit the truth. But it was more the way he looked at her, demanding complete honesty, that made her unable to lie.

"Why don't you do something about it?" His tone was challenging.

"I'm going to. I've signed up for some courses at school."

"And then what?"

"I don't know. I hadn't thought that far." She hadn't and didn't want to.

"What do you think about?"

"Oh, the national debt, OPEC, the European Common Market, the usual things." No man ever spoke to her this way. Asking her about herself, about what she thought. It unsettled her. Alex unsettled her.

''Your interests are so encompassing. And here I thought you were only interested in shopping.'' One side of his mouth lifted in a grin.

''On the contrary. It's only a means to an end.''

''And a successful end at that.'' He glanced down at her legs and commented smoothly, ''Fogal never looked so good.'' He raised his gaze, the silver eyes penetrating, and added, ''And in stockings too.''

Ariane looked down and, seeing the outline of her garter revealed by the snug fabric of her dress, blushed hotly. He did remember her. Down to the brand of her stockings.

As dinner was being cleared away, the light classical music was replaced by the livelier sound of Vince Giordano and his Nighthawks.

Much to Ariane's amazement, Craig asked her to dance. He almost never danced, as he was always too busy working the room.

As they moved together on the dance floor, Ariane soon learned the reason for Craig's unusual invitation as he whispered to her, ''I want you to be nice to Alex. He could be very important to me.''

Ariane's heart sank even as her temper flared. Every time she thought they were getting closer, Craig would do something to ruin it. ''Of course, Craig. I'm yours to command,'' she replied, her voice bittersweet.

So Craig wanted her to be nice to Alex. That wouldn't be so difficult. Aside from being ruggedly handsome, Alex radiated a maleness that was impossible to ignore. Be nice to Alex Savage? Sure, Craig. No problem. No problem at all.

''Tell me, Alex, do you live alone on your ranch?'' she asked, when she returned to the table. The tone of her voice made it sound like anything but an innocent question.

His silver eyes glittered with interest as he watched her raise her champagne glass to her lips—her third glass in less than an hour.

"No," he replied carefully. "A ranch the size of mine takes a large crew to run. Ranch hands look after the cattle and horses, men who—"

"No," she interrupted. "What I meant was, is there a woman in your life?" Her dark, almond-shaped eyes looked steadily into his.

He returned her gaze and held it for a moment, as though suspicious of this sudden friendliness that bordered on flirtation . . . even seduction.

"No," he answered simply, then added, "Would you care to dance?"

"I'd love to."

The orchestra was playing Gershwin's "Embraceable You" as he led her to the dance floor, his large hand on the smooth nakedness of her back, his warm touch sending a shock wave through her. Suddenly, Ariane couldn't breathe very well. A terrible rush of excitement filled her, overwhelmed her.

Being in Alex's arms shook her to her very foundation. She realized belatedly that her plan had backfired. Being in Alex's arms was dangerous. She liked it. She liked it too much.

He held her a bit more closely than propriety allowed, so that she sometimes brushed against his body. The contact disturbed her. Each brush against his hard, lean body caused her heart to beat faster as she felt herself growing warmer in his arms; a hot pulsing sensation throbbed deep inside her.

I definitely drank too much, she thought. But she knew

it wasn't the wine. It was the silver-eyed stranger who had stepped out of her fantasies and taken her into his arms.

Ariane glanced up at Alex's hard, chiseled face, and she thought she saw a flash of something in his cool eyes. Then it was gone and he was regarding her in a half-amused, sardonic way she didn't understand.

"It's rather warm in here," he said, his voice husky. "Why don't we step outside for some air?" Not giving her a chance to reply, he gripped her elbow and led her through the ballroom.

They entered the Cotillion Room, which was now cleared of any remnants from the earlier cocktail hour. A scattering of couples in the room were also seeking relief from the overcrowded, smoke-filled ballroom. Still holding her arm, Alex guided her out of the room and down a wide hallway to a set of closed doors. Holding the door open for her, he motioned her through and followed.

Ariane found herself standing on a small balcony that overlooked a plant-filled lobby leading to a bar on the floor below. It was a private spot hidden by the foliage and closed doors behind them. They were alone, and she was being "nice" to him. Wasn't that what Craig had wanted? Her thoughts swirled through a champagne-induced haze. This game they were playing both stimulated and frightened her.

"It's more comfortable out here, don't you think?" Alex asked, his voice deep and smooth as he draped his arm on the railing.

"Yes," was all she could answer. Something had changed, and she didn't think they were playing a game anymore. Standing so close to him, she noticed the silver strands at his temples, nearly hidden by the thick blackness of his hair. She glanced at his mouth and wondered how it would feel to be kissed by him. Probably hard and brutal, she thought. He seemed like a hard man.

"It's cooler out here," he said.

Was it? The air felt cool. So, why did she feel so warm? She could swear she could hear her heart beating. "Yes. And quiet," she said.

"It's the contrast that's nice. I think we all need a change from time to time, don't you?" His silver eyes regarded her intently.

"Yes. I suppose so." What were they talking about?

"Changes from things we know, things we've grown bored with, things we take for granted."

"Some things can't be changed," she said without thinking.

"Everything can be changed. Nothing is forever." There was a hard coldness to his words.

"Nothing?"

"No. It's supposed to be forever, but it's not."

Ariane heard the cynicism in his voice and wondered at its cause. And while his bitterness frightened her just a little, there was something sad about it that touched her, moved her. She was about to disagree when voices from below diverted her attention.

Looking down onto the lobby below, she watched as a man and woman left the bar. When the man embraced the woman and began kissing her, Ariane was mesmerized. She watched, unable to tear her eyes away as the couple kissed.

Suddenly embarrassed at spying on them, she glanced up to find Alex staring at her. "I think we ought to be getting back," she said.

"But it was just getting interesting," he said, one side of his mouth lifting in a grin that instantly put her at ease.

"But maybe we should leave before it gets too interesting," Ariane said with a self-conscious laugh.

"They don't interest me at all."

The look on Alex's dark features made Ariane's breath

catch in her throat. He wanted her. She could feel it. And what disturbed her most was that she wanted him.

"Shall we?" Alex switched moods abruptly as he gestured toward the closed door.

When Ariane passed him she felt him place his hand on the small of her back to guide her. There was something safe, comforting, yet possessive about the touch of his warm hand on her cool flesh. Something stirred inside her. Something that had never been touched before. Not by Craig, not by any man. Until that moment.

Ariane sat in bed, waiting, as Craig turned off his bedside lamp and adjusted his pillow.

"I'm bushed," he said, as he slid deeper between the fine linen sheets. "Sometimes I think those parties will never end. And tomorrow I have to meet with Brad."

Ariane switched on her light. "Tomorrow is Sunday."

"I know, but it can't be helped. I've got a new issue breaking Monday, and Brad and I have to take care of some things before the market opens. I'll try to be home for dinner."

"Are you sure you don't want me to go with you? Maybe I could be nice to Brad," she said sarcastically as she punched at her pillow.

"And just what is that supposed to mean?" Craig propped himself up on one elbow.

"As long as you're ordering me to be nice to strange men, maybe I should be nice to your friends as well."

A look of irritation crossed Craig's face. "Honestly, Ariane, I don't understand you at times. I only wanted you to entertain Alex socially so he wouldn't feel neglected if I was called away. I didn't think it was any big deal. Certainly nothing for you to start a fight over. Is it so terrible for a man to expect his wife to help him with his business dealings?"

Craig's logic confused Ariane, deflating her anger. Had she really misunderstood? It hadn't sounded like that at the time. "No," she said, feeling like a fool when she remembered how she had flirted with Alex to punish Craig.

"First you complain I exclude you from my life and then when I ask you to do one simple favor for me, you complain. I don't know what you want from me."

"I'm sorry." Ariane didn't want to argue. They were fighting too much lately. "Where are you meeting Brad?"

"At his house."

Maggie and Brad had a magnificent estate in Pound Ridge. "Why don't I go with you? I could keep you company in the car. And I could visit with Maggie."

"Brad said that Maggie's taking the kids to visit her folks, so you'd be all alone."

"I don't mind, really I don't," she said, warming to the idea. "I'll bring a book and stay out of your way. I can fix you and Brad a snack when you take a break."

"You'll just be bored. Look, why don't you call Jessica and do some girl things? I'll make it home for dinner and we'll spend a quiet evening at home, just the two of us."

A quiet evening at home did sound tempting. Ariane couldn't remember the last time they had been alone. "Okay. But you'd better be home for dinner."

"I promise." Craig smiled and leaned over to kiss her good-night.

His lips brushed hers in the usual brief fashion, but Ariane refused to relinquish the contact, holding it, forcing him to kiss her back. She wrapped her arms around his neck and pressed her body against his, hungry for the feel of him, longing for his embrace and the reassurance of his love. She couldn't remember ever feeling like this before, the desire rippling along her body, a hot passion urging her on.

But Craig broke the kiss and, after a chaste peck on her cheek, said, "Good-night."

Ariane turned on her side, away from him, and lay there thinking, long after he began to snore. His sleeping form irked her. Her frustration turned to discontent, driving away sleep. Images of Alex came unbidden into her mind. Alex with his dark, rugged looks. The hardness about him in direct contrast with the elegant surroundings of the ballroom. He had seemed out of place, yet he had moved with a grace that surprised her.

She had liked the way he'd held her in his arms on the dance floor. But it was his eyes that kept coming back to haunt her. Silver-gray, appraising eyes. One minute they were coldly assessing her and the next, they were alight with fire.

Ariane finally drifted off to sleep after assuring herself that nothing had happened between them. She had nothing to worry about. Then why did she feel so guilty?

chapter 4

He had work to do but images of her kept intruding his mind, breaking his concentration. Disgusted with himself, Alex threw down his pen and leaned back in the leather desk chair. If he closed his eyes he could see her flashing black eyes, her becoming smile. The naked column of her back.

Holding her in his arms had affected him. He wasn't surprised that he had wanted her. Why not? She was a beautiful woman. But he hadn't counted on the tightening he'd felt inside or the way the blood had pulsed in his body.

Her flesh had been cool at first but had warmed quickly, the skin on her bare back smooth like satin. He had been tempted to trail his fingers lower, inside her dress, to see how warm she was.

"Thinking of something?" Travis interrupted.

Alex quickly leaned forward and picked up his pen. "What's up?"

"How did it go last night?"

"Fine."

"Do you think Wakefield will bite fast enough?"

"No problem. Anyway, I can always use his wife for a connection. She's only too game."

"You sure? Not all women are alike, you know."

"Aren't they?" The silver eyes turned hard.

Travis sighed and shook his head. "No."

"Spare me your lectures on the virtues of women. It's a contradiction in terms."

"Have it your way. You know where I'll be if you want me."

Sure, he wanted her, Alex thought. Wanted to feel her naked in his arms. Wanted to feel that tempting body writhing beneath him.

She had charmed him, on cue, as if he could be bought. She wasn't merely a flirt enjoying the game but a whore sent to work by her husband.

Craig stood at the entrance to the Plaza Athenee's bar, letting his eyes adjust to the dimness. He recognized the tall man and headed for his table, taking the empty club chair next to him.

"Sorry I'm late, but the traffic was brutal." Noticing that his companion had already been served, Craig signaled for the waiter and ordered a scotch.

"I could have met you downtown if you'd preferred," Hassan offered, his long bony fingers toying with his champagne glass. Everything about him was sharp and pointed, his slicked-back hair accentuating his thinness.

"No. I'd rather meet up here, away from any prying eyes." Craig glanced around the dimly lit bar. The paneled walls and dark carpeting met with his approval. "I'm in the process of acquiring a new account and I think it could be very beneficial to us."

"How's that?"

"I met this Texan the other night. He runs a wealthy syndicate out of Texas and handles some major money. Not only that, but his return is excellent."

"How does that help us?" Hassan leaned back in his club chair, idly toying with the Burmese ruby he wore on his pinky.

"Simple. When he gives me an order I'll run ahead and take care of my own position first. And yours, of course. I'll be buying and selling one step ahead of him. If worse comes to worst, I can always unload my position into his account. He'll never know. What's a little front running between friends?"

"Sounds good. By the way, are the new insider trading penalties going to affect you?"

Craig reached forward to retrieve his drink from the low round table. "Only if I get caught. What bothers me is the thought of every disgruntled employee and shareholder turning into a goddamn bounty hunter. They're turning the Street into a damn police state and making it too financially appealing for people not to turn in their co-workers. Shades of Orwell's *1984*." Craig put his glass down. "It's deputized every idiot in the Street."

"That's not going to be a problem?" Hassan's black eyes narrowed slightly.

"No. Not for us. Nothing's going to be a problem for us."

Alex dashed across Park Avenue and narrowly missed being hit by a swerving taxi. He ignored the driver's screamed epithets and entered the towering glass and steel office building.

The elevator let him out on the twentieth floor, and he walked to the double glass doors that read "Creative Consultants."

The large, plush reception area was a luxurious combination of gray and black, dotted with the obligatory exotic floral arrangements.

The young, pretty receptionist flashed a flirtatious grin at the attractive visitor, but her smile disappeared when she saw the coldness in his eyes.

"I know my way," he said over his shoulder as he turned down the long carpeted corridor.

He reached the gray metal door marked "Numbers" and entered the windowless, soundproof room.

"You're late," said the heavyset man sitting at the large table.

Ignoring him, Alex faced his superior and said, "I'm in," before sitting down.

"How did the contact go?"

"No problem. Wakefield bought it all and can't wait to get his hands on my money. I could wrap this up in a few weeks."

"No. Don't rush it. Let him pursue you and let him beg. I don't want to rouse his suspicions by making it too easy. I don't want the Arab getting nervous." Alex's boss removed his glasses and tapped them on the table. "Looks like you didn't have to invest in Blakely's movie after all."

"It can't hurt to come out of this with a little profit."

"You're not in it to make money. You've got a job to do," the other man said, tugging the vest that strained across his round belly.

"Don't presume to tell me my job." Alex's eyes turned cold, his jaw rigid. "Remember, I didn't ask for this assignment. You came to me."

"Gentlemen," the superior interrupted, replacing his glasses. "Please, we're all on the same side."

"Tell *him* that," Alex said. "I've had it with the sanctimonious pencil pushers of his department that don't know what the hell it's all about. Anytime you want me out, just say so."

"Easy, Alex. He's just a little nervous about this one, aren't you?" He glanced at the man who avoided answering by picking at a mustard stain on his tie.

"How do you want me to proceed from here?" Alex asked.

"Do nothing. Let Wakefield come to you. He's really rolling now. He hooked up with Donald Hayes, the blind pool king."

The heavy man looked up from his tie. "What's a blind pool?"

Alex shot him a contemptuous look. "Where the hell did you get him?"

The superior drew a long patient sigh, then explained, "A blind pool is a shell corporation usually without any assets other than its name. Hayes puts his friends in as officers and brings it public. Once it's registered with the SEC he sells it to Newman Brothers in a package known as 'stox in a box.' Then Newman's salespeople push it on their customers. Hayes makes a bundle inventing worthless companies, Newman makes a bundle marking up the stock, and the customer owns something that's worth nothing."

"I presume you told the SEC boys to keep their hands off of this one," Alex said.

"No." The man shoved his glasses higher.

"What do you mean 'no'?"

"The less people who know about this the better. I couldn't risk having this leaked, even to another government agency."

"Great. I just hope some ambitious hot shot doesn't try to make his name by hitting Newman Brothers."

The meeting was over. As Alex got up to leave, the man with the glasses asked, "By the way, how do you like hobnobbing with all the high rollers?"

"It has its moments," Alex said glibly and then thinking of a particular raven-haired beauty the harshness left his face. "It definitely.has its moments."

Ariane was reading in bed when Craig came upstairs after working in his study until midnight.

"You're still awake," he said. "I thought you'd be asleep by now, what with school and all."

"I'm not tired. Besides, I'm doing my homework." Ariane held up her *Vogue* magazine as proof.

"My wife, the designer," Craig said with a laugh. "Next thing I know you'll be setting up a sewing machine and making my suits."

"Well," Ariane began, "I was thinking of setting a sewing machine in the maid's room downstairs. After all, I can't expect to design clothes if I don't understand how they're held together."

Craig raised one eyebrow. "Wait a minute. Do you really expect to be designing clothes? For whom, may I ask?"

Ariane shrugged. "I don't know. I'll worry about that later. First I have to know what I'm doing. Anyway, that room's sitting down there empty. What's the difference what I do with it? You're hardly ever home, so why should it matter?" Ariane regretted her last comment the moment it slipped out. She wasn't in the mood for one of Craig's speeches about how hard he worked.

Luckily, he chose to ignore it. "All right, go ahead then," he said, dismissing the subject as he walked into his dressing room to put on his pajamas. "But why do you want to waste your time with that? Wouldn't you rather spend time with your friends?"

"What I'd really like to do is spend more time with you," Ariane admitted.

"We haven't been spending very much time together

lately, have we?'' Craig said as he walked out of the dressing room.

"No, we haven't." Ariane didn't try to hide her dissatisfaction. She was tired of hiding her feelings.

"Working out this new deal hasn't been easy," he said and then, changing the subject, added, "I've been meaning to ask, do you know a single woman we could seat with Savage, or do you think we should just seat him with us?''

"You mean Alex?" Ariane asked dumbly, surprised and unaccountably agitated to find out he had been invited to the Newman Brothers' upcoming dance.

"Of course I mean Alex." Craig got into bed. "Well, what do you think?''

"We could invite Jessica." Why did the mere mention of his name cause a tightening deep within her?

"Yeah, maybe." Craig paused. "No, on second thought I don't think it would be a good idea. I don't want Savage so wrapped up in a woman that he's too busy for me. No, forget it. I'll seat him with us.''

"Whatever you think best.''

"Good-night, dear." Craig's lips brushed Ariane's bare shoulder.

He went to sleep immediately, but Ariane lay, thinking, for a long time before finally drifting into a restless sleep. She dreamed she was dancing with Craig at the Newman dinner. But when she looked up into his sapphire blue eyes she was confused. The eyes looking down at her were silver.

All of the guests had arrived at the Plaza Hotel. Craig was deep in conversation with the owner of McCauley Philips. Ariane had begun to circulate when a deep voice behind her said, "Excuse me, do you know where I might get a drink?''

She turned and smiled as she looked up into the dark chiseled features of Alex Savage. God, he was good-looking, she thought, feeling her breath catch in her throat.

"Hello. Welcome to our little party." Her voice sounded high and tight, almost a squeak. Why couldn't she talk naturally around this man?

"Thank you. Care to join me for a drink?"

"Sure."

Ariane and Alex made their way through the now crowded room to the bar and ordered a white wine and bourbon respectively.

"Quite an impressive turnout," Alex commented, surveying the crowd that included several of Wall Street's more infamous luminaries.

"Yes, it is." Her head felt light, as if all the blood had rushed out of it and she couldn't think.

"Perhaps you'd do me the honor of sharing a dance with me later," Alex asked, overly gallant.

"Yes, of course." He was joking, but the look in the silver eyes was at odds with his banter.

"Good. Because I've been looking forward to holding you in my arms again." He lightly stroked her bare upper arm.

The moment of joviality stopped abruptly to be replaced by something quite different. It was only the barest brushing of his fingertips on her arm, yet she felt a thrill at his touch. It was exciting, intimate.

"Here you are," Kristen said, appearing out of nowhere. "I've been looking all over for you. Oh Alex, what a surprise finding you here, with Ariane. Ariane dear, I hope you're not going to try and keep Alex to yourself tonight like you did at the Opera Ball. Why, that was positively selfish. After all, we must share and share alike. Tell me, Alex . . ."

Ariane couldn't understand how a man could fall for

such empty-headed flirtation. But Alex didn't seem to mind at all. In fact, he seemed to enjoy having Kristen drape herself around him, which annoyed Ariane.

"Well, Ariane?" asked Kristen.

"I'm sorry, I didn't hear you above all this noise," she answered sweetly. "What did you ask me?" She absently touched the rhinestone-embroidered waist of her Ungaro white crepe satin gown.

Alex smiled, amused, which irritated Ariane even more.

"I asked you if you didn't think it was a good idea to invite Alex out to the house for the July Fourth weekend," Kristen said. "After all, positively nobody spends the Fourth in the city. It's just too dreadfully hot and depressing. I know I'd love to have you, at the house that is," Kristen finished as she rubbed herself against Alex and gave him a knowing look with her round blue eyes.

I bet you would, Ariane thought, *just like you loved the waiter and the bartender and anyone else who crosses your path.* Her smile fixed, she answered, "Yes, do come. Kristen always has room for one more."

The Terrace Room was an elegant, softly lit room with a wide balcony running the length of the room from where one could watch the festivities below.

Craig arranged to have Alex sit next to Ariane so he could speak to him while Kristen arranged to seat herself on Alex's other side. Kristen rambled on while Craig leaned across the table, trying to engage Alex in a conversation about business, all of which made Ariane feel as if she were in the middle of a tennis match. God knew how Alex felt.

"The duck is rather good, don't you think?" Alex asked Ariane when Kristen finally left him alone long enough to eat.

Ariane turned to look at him. "But it's lamb."

"I didn't think you'd noticed." His mouth curved in a knowing smile.

When Alex looked at her as he was now, with those intense silver eyes of his, she felt as though they were alone and that the things he said to her held some secret meaning known only to them.

"I get the impression that the party is not exactly to your liking," he said.

The smile faded from Ariane's face, to be replaced by a closed tightness. "No, I think the party is just fine."

"Oh?" Alex asked, raising one black brow.

"Yes."

"Perhaps it's not the party that's your objection but rather the seating arrangement," he said smoothly, piquing her interest. "Possibly, the table is too crowded by one?"

"Oh? And whom did you have in mind?"

"How about the one you've been shooting daggers at?"

Was she that transparent? "Why, whatever makes you say that?" Ariane asked with pretended innocence.

"Oh, just a hunch."

"Well, Mr. Savage, I suggest you play your hunches."

He regarded her a moment then asked, "Tell me, what does a beautiful woman do all day to stay out of trouble, or do you?"

He was flirting with her. She wished she could respond in kind with a witty retort, but she didn't know how. "I'm going to school. Would that constitute staying out of trouble?"

"Well, that would depend on the subject matter." His eyes peered at her intently.

"I think fashion design is safe enough, don't you?"

"Could be. Unless, of course, one was designing ladies' lingerie."

Ariane had to laugh at his relentless pursuit. "You're impossible, you know that?"

"Am I?" he returned innocently. "Perhaps. But at least I got you to laugh."

As she responded to his questions she found herself telling him about her classes and her secret ambition to be a fashion designer. They drifted from one subject to another, finally discussing the latest movie releases.

"That may be so," she said. "But I still say there are entirely too few adult films made. I'm tired of all the violence for shock value and drawn-out absurd car chases. I like a film with a story about people. Like my friend, Justin, is making."

"Oh? Who's that?" Alex asked, glancing down into his drink.

Ariane told him about Sloane and Justin, flattered at his interest. "As a matter of fact," she said, "Sloane has invited me out to watch them shoot."

"Oh? Will you go?"

"I don't know. I have my classes . . ." Ariane's voice trailed off quietly. She knew Craig would never agree to take time off for such a frivolous reason, and she had never thought of going alone.

The waiter's intrusion ended their conversation and Kristen seized her chance by asking him more inane questions about his ranch. Rather than sit and listen to her chattering, Ariane left the table for some air.

As she passed a mirror she checked her reflection, idly smoothing the back of her hair. The French twist of her hair, combined with the low plunge of her white halter dress, bared her back to its best advantage. The diamonds at her wrists glittered as she moved her arm, but she didn't notice.

As she stood on the balcony and looked down on the merrymaking below, Ariane smiled to herself and thought "arena" was the perfect word to describe the festivities. Small cliques had formed around the room as guests sought their enjoyment, whether it be business or personal. Women formed small groups, discussing the latest gossip, while the men formed tentative alliances that could be broken with the rise and fall of a stock. Promises, made by smiling faces behind puffing cigars, could make one man millions while destroying another.

Unnoticed, Alex observed Ariane from afar, yet close enough to see the tension in her. She appeared to be cut from marble, the long white column of her dress and the paleness of her skin accentuating her remoteness. He wondered how much she knew about her husband's dirty dealings. He wondered about their marriage.

She seemed removed from the crowd, different from the others. She intrigued and fascinated him. Her aura of cool sophistication made her refreshingly unique among the roomful of black. But it was more than that. He remembered the way she had flirted with him at the Pierre, seemingly on cue from Craig. Interesting game the Wakefields played. A game he wouldn't mind playing at all. No, not at all.

"Enjoying the display below from a safe distance, I see," Alex said, taking Ariane by surprise.

"Just catching a breath of air."

Alex moved to stand next to her at the balcony railing. He stood close to her, without touching her.

"Are you enjoying the party?" Ariane asked.

"It's not exactly a down-home barbecue, but it'll do." A small smile lifted one corner of his sensuous lips. *You'll more than do,* Alex thought, gazing at her arresting features.

"I'd imagine you'd rather be home in Texas now than

here in the middle of this.'' Ariane gestured to the room below.

''Not at all. I'd rather be right here than anyplace else.'' His intense gaze held Ariane's, searching her face for a sign of the coquette. But she surprised him. She seemed to pull back from him, distancing herself, hiding behind a wall of reserve.

''I believe this is our dance,'' Alex said, not taking his eyes off her as he offered her his arm.

''It is?'' Her eyes questioned his.

''Most definitely. Isn't it your obligation as hostess of this party to see to it that your guests are having a good time?'' His intensity dissolved into teasing mischievousness.

''I suppose so.''

''I'm not having a good time because I'm not dancing with you.''

''Well, if you put it that way how can I refuse?'' Ariane smiled.

''I didn't think you would.'' The teasing was gone, a hard edge of sarcasm tingeing his voice.

Her smile faded. ''What do you mean by that?''

''Just that I know all about you.''

''Oh really?'' She hesitated. ''What do you think you know?''

''I know you're unhappy. More than you care to admit.''

''I'm not. And even if I was I certainly wouldn't admit anything to you.''

''But you don't even admit it to yourself, do you?'' He paused and then added lightly, ''Our dance?''

The band was playing Glenn Miller's ''Sunset Serenade'' as he led her onto the crowded dance floor.

He looked down into her face as he slipped his arm around her back, and his large, warm hand came into contact with the smooth, cool flesh of her back. He drew her closer and breathed in the tempting fragrance of her scent, a light green fragrance with a subtle, seductive undertone. It suited her perfectly, he thought as his fingers began to discreetly stroke her back. He felt her stiffen and her dark eyes stared up at him with surprise and then annoyance.

"Alex," she whispered. "Please."

"Sorry, it's just that it's hard for me to keep my hands off that beautiful back of yours." He could feel the heat rising in her body, feel her growing warm in his arms. She didn't look like a game player, but she had to be. All women were.

Looking down at her ripe, seductive mouth, he thought, *What an enchanting creature. This is going to be easy.* He hadn't met a woman yet who couldn't be seduced. The end result was always the same, only the strategies were different.

Across the room, Craig had finally cornered Roger McCauley of McCauley Philips.

"Maybe we could get in a game of tennis at Russ's party," Craig offered.

"Sounds good. Only this time, do me a favor and have a little respect for your elders."

"You shouldn't work so hard, Roger. Too many late-night meetings aren't good for you. Why don't you try and get out of Manhattan for a while? Take some time off and go to Europe, maybe?" Craig watched Roger closely for any reaction. He was rewarded with a flicker of recognition in his brown eyes and a tightening of his fleshy jaw. So, Matt's hunch was right, Craig thought triumphantly as he mentally tallied all the Bank of Manhattan he'd been buying.

"Good idea. Maybe I will. Er . . . if you'll excuse me,

I think my wife is looking for me,'' Roger said as he made a hasty retreat, leaving a smug Craig to search out Brad.

"They're freezing Ralston Price's assets,'' Craig whispered.

"You're kidding! How can they do that?'' Brad asked.

"They're invoking RICO.''

"What the hell is going on downtown? Has that idiot lost his mind? I thought it was 'innocent until proven guilty' in this great land of ours.'' Brad paused and studied Craig sharply. "Wait a minute. How do you know?''

Craig looked smug. "I have friends in low places.''

"I still don't understand how they caught Price.''

"His wife. Actually, it started with her brother. He worked for Luft's, heard about the takeover and told Price. Price started buying up the stock but to be on the safe side put it in his wife's maiden name. There was too much activity in the stock and the boys traced it and subpoenaed Price's wife. She screwed up big on the witness stand. Blew everything.''

"What an idiot. But they couldn't invoke RICO just for that.''

"They would if they found a pattern of racketeering. Once they got Price on insider trading, he turned over faster than you can say Benedict Arnold. Gave up his uncle who started the firm, who took him in when he was nothing.''

"Price always was a lowlife,'' Brad interjected.

"They got him on creating illegal tax losses through fraudulent tax deals.''

"They have proof?''

"Yeah. They seized the tapes Price was making.''

Brad's complexion turned two shades lighter. "Oh Christ.''

• • •

Spying Alex and Ariane at the table, Craig crossed the room to join them.

"I'm sorry I haven't been able to spend as much time with you as I would have liked, but I'm sure you understand." Turning to Ariane, he continued, "I hope you've been entertaining our friend while I've been busy, darling."

Alex gave Ariane no chance to answer as he commented smoothly, "This has been one of the most enjoyable parties I've attended. Your wife is a lovely and charming dinner companion and has been amusing me with her delightful anecdotes on a variety of subjects."

"Thank you. I hope you weren't too bored," Craig replied.

Ariane shot Craig a scalding look, but Craig didn't notice.

"I'm never bored in the company of a beautiful woman, especially one that has so much to offer," Alex said.

Craig heard the implication but chose to ignore it. He angled his body toward Alex, fairly pushing Ariane behind him. "You know there are a variety of ways for you to increase the earnings of your fund that I'd like to go over with you. Of course, now isn't the time. But I could just briefly . . ."

"It's a great party, Ariane," Joanna complimented. "I've always loved the Terrace Room."

"I know. Me too. I missed you at the last meeting." Ariane referred to the working lunch the museum committee had held two weeks ago. "How did you get so lucky? It was boring."

"I haven't been going out lately. Haven't been doing anything lately. God, that Kristen is revolting." Joanna's voice sounded slurred.

Ariane followed Joanna's gaze to the dance floor, where Kristen was wrapped around Eric.

"Yes, but she's harmless. She just loves to flirt."

"I wouldn't be too sure of that if I were you." Joanna's voice held a hint of warning.

"What makes you say that?" Ariane was sorry she asked when she remembered what Kristen had said about Stuart.

"Just take my word for it. Sometimes the truth is so obvious you think it can't be. But it is."

"If that's true, why does Russ put up with it?"

"You'd be surprised at what some of us put up with. They're all no good. Every last one of them."

"Not all of them."

"Oh? And I suppose you think your precious Craig is above it all? Please, he'd sell you for an eighth."

"That's a disgusting thing to say. And completely untrue." But even as she spoke the words, Ariane knew that Joanna was right. Craig would sell his soul for an eighth— and had, many times. And he would sell her and their marriage in a minute.

Ariane leaned her weary head against the back seat in the car. They had stayed to see the last guest out and it was now after three as they rode home through the deserted city streets. She felt too tired to speak and closed her eyes as images of the party flashed in her mind's eye. Alex, Kristen, Alex, Craig, Alex.

By the time she entered the apartment she was furious.

"I'm too keyed up to sleep," Craig said as he walked to the built-in marble bar in the living room. "I think I'll have a brandy. Care to join me?"

Following in his wake, Ariane said sarcastically, "If you wouldn't feel that I was boring you."

"Why would you feel that you bore me? Whatever gave you that notion?"

"I'm only repeating what you said tonight in front of Alex. That you hoped I wasn't boring him. Would you mind explaining that remark?"

"Ariane dear, you completely misunderstood me. I meant the roomful of strangers was boring, not you. How could you think such a thing?" He stroked her bare arm with his cool fingers.

Though somewhat appeased by Craig's explanation she shrugged away from his hand.

"You know, you've been very testy lately," he said, obviously annoyed at being rebuffed. "You jump at everything I say or do. Is something bothering you?"

Yes, Ariane thought, *everything.* "No."

"Then why don't you stop looking for trouble where there isn't any? I've been ignoring it and letting you get away with it for quite some time now. Don't you think you owe me an apology for thinking so little of me?"

Ariane had been drinking, she was tired, and now Craig made her feel as if not only had she wrongly accused him but had insulted his integrity as well.

"All right, Craig." She sighed. "I'm sorry that I thought you thought I was boring. I'm going to bed."

Craig reclined on the white silk sofa, enjoying his brandy, feeling quite pleased with himself. Everything was progressing smoothly, just as he had planned. And if Alex wasn't interested in Craig for business, Craig would just have to dangle Ariane under his nose for bait. Sometimes it was convenient, having an attractive wife . . . even a testy one.

Having undressed and showered, Ariane slipped on her nightgown and began brushing her hair. It felt good to have it falling freely about her shoulders and down her back after having it pinned up all night. She shook her head, and as an afterthought, she swept the heavy length to one side and thoughtfully scrutinized her back in the mirror.

chapter 5

The black ball crashed against the marked white walls as the two men took turns slamming it to each other. Sweat poured as they strained for the hardest hit and tried to outmaneuver each other.

An hour later Craig and Hassan sat at the Vertical Club's health bar, drinking orange juice.

"How are we doing with Hazelton Loran?" Hassan asked, referring to the brokerage house they planned to buy.

"Not good. I put a trader/salesman in there and turned him loose. If he'd known what he was doing we could have made a mint with him. Unfortunately, he screwed up and the firm lost its capital."

"Now what?"

"Now we walk away and let them go under. I can't believe they were that stupid not to ask for any front money. Lucky for us they were," Craig mused as his attention drifted to the two women at the other end of the bar.

"Something catch your fancy?"

"Could be." Craig smiled at the auburn-haired woman in the shimmering blue leotard. She smiled back and nodded.

An aerobics class ended and the bar became crowded and noisy as the women filled the area.

Craig eyed the crowd of fit females clad revealingly in skin-tight workout clothes that left nothing to the imagination. The yellows, greens, reds, and blues jostled against each other, the well-developed bodies damp with perspiration.

"I had no idea this place offered such a wide variety of activities," Hassan said, viewing the crowd appreciatively, his gaze settling on a woman with long, black hair.

"You bet. They don't call it the Horizontal Club for nothing."

"You haven't mentioned my name to Hayes, have you? I don't understand why you brought him in. Couldn't you have created the blind pool yourself?" Hassan asked, with barely concealed annoyance.

"Yes, but there's no sense in calling undue attention to Newman Brothers. Besides, by letting Hayes do it I can avoid federal disclosure laws and ownership restrictions that would cut into my profits. Don't worry. He doesn't know anything about you."

"Have you thought about how you're going to dispose of my newest deposit?" Hassan asked.

"Yes. I think the best way is to start an endless paper trail. We'll deposit it first in a Swiss bank and then transfer the funds through Europe, the Caymans, and Panama. Sort of what E.F. Hutton did."

"But didn't they get caught?"

"Yeah. But we won't."

• • •

On July Fourth, Ariane and Craig drove to Russ and Kristen's neighborhood where the manicured, well-tended estates of Gin Lane gave way to the more rustic beach-type homes along Dune Road.

The entrance to the Newmans' house in Southampton was almost totally hidden by the heavy growth of Japanese pines and junipers. Craig pulled the Mercedes convertible coupe into the driveway and parked it behind the usual array of expensive cars.

Ariane and Craig approached the house, passing Russ and Eric, who were playing tennis. The house was a rambling two-storied structure of weathered cedar. Nearly every room sported a balcony. The back of the house was almost all glass.

A large expanse of wood deck, littered with lounges, surrounded the swimming pool, affording the guests a view of the pool or the beach. Kristen loved red and left no doubt about it. She used it generously, in the flowers, the towels, all the accessories. Ariane thought the effect was too bright under the harsh light of the sun, the whole impact gaudy.

Having lost Craig to Clayton, Ariane drifted away.

"I swear she is such a wiz in the kitchen I can't believe it," she overheard Denise telling Madelyn. "Do you know I had to go out and buy her a set of her own Cuisinart cookware? She told me she didn't like the way the housekeeper kept mine and wanted her own. She's only twelve! When I was her age, I wasn't even allowed in the kitchen."

"I know. Lisa is nagging us about getting a horse. She rode in camp, and now she wants her own. First it was tennis lessons, then the computer, then the dog. What's next?"

Bored, Ariane found a secluded lounge and sat down. She closed her eyes against the glare of the burning sun, letting its heat soak into her bones. In her mind's eye she saw the other guests stretched out on Kristen's outlandish red towels, their bodies oiled and greased, looking like pagan sacrifices to the sun god.

She thought of Joanna's remark about Craig cheating on her. Was it possible she was right? Ariane had thought about it in passing, always dismissing it. But what if he did? Could she survive? What if she were forced out of his life? But Craig wouldn't. Or would he?

"Ariane, about what I said at the party," Joanna said, taking Ariane by surprise as she sat down on the lounge beside her. "I'm sorry. I guess I had too much to drink and got carried away. I shouldn't have taken it out on you."

"Forget it." *I was right,* Ariane thought. *Craig wouldn't cheat on me and even Joanna realizes it.* "How's everything?"

"Swell. Couldn't be better." Her bitter tone was impossible for Ariane to ignore.

Joanna had become increasingly morose over the last several weeks. The ring of truth in her caustic remarks upset Ariane. More than she wanted to admit.

"I saw Jessica the other day. She asked me to send you her regards," Ariane said, hoping for a safe subject as she idly adjusted the strap of her Giorgio di Sant'Angelo bronze maillot. "She said she tried to call you several times but you're never home."

"I'm home. I just don't answer the phone." Suddenly, Joanna sat up straighter and leaning forward asked, "How is Jessica? Does she mind being divorced?"

"I think she's all right now. At first she said it was hard. The shock of finding out that Martin had been having an affair for a year made her sick. But the worst part was finding out who her friends were . . . or rather weren't."

"There are no friends in this group."

"What do you mean?"

"Without them we don't exist. Look at them," Joanna snapped, indicating the cliques of men scattered around the deck with a wave of her hand. "They don't even know we're here and couldn't care less. Deal, deal, deal. That's all they know."

Ariane wondered at Joanna's words. Was that all they cared about? The market certainly seemed to be Craig's obsession.

"Hi, girls." Lydia joined them, sitting down with her gin and tonic. "Did I miss anything? I couldn't get away from Melissa. She's so boring. All she talks about is exercising. She drives me crazy."

"Well, with what she has to contend with, can you blame her?" Joanna asked.

"No. I guess not. But I heard she's beginning to enjoy it more than Eric," Lydia replied.

"Enjoy what?" Ariane asked, completely lost as to what they were discussing. Someone had turned up the stereo, forcing Ariane to raise her voice.

"Enjoy making love to another woman," Joanna explained. "Eric likes to watch Melissa having sex with another woman before he joins them. Didn't you know?"

"Eric alluded to it once but I thought he was kidding," Ariane said.

"Nope. It was Eric's idea in the first place. But it looks like he created a monster. Melissa told me she and Hilary, her personal trainer, have been meeting several afternoons a week without the benefit of Eric's presence. Now she says she prefers Hilary and has been trying to stay away from Eric. I don't know how long he'll stand for that. If it was Clayton, I'd never get away with it."

"Oh, Lydia, you're such an animal," Ariane said jokingly.

"Maybe, but it's what keeps them home on the farm."

"Hi, ladies," Kit greeted them as he sat next to Ariane on her lounge. "Dishing the dirt?"

Kit Marshall was Craig's top salesman and ran the Long Island office. He and his new wife, Ellie, were both in their mid-thirties and married for the second time. He was always talking about sex and constantly grabbing Ellie.

"No, the weather," Lydia quipped.

"Cute." Turning to Ariane, Kit fingered the sheer bronze chiffon of her sarong. "Love this fabric. I bought Ellie some underwear made out of this. I love the way it feels. And she loves the way I feel."

"Jesus, Kit. Give it a rest, will you?" Lydia said.

"What's the matter, Lydia? Not getting enough?" Kit teased.

"I get as good as I give," Lydia returned, smiling.

"What do I have to do, throw water on you two?" Joanna asked.

"No, but it does sound tempting. What do you say, Lydia, a little dip in the hot tub?"

"No, thanks. We were just about to settle the national debt."

"How about you, Ariane? Tired of that superstar husband of yours yet?"

"No, not yet. I'll be sure and give you a call if I do. But please don't hold your breath on my account."

"Okay. I can take a hint," Kit said good-naturedly. "Catch you later."

"What a joke," Lydia said when Kit was safely out of earshot.

"Does he really think he's fooling anybody with all that sex talk?" Joanna speculated.

"You mean he doesn't fool around?" Ariane asked. Kit regularly came on to all the women, in an offhanded manner.

"Of course, he fools around," Lydia responded. "With other men."

"Kit's bisexual," Joanna whispered. "It's supposed to be a closely guarded secret. I don't even think Ellie knows."

Ariane was shocked. Not about Kit's sexual preference, but the fact that everybody seemed to know. Everybody except her.

"Anything else going on around here that I don't know about?"

"No. I think that about covers it," Lydia responded. "You know you ought to hang around more often. You never know what you might learn."

"Thanks for filling me in. Excuse me." Ariane left, feeling completely alienated from the people she had considered her friends.

Things were changing. Lately she had noticed a subtle shift in Kristen's usual harmless digs and sexual innuendoes. Her comments had once been amusing and harmless; now they seemed mean-spirited and malicious.

All of a sudden the heat of the sun, the blaring rock music, the laughter, and the nearly naked tanned bodies became too much for her. She had enjoyed as much of this party as she could stand.

Waves crashed on the beach, powerful and fierce. The water was a dark gray-blue flecked with foam. But the day had turned hot and bright, as promised, causing heat waves to shimmer off the sand; the water beckoned Ariane. It was cold, as she knew it would be when she walked into the surf, but once she began swimming she grew accustomed to it and was refreshed by the waves that tossed her around.

Ariane swam for some time and was growing tired. She tried to stand but found that she had drifted out too far and was in deep water. When she turned to swim toward shore a huge wave caught her, slammed over her, and dragged her under.

She tried to right herself, but she was disoriented. She couldn't see which way was up in all the turbulence. Spinning water caught her in its powerful undertow.

She panicked. She wasn't going to make it. Her lungs felt near to bursting. In a minute she'd have to breathe and she'd drown. The salt water burned her eyes, filled her nose, her ears. She had to breathe. She couldn't hold her breath any longer.

Suddenly, the stale air burst from her as a strong arm encircled her waist and propelled her upward.

She broke through the surface coughing, panting, and trying to fill her lungs with air all at the same time. As she reached out blindly for support she encountered a pair of wide, strong shoulders. Leaning on them, she gulped the sweet air. She sobbed uncontrollably, clinging to her lifeline, thankful to be alive.

"Are you all right?" her rescuer asked as his arm buoyed her.

She knew that voice; it was Alex. She was breathless, her throat ached and all she could do was nod her head.

As soon as they reached shore, Ariane collapsed onto the sand, knees up, her head bowed, still shaken. Alex sat down beside her and waited for her to compose herself.

She looked into his deeply tanned face. Gratitude and a number of other nameless emotions overwhelmed her. "Thank you for saving my life."

"Think nothing of it. I try to make it my business to rescue at least one damsel in distress per beach party," Alex joked, his lips twisting into a smile, revealing strong, white teeth.

Alex's remark hurt her, crushing the warm feelings she had. Why did he always have to answer with that easy adroitness? He was all surface charm with no depth, always tossing a glib remark.

"You may choose to make light of it but I assure you I take drowning very seriously. So thank you anyway."

"Well, in that case you're quite welcome. But if you're going to swim alone in the future, you should know better. Little girls shouldn't venture out into deep water. You might get in over your head, and I might not be around to save you the next time." His drawl sounded sanctimonious.

In an instant Ariane was standing, hands on her hips, dark eyes blazing.

"Thank you for your concern, Mr. Savage," she said between clenched teeth, her color rising. "But you needn't bother. I do not get in over my head. But if I did, I certainly wouldn't expect a shallow, arrogant fool like yourself to save me."

"My dear Mrs.—or is it Ms.?—Wakefield," Alex said, coming to his feet in a smooth, catlike motion. "I'd suggest you clean your own house before you start hurling names. After all, you know about 'people who live in glass houses.' " His eyes seemed to burn into her.

"And what is that supposed to mean?" she snapped.

His silver eyes searched hers, probing. He seemed to always be evaluating her, weighing, judging. He seemed to think her guilty of something. But what?

Then the sneer fell from his lips and a shutter seemed to pass in front of his eyes, shielding his thoughts and emotions.

"It means," he said, "that you are one of the most innocent people I've ever known, or lady, you're one hell of an actress."

Then he walked away, leaving her with as many doubts about him as he seemed to have about her.

• • •

Two days later Ariane idly flipped through the *New York Times* while she drank her orange juice. Bored, her glance kept drifting to the backyard, to the rhythmic breaking of the waves. And her thoughts kept returning, unbidden, to the memory of Alex's strong arm around her waist, propelling her toward the surface, toward life itself. Why did he have to be such an insufferable bastard?

Craig wasn't coming to the beach house this weekend because of a business trip to Delaware. Another business trip. Did it really matter?

Turning back to the paper, her interest was caught by a story on California designers. There was an upcoming show at the Beverly Hilton.

Before she knew it she had reached for the telephone and dialed.

"Reservations? I'd like to make a reservation on the first flight to Los Angeles, please."

The old bank on lower Fifth Avenue had been converted to MK, this year's hottest night spot. The four-storied building retained some of the bank's original flavor, including the brass and glass doors, the white marble floors, and the vault which now served as the coat check room flanked by the immense time locks.

Dominick, the manager, kept the club jumping by choosing the right mix of celebrities, models, Europeans, and businessmen from the crowd that gathered outside.

Hassan lit a Gauloise and leaned back in the booth. From the balcony he watched the fashionable crowd below, his eyes narrowing as an attractive, long-haired redhead entered the main room. She was wearing a black leather halter dress. The short, tight skirt rode up, revealing long white legs, as she sat on the blue satin love seat. His portable phone rang, disturbing his fantasy.

"Yes." Hassan listened for a moment, muttered, "Thursday," and broke the connection.

"The shipment has arrived. Delivery will be Thursday," he told the two men seated with him. They were both dark with sallow complexions. Even sitting, it was obvious Khazi was tall, with long arms and extremely large hands, hands that could crush a man's windpipe—and had on occasion. His face was pockmarked and he was constantly running his fingers over the scars.

Sayed was short and square, compensating for his lack of stature by body building. He had enlarged his body into gross proportions. His close-cropped hair, thick neck, and broken nose gave him the appearance of a bull dog.

"You sure she won't give us any trouble?" Khazi asked, raising his voice just enough to be heard above the din.

Hassan absently stroked the cold metal of the brass railing. "She can't give us trouble when she doesn't know what's going on."

Khazi shook his head in disbelief. "How can she not know?"

"Because she believes what I tell her. It suits her. She'd rather believe I backed her in an antiques store because she's talented. Talented . . ." Hassan made a derisive sound. "I can find better talent than that at the Square." He referred to an area in his hometown of Ramir that was known for its prostitutes.

Hassan saw Sayed's eye twitch. Sayed had a facial tic that became more pronounced when he was nervous.

"Missing home, Sayed?" Hassan baited him. Sayed rarely spoke and Hassan enjoyed making him uncomfortable.

"No," came the quick reply.

"Good. Because I think it will be a while before we see home again." Hassan's voice was brittle with anger.

They finished their dinner and moved upstairs, passing

the library's pool table and painted ceiling adorned with oversized pictures of insects. They entered a private room known as the Cabaret, which had been set aside for special customers.

"Have you spoken to your uncle lately?" Khazi asked once they were settled in the green leather booth.

"No. But I'm sure it will blow over. It's only a matter of time and money." Hassan took a drag of his cigarette and released the smoke slowly. The music pounded mercilessly, drowning out any hopes for a normal conversation.

"I don't know," Khazi shouted. "The others didn't matter. No one cared about a few prostitutes. But this one . . . her husband is in the government."

"No one forced her." Hassan smiled and then, as though to himself, added, "In the beginning anyway. Besides, they're only women. What's one woman more or less? My uncle will take care of it." The redhead had made it upstairs, Hassan noticed. She was dancing, the tight leather straining against her body.

"Supposing he can't?" Khazi sounded worried.

"Then we'll just have to stay here, I suppose." Hassan gazed at the crowd, searching. When he had been forced to flee Ramir, just because he had murdered the wrong woman, he hadn't been happy about relocating to New York. True, New York offered the perfect setting for his money laundering and drug operation. But he had been concerned about the New York liberated women. He'd read that they were smart, savvy, and independent. He needn't have worried.

The fools. They were no more liberated than the prostitutes of the Square. Finding the right woman was nothing more than a matter of displaying his wealth. With a flash of his platinum card, a bottle of Cristal champagne, and his stretch limousine he could buy any woman he desired. They were his for the taking.

Hassan squinted, watching his choice through the thick haze of blue smoke that hung over the crowd.

"That one," Hassan said, nodding in the direction of the woman with the waist-length red hair.

Khazi followed his gaze, rose, and made his way through the dancing bodies.

The music was loud, the heavy bass making the wood floor vibrate. Hassan could feel it reverberating through his body, pulsing in him, making him ready.

"I can't believe you're here," Sloane said from their table at Spago. They sat in the front room, Justin's reputation earning them the coveted location. "Why didn't you tell me you were coming to LA?"

"I wanted to surprise you," Ariane answered. "So why are you here if Justin's on location? Isn't the producer supposed to be watching out for her interests or something like that?"

"Yes, yes. Justin's been shooting up north for a while. I was supposed to follow immediately, but I just got word tonight that one of our backers is flying in and wants to discuss his deal. So, I planned a party for tomorrow night. Hey, why don't you come?"

"I don't know. If it's a business party I don't want to intrude." Ariane glanced around the crowded room. The bare walls and wood floors did nothing to muffle the noise level. A changing exhibit of contemporary art hung on the white walls.

"No, no. A few people from the industry are coming, but it's not business. We're friends and you'll know some of them. Come on. Besides, I might need your help. If the backer gets cold feet, you can always vouch for my frugality and honesty."

Ariane laughed, thinking that once Sloane set her sights on this poor, unsuspecting backer he couldn't do anything but say yes. "All right. I'll come."

Sloane picked up a slice of broccoli pizza and bit into it.

"So, when is Craig coming?"

"He's not."

Sloane lifted her auburn eyebrows in surprise. "All right, Kingsley. Would you mind telling me what's going on? You never travel without Craig."

"What do you mean 'what's going on?' Nothing. I just missed breathing your famous brown smog and decided to fly out," Ariane replied half-heartedly, trying to force a lightness into her voice.

"Right. After all your years of marriage you suddenly decided to travel alone, leaving Craig home so you can breathe smog. That's a good one. Now why don't you tell me why you're really here?"

"Look, can't I just come visit an old friend without you reading something into it?" Ariane snapped. "I'm a big girl now, and I hear they let us travel alone and everything these days."

Ariane turned away to stare out the window. Across the street the fluorescent glow from Tower Records lit Sunset Boulevard. She felt terrible. She didn't know what was wrong with her lately. "I'm sorry," she said, toying with her napkin edge.

"You know, Kingsley, you're my best friend. And contrary to popular opinion I can keep my mouth shut."

Ariane had confided in Sloane over the years but never her innermost secrets. There were some things she would never tell anyone. "I know. Don't pay any attention to me. I must be tired, what with the flight and the time change."

"Are you sure that's all it is, the time change?" Sloane

asked softly. "You seem to be down a little, and you were the last time I was in New York. Oh, you smile and laugh in all the right places, but something's wrong and I know it."

Ariane shrugged her shoulders. "I just felt like getting away for a while, but I don't even know what I was escaping. Craig and I are fine. We hardly see each other, so how could we fight?"

"Is it Craig you miss, or a husband?"

Back in the apartment, Ariane lifted the phone and dialed Craig's number.

I miss him, she thought. *I really do.*

The phone rang eight, nine times. Ariane hung up and sighed. So, if she missed him so much, why was she relieved that he hadn't answered?

chapter 6

Most of the guests had already arrived when Ariane's taxi pulled up to Sloane's English Tudor home in Beverly Hills.

"Perfect timing," Sloane said, meeting her at the door. "Everyone's here. You look great. How about a glass of wine? Richard and Emily are here. You remember them?"

Ariane listened to Sloane's nervous rambling, not paying attention to where she was leading her.

"Ariane, I'd like you to meet . . ."

Ariane looked up to find herself staring into a pair of cool gray eyes she had hoped never to see again. She didn't hear the rest of Sloane's introduction, preoccupied with holding her temper in check. Standing in front of her, wearing black linen slacks that clung to his narrow hips and a gray linen shirt opened at the neck and somewhat lower was ". . . Alex Savage."

Alex grinned. "The lady and I are acquainted," he drawled.

"Oh, you are?" Sloane said, obviously surprised.

"Yes, he's a business acquaintance of Craig's," Ariane explained, refusing to use Alex's name or elaborate. Alex looked as if he were completely at ease in the situation, while she could feel her anger pulsing in her veins. She hated him for his coolness.

"Actually, the lady and I have grown to be quite good friends, having spent time together on numerous occasions," Alex said, his penetrating eyes never leaving Ariane's face.

"It was only three occasions, if I remember correctly."

"Was it? Seems like more. Anyway, you know what they say, it's the quality of time one spends, not the quantity. And I did so enjoy our swim together that last time." Alex's mouth lifted on one side in a cynical, knowing smile.

The nerve of him. Why, he's actually enjoying this, she thought. "Did you? I wish I could say the same." A malicious gleam danced in her eyes.

"Alex, are you still coming up tomorrow to watch us shoot?" Sloane asked with a conciliatory tone.

"Sure, I have a few days free and I hear the country's beautiful up north. Say, I have an idea." Alex paused and turned his gaze back to Ariane. "Why don't you come up with me and take a look?" He was the vision of politeness.

"Oh, no. Ariane, didn't you tell me you had some appointments in town?" Sloane said. Ariane knew that she was offering her a way out because she obviously disliked Alex.

"Forgive me," he said. "I should have realized a busy woman like yourself must have many things to do on Rodeo Drive. And I'm sure your husband would never permit you to travel with a man, even if it was just to visit your friends and lend support."

Ariane fairly bristled at his words and their implication, his cool insolence nothing short of an insult.

"I'll have you know, Mr. Savage, that my husband and I enjoy a marriage built on trust and he would no more question my motives than I would question his. He's not my keeper, as you implied, nor I his."

"Forgive me, again." Alex's dark features hardened for an instant before he continued smoothly, "I was only offering you a ready excuse to beg off from a situation that might upset you. I wouldn't want you to feel that you have to come along just to prove that you aren't afraid."

"I'm staying at the Beverly Wilshire. What time will you pick me up?"

"Shall we say ten o'clock?"

"Fine. Good-night," Ariane snapped. But as she turned on her heel and walked away, she heard his low chuckle. And she had the sinking feeling that Alex had won this round too.

Walking through the open glass doors in the lobby, Ariane saw Alex's tall, lean form lounging against a sleek black sports car. They both reminded her of predators. And she felt like the prey.

Alex pushed himself off the car to take Ariane's bag and put it in the luggage compartment.

"Good morning," he said pleasantly, seeming to enjoy her discomfort.

"Morning," she mumbled, as she slid into the low black leather seat and closed the door. She placed her Hermès ostrich tote on the floor and smoothed her tobacco-colored suede shirt as she buckled her seat belt.

Alex slammed the trunk and slipped behind the wheel of the Ferrari Testarossa. After starting the powerful engine, he put on a pair of black aviator-style sunglasses, almost at the same time Ariane was slipping on her sunglasses. Ariane caught the identical action and had to smile inwardly as the image came to mind of two knights, lowering their visors before they clashed in battle.

"Ready?" Alex asked as he prepared to shift gears.

"Ready."

They had been driving for two hours when he turned off the road in Santa Barbara and headed the car toward the beach.

Pulling up in front of a large, Spanish-style stucco hotel, Alex stated, "I thought this would be a good place to stretch our legs and rest a while. There's an excellent restaurant in the back on the beach."

Ariane stood at the entrance of the open-air restaurant and looked around appreciatively. The restaurant was blue and white, decorated with fresh flowers and country patterned china. The French doors at the back of the restaurant were thrown open to the beach; a painted white wood railing edged the area. Their table was at the railing, affording them an ideal view of the beach and ocean.

As soon as they were seated, Alex removed a white envelope from his jacket pocket and handed it to her. She raised her eyes questioningly but his expression was blank.

On the cover was a picture of a white dove carrying an olive branch in its talon. Inside was one word: Peace. She stared at it, bewildered for a second, until its meaning became clear. As it did, she couldn't help but smile.

"And just what does this mean?"

"Well, I was going to suggest that we bury the hatchet but I felt this would be a much safer offer of peace. You see, I was afraid I knew exactly where you'd like to bury it." A small grin touched his sensual lips. "Will you accept my peace offering?"

"I suppose that since you went to all this trouble, I can't very well refuse. Wherever did you find this on such short notice? Or do you keep a ready supply on hand for all the people you insult?"

"Madame, you wound me grievously," Alex said with feigned indignation. "I assure you I am not in the habit of insulting beautiful women such as yourself. A man would have to be a fool to insult you." He peered intently at her and she blushed at his compliment.

The ocean breeze blew gently across the nape of Ariane's neck and she turned her face toward the beach to enjoy it. The stream of warm air brought the sweet scent of the gardenias that surrounded the patio.

"Like the view?" Alex asked.

"It's a beautiful spot. It reminds me of a vacation place my parents and I used to visit." Ariane's voice was soft and her eyes dreamy as she remembered one of those rare idyllic times.

"You must be very close to them."

"I was," Ariane corrected, her face tightening as she looked down and fidgeted with her napkin. "They died six years ago."

"I'm sorry." She looked into his eyes and saw that he meant it. "At least you have pleasant memories to comfort you." His voice was cold and flat.

Not all of them. There were some things she would rather not remember. And those were the memories she couldn't forget, the memories that haunted her into the present, that wouldn't let her live in peace. "How did you find this place?" she asked, wanting to change the subject.

"That was easy. I'm one of the hotel's investors."

"So you're involved in hotels, films, Wall Street, oil . . . You're full of surprises. Anything else?"

"I quickly grow bored with any one thing. I found that by diversifying my investments I'm able to meet new challenges. It keeps me busy," Alex finished with a nonchalant shrug of his broad shoulders.

Did he also quickly grow bored with his women? Ariane wondered. What kind of woman could keep Alex interested? Was she that kind of woman?

The two men passed through the brass doors of Grand Central Station, pushed along by the rush-hour crowd that was eager to escape the frenzied madness of the city for the tranquility of the suburbs. The anonymous sea of humanity made it the perfect place for Khazi and Sayed to meet their contact and receive his package, a small sample of the delivery that had arrived.

The noise level in the Rotunda, so named for its huge domed ceiling, echoed around them, bouncing off the marble walls and floor. Khazi and Sayed stood at the appointed spot in front of the small corner bar. Light streamed in from the huge arched windows, the black cross bars throwing patterns of shadows on the stone floor. The hurrying crowd paid no more attention to the men than they did to the official yellow police tape that cordoned off an area. It was New York City. Nobody wanted to notice anything. It was safer that way.

Khazi gazed at the clock above the information booth in the middle of the Rotunda. They were early. Bored, he looked up at the green ceiling painted with the zodiac signs and waited patiently.

Later, their task completed, Khazi and Sayed were on their way out when Khazi grabbed Sayed's arm. Sayed followed Khazi's gaze to the evening edition of the *Daily News* displayed at the newsstand. "Rapunzel Strangler Strikes Again" was splashed across the front page. Beneath the headline was a photograph of an attractive redhead. A redhead with waist-length hair.

They continued walking and didn't speak until they were outside on Forty-second Street.

"I'm getting tired of cleaning up after him," Khazi said.

Sayed's eye twitched furiously. "Why couldn't he have stuck to prostitutes? Why'd he have to do Wattari's wife? If it wasn't for him, we'd still be home."

Ariane and Alex arrived in Pacifica, a small town between Big Sur and Carmel, and found the small motel Sloane had described. Alex pulled into its driveway, which was filled with campers and trailers.

The view was breathtaking. The grounds of the motel, cut into the mountain, were surrounded by a thick forest of vibrant green, the towering oaks, sycamores, and Chinese elms so dense one couldn't see through them. Behind the motel, sheer cliffs fell to the beach below. The ocean was wild and rough, the waves spewing foam and spray.

They found Sloane sitting at a redwood table, going through some papers.

"When did you get here?" Ariane asked.

"I flew in early this morning. How was your ride up?" Sloane asked apprehensively.

"Fine," Ariane answered.

"Couldn't have been better," Alex added. "How about our rooms?"

Sloane looked somewhat nervous and hesitated. "Well I can show you to . . . a room."

"What?" Ariane asked very quietly through clenched teeth.

"You see, I forgot last night that I had only saved one extra room for Alex because I didn't know you were coming. By the time I got here this morning it was too late to find another room. Everybody's doubled and tripled up as it is."

"Look, I'll bunk with the crew. There has to be at least one spare bed around, and Ariane can have my room," Alex suggested.

Ariane turned and looked at him, her manner softening

at his offer. "Oh no, I couldn't let you do that. You don't have to give up your room for me. There must be some other way."

"There is. We could share the room together," Alex said seriously, never taking his eyes from Ariane's face. "Unless, of course, you snore."

"I do not!" Alex's jest seemed to break a spell over her and she realized she had been holding her breath at his proposal.

"All the same I suggest we find a room that I can share with someone."

Taking charge, Sloane said, "All right. That's settled, so let's get you settled. Alex, I'll put you in with Hank and Willy. Why don't you get the bags and meet us at Room 15?"

"Don't forget my card," Ariane called after Alex. "You never know when I might need it."

"We have another one."

Alex let the air out in a rush. "Same MO?" He gripped the telephone receiver tighter, already knowing the answer.

"Yes." There was a pause. "Alex, what are you doing up there?"

"Endearing myself to Wakefield's wife."

"And how's that going to help?"

"It's part of the game they play. She's the bait and I'm the prize."

"Well, good fishing then."

"Yeah." Alex slammed down the receiver with more force than was necessary.

The next day Ariane spent the afternoon alone, watching the filming from her position on a sand dune. She couldn't help wonder at Alex's abrupt change of mood last night.

The two of them had joined Sloane and Justin and the rest of the cast and crew for dinner. Seated next to Carlo Orsini, she had found the handsome movie star to be charming if somewhat of a flirt. Alex's early pleasantness had fled and darkened until by the end of the evening he was positively glowering at her.

When Justin finally yelled "cut" for the day, she went for a walk on the beach. She sat on the warm sand, watching the changing shades of the sunset. The sky was ablaze with glowing oranges, reds, and purples, reminding her of a kaleidoscope as the patterns quickly changed and intensified. Suddenly, the colors blurred, her eyes filled with tears, and she felt like crying—crying for her perfect life.

Angrily she brushed her tears away, annoyed at herself for becoming so morose. She got up, brushed herself off, and started back to the motel. As she walked she noticed the figure of a man sitting on the beach. Drawing closer, she recognized Carlo and called out a greeting.

"I thought you were very good today," Ariane said sincerely as she sat beside Carlo.

"Did you?" he asked.

"Yes. I believed you completely, even with all the crew around and the distractions. I think you and Samantha were both perfect."

"Thank you. You are very kind to say that. This movie means a great deal to me." Looking out over the ocean, Carlo continued quietly, "Acting is all I've ever had. Now finally this, a real chance. If wanting something badly enough can make it happen, then surely this will." There was a quiet, fierce note in his voice.

What did she want? Had she ever wanted anything that badly? "It will happen, Carlo. I saw it today in your performance, and so will others."

"You are a very special woman, Ariane. I envy your husband."

"Alex isn't my husband," Ariane corrected, assuming that Carlo had made a mistake.

"I know that. I mean the man you wear this ring for," Carlo explained as he touched Ariane's hand and fingered the thin diamond wedding band. "If Alex was, you wouldn't be sitting here with me." With that he raised her hand and touched his lips to the back of her hand.

The cold silver eyes missed nothing, not Carlo's gesture nor the soft smile on Ariane's mouth. Alex had also watched the filming and had followed Ariane onto the beach. Now that he knew her destination and the reason for it, he could forget her. Forget how her eyes sparkled when she was angry, forget the deep sadness that clouded them. For a moment he had almost forgotten what all women were like.

Suddenly, he remembered another pair of lying lips. Seemingly innocent, but truly traitorous. He'd only been seventeen at the time, but he'd learned plenty from her, all he needed to know about women. Enough to last a lifetime.

In no mood for sleep or the good-natured banter of his roommates, Alex decided to take the Ferrari for a spin. Opening the windows and racing along the tight, treacherous curves of the highway should have made him feel better, but it didn't. He kept seeing Ariane's seemingly guileless face, her dark eyes clear and innocent. How could such a little cheat appear so honest and sincere? For a moment, she almost had him believing her act. He gripped the leather steering wheel tighter, as he remembered her rendezvous with Carlo.

Why should I care? he wondered grimly as he raced the car around a hairpin turn. *I have a job to do, and that's all there is to it.*

He knew all about women, all about wives. He had

learned plenty from Sueanne. There was nothing like finding your bride of three weeks in bed with another man to set your head straight. Amazing how fast one can learn.

Let Ariane's husband worry about her, he decided. *I don't care how many men she sleeps with.* So, why was he doing one hundred miles per hour around a hazardous turn?

Ariane stood in the middle of her living room in the apartment. Something was wrong. She leaned on the sofa and her hand sank into the fabric that had somehow become liquid. Horrified, she got up from the sofa but she couldn't stand. The floor was quicksand. She was sinking. Oh God, she had to get out. She tried to run but the sand grabbed at her feet, her ankles. She was stuck, sinking into the thick, viscous mass.

The whole apartment turned to quicksand around her. The furniture melted down, dissolved into it. When she tried to run, her feet sank deeper and deeper. She was caught by the gelatinous body, trapped in its deadly grasp. She screamed for help, but she knew no one would hear her. No one ever heard her. There was no way out.

She woke with a start, her heart pounding, her eyes wide with fear. She recognized the dream as her familiar nightmare. It had started some time ago, but lately she had been troubled with it more frequently. She lay there, her eyes staring into the darkness, afraid to go back to sleep, afraid the nightmare would return.

She chided herself for being so foolish as to let a dream upset her. After all, dreams don't mean anything, she told herself without much conviction. She tried to think of Craig, but his face eluded her.

chapter 7

Alex and Ariane spent most of the drive to Los Angeles in silence.

Ariane was anxious to get away from him and the strange stirrings he caused within her, back to the safety of her marriage, back to Craig.

Trapped within the narrow closeness of the small car, it was impossible not to notice Alex, not to be totally aware of his almost animallike maleness. The breadth of his wide shoulders fairly filled the narrow, black seat. A few buttons of his denim shirt were open to reveal a tanned chest covered with soft, black hair. The sleeves of his shirt were casually rolled up, displaying strong forearms. A deeply tanned hand with long tapering fingers rested on the gear stick, expertly shifting the car, while his long, strong legs worked the pedals. She watched the play of powerful thigh muscles move beneath the tight confines of his jeans.

It wasn't merely his rugged hard looks that affected her, drawing her against her will. It was as if there was a current of excitement running through him; by just being near him she could feel its vibrations reach out, touch her, and move over her. There was potential danger there, a reckless streak beneath that cool exterior that had been evident in the way he had handled Craig.

Ariane suddenly remembered a theory held by the girls at college: You could tell how well a man made love to a woman by how he handled his car. Alex handled the sports car well. Very well.

It was some hours later when the Testarossa pulled into the driveway of the Beverly Wilshire Hotel. Alex retrieved Ariane's bag from the luggage compartment while she stretched alongside the car, grateful for the freedom of movement after the car's cramped quarters.

As he handed her the bag, Ariane thanked him for taking her up to see Sloane. "I really appreciate it, especially knowing how you feel about me," she added.

"Oh? And how do I feel about you?"

She was tired, tired of his word games. "It's obvious, isn't it? You just don't like me very much. I just wanted to say thank you, not start another argument with you."

"You're wrong . . . about my feelings, that is." For a moment Ariane thought she saw a glimmer of warmth in the cold, silver eyes. "And to prove it to you, why don't you let me take you to dinner tonight?" He held up his hand when she started to shake her head. "There won't be any arguments tonight. Just a nice, pleasant dinner. Trust me." He smiled his most disarming smile.

No, she couldn't go. "All right, but you're asking a lot."

Alex's silver eyes gleamed. "I know. I always do."

In her bedroom, Ariane unpacked and called the desk to check for telephone messages. There were none. Surely Craig had called. Perhaps the front desk had lost the message. Checking the time, she decided to call him at the office. He was out. Again.

Alex took Ariane to Shell's, a small intimate restaurant with dark wood paneling and red leather banquettes.

Following Ariane to their table, Alex eyed the alluring body molded in a bare slip of a dress of black silk.

"You seem to know all about me," she said in the middle of dinner, "yet I don't know anything about you. Have you always lived in Texas?"

"Yes." All during dinner Ariane had amused him with stories about Sloane and Justin and, surprisingly, he found himself enjoying them, enjoying her.

"On a ranch?"

"Yes." No one had ever shown so much interest in him before and it unnerved him.

"Cattle or oil?"

She didn't really care. It was part of the game. Dark memories made his tone clipped. "Little bit of both."

"I'm sorry. I didn't mean to pry." She looked away, concentrating on her food.

"You weren't prying. I just don't like talking about myself." There was a hard flatness to his voice.

"I'd love dessert. Do you think they have something rich and sinful?"

Ariane's request brought a wry twist to Alex's lips as he thought to himself that he fit the bill perfectly. His silver eyes glinted with suppressed amusement. "I'm sure we can find something to fit the bill."

Standing at the door to her apartment, Ariane thanked Alex for dinner.

"I think I should see you in safely," he said. "How about sharing a nightcap with me?"

"Okay."

Alex's dark presence dominated the pale living room while Ariane poured his brandy. He was standing at the huge expanse of glass, his broad back to her, admiring the view. He took the glass from her and opened the sliding terrace doors.

Downing half his drink, he seethed with anger. The moment she had let him enter the apartment, he had felt something ugly begin to fester in him. He didn't know what it was, only that for some unfathomable reason he was disappointed she had let him in, disappointed she was like the others.

He stared at her as he carelessly tossed down the remaining brandy, and smiling, not a nice smile, motioned with his glass toward the bar. "May I?"

"It's getting late," she said.

In two swift strides Alex was standing in front of her, his mouth twisted downward. "But not too late. It's never too late for women like you." His hand reached behind her and pulled the comb from its place, causing her long hair to tumble down her back. He hadn't planned to do this and knew it was against his better judgment, but suddenly he didn't care.

She slapped his hand away. "Stop it. What do you mean, women like me?"

He grabbed her wrist so swiftly she didn't have time to react. His hand easily encircled its narrowness, his tight grip making her wince in pain. His eyes were cold and hard, and a muscle jumped in his jaw as he said, "You can stop the play-acting now, Mrs. Wakefield. It's just you and me." He punctuated his remark by pulling her against him.

"I don't know what you're talking about. Let me go," she ordered.

"But that's not what you really want, is it, my dear? If you'll drop your phony act of respectability, we can get down to the matter at hand. This is what you've wanted all along,'' he said as his hand slid up her back, burying itself in her hair.

''You're either drunk or insane!'' she cried, pushing against him. The useless motion made him aware of the soft flesh of her thighs pressing against him.

''Perhaps a little of both.'' He bent his head to claim her tempting, generous mouth.

She went rigid as his mouth took hers in a savage kiss. It was a kiss that took everything and gave nothing as his lips moved possessively over hers.

When he had first kissed her, Alex had meant to punish her and use her, but as his mouth tasted her sweetness, all thoughts of hurting her fled. An unexpected passion that was alien to him spread throughout his body, consuming him. Strange ideas entered his mind, ideas so foreign to him that his mind refused to accept them. What he wanted to do was possess her completely, to make love to her until she cried out his name in surrender.

The fight left her body and she swayed into him, her form yielding as her arms went around his neck. She surrendered, her lips parting beneath his as he sought the warm recesses of her mouth. He could feel the rush of heat in her body through the fine silk of her dress as she returned his passion.

His lips left hers to trace a hot, fiery path across the fine line of her jaw and down the smooth column of her neck. Her skin was incredibly soft as his warm lips found her pulse and felt its erratic beating. When she arched her neck backward, he felt the thrust of her full breasts against his chest. The contact set his hardened manhood throbbing with desire.

He moved his hand down toward her buttocks and crushed her to him. Rubbing himself against her, the contact had the effect of ice water thrown in her face. She pushed against his chest, struggling to break the embrace.

"No, stop. Please," she begged. "I-I'm sorry." Her breath sounded labored. "But I can't."

"Can't or won't?" He released her abruptly. He saw the flush of passion on her face and was hard-pressed to comply with her pleading. But he had never forced a woman before and, even though he thought she deserved it, he held himself in check. The lust faded from his eyes, their look cold and distant, as his features set themselves in hard, implacable lines. "Well, which is it?" he said with loathing in his smooth voice. "Or do you always go around leading men on, flaunting yourself and then pushing them away? There's a name for women like you."

"You're crazy! I never led you on. I never did anything to encourage you."

"No? Think again. What about throwing yourself at me at the Pierre, going away for the weekend with me . . . and what about tonight?" His eyes narrowed, his mouth was taut with anger.

"You interpret and twist everything for your own benefit. I only went with you to visit Sloane."

"Cut the crap. You don't expect me to believe that, do you?"

"It's true and I don't care what you believe. You can't conceive of honesty and decency in anyone because you're so vile and disgusting."

"Is that so? And this coming from a happily married woman, alone in a hotel, with a man definitely not her husband, and definitely enjoying every minute of it."

Her hands balled into fists. "Get out of here."

"Gladly," he said and moved toward the door. His hand rested on the doorknob of the opened door as he turned to face her. Now he knew that those tightly drawn lips could open softly and taste so sweetly. He snorted with derision when he thought that all that lovely packaging couldn't make up for the lying whore inside. "By the way, if you ever decide to finish what you started, give me a call. If I'm busy, I can always have one of my ranch hands fill in. I'm sure anything in pants will suit you." With that he slammed the door behind him.

Ariane stormed around the room in a rage, shaking with frustration until, without thinking, she grabbed Alex's brandy glass and threw it against the door with all her might. The sound of the fine crystal shattering into a thousand pieces satisfied her somewhat, cooling some of her temper. But it did nothing to cool the heat within her.

Alex took the package from the messenger boy and closed the door to his town house. He opened the box and dumped the contents on his desk.

Another morgue shot. This one of a redhead, her waist-length hair still wrapped around her throat as she had been found. Her file was included: name, address, occupation, friends, habits. But there was no connection with the other murder victims, just as he knew there wouldn't be. Nothing except her age, wealth, and long hair.

There were other reports in the package, updates on Hassan and Wakefield. He read them quickly, his gaze drawn back to the redhead.

As soon as Ariane arrived home, she telephoned Craig at the office. Martha told her that he had just left for Delaware and was not expected back for at least a week.

Ariane spent her first day home taking a ballet class, visiting the Whitney, and condemning herself for having allowed herself to kiss Alex. Whatever had she been thinking of? Well, it would never happen again. She had seen first-hand how adultery could tear a family apart, and she wasn't about to jeopardize her marriage—her life—for a

night of meaningless sex with a stranger who offered her
nothing more. She walked home, the hot summer heat of
August enveloping her, wilting her. What she needed was
something cold and wet to drink and then a cool refreshing
shower.

She picked up a Baccarat glass and noticed the red lizard Filofax on the bar. It wasn't hers. It wasn't Craig's.
There was only one person she knew who owned a red
lizard Filofax. Kristen.

Her hand trembled slightly as she picked up the book
and looked inside. It was Kristen's, all right. The bold,
florid handwriting left no doubt.

Forgetting her thirst, Ariane slowly walked to the sofa
and sat down, holding the agenda in her hand, staring at
it.

How had Kristen's Filofax found its way into her apartment? Why had Kristen been here?

Calm down, she told herself. There must be a million
reasons why Kristen left her Filofax here—a million. Then
why couldn't she think of even one?

The questions tumbled over and over in her brain. Kristen was checking up on Craig to see how he was faring
during Ariane's absence? Hardly. Kristen was dropping
something off? What? Picking something up? What?
Looking for Ariane? Not likely.

Ariane went upstairs to take a shower, leaving the
agenda on her peach marble vanity so it was never out of
sight. She took it downstairs when she went to make dinner, stared at it while she picked at her food. Back upstairs
in her bedroom she slipped between the Porthault sheets
and put the agenda on the bed. The red book glared at her
brightly, defiantly, on the sea of pale peach, its electric
color out of place, not belonging in the soft pale room.

And then the logical conclusion she had fought so hard
to keep buried began to work its way to the surface, break-

ing down the barrier she had built, cracking the protective shield she had erected.

Craig and Kristen. Together.

It couldn't be. She wouldn't let it be. There had to be some logical explanation. What? What!

Craig hurried through Eastern Airlines' gray and red terminal, anxious to be on his way. His flight from Delaware had been delayed and he wanted to make it to the bank before closing time. He could have had Martha phone ahead and arrange things, but she didn't know he was in Florida. He had told her, and everyone else for that matter, that he had business in Delaware and then would probably take a few days to visit some horse breeding farms in Kentucky. What he did in Florida was his own business and no one else's.

As Craig emerged from the terminal building and the humidity enveloped him like a sauna, he remembered his vow never to come to Florida in August. The air seemed too thick to breathe and he was thankful when he quickly found the waiting limousine he had hired. The chauffeur held up a sign with the name "Lynch" written on it, and Craig walked swiftly to it, smiling inwardly at his choice of alias. Gary Lynch was the former chief enforcer for the SEC.

The dark coolness of the United Caribbean Bank offered a pleasant respite from the bright heat of downtown Miami. Craig shook hands with his banker, Mr. Poole, who knew him as Mr. Breeden. Again, the choice of name amused Craig; Richard Breeden was the chairman of the SEC. It didn't really matter what name Craig used. Mr. Poole was quite agreeable, for a small fee of course, to conduct Craig's business exactly as specified. Craig brought him a suitcase full of cash, skimmed from Hassan's money, and Mr. Poole deposited the money into

Craig's account in increments of $9,999. Keeping the deposits under $10,000 meant the bank wouldn't have to report it to the federal government.

No sense in having them know everything. What they didn't know couldn't hurt him.

Ariane woke exhausted. She had barely slept, waking every hour with visions of Craig and Kristen together, the images tormenting her, making her sick.

How could Craig prefer Kristen to her?

Obviously she was inadequate and Craig had needed, wanted, someone else. She had failed Craig. Failed herself.

Maybe if she had been more open, more giving in the beginning; if she hadn't allowed those painful memories to intrude on her marriage. Craig had accused her of being frigid. Maybe she was. Then memories of Alex's kisses flooded her mind. She hadn't been frigid with Alex. Not at all. He had set her on fire.

Ariane felt as though she were suffocating. She had to get away from the city, the heat, her own thoughts.

She packed her things, picked up the Mercedes from the garage, and drove out to the house in Southampton, hoping the solitude would help her. It didn't.

She couldn't eat or sleep. The pain of betrayal, of rejection, gripped her. Her mind tormented her with scenarios of Craig and Kristen. Craig disappearing at parties to be with Kristen, Kristen laughing at her, Kristen saying, "If a woman can't satisfy her man in bed, he deserves to find satisfaction elsewhere."

But always at her lowest point, after the spent tears, after the self-pity, Ariane grasped the one thought that was her lifeline. There was no affair, just a forgotten Filofax. Maybe it meant nothing. There was only one way to find out. But did she have the courage?

• • •

Craig was comfortably settled in his aisle seat for the return flight home when he realized someone was standing next to him. Glancing up, he found himself staring at a tall and stunning blonde who appeared to be in her mid-thirties. She was wearing large tortoiseshell sunglasses and a trim white linen suit.

"Would you mind? That's my seat." She barely gestured toward the empty window seat. Her voice was more than cool; it was cold and demanding.

"Go right ahead," Craig offered too pleasantly as he picked up his papers and barely moved his legs. He had no intention of jumping to this cold beauty's command.

The blonde fixed Craig with an imperial stare and attempted to step across his legs. Her short tight skirt and the narrow spacing between the seats made it nearly impossible.

Craig watched her struggle, enjoying the perfect view of her splendid rear, watching her thighs spread and stretch the skirt tightly as she stepped over his feet. When she stepped on his foot with her white pump, he knew it was no accident.

The L1011 took off and Craig busied himself with his papers, taking note of the two vodkas the blonde ordered and how quickly she drank the first one.

"I'm sorry."

"Excuse me?" Craig turned to look at her. He had scarcely heard her mumbled words.

"I'm sorry. It's just that I really despise flying and I tend to get a little tense." She slowly removed her sunglasses, revealing pale green eyes that peered intently at Craig.

Craig was taken aback by her striking good looks. He felt his anger melt in the face of such beauty.

"That's all right. I don't think anybody in their right mind enjoys flying."

"Yes, but I shouldn't have taken it out on you. I didn't mean to disturb you. Please go back to your work." She turned her face toward the window.

"You're not disturbing me. Besides, work can always wait. You live in New York?"

"Yes." She turned her green eyes on him and Craig felt his blood rush out of his brain. "I had business in Miami. I flew in last night and couldn't wait to get out."

"I know what you mean. The weather is sweltering. What kind of business are you in?"

"Interior design."

"Really? What a coincidence."

The green eyes swept over him. "You're a designer too?"

He smiled. "No, but I was just thinking of redoing my executive offices." His tone didn't exactly ring true.

"That is a coincidence. But I don't know if you'd appreciate my method of working."

"What's that?" Craig asked, intrigued by this self-assured, independent woman.

"I believe in a very close designer/client relationship. I like to get to know my client as intimately as possible." Her voice fairly caressed him as she continued, "Learn his needs, his wants, his desires. That way I can give him exactly what he wants."

Craig felt a pleasant tightening. "Well, I only foresee one problem."

"What's that?"

"I don't know your name."

The blonde laughed, a cool rippling sound. "Dulci Ryder."

chapter 8

The Labor Day party proved to be a mixed blessing. Ariane certainly wasn't in a party mood and entertaining one hundred people in less than two weeks was the last thing she would have wanted. But the preparations gave her something to do.

As usual, Martha had sent out the invitations from the guest list that Craig had submitted and she had arranged for the caterer, florist, and musicians.

The telephone was ringing as Ariane entered the house, an altered dress draped over her arm. Dropping the dress on the sofa, Ariane grabbed the phone.

"Hello. Remember me?"

She froze, her stomach muscles tightening. Craig. She forced her voice into a semblance of normalcy. "When did you get back?"

"This morning. And I'm exhausted. I couldn't wait to get out of there. How are the party preparations? Everything under control?"

"Yes, of course. Everything's going smoothly. When will you be coming?"

"I wanted to come out today but there's so much for me to clear up at the office, I'm afraid I won't be able to. I'll take a helicopter first thing tomorrow morning. Do you realize we haven't seen each other in weeks? I was hoping we could spend some time alone tomorrow, before the party on Sunday. What do you say?"

It was all Ariane could do to keep from blurting out, "Why was Kristen in our house?" Instead she answered steadily, "Of course, Craig. That sounds lovely." She heard the falseness in her words. Could he hear it too?

The sound of Craig's voice had brought back all her anxieties and uncertainties. What if she confronted him and he left her? What then? If she wasn't Mrs. Craig Wakefield, who was she?

Ariane woke early to a bright sunny day. With a monumental effort she pulled herself together in preparation for the party. She threw on shorts and a T-shirt, pulled her hair into a ponytail, and went downstairs.

She and Hilda, the housekeeper, were in the kitchen, going over her schedule, when the tent people arrived. Soon the house and backyard were a beehive of activity with delivery men walking in and out, questioning Ariane on every detail. Organized chaos was in progress.

Absorbed in the tumult going on around her, Ariane was thrown off guard when she turned around and saw Craig standing in the kitchen doorway.

"Anybody in there making lunch by any chance?" he called.

"Craig . . ." was all she could say.

"You needn't look so surprised, dear," he said as he crossed the kitchen to her side. He bent his head to kiss her and, seeing his intention, she quickly turned away. His lips brushed her cheek. Locking his arm through hers, he called over his shoulder, "Excuse us, Hilda. I'm sure you can manage.

"Dear, we have a guest for the weekend," he said as he propelled Ariane into the living room. "I invited him to the party and then realized he didn't know anyone in town, so I told him that he could stay with us."

Standing in the entrance gallery with his back to them was a tall man with black hair. At the sound of Craig's voice the man turned. "Ariane," Craig said, "this is Hassan Bjerabi. Hassan, my wife, Ariane."

"I am so very pleased to meet you," Hassan oozed. "I hope I will not be too much of an inconvenience, but I'm afraid your husband insisted." Hassan extended his hand.

"Of course not," Ariane answered, placing her hand in his. "You're more than welcome to stay here." He held her hand tightly, too tightly, causing her emerald ring to cut into her flesh. She winced but he didn't seem to notice as he continued squeezing.

"Dear, why don't you have Hilda prepare us some lunch while I take Hassan up to his room?" Craig asked, effectively ending the conversation.

Ariane watched their retreating backs, feeling as though an evil presence had swept over her, through her. Something about Hassan gave her the creeps. He was tall and thin, his pointed features jagged. The beady black eyes were flat, void of expression. They reminded her of a shark's eyes—that deadly, unfeeling stare. She rubbed her finger and shuddered.

Locked in the coolness of the study, Craig and Hassan sat comfortably on the sofa, the pitcher of iced tea and plate of sandwiches untouched on the antique tray table.

"I think twenty-five percent should cover your fee nicely," Hassan offered.

"I don't think so. I'll be taking all the risks. Aside from hiding it from the Feds I'll have to work around Russ. I think forty percent is more adequate for the risk involved," Craig countered. If he was going to launder Hassan's money, he certainly wasn't going to come away empty-handed. Of course, even twenty-five percent of Hassan's millions would be a tidy sum. But there was no reason to accept his first offer. He knew Hassan would be willing to go higher just as he knew the Arab expected him to turn down his first offer. After all, turning Hassan's money from drugs, prostitution, and God knew what else into legitimate greenbacks was no easy task.

"I see your point. But I hardly think Russ offers much of a problem. Thirty percent."

"Maybe not. But all the same it's not going to be easy. Thirty-five."

Hassan paused momentarily, regarding Craig, his sharp black eyes narrowing briefly before he answered, "Agreed."

"Good."

"You have a lovely wife. You're a very lucky man," Hassan said.

"Thanks. I've been giving your problem a great deal of thought and I think I've come up with another method of disposing of your excess cash."

"What's that?"

"A lot of the smaller firms ran into a cash flow problem after the crash, and those who have survived have been hanging on by a thread. I'm sure they'd be only too eager for an infusion of capital, and I know some of them won't be too particular where the money comes from."

"What good does that do me?"

"We'll take control of the firm and do some wheeling and dealing with discretionary accounts, overseas accounts, whatever. The firm won't know what hit them."

Hassan smiled. But it was an ugly smile. "I'm in your hands. Do it."

The early morning freshness of the day had given way to a hot, sultry afternoon. The blue sky disappeared as a white haze rolled in, bringing with it increased humidity.

Craig was off in a corner with Hassan when Ariane entered the garden. Their guests had begun arriving and were seeking out the bar and food from passing waiters.

The sun was a great ball of red fire as it sank and lent everything a soft orange glow. But the glow only served to intensify the heat which had not abated, the air thick and stifling.

Ariane had swept her hair up into a tight knot, anticipating the heat. Her new Zandra Rhodes dress was a cloud-like confection of layers of sheer white silk chiffon sewn with a smattering of tiny seed pearls. The dress bared her shoulders with small puffs of fabric around her upper arm, the uneven layers of chiffon floating down gently, ending just above her ankles.

She surveyed the tent and its decorations, pleased with the results. This year she had chosen white and silver as a color scheme. She enjoyed the cooling effect it lent to the hot summer night. The abundance of Renny's exquisite white floral arrangements in their Buccellati silver bowls, combined with the flickering white candles in their Lalique crystal holders, gave an aura of cool moonlight.

She glanced over at Craig and noticed Hassan walking away. She felt the anxiety ripple through her at the sight of Hassan. Something about him made her skin crawl.

Craig approached her, looking handsome in his white linen jacket and gray slacks. "You look lovely tonight," he said.

"Thank you." She absently touched the antique pearl and diamond dog collar from Fred Leighton around her neck. Matching earrings dangled at her ears. She was wrong. The Filofax meant nothing. And she would prove it to herself.

"Craig, I meant to ask you," Ariane began. "I found Kristen's Filofax in the apartment. How did it get there?"

Craig had been glancing around at the arriving guests, but he immediately swung his attention to Ariane.

"Kristen's what?"

"Her Filofax, her agenda. I found it on the bar," Ariane answered, watching him closely.

"Oh. I guess she left it there last week. She stopped by to drop off some papers about a charity or something for you. I wasn't paying much attention."

"Well, I'll have to get it back to her."

Ariane believed Craig, but all the same she kept her eye on him as they drifted apart and circulated among their guests. She wandered around aimlessly, always aware of where Craig was, where Kristen was.

She heard Kristen's laughter and watched her flit from one man to another. Her gaiety taunted Ariane, threatened her, dared her.

She had to know for sure. Craig's explanation wasn't enough. The uncertainty was driving her crazy, paralyzing her with dread. If she didn't do it now, she would never know. She squared her shoulders and walked determinedly toward Kristen.

"Kristen, I found your Filofax. You left it in my apartment," she said bluntly, wanting to take her by surprise.

A look of triumph flashed briefly in Kristen's blue eyes, and then it was gone as she answered coolly, "Oh, good. I was wondering where it was. I must have left it there a few days ago. Russ asked me to drop some papers off for Craig."

Ariane felt sick, nauseated, as if she had been punched

in the stomach and all the air knocked out of her. Her worst fears had come true.

"Excuse me. I think I'm needed in the kitchen," she said as she walked away, dazed.

She ordered a vodka at the bar; her usual white wine wouldn't do for tonight. Drink in hand she strolled around aimlessly, ghostlike, occasionally stopping to listen to a conversation.

At first the potent vodka burned her throat and stomach. Then she felt a pleasing warmth spreading inside of her. The alcohol took the edge off her misery, dulling the sharp pain. With a gracious smile frozen on her lips, she made her way to Lydia, Joanna, and Melissa.

"I couldn't believe my shoulders had gotten that much bigger. I was trying on my Bill Blass suit from last fall and it was too tight across the back." Melissa seemed obviously pleased that she had outgrown her suit.

"You keep up that weight training much longer and you're going to look better than Clayton," Lydia said lightly.

"I do it because it feels good to work out. You really ought to give it a try. Besides, what else have we got to do?"

"No thanks. I like my workouts between the sheets," Lydia replied.

"Why don't you come to the club, Joanna? We could work out together," Melissa suggested.

"No. I don't think so. If I worked on my breasts then legs would be in. If I worked on my legs then hips would be in. Besides, why bother? What's the use anyway?"

The sound of bitter resignation hit home, making Ariane's head reel with her pain. She drifted away, away from Joanna's cutting truth. Her glass empty, she made her way to the bar, careful to give Kristen a wide berth. The sight of her revolted Ariane. The sound of her insidious laughter filling the air was a knife twisting inside her. She would never be able to forget. Or forgive.

Thinking nothing could make her feel worse, she turned away from the bar only to come face to face with the one person who could—Alex Savage.

Her shock was thorough and showed in the widening of her dark eyes.

"Mrs. Wakefield," Alex drawled insolently. "Don't tell me you're surprised to see me. I'm disappointed. I thought the invitation was from you, personally." Alex leaned forward, his finely tailored black linen suit emphasizing his dark, dangerous looks.

"No, it was not." Her voice sounded flat and empty. He was standing too close to her and she couldn't think. Her brain was cloudy from the alcohol.

Alex reached out and, firmly cupping her elbow, led her away from the crowded area. "Now don't make a scene or you'll have a lot of explaining to do."

Ariane was helpless in his grip as he led them to a secluded spot at the end of the garden.

Wrenching her arm free, she asked heatedly, "What are you doing here?"

Alex took her glass from her and put it down on the grass. "I think you've had enough of that."

"How dare you!"

"Someone has to take care of you, as it seems you're incapable," he said, smiling.

"I don't need taking care of, and if I did, it certainly wouldn't be by the likes of you." Ariane welcomed the long-suppressed rage that rose to the surface. It was as if she was finally herself, saying what she felt.

"Now, now . . . don't get all ruffled." His fingertips softly traced random patterns on her bare shoulder. His silver eyes bored into her as he softly continued, "I was hoping the invitation was from you and that you had changed your mind."

"Well, it wasn't and I haven't," Ariane said, but without conviction. His fingers traveled gently up the side of her neck and down over her shoulder. She was mesmerized. She should stop him but she didn't have the will. She felt warm all over. The alcohol, the warm sultry night air, and Alex's warm fingers all combined to take the fight out of her. She felt like a butterfly trapped by the web of his silver gaze, unable to move.

"I can't tell you how disappointed I am to hear that." His fingers lightly traced her collarbone.

"Don't," she said feebly. She studied his dark swarthy face, the straight black brows over those incredible eyes. A warm ball of excitement grew deep inside her and she felt the urge to reach up and kiss that sensuous mouth, remembering how it had felt pressed against hers. His fingers moved to the nape of her neck and began to draw her closer to him.

"Oh naughty, naughty," Kristen cooed maliciously.

Ariane blinked her eyes as if the spell over her had been broken. She suddenly heard the noise of the party around her again and felt the warm glow she had been feeling fade to coldness.

"Aren't you two the cozy pair. Ariane, really you mustn't monopolize Alex like that. After all, he came here to have a good time. Didn't you, Alex?" Kristen purred.

"Then you show him a good time. You two deserve each other." Ariane jerked herself free of Alex's hold and stalked off angrily.

Ariane tried to rejoin the party and socialize, but her throbbing headache made it impossible. Finally, unable to stand the pain any longer, she went into the house in search of some aspirin.

She stood gripping the granite counter, having just

swallowed her pills. She squeezed her eyes shut, trying to will her headache away, but unwanted images flickered across her mind. First it was Craig and Kristen, then Kristen rubbing herself against Alex. Then Alex's hard sardonic face mocking her. At that moment, with one hundred of her closest friends outside, Ariane felt utterly alone. She heard her name called and turned to find Russ standing behind her.

"Are you all right, Ariane?" he asked solicitously.

"Oh . . . Russ. Yes, I'm fine," she whispered, afraid of aggravating her headache.

"You don't look fine. I mean, you don't look well," he explained.

"It's nothing really. I just have this awful headache. Are you enjoying yourself?" she asked. Searching his soft hazel eyes, Ariane wondered if he knew about Craig and Kristen. But he couldn't, she thought, otherwise how could he be acting so normal when she couldn't seem to function?

"It's a great party. You've really outdone yourself. But then you always do." He lowered his voice. "You know it really doesn't matter . . . about them, I mean. It doesn't mean anything."

Afraid that she understood, Ariane stalled, "Them? I don't know what you're talking about."

"I think you do, Ariane," he said sadly. "And I can see that it's tearing you up. But I know Kristen and, believe me, it's nothing."

Ariane's eyes widened in amazement. Russ knew about them. What? Did everybody know and she was the last to find out? Her humiliation was complete. She felt like a fool.

"Nothing? How can you say it's nothing?"

"Because I know Kristen. And I'm sorry to say, Craig isn't the first, and he won't be the last. They're just conquests to her. They don't mean anything. It's just something she has to prove to herself.''

"How can you accept that? Why do you accept it?''

Russ's face had a pained look of resignation as he explained, "I had to either accept it or end my marriage. I don't mean to blame it on Teddy's death, but that's when everything changed. Before our son died, Kristen always flirted, but it was harmless. Afterwards she seemed to have this terrible need, a kind of desperation that made her seek out other men. It never lasts long and then she's sorry. It wasn't easy, but I decided it was better for our daughter if we stayed married.''

"But what about you? Don't your feelings count?'' Ariane asked, searching for her own answers as well.

"The sad truth is that I love Kristen, and I know she loves me. At least as much as she's capable of loving anyone.''

Ariane reached out and rested her hand on Russ's arm. "I'm sorry. I really had no idea. I always thought Kristen was just a tease.''

"It's not that bad really.'' Russ shrugged and covered her hand with his own. "We all make our choices and we have to live with them. What about you?''

"I don't know,'' Ariane answered honestly.

"Have you spoken to Craig about it?''

"No. At first I was afraid to, and now I don't know what to do. I feel so helpless and inadequate.''

Russ's hands gripped Ariane's bare shoulders, and he gave her a light shake. "Stop it! What they did is no reflection on you. You're a young, beautiful, desirable woman, and Craig's a fool if he doesn't see that.''

A wan smile played at the corners of her mouth. "Thanks, Russ.''

He held out his arms to her and she went to him, grateful for the feeling of warmth and friendship, longing for the contact of another human being. She closed her eyes and felt her body relax for the first time in weeks.

Enjoying the solace of Russ's arms, Ariane was oblivious to the caterers in the kitchen and a pair of silver eyes watching her.

Alex tore himself away from the telling scene he'd witnessed, the obvious conclusion leaving a bitter taste in his mouth. After freeing himself from the none too subtle Kristen, he had gone in search of Ariane to finish what he had started. Finding the very moral and virtuous Mrs. Wakefield in the arms of another man sent his temper soaring. He had been right after all. The soft mouth trembling beneath his, the candid look in the dark eyes, the cries of moral indignation, had all been an act. A very good one, indeed, for he had almost forgotten what lying and deceiving creatures women were.

Downing his bourbon, Alex pushed thoughts of Ariane aside, wanting a clear head now that the investigation was proceeding. With Hassan's surprise appearance tonight, things were taking an interesting and critical turn.

As she hurried to get out of the kitchen Ariane collided head on with Hassan.

"Oh, I'm sorry," she said, automatically pulling back. But Hassan had reached out and grabbed her, his hands gripping her upper arms.

"Please, don't apologize. A woman as beautiful as you should never have to apologize." His eyes swept over her figure.

"Thank you. If you'll excuse me." She wanted to get away. She didn't like the black ice in Hassan's eyes, didn't like being this close to him, didn't like being touched by him.

Hassan's mouth twitched in what was supposed to be a

smile. "I want to thank you for your hospitality. Most wives would have been put off by an unexpected houseguest. But I can see you don't mind having an extra man around, do you?"

He was purposely trying to unnerve her, Ariane realized in a flash. He meant to disturb her. She squared her shoulders and tilted her head back, looking him straight in the eyes.

"I'm accustomed to Craig bringing his business associates home. They come and go." He was holding her too tightly. Her arms hurt.

"Yes. I suppose they do. But I expect to be more than a business associate, much more." Releasing her abruptly, he turned and walked into the kitchen.

Ariane rubbed her arms, massaging away the pain caused by his hurtful grip, trying to erase his touch. If his words hadn't frightened her, his eyes certainly would have. There was something inhuman about them, as if the man had no feelings, no emotions. Hassan had dead eyes.

chapter 9

The warm night air was still. Without a breeze and with so many people around her, Ariane suddenly felt as if she were suffocating. The music, the laughing, jeering voices, all laughing at her. The burning candles seemed too hot and too bright. She felt lightheaded and knew if she didn't get away from the crush of people, she would go mad. She had to get away, to be alone.

She walked down the wooden path, slipping off her white silk sandals and leaving them on the bottom step as she stepped onto the beach. She pulled the pins from her hair, running her fingers through it, letting it fall loosely down her back. Maybe that would lessen her headache. The sand felt good on her bare toes as she walked toward the water. The ocean was relatively quiet tonight with softly breaking waves foaming at the shoreline. She looked up at the brightly lit house, with its perfect decorations, the perfectly clad guests dining on the perfect cuisine, and felt alienated and completely alone.

The cold, dark water swirled at her ankles and wetted her hem. She was ruining the dress, but she didn't care. The water felt good and refreshing. Besides, it was her dress and she could do what she wanted, she thought a little drunkenly.

Not paying attention to where she was walking, she jumped when something cold and wet touched her hand. Looking down, she saw that it was Max, the neighbor's golden retriever. She smiled.

During the past several weeks when she had frequented the beach with her long, solitary walks, Max had taken to joining her. He followed her quietly, occasionally nudging her hand with his wet, black nose. If she sat and stared at the ocean he did the same. Sometimes he would rest his large head on her lap and she would pet him, enjoying his company, comforted by his presence. She had the eerie feeling that he knew he was comforting her and that was why he joined her.

Tonight she greeted him warmly, scratching him under the neck, and was rewarded with a lick and the exuberant wagging of his tail. They walked down the beach together a bit and then, suddenly tired, she sat down on a small dune. Max joined her and nudged his big body against her until she wrapped her arm around him and petted him.

"There, is that what you want, Max? What a big baby you are."

Max looked up at her with what looked like a grin, drawing a weak smile from her. She knew dogs didn't grin, but Max always looked as if he did.

Max's ears suddenly picked up as he stared out into the blackness listening to something. He let out a low growl and she turned to see a figure approaching. Instantly, Max was on his feet.

"I didn't realize you felt you needed protection," the unwelcome voice said sarcastically.

She rested her hand on Max, who continued his low, menacing growl.

"Just go away, Alex, and leave me alone. It's okay, Max." She petted his head, trying to calm him.

Bending over, Alex extended his hand for Max to sniff. Scratching him under the neck, he spoke to the animal softly in a voice she had never heard him use before. Soon Max began wagging his tail.

She was annoyed by Max's quick siding with the enemy. The two were playing and acting like old friends, and she felt betrayed.

"Thanks a lot, Max," she said disheartedly.

Max turned to her and, giving her a spirited wag of his tail, trotted home.

As Alex settled beside her, she looked straight ahead and refused to acknowledge his presence.

"Perhaps I offended you before. Could that be why you're so angry with me?" he asked innocently.

"I am not angry with you and I am not offended." She continued to look straight ahead. If she refused to argue with him, maybe he would go away.

"I didn't think I had. Perhaps it was Kristen's presence that annoyed you?"

She turned her head sharply to look at him, only to be met by a placid expression.

"No." She turned back to study the ocean, her nerves stretching at the mere mention of Kristen's name. *If he doesn't leave now I'll scream,* she thought.

"Then what are you doing alone in the dark?"

"But I'm not alone. I'm keeping one of my guests company," she replied, momentarily forgetting her anguish.

"Ah, yes. And an uninvited one at that."

"You bring that on yourself, you know."

"Mm . . . I do, don't I?"

"Yes, you do. And I think you enjoy it, enjoy making

trouble.'' She was aware of the soft night air, warm and soothing, the gentle breaking of the waves, the clean scent of the ocean, his nearness.

"Well, life is so boring otherwise, don't you think?"

"I don't know. Is it?" Was that the problem? That her marriage was boring, that she was boring?

"Is your life boring?" Alex asked.

Not now, thanks to Craig. "No."

"That's good. I wouldn't want you to be bored. You should always be excited, stimulated." His words sounded innocent enough but the look in those silver eyes meant something else and sent her heart beating furiously.

"I think I should be getting back to my guests." Sitting alone in the dark with him was too disturbing, too exciting. The way he stared at her, his heated gaze glancing at her mouth, his words a passionate promise, caused a rush of heat within her. She knew he wanted her, felt his desire pull at her, drawing her closer, tempting her beyond her control. She sprang to her feet and rushed off, leaving him alone in the dark.

"Craig, there's something I'd like to discuss with you," Ariane said when she found him in the gallery the next morning. She had found the other side of the bed empty when she awoke, and she had been relieved. Lying there beside him all night had been difficult enough.

"Okay. What is it?" Craig answered pleasantly, walking into the living room. He was looking handsome and pristine in his tennis whites.

"Not here. Let's go into the study." Ariane led the way.

Craig followed her into the blue and white room and sat on the plaid sofa as she closed the door.

This was Craig's domain, and suddenly Ariane was sorry she had chosen this room. But it was the only room downstairs that afforded any privacy, and she refused to discuss Kristen in her bedroom.

"Well, what is it?" Craig asked as she hesitated at the door.

Now that she was finally confronting him, she was scared, her insides shaking. She still had the nagging fear that, once confronted, Craig would leave her.

"I know about you and Kristen," Ariane stated without preamble.

His face went blank. Too blank. "Know what?"

"I know how her Filofax came to be in our apartment. Your stories didn't match. The least you could have done was come up with a well-rehearsed alibi." Her words brought a welcome heat of anger, taking the chill out of her. There was no going back now.

"Oh, God, Ariane, I'm sorry." Craig rubbed his hand across his eyes.

"Sorry you did it or sorry you got caught?" Ariane lashed out, her pain fresh and raw. His easy admittance and apology infuriated her. She paced in front of him, trembling with the force of her anger.

"Both, I suppose. Look, it only happened once and I don't even understand why it did. She came by the office and I gave her a ride home. We stopped at the apartment for something and wound up in bed."

"That's all? How could you? And in our bed!"

"Would it have been any better in some sleazy motel? What's the difference where it happened? It happened and that's it. I said I'm sorry. What more do you want from me?" He was on his feet, glaring defiantly at her.

"I want your head on a platter," she cried. "I want you to hurt like you've hurt me."

Craig's stance relaxed. "It meant nothing. I swear to you, it'll never happen again."

Words. Empty words. "But what about *us*? How could you have done this to us?" Her voice choked with pain.

"It had nothing to do with us. Forget it . . . it's not important." An irritated note of impatience crept into Craig's voice.

"Not important? Are you crazy? You cheat on me and tell me it's nothing. And you expect me to forget it just like that?" She wanted more from him, needed more.

Craig's voice turned clipped. "All right then. What do you want, a divorce?"

Divorce? The thought terrified her. She'd be all alone. "No."

Craig put his hands on her shoulders and smiled easily. "Well, neither do I. Let's not let one night ruin seven years. We can go on, can't we? You want to, don't you?" When Ariane didn't answer immediately, he put his arm around her shoulder and attempted to hug her to him. She shrugged out of his grasp. "You do want to go on, don't you?"

Wanting to feel reassured by his explanation, Ariane looked at him, searching his face for reassurance, and muttered a halfhearted, "Yes."

"Good," he responded cheerfully, as though the argument was already forgotten. "Just put it out of your mind. I did. Listen, I have a tennis game with Eric, but if you'd rather I can stay home with you."

"No. Don't bother." The last thing she wanted was to be with him.

The holiday traffic home from Southampton had been brutal and she was exhausted. Craig went to work in his study while Ariane went upstairs to bed.

In a while she felt Craig's lips on the side of her neck, gently moving upward toward her ear, planting light feathery kisses along the path. She jerked away.

"What's the matter?" Craig was propped on his elbow, looking down into her face.

Ariane glared at him, almost unable to find the words. "What's the matter? Are you kidding?"

"I said I was sorry."

"Great. But I'm not in the mood. Good night." Ariane rolled to the edge of the bed, yanking the blanket over her shoulder.

Suddenly, she felt terribly alone and sad, a crush of tears choking her throat. Craig had shattered her pride, her self-respect, her identity. The anger at his betrayal bubbled up, and tears of frustration filled her eyes. She had centered her life on him and she saw now it had been a mistake.

Her marriage, her life, wasn't what she wanted it to be. It was time for her to take responsibility for it and do something about it.

An idea had been teasing at the edge of her mind for some time now and she decided to act on it immediately. Satisfied with her decision, she fell into an exhausted sleep.

Walking past the mirror in the office building on Seventh Avenue, Ariane checked her reflection before entering the crowded elevator. She was wearing a trim black and gray tweed Armani suit over a white silk blouse. As her gray kidgloved hand reached out and pushed the penthouse button, nervousness quivered in her stomach. When the doors opened, she took several deep breaths to calm herself and stepped into a spacious reception area.

An hour later, a radiant Ariane fairly floated out of the building. She paused on the sidewalk outside, too happy to go straight home. She had done it, she thought triumphantly. It had taken weeks and at times she had been ready to give up, but she had persevered. She had gotten a job! Not just any job, but something she had always wanted—a career designing clothes. And she had done it all on her own with no help from anybody. She knew many women whose husbands owned firms on Seventh Avenue. It would have been easy to make a few phone calls and have one of them prevail upon her husband to help set up an interview and call in a favor. But she didn't want it that way. This had to be something she did entirely on her own.

Looking up into the brilliant blue sky, she decided to walk, too excited to be confined in a taxi. It was an early fall day and the crispness in the afternoon air enlivened her step. She smiled to herself as her mind replayed the events that led to today's victory.

For weeks she had poured her anger, her frustration and fear about Craig and Kristen into the task of job hunting. She was going to make a new life for herself one way or the other. Finally, today, in Logan Townsend's office it had happened. Townsend was the founder and president of LT, Inc., a manufacturer of moderately priced women's sportswear.

Logan Townsend had intimidated her a little at first. He was in his early sixties, standing shy of six feet and powerfully built. His sharp blue eyes sparkled beneath black brows and brightened a tan, ruddy complexion. The only giveaway as to his age was his head of pure white hair.

The interview had gone smoothly as Logan had asked her about her background, schooling, and job experience. He looked through the portfolio of the sketches she had brought with her and seemed especially interested in her evening wear. When he had mentioned the salary he was willing to pay and offered her the job, she'd accepted on the spot. They had shook hands on their agreement, and Ariane had positively beamed with happiness.

There was a spring in her step as she walked home. She couldn't wait to tell Craig. She would fix a special dinner for the two of them, sort of a victory celebration. With all the stress that had been between them lately, a romantic dinner would be nice . . . like a new start to her new life.

An hour later champagne was on ice, the miniature orchids in their Baccarat vase, and the table set with the Cristofle silver.

She would eat alone. Craig had to work late.

Craig pushed Brad's private telephone number and drummed his fingers on the desk, waiting for him to answer. "Oh good, I was hoping to catch you before you went home," Craig said when Brad answered.

"I wish I had left. I can't seem to get out of here any night before ten."

"I know just how you feel. How have you done in Tripton?" Craig asked, referring to the stock they had bought up and manipulated with a short squeeze.

"Great. I'm up an average of forty-five dollars. How much longer do you think we should hold out?"

"I think it's about that time. We can't squeeze any more out of Tripton. It's overvalued as it is now. Let's start unloading tomorrow. I'll sell out my position first and then start unloading my customer accounts."

"I'll do the same. Without us around to support the stock, coupled with the huge block we'll be dumping, Tripton will fall like a rock. Those guys that started buying the stock on the way up are going to lose their shirts."

"Look, they know the Street's a gamble. There's no such thing as a sure thing." Craig paused, then added with a smug note of satisfaction in his voice, "Unless, of course, you can control the situation."

Craig replaced the receiver, glad he hadn't gotten involved with the latest craze on Wall Street and had the phones tapped. Lots of firms did it, including some of the big board companies such as Merrill Lynch. They tapped all the phones, storing the conversations on tape. Since the October 19 crash more firms had been jumping on the bandwagon, installing the sophisticated equipment, hoping the taped conversations would explain away the mountain of trade problems that turned up after the monumental volume.

He knew of one firm where the traders had all started using portable phones to avoid having their business dealings permanently recorded for posterity.

But he had more important things to deal with as he turned to Newman Brothers' latest underwriting. He had already set his fee and the amount of free warrants the firm was getting from the company. Now he had to bill out the underwriting to the firm's customers, his friends, so he could maintain control.

Craig had finished the preliminary draft and was getting ready to leave when his private line lit up.

"Yes."

"Do you know who this is?"

"Yes," Craig answered, recognizing the voice.

" 'Wall Street Examined' is doing their feature on TVC this week. Thought you'd be interested."

"Yes, very," Craig said. TVC was a stock Newman Brothers traded. "What's their stand?"

"I'd buy as much as I could, if I were you."

"I understand, and thanks for the call."

"My pleasure, and I assume you'll make sure it is."

"As our usual arrangements. Thanks again." Craig replaced the receiver, an excitement surging through him.

"Wall Street Examined" was a highly regarded and well respected weekly television show on Friday night. First, the commentator discussed and examined the past week's activities and events on Wall Street. Then each week there was a different guest speaker, offering views and advice on different stocks, industries, or whatever was his field of expertise.

This week the guest speaker was obviously going to tout TVC as a "buy." Today was Thursday, which gave Craig all day Friday to buy as much TVC as he could get his hands on. By Monday, after the recommendation had been made public, the stock was sure to open higher and take off as the average citizen sought to fatten his portfolio.

Cultivating "the voice" on the phone as a friend had paid off well. This wasn't the first time Craig had used his services. Each time "the voice" had been richly rewarded for his information. After this bit of information he would be expecting a bonus and he'd get it. He was worth every penny.

It was a little after eleven o'clock when Ariane heard Craig's footsteps on the stairs. He entered the bedroom, looking exhausted. "You didn't have to wait up."

"I know, but I wanted to. I have something to tell you." She could hardly stop herself from blurting out her news.

"I'll be right in," he called over his shoulder as he walked into his dressing room. Moments later he emerged, wearing his Sulka silk robe. "So, what is it?"

"I got a job today," she said, her eyes shining.

"Oh? What hospital?"

"No, not that. A real paying job. I'm going to be an assistant designer for LT, Inc."

"Why in the world would you want to do that?"

"You know I've always wanted to design clothes, and I just decided to get a job."

"You realize, of course, that means getting up early every morning and going in every day, even if you'd rather go shopping."

"I assure you I'm capable of rising early, and Logan

Townsend wouldn't have hired me if he didn't think I could handle the job.''

"All right . . . Fine, then. Enjoy yourself," Craig said as he strode from the room.

Ariane could hardly go to sleep that night, as conflicting emotions bombarded her. She was still proud that she had gotten the job, but Craig's remark had planted a seed of doubt. Maybe he was right. Maybe she couldn't hold a job.

Ariane loved work. In fact, sometimes she felt guilty calling it work because it didn't seem like work at all. It was more like an exciting new world that had been opened up to her and she was enjoying every minute of it. Sometimes, when five o'clock came she had to be reminded it was time to leave. She grew restless on the weekends, missing her job, anxious to return.

She had been on the job for almost two months, and she felt like a professional now, compared to her nervous beginning. As she sat at her desk she smiled, remembering how anxious she had been. On that first day Logan had led her into the designing room and she had looked around in awe at the large room. It was bright and airy, painted white, with bare, ash floors, one end framed with towering windows. The models' fitting area was cluttered with three-way mirrors, stools, and dressmaker dummies. The middle of the room held tall architect tables and stools. The walls were nearly covered with sketches of clothing and swatches of fabric.

Logan introduced Ariane to the head designer, Gordon Friedman. Gordon began Ariane's education immediately.

"Choosing the right fabric is just as important as the design of a garment," he explained. "A material that's too stiff or too limp could ruin the finished product. I'm afraid your designer clothes of silk and cashmere and linen will never work for the LT customer.''

"So we have to blend wool and polyester to keep the price down,'' Ariane said.

"Exactly,'' Gordon said. "Today I want you to go to Macy's and scout the competition. Then visit your designers and see what they're up to.''

"And here I thought you designed everything yourself,'' Ariane teased.

"I do,'' Gordon had said with a teasing smile. "I just want to see what they stole from me.''

Craig and Ariane sat at the table in silence, sharing a rare dinner together at home. His early attempt to spend more time with her, to make up for his transgression, had quickly faded. He stopped coming home early, stopped calling as frequently, and reverted to making appointments on the weekends. Only this time Ariane didn't seem to mind as much. She had her own life.

"Ariane, don't make any plans for next weekend because I've accepted an invitation for us to go to Texas.''

Her heart lurched. "Oh?'' she said casually. "Whose invitation is it?''

"Alex Savage.''

With a great deal of effort she forced herself to remain calm.

"Russ and Kristen were invited too, and we'll be flying down together,'' he added.

"Do we have to go?'' She tried to think of an excuse that would save her from what would most assuredly be a disastrous weekend.

"No, of course not. I could always insult Savage by telling him my wife didn't feel like coming and let some other firm pick up his multimillion-dollar account,'' Craig said.

"I didn't mean for you to insult him. I'd just rather not go if we don't have to."

"Look, Ariane, there are lots of wives who do much more business entertaining than you. This is one of those invitations that I can't afford to turn down. I don't think a weekend in Texas is too much to ask."

No? Then why was she so afraid? Not only of Alex, but of herself as well. She didn't know what frightened her the most—Alex, or her reaction to him. Both were dangerous. But how could she avoid either one?

chapter 10

Ariane settled herself on the large, comfortable seat in Alex's private plane for the hour flight to his ranch. He had been unable to meet them when they arrived at the Dallas/Ft. Worth airport and had sent his friend, Travis Taylor, in his place. Travis, tall and muscular with brown wavy hair and amber-colored eyes, was very friendly, keeping up a steady stream of conversation.

Locked within the confines of the cabin, Ariane couldn't help but catch the heavy musk scent of Kristen's perfume. Unconsciously, she turned her nose up at the potent fragrance. This was the first time since she had discovered Craig's adultery that she had not been surrounded by a large crowd when Kristen was present. There had been none of the usual dinner dates with just the four of them. She assumed she had Craig to thank for that, but the thought did nothing to stop the bitter wave of resentment churning in her stomach.

A station wagon was waiting for them at the airstrip for

the drive to the ranch. They rode for some time before Travis turned the car onto a long, straight road lined with towering oak trees, their overhead branches forming a canopy of shade from the hot sun. Kristen complained about the heat, and Travis explained that it was unusually warm because they were in the midst of one of their occasional hot spells.

The house came into view and Ariane was surprised at the elegance and size of it. Done in the Spanish style, it was a sprawling white stucco with a red-tile roof. A white wall surrounded the house, and as they drove through the black wrought-iron gates the courtyard became visible, revealing a large fountain surrounded by myriad blooming flowers.

The large carved mahogany door opened and an elderly Spanish woman appeared. Dressed in a black uniform, she was short and plump, her gray hair pulled tightly into a bun. She introduced herself as Consuelo Ramirez and greeted them warmly, apologizing for Alex's absence.

The interior of the house was invitingly cool, and as they passed through the large entrance gallery Ariane noticed the polished dark wood floors and handsome antique furniture. They climbed up the wide staircase to a spacious landing where Consuelo led them to the left, explaining that Mr. Savage's quarters were to the right. At the end of a long, wide hallway, Consuelo stopped and opened the door to the room that was to be Kristen and Russ's. Ariane caught a glimpse of a brightly colored bedspread on a double bed before moving two doors down.

Their room was large and airy, the light streaming in through the French doors, framed with sheer white curtains, leading to the balcony. The soft rose and white room was furnished with antique pine furniture, the twin beds covered with antique quilts. There were low bowls of fresh flowers everywhere and antique prints on the white walls.

"I'm sure you would like to freshen up after your long trip, so I'll leave you. Mr. Savage would like for you to join him for cocktails in the living room at seven o'clock," Consuelo said as she left.

"Well, he certainly likes playing hard to get," Craig said.

"Who?" she asked, as though she didn't know.

"Alex. Who else?" Craig replied with irritation. "First he doesn't meet us at the plane and now this. I guess when you run that kind of money you can afford to be independent."

Ariane busied herself with unpacking while Craig grumbled his annoyance. As far as she was concerned she'd be only too happy if Alex never appeared.

"Good to see you, Craig," Alex said when Craig and Ariane entered the living room. He nodded curtly in Ariane's direction. "Welcome to Texas. I'm sorry I couldn't meet you before, but there was something I had to take care of personally. I hope your trip was comfortable. Kristen was just complaining about the hot spell we're having. I'm afraid I can't do anything about that. But I can offer you a drink. What will you have?" Alex turned his glance toward Ariane.

"White wine, please." Why did her heart leap in her throat at the sight of him? She could feel her skin flush hotly at the look in his silver eyes.

Craig and Ariane joined Kristen and Russ, who were being regaled by Travis's amusing stories. Alex came over with their drinks and as he handed the crystal goblet to Ariane, she felt his lingering look.

"Thank you," she murmured, growing uncomfortable at his sharp perusal.

"You're welcome," Alex replied, overly polite as one corner of his mouth lifted in an amused smirk.

What a miserable weekend this was going to be, Ariane thought. Alex and Kristen. Alex.

After dinner they adjourned to the patio to enjoy the warm night air.

The house was U-shaped, with the two wings of living quarters flanking the patio and fountain. Terraces, covered with blooming flowers, ran the length of each wing. Small lights on the grounds of the garden threw occasional pools of light into the darkness.

Ariane commented on the exotic plants she had never seen before.

"There are probably thousands of plants native to Texas that you've never heard of. I bet you've never even seen a mesquite tree. You probably think it comes packaged in bags." Travis laughed good-naturedly.

"If you'd be interested, I'd be glad to take all of you riding tomorrow," Alex suggested.

Interested in seeing more of Texas and momentarily forgetting her anxiety about Alex, Ariane was the first to answer, "That sounds wonderful. I'd love to."

"Well, count me out. You wouldn't catch me on a horse. I don't deal with four-legged animals," Kristen finished suggestively, peering at Travis, who pretended not to notice.

"If you're not going, dear, then I'll stay here and keep you company," Russ said, with a sharp look at Kristen, obviously dashing her hopes of getting Travis alone.

"Count me in. Sounds like fun," Craig said.

"Good. Consuelo will serve you breakfast in the dining room or, if you prefer, call and she'll bring it up. Just ask for anything you want. Say we meet at the stables, nine o'clock?"

As Craig and Ariane both nodded in agreement, Travis rose and said, "I guess that's my signal. Sorry to have to leave you nice folks, but I have a lot of work to do tomorrow."

Kristen pouted and cooed, "Oh no. Just when I thought we were getting friendly."

"Don't worry. I'll be back tomorrow before the party."

"Party? What party?" Kristen turned her attention to Alex.

"Just some neighbors of mine who are coming by for dinner tomorrow night. I thought you'd be interested in meeting some of the local people."

"Only if they're as charming and good-looking as you two," gushed Kristen.

Oh please, Ariane thought, *if it breathed it would be charming to you.*

Ariane and Craig passed each other in the small room while they undressed and prepared for bed.

"How did you like the food? I thought it was very good." She felt as if she had to make conversation.

"I suppose, if you like Spanish food. Give me Le Cirque any day."

"Travis seems very nice, doesn't he?" She couldn't believe they could sound so casual when their life together was coming apart.

"Yeah, but a little too much of that good old boy routine. When Alex said he had a ranch I didn't think he meant in the middle of nowhere. I guess that's why he comes to New York, to get away from all the desolation."

"I don't know. It doesn't feel desolated to me. I kind of like it." There was something about the wide open spaces, whether it be at the beach or in the country, that appealed to her.

"Oh really? Come on, Ariane, you wouldn't last two days out here without your string of designer boutiques."

Craig smiled, but there was an undertone of sarcasm in his voice, telling Ariane just how little he thought of her.

"Is that a fact? For your information I happen to be working now, and I haven't been in a store since I started," Ariane snapped, her anger surprising them both.

"There's no need to take my head off. I was only kidding. You know, you've been very touchy and uptight lately. Maybe this job is more than you can handle. I suggest you take a Valium and calm down." He patted her on the arm and left her alone in the bathroom.

When she came out of the bathroom, Craig was already in his bed. The separate beds would prove no hardship on their relations. They hadn't made love since her discovery. And she didn't seem to miss it. Or was it Craig she didn't miss?

Ariane pulled the lace-edged covers down and settled herself in the strange bed. She fell asleep almost instantly, only to wake up sharply, her heart pounding in her throat. She looked at the clock in the dark room and read three o'clock. The sickening anxiety made her shiver. Her body was cold and damp with perspiration. She had had the nightmare. Again.

The apartment had turned to quicksand. The walls, floors, furniture, everything. There was nothing solid to hold onto. The more she tried to run, the deeper she sank. The quicksand was alive, grabbing at her ankles, sucking at her calves. She screamed but no one heard. She was alone. Helpless. She was being pulled lower, lower, the thick ooze tugging at her knees. There was no escape.

Just when the fear overwhelmed her, she had woken with a start, her body trembling. Lately the dream had been coming more often and more terrifyingly vivid. And each time she sank deeper and deeper into that morass.

It's only a dream, she told herself. *You can't die from a dream.*

• • •

Craig had already left the room when she woke in the morning. It was eight o'clock and she knew she'd have to hurry not to be late.

The dream always left her shaken with a hangover of anxiety she had to fight hard to dispel. She washed and dressed quickly, choosing a pair of snug-fitting faded jeans and a chambray cotton shirt. After she plaited her hair into a thick braid, she made up her eyes lightly and slipped her small feet into brown lizard cowboy boots.

Craig was in the dining room finishing his breakfast when Ariane joined him. While she was still eating her grapefruit, he excused himself, explaining he wanted to make a few calls before they left.

He returned moments later and said, "Sorry, but something's come up and I have to stay by the phone. Looks like you'll have to take your ride without me."

"No," Ariane answered quickly. "I mean, why don't we wait until this afternoon, and then we can go together?" She didn't want to be alone with Alex. Whenever they were alone together they either fought or . . . There was definitely safety in numbers where Alex was concerned.

"I wish I could, but I have to be by the phone all day. Look, you love to ride and I'm sure Alex is a great guide, so go ahead and enjoy yourself."

Craig crossed to where she sat and rested his hands on her shoulders. "Go ahead. After all, it's not every day you have the opportunity to see Texas. It would be a shame for you to miss it just because I have to work. Besides, it would be insulting to Alex for you to cancel just because I can't go. And I'd rather not insult him. You do remember why we're here in the first place?"

"Yes, I remember," Ariane replied, seeing no way out.

If she refused to go, she'd have to contend with Craig's anger and Alex's ridicule. At that thought, she sat up a little straighter and said, "I'll make your apologies to Alex."

Ariane was surprised at the vastness of the stables. On this ranch, raising horses was apparently more than a hobby; it was a profitable business. The large horse breeding farm had rows of barns, neat white fencing, and surrounding lush green grass. There were a dozen or more ranch hands about and as she walked nearer, she recognized Alex in a corral with a honey-colored palomino.

She walked directly to the ring and stood unnoticed as she watched Alex attempt to quiet the bucking horse. He was holding onto the horse's bridle while the animal jerked and reared. The horse's hooves pawed the ground, raising clouds of dust.

Ariane watched, amazed as the horse's frantic efforts seemed to lessen as the beautiful creature appeared to be listening to Alex's quiet words. He gradually tightened the reins and gently stroked the horse's nose.

Slowly, Alex began to lead him around the corral. Again, the horse tried to fight him but Alex held him firmly and continued talking to him. When the animal had quieted sufficiently, Alex motioned to a tall lanky boy who had been watching. Giving the boy instructions, he handed him the reins, then walked over to where Ariane was standing.

As she watched him walk toward her, Ariane thought Alex looked more like a ranch hand than a sophisticated businessman. Dressed in well-worn Levis and a faded denim shirt with its sleeves rolled up, his face sun-bronzed, he looked perfectly at home in the dusty corral. Running a hand through his thick black hair, he casually pushed back a stray lock that had fallen across his forehead.

"That was quite impressive," she said.

"All in a day's work," he replied. Then, glancing around he lowered his voice and added teasingly, "Are we alone?"

In spite of herself, Ariane could feel the hot blush rise to her face as she explained Craig's absence.

Alex gave her a lazy smile. "Then I suppose you'll have to cancel our ride. Surely Craig wouldn't let you go riding with me alone."

"Don't be ridiculous. Of course I'm still going."

It was ironic, she thought, that Alex kept assigning traits of jealousy and possessiveness to Craig, assuming Craig wouldn't let her out of his sight. But it was Craig who kept pushing her to be with him.

"Good. For a moment I thought you'd be afraid to be alone with me," Alex said, his face inscrutable.

"I am not afraid of being alone with you." She rankled as his words hit their mark. Then, deciding on a different tactic, she asked with a playful note in her voice, "Maybe it's you who's afraid to be alone with me."

Alex's gray eyes stared hard at her, an odd glint in them.

"Maybe you're right." His expression was quickly replaced by the mocking sardonic look that she knew all too well. "If I promise not to take advantage of you and to behave myself, would you do me the honor of allowing me to show you my humble ranch?"

His sensual mouth twisted in a teasing smile that she couldn't help returning. "I doubt if you could ever behave yourself, but as long as you've offered me your promise, I know I'll be safe."

Ariane followed Alex to the stable, where he selected a gentle chestnut mare for her. Alex's horse was barely under control as it was led out by a stable hand, and he quickly took the reins of the large black stallion from the boy. The horse was magnificent, tossing his beautiful head, his black mane flying until he recognized Alex. He quieted somewhat as he allowed Alex to stroke his nose.

"Do you have to go through that every time you ride him?" Ariane asked from on top of her mount, Bluebonnet.

"He doesn't like anybody to handle him except me. Sort of a one-man horse. He doesn't trust anybody but me, do you, Thunder?" It was almost as if Thunder understood as he gave his regal head an answering toss.

Ariane took the opportunity to observe Alex on Thunder's back and thought how alike they seemed. They were both arrogant, independent creatures with a wild, reckless streak. It was obvious they were well-suited for each other, Ariane thought as she studied Alex's proud profile. The virile quality in him was almost animallike, frightening in its intensity. He had seemed to enjoy the fact that Thunder couldn't be handled by anyone but him. Well, at least one of them could be tamed, Ariane thought, bemused. Certainly no one could tame Alex.

They rode for some time, not talking, the hot Texas sun beating down on them. Ariane was surprised by the sharply rolling land covered with thick grasses. She had imagined all of Texas to be flat, open. She felt deeply contented as she looked about the vast open space. It was the same feeling she experienced sitting on the beach in Southampton, looking at the ocean.

They passed a small herd of cattle grazing peacefully, then rode beneath trees that Ariane had never seen before. Alex explained they were pecan, walnut, and hickory.

Alex stopped at a stream, dismounted, and led his horse to the water to drink. Ariane followed his lead and did likewise, dipping her hands into the clear, running water and cooling the back of her neck. Straightening up, she walked toward Alex, who was sitting in the shade of a large oak tree. She sat opposite him, giving him a wide berth. It did nothing to lessen the pull of his sexuality.

"Well, what do you think?" Alex asked, gesturing wide with his arm, apparently anxious to hear her reply.

"I think it's beautiful. I had no idea it would look like this," Ariane answered honestly as she sat enjoying the coolness the shade offered. "It's much warmer than I expected." She opened the cuff of her shirt and rolled it back, trying to ignore Alex's intense stare.

"We're in the last throes of an Indian summer," Alex explained. "Any day a norther could blow in and bring the chill of winter. Texas weather is very unpredictable. I guess that's why they call it 'Mother Nature.' "

Ariane saw the familiar teasing glint in Alex's eyes and had to laugh. "Oh, but you're wrong if you think that's the reason. It's because she's so strong and powerful and everyone depends on her."

"And I suppose you believe men and women should be treated as equals?" He laughed. "Heaven help us, a red-hot feminist in our midst."

"And what's wrong with being treated as equals?" Ariane asked hotly, still smarting from Craig's remark about her not being capable of handling her job.

"Now don't get excited. I just don't think that women were cut out for certain jobs, just as men weren't cut out for others. Now, take you, for instance. I don't think a man could sit around all day being a man of leisure. There's nothing wrong with it, if that's what you want, mind you, but I don't think a man would find it stimulating enough."

"First of all, there is no reason why a man would need any more stimulation than a woman. Secondly, as a so-called woman of leisure I didn't spend my time staring at the walls. I did volunteer work in a hospital, I sat on committees to charities and took courses at school. And anyway, I'm working now." Ariane was surprised at the anger she heard in her voice. She was tired of being thought of as worthless.

"You are? Doing what?"

"I'm an assistant designer at a sportswear house," Ariane answered with pride.

"And exactly what does that entail?"

As she told Alex about her job she found him to be a good listener. He asked questions when she used terms he didn't understand. She told him things she hadn't meant to, things she hadn't told anyone, such as how determined she was to get the job on her own, and her fear at each interview.

"I thought all little girls wanted to be ballerinas when they grew up," Alex teased when Ariane told him she used to make clothes for her dolls.

"Oh, that too. I've always taken ballet lessons. The only reason I stopped is that I don't have the time now." Embarrassed at how much she talked about herself, she sought to change the subject. "What did you want to be when you grew up?"

A dark look passed over Alex's bronzed face and his jaw grew rigid. He had a faraway look in his eyes and when he focused on her, she shuddered inwardly at the cold, empty stare. Then, just as quickly as it came, his grim look disappeared as his features smoothed themselves into a bland expression.

"I wanted to be a writer."

"Really? Do you ever write now?"

"No, I don't have the time." With one fluid motion he rose and offered her his hand. "And if I don't want Consuelo to bite my head off, I'd better get us back for lunch." Ariane accepted his hand and as her eyes locked with his, she felt something warm and vital pass between them. She thought Alex felt it too before he dropped her hand and looked away.

Mounted on their horses, they began a leisurely ride back to the ranch. Ariane's mind drifted as she rode, the sun pleasantly warm on her back. The sky was an incredibly clear cornflower blue, spotted by an occasional white cloud. The land and sky seemed to roll on forever, with no end in sight, and she somehow felt a part of it.

Lost in thought, Ariane failed to notice the dark shape in the grass, but Bluebonnet saw it and reared in fear at the sight of the snake. The terrified horse took off at a fast gallop, racing flat out. Ariane held on tightly and bent low to avoid low-hanging branches. Suddenly, Bluebonnet stumbled over a large root and lost her footing. Ariane flew through the air.

She landed on her back with a thud, the breath momentarily knocked out of her. Slightly dazed, she felt strong arms around her.

"Are you all right?" Alex demanded, his face full of concern as he bent over her and helped her into a sitting position. Ariane shook her head to clear it and answered a hesitant, "I think so."

"Just rest a minute. I think you're probably all right, but that was quite a dive. I'll have the doctor check you out when we get back."

"No, no," she protested, struggling to rise. "Really, I'm fine."

Alex's arms held her back and he spoke softly as if to a child, "All right. No doctor. But stay put and relax for a moment."

Taking a deep calming breath, Ariane smelled the pleasing scent of Alex mingled with horses and fresh grass. She felt the heat emanating from his body and noticed the mat of black hair on his chest left exposed by his partially opened shirt.

"You should have told me you were a beginner rider," he chided.

Annoyed, Ariane sat up. "I am not a beginner rider. I've been riding since I was a child."

"Well, that couldn't have been very long ago."

"You really are infuriating, you know that?" She scrambled to her feet. Looking down at Alex resting complacently in the grass, her temper flared. "I should have known better than to expect anything more of you," she said. "You just can't control that superior male attitude of yours. No wonder you hide out here in the middle of nowhere. You just can't make it in the civilized world."

With a catlike grace, Alex rose to his feet and stood in front of her. "And can you make it in your civilized world?"

"Of course I can."

"Well, I don't believe the old adage, 'Clothes make the man.' There's a lot more to being civilized than wearing a pin-striped suit and dining in the best restaurants. Don't you think?" She knew he was baiting her. "Or is that all you want from life?"

"No, I have my job," Ariane answered defensively. Alex's question was a little too close to her own recent doubts. Deciding to recapture the offensive, she said, with her arm gesturing widely, "And is this all you want?"

"Yes," he answered simply.

"I . . . I'm sorry. I didn't mean that the way it sounded." She was ashamed to meet his eyes.

Alex reached out and, placing one finger under her downcast chin, lifted her head so that she was forced to look at him.

"I know," he said with surprising gentleness.

"It's just that you get me so angry that I don't know what I'm saying," she said.

"I know." The corner of his mouth lifted in a mocking smile.

Sensing a heretofore unknown honesty between them, she continued, "Sometimes I think you do it on purpose."

"I know." His eyes twinkled. "I do."

"You really are a rat," she said, smiling up at him.

"I thought we had already established that. You've certainly told me so . . . many times."

"You deserved it."

"Right again. And now that I've used up my quota of agreeability for the next ten years, I think we'd better get back."

Alex turned away and walked over to Bluebonnet, leaving a bewildered Ariane staring after him in confusion. She watched as he bent down and expertly went over each of Bluebonnet's legs, feeling for injuries. When he got to her right front leg, Bluebonnet raised her head and tried to shy away. Alex patted her gently on the neck and walked back to Ariane.

"There's nothing broken, but it's a pretty bad sprain and I don't think you should ride her."

"Then how will I get back?"

"You'll have to ride with me. I suppose Thunder can handle the extra weight." Alex's eyes raked her from head to toe, causing a hot blush to spread over her features. "We'll leave Bluebonnet here for now and I'll have one of the ranch hands come out this afternoon and tend to her. Unless, of course, you have any other suggestions?"

"No, that's fine," she answered, trying to hide her reluctance.

"Good. Come over here," Alex ordered as he stood next to Thunder.

Ariane obeyed, feeling like one of his cattle on the way to the slaughter house. Alex gave her a lift up, causing

Thunder to snap his head around, unaccustomed to having anyone but Alex on his back. The stallion tossed his head and began dancing nervously. Alex grabbed his bridle, holding it while he stroked his nose, trying to calm him.

Ariane felt Alex's lean, hard body press intimately against her back as he eased into the saddle. His muscular thighs curved around her and as he leaned forward to gather the reins, she could feel his warm breath on her cheek. She looked down as his strong arms came around her and rested nonchalantly on her thighs. His hands loosely held the reins.

"Ready?"

"Yes." Her mouth felt unaccountably dry.

Alex clicked to Thunder and started him walking in the direction of the ranch. Ariane was all too aware of the pressure of Alex's body against the small of her back as they swayed gently with Thunder's rhythm. She found herself studying the brown, sinewy arms that surrounded her, trapping her in their circle. She sat up perfectly straight and tried to lean forward to put some space between them, but there was no room. Alex's thighs felt like granite pushing against her legs and she could feel the powerful muscles work as he directed Thunder. She had the strangest feeling in the pit of her stomach. It was much warmer out than she had realized, and she could feel tiny beads of perspiration forming between her breasts. If only he weren't sitting so close to her.

"Relax," Alex commanded, his voice sounding annoyed.

"I am relaxed."

"No, you're not. I don't mind if I make you nervous. I just don't want you to spook Thunder," he said as he leaned forward.

Ariane whipped her head around only to find herself inches from Alex's hard-set face. The cool, gray eyes glowed with a malicious gleam. "I am not nervous and there's no reason why you would make me nervous. If you'd just give me a little more room, I'd be more comfortable." Ariane focused on her anger to dispel other unwanted feelings.

"Sorry," Alex said sarcastically and leaned still closer to her. "But I thought you enjoyed being embraced by men." His eyes narrowed.

"I don't know where you get your ideas, but the only man who embraces me is my husband," Ariane said. God, she could feel the heat from his body.

The look on his face changed and Ariane saw a smoldering flame in the depths of his eyes that frightened her more than his cutting words. She turned around so quickly she startled Thunder. She was hot. The small beads of perspiration formed tiny rivulets as they trickled down between her breasts. The day was uncomfortably warm, but she wasn't sure if the heat came from the burning sun or the heat burning within her.

At last she caught sight of the stables. Just a little longer and she'd be free of him.

They rode through the opened white gate toward the stables. Alex pulled Thunder to a halt and slid off his back before Ariane had time to react.

"Swing your leg over," he ordered, his voice sharp as he stood on the ground looking up at her.

"I can do it," she answered stubbornly as she tried to maneuver on the tall horse.

"Don't be ridiculous," he said. "Thunder's too big for you."

Before she realized what he was about, Alex reached up and, grabbing her firmly about the waist, pulled her from Thunder's back. She landed forcefully on the ground, her waist hurting from the grip of his hands.

"Tell Consuelo not to hold lunch for me, I have work

to do.'' Not waiting for an acknowledgment, he turned on his heel and walked away.

She had been right from the start. She shouldn't have gone riding with Alex. She shouldn't be alone with him. This man was definitely dangerous.

chapter 11

When she entered the dining room Craig, Kristen, and Russ were already seated. While one of the maids served the well-chilled spicy gazpacho, Craig asked Ariane about her ride.

"Well, I'm glad I didn't go," Kristen said, interrupting Ariane. "This place is probably crawling with snakes and God knows what other horrid creatures."

"You're right, there are snakes," Ariane replied. "As a matter of fact my horse threw me when she was spooked by one."

"Are you all right?" Craig asked.

"Yes, I'm fine. Just embarrassed, really."

"Are you sure? Maybe we should call a doctor . . ." Russ suggested.

"Don't make such a big deal," Kristen cut in. "If Ariane says she's fine, she is. Anyway, she shouldn't have gone riding in the first place if she couldn't handle it."

"Oh, I can handle it," Ariane replied pointedly. "It's just that snakes are such sneaky, slimy things that one never knows where they'll turn up. And they do turn up in the oddest places . . . even in the best homes.''

Alex led Thunder into his stall. The dark, cool stable offered a welcome respite to the bright heat.

"Damn foolish woman," he muttered to himself as he removed Thunder's saddle and pad, flinging them over the railing.

He picked up two combs and began grooming Thunder. The action of the long strokes should have been comforting, but he couldn't rid himself of the tearing fear he'd felt when Ariane took her fall. He had thought she was lost. And he didn't like the feeling, didn't like caring.

She's a married woman, he reminded himself. He knew all about married women. Let her husband worry about her. His brushing became more forceful and Thunder whinnied his protest. Why should he feel anything? Why should he care?

The pool and its surrounding terra-cotta tiled patio were set beyond the garden, insuring privacy from the house. The pool was at least seventy feet long. The interior was a dark blue mosaic tile, turning the ordinarily bright turquoise water into an inviting dark blue reminiscent of a lagoon. There were arrangements of white tables, chairs, umbrellas, and lounges. On one of the tables was a large pitcher of frosty tea, several glasses, and an ice bucket. The area was saved from starkness under the hot afternoon sun by a profusion of terra-cotta tubs filled with brightly colored flowers.

Lying on one of the chaises, Ariane smiled as she recalled the look of shock on Kristen's features at lunch. *Let that be a lesson to you,* she thought, *you bleached blond witch.*

It was ironic that she probably owed the tramp a vote

of thanks. If it hadn't been for her, Ariane never would have stepped out from behind Craig's shadow. When she had married she had centered her life on Craig, sublimating all that she was, content to become a reflection of him. Her friends were the wives of Craig's business associates. They dined together, partied and vacationed together. Sometimes she thought all the women were interchangeable pawns on a chess board controlled by the men.

Now, for the first time since she had married, Ariane was accepted as Ariane Wakefield, without the trappings and influence of Craig's power and wealth. And she liked it.

The combination of the lazy afternoon, the bright sun warming her body, and self-satisfaction left her feeling charitable. She rose and walked over to where Craig and Russ were sitting. Sidling up to Craig in her shiny cobalt blue maillot, she said, "Excuse me, gentlemen, but I believe this was supposed to be a vacation. I think it's time the vacation part started."

Shifting her gaze to Craig, she asked, "How about a swim?"

Craig glanced up at her then over at Russ. "Well, you heard my wife, Russ. Looks like work will have to wait."

The dark blue water was warm and inviting. They leisurely swam two laps before stopping on the tiled steps that ran the width of the pool at the shallow end. The hot air dried their exposed skin almost immediately as they sat on the step, leaning against the edge.

"Mmm, this is nice." Ariane enjoyed the combination of the warm lapping water and the hot sun beating down on her.

"Yes, it is," Craig agreed, tilting his face up to catch the sun's rays.

"You know, I think we need a vacation. I can't remember the last time we went away."

"Oh? What about the week we spent on Mustique and the two weeks in St. Moritz? Doesn't that count?"

"I meant alone," Ariane replied deliberately, not wanting to mention their companions on both trips. They both knew it was Kristen and Russ.

"Sure, we could do that. Where would you like to go?"

She was pleasantly surprised at Craig's easy acceptance, having expected him to argue that he couldn't get away. Maybe all he had needed was a little nudge in the right direction after all.

"Oh, I don't know. Someplace new where we've never been and someplace warm with a white sandy beach."

"What about your job? Do you think you'll be able to take time off?"

"I'm sure I'll be able to work something out."

"If this job is just a plaything to you I don't know why you're bothering."

"My job is not a plaything! I'm very serious about it and if you could give me one-tenth of the attention you give your work you'd know what it means to me. You think if a *man* isn't doing it, it can't be important. In case you hadn't realized it yet, there are women who run entire countries!"

"Jesus, Ariane, calm down. Someone will hear you. I didn't mean to cast dispersions on the entire gender. I only meant that if you're only going to work for a while, why take it so seriously?"

"What makes you think I'm only working for a short time?"

"I assumed you were only doing this as a way of getting back at me for Kristen."

Dumfounded, she asked against her better judgment,

"What in the world does my working have to do with getting back at you?"

"You know I never wanted you to work. We've had that discussion on numerous occasions. I provide for you handsomely and I don't like the idea of my wife working. After you found out about . . . about me, you got a job out of revenge. You knew I wouldn't like it, yet you deliberately went against my wishes. I only let you because I felt it was something you had to get out of your system," Craig explained, using his familiar condescending tone.

Ariane felt her simmering temper turn to a fast boil. She looked at him as if seeing him for the first time. And she didn't like what she was seeing.

"I don't think this is the time or place to discuss this any further," she said stiffly, afraid if she said any more she'd explode with rage.

"Why? Is it something I said?" Craig asked innocently as he stepped from the pool.

For a moment Ariane thought he was being sarcastic until she realized he really had no idea of the implications of his words. She looked at him with amazement. Knowing it would be useless to explain, she said, "No, Craig, it's nothing you said."

Ariane swam several laps and, after tiring quicker than usual, decided to quit. As she stepped out of the pool she was dismayed to see Alex sitting with Craig and Russ. Standing a little straighter, she walked to where the three men were sitting.

She felt Alex's appraising silver eyes rake over her body and wished she had something on over her bathing suit. She felt positively naked as she read the unmistakable look in his eyes. How dare he look at her like that in front of her husband! She wished Craig would look up from his papers so that Alex would have to refrain from looking at her. But somehow she didn't think that would stop him.

"Enjoy your swim?" Alex asked casually, the heat gone from his eyes as he set his dark features in a bland expression.

"Yes," Ariane replied, resting her hand on Craig's shoulder.

"Look out!" Craig exclaimed, pulling his shoulder away, causing Ariane to flinch. "You're getting my papers all wet."

Ariane felt her heart sink, shamed by Craig's insult, mortified that Alex was there to witness it. She glanced at him, her humiliation complete as Alex looked away, refusing to meet her gaze. Furious, she said tightly, "I'm going in."

"Okay. I'll be up later," Craig answered absently, shaking off his papers.

It startled her to realize that Craig's contempt no longer had the power to hurt her. It was Alex's pity that cut so deeply.

"Ariane, wake up. We have to be downstairs in half an hour. Shouldn't you be getting dressed?" Craig shook her awake.

"Is it that late? Why didn't you wake me?" She had showered and fallen asleep on the terrace.

"I only just got back myself," Craig explained. "I spent the rest of the afternoon with Alex in his study, trying to convince him to turn his account over to us. It wasn't easy, but I got it. We'd better put a move on. Alex has some of his investor friends coming over tonight and I don't want to be late."

Ariane followed him into the bathroom, where he stepped into the shower and she began applying her eye make-up.

"By the way," he shouted over the running water, "I meant to discuss that incident at lunch today. I don't think it would be a good idea for you to start up with Kristen tonight." He stepped out of the shower, wrapped a towel around his waist, and walked over to the sink. "It doesn't look good to have the two of you at each other's throats."

Slowly, Ariane put down her mascara and turned to face him. "For your information I wasn't the one who started it. I was only answering one of the cunning remarks she's so fond of making. And if the situation makes you uncomfortable, it's a situation of your own making. I think I've been pretty damn good about the whole thing."

Craig moved to stand behind her and, placing both hands on her shoulders, looked at her reflection in the mirror.

"You're right. I just don't want her to upset you. She doesn't mean anything to me and I don't want her to mean anything to you. Can't you just forget what happened?"

"I'm trying. But it isn't easy," she admitted. "I'm sick and tired of having to listen to her nasty comments. It was bad enough before, but now it's worse."

"Do we have to go through that again?" Craig asked, irritation creeping into his voice. "How long are you going to hold it over my head? I thought we agreed to let it rest."

"We did. But that doesn't mean Kristen can use me for a dart board and that I have to like it."

"But you know that's just Kristen's way. She's like that with everybody."

"Fine. Then let her be like that with everybody, but not with me, not anymore."

Craig studied her determined face, then sighed heavily. "All right, then. But maybe if you steered clear of her you wouldn't be open to one of her comments. I don't want you to have to spend the evening fighting with her. With

Alex's friends there it wouldn't do to have you and Kristen sniping at each other.''

As usual Craig was more worried about what people thought than how she felt, constantly concerned with making the right impression. "All right, Craig. Whatever you say,'' Ariane conceded.

"Good girl,'' Craig said as he kissed the top of her head and walked into the bedroom to dress.

Ariane's hand shook with suppressed anger at Craig's predictable manipulation. But things were changing between them. This time she easily saw through him.

Downstairs in the oak-paneled study, the two men stood facing each other, the unlit fireplace between them a testimony to the warm Indian summer. The room was dimly lit by a single lamp on a massive antique walnut desk placed near the bay window. If the room was uncomfortably dark neither man noticed, so intent were they in conversation.

"Did he bite?'' Travis asked.

"Hook, line, and sinker,'' Alex answered, the dim light throwing an ominous cast on the harshly defined features. There was a darkness about him that had nothing to do with the poor lighting.

"Good. How soon before we'll know anything for sure?''

"Not too soon, I'm afraid. I don't want to rouse his suspicions. Although the little bastard's so greedy, I doubt if he could smell anything except money.''

"I still can't understand how Wakefield can pull this off without his partner suspecting a thing.''

"Beats the hell out of me. I just hope this time they put the evidence in a fireproof safe,'' Alex said, referring to the previously gathered evidence that had been suspiciously destroyed when the agency's office was burned.

"You know Newman ought to thank you for getting the goods on Wakefield. If you don't take care of him soon, there could be nothing left of Newman Brothers by the time Wakefield's finished."

"True. But this time he's gotten too greedy for his own good. Did you read the latest report on that new company Anatech that he started? It seems they have a new method for converting raw sewage into cheap, usable fertilizer. Between every city in the country wanting to set up a treatment plant and every farmer wanting to buy the finished purified product, he could make millions with the process. The new issue opened at six and climbed to fourteen in two days. The stock's so hot there's already talk of a secondary. Only problem is there's no method."

Travis shook his head in amazement and said, "At least you have to admit the guy's an original."

"Yeah, about as original as the Arab," Alex answered grimly. He couldn't get the morgue shots out of his mind.

"Any more information on him?"

"Nothing. Just the usual meetings with Wakefield in dark bars."

"I wonder how his wife will bear up when this hits the fan. He's sure to do time. Do you think she'll stick by him?"

"Stick by him? She can't even stick by him now," Alex answered vehemently, his lips thinned in disgust.

"What do you mean?"

"I mean she's nothing but a common tramp. Wakefield's going away won't make one bit of difference to her."

"Ariane?" Travis asked incredulously. "Look, I know your feelings on the female species, but surely you don't mean to include Ariane?"

"Take my word for it. I've seen her in action and she ranks right up there at the top of her class," Alex fumed. "I have to fill out these forms to open an account with Wakefield and I want to do it before he leaves. Do me a favor and attend to any guests that arrive early. I'll only be a few minutes.''

''Sure,'' Travis agreed and closed the study door behind him after he left.

Enjoy yourself, Wakefield, Alex thought, *your days are numbered.*

Ariane dressed quickly, slipping into a Calvin Klein strapless black cashmere dress, cinching in her narrow waist with a black alligator belt. Sheer black stockings and black alligator pumps completed her ensemble. Her long, black hair had dried in soft glossy waves and, not having time to put it up, she decided to wear it down, brushing it back from her face and letting the heavy, lustrous mass fall down her back. She slipped her gold and diamond Bulgari watch on one wrist and several Bulgari gold and diamond bangles on the other.

On the way downstairs she met Craig on the landing above the foyer. With one hand clasped around her wrist he said, ''Now these people are very important to me, so remember what we agreed to upstairs.'' Met with silence, he persisted, ''You're going to do what I told you, aren't you?''

''Yes, Craig, I will.''

A shadow moved under the landing as Craig and Ariane passed through the foyer and entered the living room. Alex had been on his way into the living room when he heard Craig's voice and paused beneath the stairs to listen. What he heard caused a white hot rage to spread through him. They were in it together.

This fascinating bit of information was going to make his job even more enjoyable. With the evidence he was collecting there was no way Craig was going to get away with his schemes indefinitely. It was just a matter of time. Only now there would be three defendants sitting in the courtroom: the Arab, Wakefield, and the lovely, lying Mrs. Wakefield. The image of Ariane sitting in the witness chair passed through his mind. For a second he saw her features clearly, the expressive black eyes wide with fear. Then he brushed it from his mind, refusing to acknowledge the uneasy feeling it brought.

"Can I offer you two a drink?" Travis asked when Ariane and Craig entered the living room. He led them through the crowded room, stopping occasionally to introduce one of the thirty-odd guests. Ariane lost Craig to Kyle as she and Travis continued to the bar.

"I think I'll try one of those," she said, motioning to the pale frosty drink the bartender was handing to a guest.

"Good choice," Travis said.

"Travis, are you cheating on me?" a woman's voice accused.

Ariane turned to face a woman who appeared to be in her mid-seventies.

"Maybelle, darling." Travis bent and kissed her cheek. "You know you're my true love."

"Well, try and remember it," Maybelle warned, her blue eyes twinkling mischievously. "Although with this kind of competition . . ."

Travis laughed and introduced Ariane.

"I won't steal him, I promise," Ariane said.

"Good. I believe a woman should fight for her man and I wouldn't want to have to call you out."

Ariane laughed and absent-mindedly reached for her earring, only to realize she had forgotten to put them on. Feeling unfinished without them, she excused herself to go upstairs.

Putting down her empty glass, she threaded her way through the crowded room and reached the arched entrance to the foyer to find Alex leaning indolently against the frame. There was a tight grimness to his dark features that was intensified by his black linen shirt and black slacks.

Ariane offered him a radiant smile as she said, "Good evening."

He stared hard at her from beneath his brooding black brows. "Successful, then?" Alex quipped, his voice harsh.

She looked at him oddly, not understanding. "Yes, it's a lovely party. It was really very kind of you to go to all this trouble just for us."

"No trouble at all."

"Well, if you'll excuse me, I was just on my way upstairs." She wanted to get away from him. She could feel the waves of hostility emanating from him and she didn't understand why.

"By all means." He swept his arm toward the foyer. "Don't let me interfere with your work."

As she walked past him and started up the stairs, she could feel his eyes on her. He seemed different somehow tonight. Usually when he was in a foul mood he was biting and sarcastic, but tonight he seemed morose. In his present sullen mood he seemed far more dangerous, his suppressed violence barely contained. He reminded her of a volcano, simmering, waiting to erupt. *And I don't want to be around when he does,* she thought.

The party was in full swing when Ariane returned downstairs and dinner was being announced. As people began milling about, making their way into the dining room, she scanned the crowd looking for Craig.

"Excuse me, Ariane, have you seen Kristen?" Russ asked.

"No, I haven't," Ariane answered offhandedly, wondering where Craig was.

"Oh, I think I saw her leave with Craig," Kyle said.

Ariane came up sharply. She watched Russ walk away

in search of his wife, afraid she knew exactly where she was, exactly where Craig was.

The affair wasn't over. It had never ended. She waited for the familiar anguish and pain to return, but there was nothing. Nothing but revulsion.

Well, he could go to Kristen and he was welcome to her. They were one of a kind—selfish, self-serving liars who would probably end up cheating on each other. The thought brought a grim smile to her mouth. Good riddance to both of them.

She should have left Craig this summer but she had been too afraid. It had been easier to go on with their sham of a marriage no matter how much he had hurt her. She had taken the easy way out before, but she wasn't going to this time.

She made her way to the bar and ordered a margarita. She couldn't do anything now. She would just have to wait until they got home. Until then she would act as if everything was normal, as if her life hadn't just come down crashing around her head. And the hot, spreading warmth of the chilled drink wouldn't hurt at all.

Ariane stood with Maybelle and Nadine in the living room after dinner. She barely heard their words. She was drunk. The softly lit room was blurry around the edges. There was music playing, but, combined with the sounds of the guests' voices, she could discern neither clearly. She liked being drunk. She was pleasantly numb, her mind and her body. She couldn't think, even if she had wanted to, and she was glad.

As she looked about the crowded room, her eyes were caught by a sight that made her stiffen with revulsion. There, standing by the French doors, was Alex. And leaning against him, her intentions all too clear, was Kristen. The bitch! She hated her.

Someone had to put a stop to Kristen and she was just the one to do it.

Excusing herself from Maybelle and Nadine's company, Ariane started toward Alex and Kristen. It took some effort not to sway, but she managed well enough and found herself standing in front of the bar. One more drink couldn't hurt. She was thirsty.

Kristen's hand was resting on Alex's upper arm while he looked on, a slightly bemused expression on his bronzed features. As Ariane approached them, Alex turned his attention to Ariane and a look of annoyance crossed Kristen's face.

"Kristen, Russ's been looking for you," Ariane said pleasantly, carefully enunciating each word.

"Has he?"

"Yes. I told him to check the street corners." Ariane smiled with satisfaction, enjoying the look of shock on Kristen's heavily made-up features.

"How d-dare you!" Kristen sputtered, at a loss for words for the first time.

"Oh, I dare, Kristen. The question is how dare you?"

"I don't know what you're talking about. Alex was just telling me about the ranch, weren't you?" Kristen looked at Alex and moved closer to him, making it clear it was not the ranch that interested her.

"Kristen, the only aspect of a ranch that would interest you would be the stud barn, and you could give them a lesson or two in coupling."

"Maybe so. But at least I can attract a man and hold on to him. Which is more than I can say about some people . . ." Kristen murmured maliciously.

The truth cut Ariane. But two could play this game. She placed her hand on Alex's arm and leaned into him as she breathed suggestively, "I'm sorry I was late, Alex. I know how you hate waiting and with the present company it must have been intolerable.''

Alex shot Ariane a cool, long look and smiled.

''Is that true?'' Kristen demanded of Alex. ''You were just waiting here for her?''

Alex looked at Kristen and gave a small noncommittal shrug of his shoulders. She lifted her chin, thrust out her ample bosom, and stormed off in a snit.

Ariane raised her glass in mock salute to Kristen's retreating back and downed the rest of her margarita. Now that she had won, and a prize at that, she didn't know what to do with him. She looked up at Alex and his face swam before her. Blinking her eyes she tried to focus, but her head was too clouded. His harsh features were set in a brooding scowl as he stared intently down at her. The black shirt accentuated his darkness, and it occurred to her that he looked like the devil. Her eyes were drawn to his sensuous lips, set in a tight line, and her fingertips itched to touch them. She asked coquettishly, ''Looks like I won. What do I get?''

Alex took the empty glass from her hand and set it down on a nearby table. ''You can have whatever you like. What did you have in mind?''

''Oh, I don't know,'' Ariane answered. ''What do you think I deserve?'' She grinned up at Alex, her lustrous black eyes shining.

Alex smiled, not a nice smile, but Ariane was too high to notice. ''I know what you deserve. The question is, do you really want it?''

She was fascinated by the hot glitter in his silver eyes. He had wanted her once. And he still did. She stared at him, noticing his incredibly thick lashes and thought them too long for a man. Without thinking, she started to reach up and touch them. ''You have the longest eyelashes.''

Alex's hand whipped out and grabbed her wrist before

she could touch him. Still holding her wrist, he turned and walked through the open French doors, pulling her behind him.

He led her to a dark secluded spot in the garden, away from the house. Soft pools of light spilled from the windows of the lit house.

"What are we doing out here?"

With his hand still tight around her wrist, he pulled her against him. One arm wrapped around her narrow waist while his free hand tilted her head back. He lowered his face to hers, murmuring huskily, "Your prize, remember?" The deep voice had a cruel edge to it.

His mouth took hers in a savage and fierce possession. Her brain fuzzy from the alcohol, she gave herself up to his assaulting mouth, having no strength or even desire to fight him. With a will of their own, her arms reached up and wound themselves around his neck. She began to feel warm all over, a hot wave of desire rushing through her, making her dizzy, causing her to hold on to him for support.

He buried his hand in the silken strands of her hair, holding her trapped, searching her mouth's inner softness. His lips were warm and demanding, and Ariane wanted more of him as she kissed him back. She was tired of thinking. She only wanted to feel. She reveled in his hard chest pushing against her, his crisp straight hair between her fingers, his hard thighs pressing against her. There was an ache deep inside her, a pleasant throbbing ache.

His hand was warm, possessive as it moved down her neck and her chest to touch her breast. He fondled it, caressing her, and she swayed into him.

A small gasp of pleasure escaped her as his fingers brushed the sensitive bud, teasing at it. Slowly his hand moved down her side, over her hip, and lower, rubbing, stroking. The pleasant ache took hold, needing more, demanding more.

As his mouth trailed lower, skimming the top of her dress, his hand moved to the edge of her dress and he hooked a finger in it to lower it.

"Uh-umm."

They jumped apart and Ariane whirled around to see Travis standing behind them in the garden.

"I thought you'd like to know that some of your guests have started to leave and were asking after you." Travis looked as embarrassed as Ariane felt. But he looked more than uncomfortable; he looked miserable and worried.

"Well, then . . . I suppose I'd better go tend to them. Why don't you and Ariane enjoy the night air a bit while I go inside?" Alex suggested smoothly.

Without so much as a backward glance, he walked away toward the house.

Dazed by Alex's abrupt departure, Ariane gathered herself together, smoothed her dress, and started to follow his path through the garden. She couldn't stay out here with Travis, not after what he had seen. Her head held high, she walked past him, refusing to look at him.

She was shocked to feel his hand tightly grip her arm.

"And just where do you think you're going?"

"Back inside," Ariane answered as she twisted around to face him, annoyed at his hold.

"Do you think that's wise?"

"Of course, why wouldn't it be?"

"I mean, Alex has been missing for some time and everyone was looking for him. Now he's coming back into the house with you all flushed hot on his heels. How do you think that would look?"

"Oh . . . I hadn't thought about that."

"I didn't think so." Travis dropped his hand. "Why

don't we go into the kitchen and get some coffee? We can go through the back door so no one will see us."

"Look, you really don't have to babysit me. I'll just wait out here for a while and then go back."

"I know that. But I'd really like to have that coffee with you. Maybe you could give me some helpful hints on the modern-day cowboy's wardrobe." A boyish smile lit his handsome face.

They entered the large country kitchen through the French doors in the dining area. Seating Ariane at the large pine table, Travis whispered, "You stay here while I see if I can talk Consuelo into whipping us up a snack."

A few minutes later the housekeeper approached with a tray. "Ah, Consuelo, you're an angel," Travis teased. "Thank you from the bottom of my heart."

"Humph! It is not for you but for the lovely *señora*," Consuelo said sternly.

"Thank you, Consuelo," Ariane said, enjoying the easy banter between Travis and Consuelo.

Travis put down his coffee cup and looked uneasy. "I know it's none of my business and I don't want you to get angry at me, but there's something I feel I have to say about what happened tonight."

"Go on." She didn't want to discuss Alex but she couldn't help herself.

"I've known Alex for a long time. I shouldn't be telling you this, with him being my friend, but I don't want to see you get hurt. And if you get involved with Alex you will be."

"Thank you for your concern but I am not involved with Alex. What you saw was just . . ." Ariane's voice trailed off. She was embarrassed to even be discussing the subject.

"I know what I saw. All I can tell you is be careful. Look, Alex is a very complicated man. There are demons that drive him, devils that even he doesn't understand. No woman has ever gotten close to him or walked away unscathed. Besides, do you think your husband would approve?''

Her black eyes flashed with anger. ''You were right in the first place—it is none of your business.''

She started to rise but Travis reached out quickly and grabbed her arm, forcing her down again.

''You're right. I'm sorry. I'm out of line and have no business interfering, but it was only out of my concern for you. Alex isn't like other men. He lives in darkness.''

chapter 12

Upstairs in their room, Craig began to undress while Ariane nervously paced the room, the pain and bitterness filling her like acid. She was terribly agitated and didn't think she could stay in the same room as Craig without confronting him. His adultery permeated the room like a poisonous cloud. But she couldn't—not now, not here.

"Aren't you coming to bed?" Craig asked.

"Not just yet," she said. "I think I'll go for a swim."

"You're what? Do you know what time it is?"

"So, what do you care? I want to work out my soreness."

"Do you think it's safe to wander around out there in the dark?"

Ariane looked hard at Craig. "The grounds are lit." She paused and then added lightly, "And I don't think coyotes swim in pools."

• • •

Walking barefoot through the silent, dimly lit house, Ariane felt herself relax, relieved to be away from Craig. She entered the semidarkness of the garden and followed the path to the swimming pool. She sat in one of the chairs, enjoying the solitude of the night. Leaning her head back against the plump cushion of a poolside chair, she looked up at the incredible velvet blackness of the sky. It was littered with thousands of stars that seemed close enough to touch. Turning her head slightly to the left, she noticed the quarter moon shining brightly, spilling pools of silver light in the garden. She found the serenity of the night soothing as she allowed the soft evening air to wash over her and cleanse her of her tension.

The evening had cooled somewhat, and Ariane breathed deeply of the fresh night air, redolent with the fragrance of the night blooming flowers. She stood, shrugged out of her robe, and tossed it on the chair. Standing in a sleek black maillot, she reached her arms toward the dark sky and stretched her tight muscles. She stepped into the still water and, feeling no chill from the warm water lapping on her legs, she continued down the tiled steps and began to leisurely swim the length of the pool.

Forcing her body to stretch and reach at each stroke, she swam several slow laps, the movement easing the stiffening of her muscles. Satisfied with her exercise she stepped from the pool.

The night air was cooler than the warm water, forcing her to quickly don her robe and wrap it around her. She picked up her towel and was patting dry her face when she heard a noise from the shadows.

"Who's there?" she called, uneasy as thoughts of wild animals flashed through her mind.

"Just your neighborhood lifeguard," a deep voice answered sarcastically.

"Alex?"

"In the flesh."

"Where are you? I can't see you," Ariane asked, uncomfortable talking to the darkness. His voice sounded strange but she wasn't sure why.

A chair creaked and then she saw Alex's lean form coming toward her from out of the darkness. It was hard to discern his shape as he seemed darkness itself with his black hair, open black linen shirt, and black slacks. When he entered the openness of the patio and the dim light offered by the moon, Ariane saw he was holding a decanter in one hand and a brandy glass in the other.

"What are you doing out here?" Ariane asked, apprehensive as she eyed the half-empty decanter. She didn't like the look in those silver eyes, and she self-consciously tightened the sash on her robe.

"I live here, remember? But I might ask you the same question. Do you always go swimming alone, in the middle of the night?"

"No, but I couldn't sleep and I thought swimming might tire me out. It seems to have worked, so I guess I'll go back." Ariane turned to pick up the towel she had dropped on the chair just as Alex set down the decanter and glass.

"Not just yet, if you don't mind," Alex said slowly as he sat on the arm of the chair.

"Oh?" She didn't like the tone in his voice and decided to leave. The thought must have been evident on her face because before she could move, Alex reached out with lightning swiftness and grabbed the belted sash.

"What are you doing?" She could feel the waves of sexuality emanating from him, washing over her.

"Just finishing some unfinished business. Come here." He pulled her against him and brought his mouth down on hers in a fierce and scorching kiss.

Ariane's hands flew to his chest, trying to push away from him, as unwanted images of another man forcing himself on her flashed through her mind. She protested against his mouth, "No, please stop."

Alex broke the kiss and looked at her, his eyes gleaming. "Why?"

"Because." Ariane looked at his dark face made harsher by the play of moonlight across the sharp cheekbones. His icy eyes raked over her.

"Surely it can't be because you're married," he said mockingly.

"You're drunk," Ariane replied, smelling the brandy on his breath.

"Not quite. But if that's what's bothering you, let me assure you I wouldn't do anything to you drunk that I wouldn't do sober."

"You're impossible. Let me go," Ariane ordered. He was holding her between the vee of his thighs. Trying to twist out of his grasp, she felt his muscled thighs close around her.

Alex seemed amused by her struggles and reached out a finger to gently trace the line of her jaw. His velvet voice poured over her like liquid smoke, as he said, "But that's not what you really want, is it?"

Ariane couldn't answer, her throat tightening, as Alex's finger moved across her lower lip. His fingers were warm and gentle as they moved to her chin and down her throat.

He stood, lowering his head to press his mouth against her neck, then his lips moved lower, tasting the satin smoothness of her skin. Pushing her robe aside, he moved down to the delicate collarbone. As his mouth blazed a trail up the side of her neck, he found her ear and nibbled on its lobe.

Ariane's hands, which just a short while ago had been pushing him away, now rested complacently against his warm, hard chest. She was aware of the play of muscles beneath her fingers when he moved. A pulsing heat spread throughout her body and she welcomed it. Everything felt so good. She wasn't going to fight him anymore. She couldn't. She wanted him to go on touching her. She leaned forward, moving into him.

Alex tore his mouth away from her and looked at the softly flushed features lit by the clear moonlight. Heavy black lashes rested on the high cheekbones, her lips slightly parted.

"Open your eyes," he commanded hoarsely.

Ariane's eyes fluttered open and she stared at him through passion-heavy lids, a glazed look shining in her black eyes.

"This is what you want, what you've always wanted," Alex said, his words a seductive caress.

Ariane tasted the brandy on Alex as he once again plundered her mouth. Hungry for the touch of his flesh, her hands slipped beneath the linen shirt to feel the muscles across his upper back. There was a savage anger in him, a fierceness, but Ariane didn't care. It suited her own anger. All she knew was that he was kissing her and it felt right—more than right. She could hear the ocean roaring in her ears and then dimly realized there was no ocean.

Holding her against him he muttered a curse against her lips, tore open her sash, and slipped the robe from her shoulders. The garment fell to the ground in a heavy heap, and his burning eyes raked over her body.

Breathing heavily, Ariane watched Alex as his eyes seemed to devour her piece by piece. The look of raw desire burning brightly in those silver eyes sent a tremor of fear and excitement through her, an excitement she had never felt before.

The moonlight cast a silvery glow on her pale skin, turning her to marble, a startling contrast of white and black. Alex's hands moved down the column of her back. One hand moved slowly down the side of her slim body, lightly brushing the side of her breast. Then his palm slid caressingly over her hip and lower still to the bare flesh of her thigh.

His hands were deliciously warm on her cool skin. When he had first removed her robe, she had felt chilled by the night air. But the heat from his hands as they stroked her left little flames of desire burning wherever they touched her. She wanted more.

He cupped her breast in his hand, weighing it, fondling it. His thumb sought the erect nub and gently rubbed it, causing her to moan with pleasure deep in her throat.

Abruptly he took her hand and fairly pulled her along past the pool area. Stopping at the pool house, he opened the door and led her inside. Before she could adjust to the darkness, Alex had led her through the living room and into the bedroom.

He fell on the bed, pulling her down with him, wrapping his arms around her slender body, pressing himself against her.

Ariane went into his arms willingly, hungrily, needing to feel the hard length of him. Her head was swimming as if she were drugged and out of control.

He fairly ripped his shirt off, flinging it to the floor before gathering her in his arms. His body was hard and warm and she clung to him, barely allowing him enough room to peel off her bathing suit. His hands were everywhere, holding, caressing, fondling, making her writhe seductively.

Impatiently he kicked off his slacks and, parting her smooth white thighs, he buried himself in her honeyed tightness.

Ariane's gasp of pleasure was muffled against his mouth. She didn't want to move. She wanted to stay like this forever with Alex filling her, throbbing hotly inside of her.

But when he started to move she couldn't stop herself from matching his rhythm.

The painful ache filled her, knotting and twisting within her, promising, threatening. It wound tightly, curving, curling, consuming her completely. It couldn't hold her, couldn't stop . . . She broke free like a rocket shooting up, up and then exploding, splintering into a thousand sparkling fragments.

As Ariane's body began to quiver Alex let go, shuddering powerfully against her.

Ariane didn't move, not knowing what to do. Slowly the fevered heat between them cooled, and she became conscious of the dark room, the perspiration between their naked bodies, the sweet musky scent of sex. She couldn't breathe and, as she tried to shift Alex's weight, he rolled off of her abruptly and rose from the bed. He reached for his slacks and tugged them on.

"Alex . . ." Ariane had never before experienced the blinding, intoxicating passion she had experienced tonight in Alex's arms. It was as if this was the first time she ever made love, and she wanted to tell him.

But the cold, hard look on his face as he turned around and stood looming over her stilled the words in her throat.

"You didn't have to bother," he said. "I would have signed the papers anyway."

He left her alone. Alone with her confusion, hurt, and rejection. Craig didn't want her, but she had thought Alex did. She had been wrong. Horribly wrong. He had only wanted to use her. Just like Craig did.

Alex closed the door to his study, only the knowledge of his soundly sleeping houseguests upstairs preventing him from slamming the door. He threw his shirt on the burgundy leather sofa and flung himself down on the seat, raking a hand through his hair.

Christ, she wasn't supposed to feel that good. Sure, he had wanted her. Why not? She had flirted and teased him, coming on to him from the start for her husband's business.

He wanted to use her, punish her for the whore that she was. Leave it to a married woman to sneak out of her husband's bed to meet another man right under his nose.

But it was wrong. All wrong. He hadn't wanted to feel that way. To feel anything.

He had had her. The mystery was over. And damnit, he wanted her again.

Ariane pulled the blanket up to her neck, chilled despite the bed's heavy covers. But then she thought of Alex, how he had looked at her with those burning eyes, how his hands had moved over her body so intimately, so knowingly, how he had moved inside her. She kicked off the covers suddenly flushed, suddenly hot.

But he hadn't really wanted her. Only a body. She meant nothing to him. What was worse was his remark about "papers." What papers? She didn't know what the hell he was talking about.

She glanced over at Craig, asleep in his bed. She should have felt guilty. She had broken her marriage vows, cheated on Craig. But Craig was the last thing on her mind. There was no room for anything but Alex.

"Good. You're awake," Craig said pleasantly, exiting from the bathroom. "You must have gotten in late last night. I didn't hear you. What time was it?"

"I don't know," Ariane mumbled.

"How do you feel?" asked Craig solicitously as he came over to stand by her bed. "Did you swim your soreness away?"

For a moment she had no idea what Craig was talking

about. Then she remembered. "Oh . . . yes. What time are we supposed to leave?"

"Right after brunch. I'd thought we'd pack first and then join the others. Hungry?"

"No. You know I never eat this early," Ariane snapped, unaccountably annoyed at Craig's cheerfulness. How dare he be so nice to her when . . .

"Then don't eat. But get dressed and come downstairs. We're expected," Craig ordered curtly as he took their luggage out and flipped it open, preparing to pack.

She silently berated herself for reproaching Craig. She wanted to end their marriage, not argue with him. Swallowing her pride—she hoped for the last time—she slipped out of bed and walked to stand next to him at the dresser.

"I guess I didn't get enough sleep last night. Why don't you leave that and I'll finish packing after I've showered and dressed."

Her apology soothed Craig's ruffled feathers. "That's all right. There's not much to do. You get ready and we'll go down."

Travis, Russ, and Kristen were already in the dining room when Craig and Ariane entered. Everyone exchanged greetings and no one seemed to notice that Ariane and Kristen studiously ignored each other.

Travis and Russ were discussing the latest in a series of charges brought by the SEC against Island Securities. From what Ariane had gleaned from the newspaper articles, they were charging Brad and several Island Securities salesmen with misrepresentation and price rigging, as well as churning accounts.

"It's obvious the SEC has a vendetta against him," Craig said. "They've been trying to get him for years and if they really ever had anything on him, they would have put him away. This is just another witch hunt."

"Maybe so. But where there's smoke, there's fire. Maybe the SEC figures if they dig long enough they're bound to come up with something. Is he really clean?" Travis asked.

"Absolutely," Craig answered without hesitation.

"I wouldn't be so quick to absolve him. Of course, nobody knows for sure, but there is a gray area involved that could be sticky," Russ said.

"What would that be?" Travis asked.

"The charge of misrepresentation. There's a fine line between properly recommending a stock to a customer and pressuring him into buying a stock for the salesman's and firm's profit. One office recommends a buy and the other a sell in the same stock. Each trade puts a commission in the firm's and salesman's pockets. When they use the same method between firms to artificially inflate the price of stock, that's stock manipulation."

"I don't see what the big deal is," Kristen interrupted. "If customers are so stupid that they listen to their brokers that's their own problem."

"It's unethical and immoral," Ariane said pointedly, looking at Kristen.

"I just read that Ripman, Arden, and Overton were hit with a big fine by the NASD. Looks like the regulatory boards are cracking down on everyone," Travis commented.

"You mean, 'Rip 'Em Hard and Often,' " Craig corrected, using the firm's nickname on the Street. "They're charging them with controlling and manipulating a stock. It goes back to the same old story of customers crying foul."

"How much trouble are they in?"

"None," Craig said. "Ripman told me he's going to appeal. He's tough and he'll probably win. One time he got so angry he took out a full-page ad in the *Wall Street*

Journal, lambasting the SEC and NASD. At the worst he'll wind up with a fine and a short suspension, which means nothing. It's a slap on the wrist, more of an inconvenience than anything else. And he can get around that, everybody always does. It's no big deal.''

Alex entered the dining room, seeming totally at ease as he joined Craig and Travis in their discussion. He barely glanced at Ariane as he took his seat at the head of the table.

Alex ignored her as if she didn't exist, as if last night had never happened. She didn't think it could hurt so much, but it did. It's almost over, she consoled herself, their time together numbered in minutes. Maybe it was for the best. They had no future.

Ariane thanked Consuelo for her hospitality before rejoining Craig and the others in the foyer. They were packed and ready to go, waiting for the car to be brought around.

''Where have you been?'' Craig asked as Ariane appeared.

''Just saying good-bye to Consuelo,'' Ariane answered casually, not liking his tone.

''Saying good-bye to the maid?'' Craig asked, a look of distaste on his features.

She gave him a frosty look and thought how very typical. She was saved the pleasure of answering by Alex's emergence from his study.

''Everybody ready?'' asked Alex. ''I'll have Deke put the bags in the car and then we'd better leave.'' His eyes avoided her or he simply didn't notice. She couldn't tell which.

In the commotion of leaving, Travis touched Ariane's elbow and led her aside. ''About last night, I didn't mean to interfere. I had no right and I'm sorry,'' he said.

Ariane believed him. "I shouldn't have snapped at you. Why don't we both forget it ever happened?"

Travis grinned broadly and stuck out his hand. "You've got yourself a deal."

"Deal," Ariane returned as she put her hand in his large palm. They shook on it as though consummating an all-important business transaction.

"I usually get up to New York several times a year," he said. "How would you feel if I called you and we got together for lunch or something?"

"That sounds like fun."

"Great. Then don't be surprised when you hear from me, because I'm going to hold you to your word. Now you'd better get going or you'll miss your connection," Travis said as he led Ariane to the front door.

"Aren't you taking us?"

"No, I'm going home. Alex will fly you out."

Wonderful, Ariane thought, *just wonderful.*

She slid into the back seat of the car next to Russ and looked straight ahead to the back of Alex's head. As they started to move she took out her dark sunglasses and slipped them on. They wouldn't do at all. She needed something more substantial to block out the sight of his dark head.

She listened to Alex's deep voice as he conversed with Craig, and she thought how very harmless it sounded. It didn't sound at all like the cutting knife that had sliced through her last night with its sharp edge of cruelty.

The transfer to Alex's plane for the flight to the airport was quick and businesslike.

Alex landed his plane smoothly and they stood on the airstrip saying their good-byes. Craig thanked Alex for his hospitality and offered to return the favor when Alex came to New York. Kristen made her usual display.

Kristen's actions were bad enough, but Ariane had the

strange sensation that Alex was enjoying every minute of it as he watched Ariane's reactions. It was hard to tell because she couldn't see his eyes behind his mirrored sunglasses.

As she walked past Alex to get into the waiting limousine she looked up into the sun-bronzed face expectantly, hoping he would say something to her. The harsh features seemed blank and as she tried to look into his eyes all she saw were hundreds of images of her face reflected back at her. With not a word between them she got into the car and left.

Ariane was surprised when she opened her eyes and saw that it was morning. She couldn't remember falling asleep. Craig was already gone and she thought she heard Hilda downstairs. Knowing what she had to do today, she threw back the covers and went to the bathroom to splash cold water on her face.

Sitting on the bed, she picked up the phone and pushed Jessica's number, not wanting to think about what she was doing.

An hour later she met Jessica at an apartment house on Fifth Avenue. Jessica hugged her warmly, her sympathy obvious in her eyes. They swept past the doorman and into the elevator. When they exited, Jessica led her to the end of the hall where she unlocked a door and led Ariane into a magnificently furnished Art Deco apartment.

Ariane's first impression of the rust marble floors and peach-gold lacquered walls was contradictory. While the hard polished surfaces and severe lacquered furniture were cold and austere, the room glowed with the warmth of its apricot tones. She passed quickly through the living room that faced Central Park, barely noticing the priceless antiques that filled the room. Josef Hoffman. Emile-Jacques

Ruhlman. Jules Leleu. Jean Dunand. They meant nothing to her.

She gave a cursory glimpse at the deep rust dining room with its black lacquer dining set. In the apricot and gold master bedroom she briefly noted the large bed, backed by a gold leaf and tufted headboard, her eyes missing the exquisite mother-of-pearl vitrine by Josef Viban. She peeked into the gray and black library and hurried down the hall.

When they approached the kitchen, Jessica jokingly warned her to be prepared.

The kitchen was entirely black, from the granite floor to the granite countertops to the black lacquer cabinets. Ariane briefly noted the state-of-the-art appliances, from the Vulcan oven and range to the Sub-zero refrigerator. There was a small breakfast nook that contained a gray and black upholstered banquet and gray marble table.

"It's a little shocking, but I suppose I'll get used to it," Ariane said.

"Then you'll take it?" Jessica asked.

"I guess I shouldn't appear so anxious, but the truth is I want to move in as soon as possible. Is there anything else you can show me, or is this all there is for immediate occupancy?"

"This is the only one I have now and if you're in a hurry then I suggest you take it. Getting a decent furnished sublet isn't easy. How soon do you want to move in?"

"Probably tomorrow," Ariane answered, feeling nervous as a few lingering doubts pressed her.

"Do you mind if I ask you a personal question?" Ariane nodded and Jessica continued, "Why are *you* moving out and not Craig?"

"That's funny. I never even thought of asking Craig to leave." As Ariane answered, she realized she had never thought of the apartment as theirs but as Craig's. He had found it and furnished it, and she felt there was virtually nothing of herself in the apartment. With the realization came the certainty that she didn't want to live in Craig's apartment any more than she wanted to live with Craig.

"I'm the one who wants to separate and I don't think it's fair to ask Craig to leave. I'm not so sure he would anyway, and I'd rather not get into one of those situations where we live in separate bedrooms, both refusing to leave. I've heard too many horror stories about that, and I can't imagine any apartment being worth that kind of pain. This will be a lot easier on both of us."

"That's very noble of you, but most women would hold on to the apartment and insist that the husband leave. If you walk out now, you might be giving up your rights to it in a settlement. Craig might even claim desertion."

"I don't really care. All I know is that I want to get out as soon as possible." As Ariane said the words the emotions flooded her. She had not felt it before, but suddenly the fact that she was really leaving Craig hit her. She felt a lump rise in her throat and, fighting against it, she asked brusquely, "Where do I sign?"

chapter 13

Ariane was in the living room, a magazine lying unopened on her lap, when she heard Craig's key in the lock. He dropped his briefcase in the foyer before he entered the living room.

Glancing at her, he walked over to the bar.

"Am I beat. You wouldn't believe how many things went wrong because I was out of the office one day." He dropped some ice cubes into an oversized crystal low-ball and splashed a generous amount of scotch into it.

Taking a deep swallow, he loosened his tie. "It wouldn't be so bad if Russ would shoulder his share of the responsibilities, but lately he seems incapable of making a decision."

"Craig, there's something we have to talk about." Ariane hated the hesitation in her voice.

"Can it wait? I'm too tired."

"No, it can't," she said, her determination growing. Maybe this would finally grab his attention. She had rehearsed it a thousand times in her mind but suddenly she forgot all her prepared speeches.

"I . . . I want a separation."

Craig looked at her, a blank expression on his face as he let her words sink in. A look of annoyance crossed his face. "Don't tell me you're still brooding about that one night? What is this? Some form of delayed reaction?"

"No, it's not. But it's also not about one night. Look, Craig, I know all about you and Kristen. So you can drop the pretense and we can settle this like adults."

"What do you think you know about Kristen and me?" he asked.

"I know that you're having an affair and it didn't end in August as you said."

"How do you know?"

"What difference does it make? I know." Now that she had finally said it, she felt drained and exhausted.

"Does anyone else know?" Craig asked.

"Is that all you can think about—how I found out and who else knows? What about *me*? What about our marriage? Don't you even care?"

"You made up your mind you want a separation. Well, you've got it. If you thought I'd come begging, you've miscalculated. And you're right, I do worry about what people think. Why do you think I married you?" He walked over to her, his once handsome features contorted with anger. "You presented the perfect picture of what the proper wife should be. Exactly what I needed. Breeding, background, education, looks. You filled all the categories nicely—except one, that is, sex."

Ariane stared at him, her mind almost too numb to absorb all he was saying. He had picked her as if he were buying a car off the showroom floor. She was seeing the real Craig for the first time, with his guard down, the charming facade thrown aside, and she didn't like him at all. He reminded her of something safely hidden under a rock, until the rock was lifted, exposing it to the light of day. He paced the living room until he stopped in front of her. "Does that surprise you? Well, the joke was on me. How was I supposed to know that your cool reserve wasn't only skin deep but went right down to the frozen core? I admit you tried, but it was obvious your heart wasn't in it and you never really enjoyed sex. I used to think you were holding back, but now I know there's nothing there. You've played the ice princess for so long, the role fits permanently."

Craig walked over to the bar and refilled his glass. She watched him, too brutalized by his words to act. A heavy depression fell on her as she realized her whole marriage had been a sham. She rose to leave when his voice stopped her.

"I hope you're not expecting me to move out, because I don't intend to. And if you're planning to come crawling back after you're over your tantrum, you'd better think again. Once you leave, that's it. I won't have people laughing behind my back, saying you walked out on me and I took you back. Better be sure you know what you're doing."

Ariane looked at him for a moment and felt a hollow sorrow for the empty, lonely life they had shared.

"I'm sure about this," she said as she left the room.

Ariane moved the things she would need for the night into the guest room. It occurred to her that she should have been in tears. But she found she couldn't cry over losing something she never really had.

She sat up in bed, knowing she wouldn't be able to sleep. A part of her life was over, finished. And tomorrow she would start a new life, her own.

Maybe it was better her parents weren't alive to see how

she had failed them, failed herself. But still it would be nice to have someone to comfort her, to be a child again. Then she remembered the memories she had sought so hard to forget and she was glad she was no longer a child. Everything had been so perfect until . . .

Her bedroom was cheery pink and white in the house on Morning Glory Drive in Bala Cynwood, Pennsylvania. It was June, the gentle summer breeze blowing through the open window, carrying the heady scent of the lilac bushes in the garden below. Sparrows sang, their lively chirping nearly drowned out by a lawn mower groaning in the distance.

Ariane's small fingers were having trouble dressing her doll when she heard her mother call from downstairs. "Come down, darling. There's someone I want you to meet."

When Ariane bounded into the living room, she saw a handsome young man sitting beside her mother on the sofa.

"Don't tell me," he said. "This adorable beauty could only be your daughter."

"Ariane, this is your Uncle Julian. He's Daddy's brother."

Ariane sat beside her mother and buried her face against her shoulder, peeping shyly at Uncle Julian. At six years old Ariane was a quiet, cautious child, timid with strangers.

"It's okay, Ariane. Say hello," Patricia coaxed.

"Hello," Ariane mumbled. Her hands were nervously balled into tight fists.

"Hello, Ariane. I'm very pleased to meet you," Julian said as if he were speaking to an adult. "Say, I'm glad you came downstairs. I have an urge for an

ice cream and I was wondering if you could tell me where I might get one.''

He sounded so serious when he spoke to her, like when her mother and father talked to each other. Ariane loved ice cream and, forgetting her bashfulness, she smiled and said, "I know where you can go. There's an ice cream store in town and they have the biggest cones."

"Well, if you don't have anything to do, and your mother says it's okay, maybe you could show me the way."

"Could I, Mommy?" She wanted to be with her new uncle. He was handsome, and when he smiled at her, he made her feel special.

Patricia grinned. "I suppose so. Are you sure you know the way?"

"Yes, yes." She liked Uncle Julian's blue eyes that crinkled at the corners when he smiled at her.

"Okay. You two go ahead and have a good time."

"I won't be long," Julian promised, kissing Patricia on the cheek. Turning to Ariane, he said, "I have a convertible. How would you like it if I put the top down?"

"Oh yes, yes!" This was going to be the best, Ariane thought. She already knew she was going to love her Uncle Julian.

"I don't want him here," William said at the dinner table. Julian had gone out for dinner, leaving Ariane alone with her parents.

"William, he's your brother. You can't turn him away. He has no place to go," Patricia argued.

"He should have thought about that before he became a gambler and turned his back on the family.

*Christ, he didn't even have the decency to come home
for our parents' funerals.''*

Ariane didn't understand what her parents were
talking about but she understood enough to know that
something was wrong. Her father never sounded this
angry, not even when she had spilled ink on the rug.

*"He explained all that to me. He was too ashamed.
He was a failure, and you were such a success. He
knew he could never measure up.''*

"Really? So what's he doing here?''

*"He's getting older and he wanted to get to know
the only family he has,''* Patricia explained.

"And he's broke,'' William added cynically.

Ariane was suddenly afraid and put down her fork,
unable to eat. But her parents didn't notice. It was
as if she weren't there.

*"Yes. But that shouldn't make any difference. Look,
he's already here and we have more than enough
room. You can't very well throw him out now.''*

*"Fine. Let him stay. But he's not moving in. He
sponged off my parents enough when they were alive.
I'm not going to support him too.''*

"No. He'll just stay for a while, I promise.'' Patricia leaned over and kissed her husband's cheek.
"You really are a softy under that tough exterior.''

Her father didn't smile but he didn't look as angry.
Ariane decided that later she would tell him a joke
and make him laugh. As long as her daddy laughed,
everything was right in Ariane's world.

A year passed and Uncle Julian appeared for his second visit.

*"But why can't I stay up and have dinner with
you?''* Ariane asked for the third time that night.

"*Because your father and I and Uncle Julian are going to the club for dinner,*" Patricia explained.

"*But you went last night and the night before. You go all the time now.*"

"*I know, dear. But grownups like to do that. We have a lovely dinner and then we dance and dance.*" Patricia's eyes were shining.

"*You never used to go all the time,*" Ariane sulked. Her mother was never home anymore.

"*No. But it makes me happy to go. And you do want me to be happy, don't you?*" Patricia asked brightly.

Her mother did laugh more and seemed happier since Uncle Julian had come. Ariane and Patricia had spent every day with Uncle Julian—taking rides in his convertible, going to the park, visiting museums, and eating ice cream every day. Uncle Julian made her mother laugh all the time, even when Ariane didn't think something was funny.

"*Can I go with you?*" she asked, pressing her point.

"*No. I'm afraid not, my darling. But I'll tell you what. If you're fast asleep when we get home, then tomorrow we'll do something special.*"

"*What? What?*"

Patricia gave a secretive smile. "*I'll have Uncle Julian take us to the zoo. Now will you go to sleep when Mrs. Schindler tells you?*"

"*Yes.*"

Julian left a few days later and the Kingsley household returned to normal. It was funny, Ariane thought. With Uncle Julian gone, her father smiled more and her mother smiled less.

Ariane was in junior high school, and she and Sloane were supposed to be doing their homework. But they couldn't stop giggling about Phyllis and how her gym-suit had split in two.

"I couldn't believe it," Sloane squealed. "Did you see Jeffrey get hit with the ball because he was staring so hard?"

"I know. And Mrs. Kelton was so mean making her finish the exercise in front of everybody. I would have died," Ariane finished dramatically. Indeed, death did seem preferable to a twelve-year-old.

"And what do we have here? A meeting of the minds?" Julian asked from the doorway.

"Hi, Uncle Julian," Ariane said.

"Who's your beautiful friend? I just love red hair," Julian said.

"My friend Sloane. This is my Uncle Julian."

"Hi." Sloane was unusually tongue-tied.

"You can call me Julian. And I'll call you Red. You don't mind, do you, Red?" Julian winked.

"No." She self-consciously touched her hair.

"Well, back to work, girls. I've got to shower for a night on the town."

"Ooh, he's wonderful," Sloane gushed when Julian left. "Why didn't you tell me about him?"

Ariane shrugged her shoulders. "There wasn't anything to tell."

"He's so cute. Is he married? Where does he live? What does he do?"

"He's not married and he travels a lot. Now can we get back to this?" Ariane answered and opened her book, suddenly intent on study.

She didn't think she liked her Uncle Julian any-more. He was too friendly, asking her lots of questions about boys. She wanted him to act more like an uncle and less like a friend. She didn't know why, but she didn't like the way things felt when he came for *a visit. Things felt wrong. Her mother laughed too much and her father looked angry all the time. And when he did smile at Ariane, it was a sad, painful smile that made Ariane want to cry.*

Ariane had been asleep but the raised voices in the next room had wakened her and now she lay in bed, her heart pounding, listening to things she didn't understand, hearing things she didn't want to.

"Couldn't you at least have the decency to come in at a reasonable hour?" William asked Patricia.

"We were having fun. I lost track of the time." Her mother's voice sounded funny.

"Patricia, this can't go on. I can't take it."

"What can't go on?"

"Julian."

"I don't know what you mean."

"I know, Patricia. I've known for years, from the beginning."

"Julian and I have a good time, that's all. You never want to go out. You're always too tired. You act old." Patricia said the word as if it were poison.

Daddy's fun, Ariane thought. He took her to the carnival and went on the rides with her, not like the other fathers who were always too busy.

"I am old. I'm forty-six. And so are you."

"I'm not old!" Patricia yelled. "You're only old because you make yourself old. Well, I'm not going to get old. Julian thinks I'm beautiful, even if you don't."

"I think you're beautiful, Patricia. I always have," William answered. Her father sounded so sad, and it made Ariane want to cry.

"Then why don't you take me dancing like Julian? Why don't you take me out more?" Patricia whined.

"Because I'm tired. I work hard all day and I'm just not able to keep up with your young friends."

"That's all I ever hear—how tired you are. Well, I'm sick of hearing it. Julian's never too tired for me."

"I'll bet he isn't."

There was a sound like hands clapping once and then silence. Ariane gripped the covers tightly, waiting. She was so scared she wanted to run into their bedroom but she didn't dare. She was afraid of what she might see.

"Oh God, William. I'm sorry." Ariane could tell that her mother was crying. *"I'm so sorry. I didn't mean to hurt you. I don't know what's wrong with me."* She was crying harder, her words now sounding choked. *"I love you."*

Suddenly, Ariane was crying too. She had never heard her parents fight like this. Ariane was afraid, more afraid than she'd ever been.

"I know, darling. It's all right," William said.

Ariane yanked the blankets over her head, wanting to hide from what she had heard. She sobbed into her pillow, her heart breaking, but not knowing why. Something bad had happened between her parents and it had to do with Uncle Julian. But what could he have done? He was always smiling and happy, too happy. Maybe she could find out what he did and make it better. She'd have to try.

"Hello there," Julian said, peering into Ariane's bedroom.

"Hi, Uncle Julian." Ariane's face tightened as she looked up from her homework.

"How about a kiss?"

"Sure." Ariane hopped off her bed, pecked Julian on the cheek, and turned.

"Wait a minute. Let me get a look at you." Julian took her hand and held her at arm's length. *"I think you're growing up nicely, niece, and quite nicely too."*

"Thank you," Ariane mumbled and pulled her hand away so she could return to her bed. She was fourteen and well aware of the changes taking place in her body. Sometimes she was glad it was happening and sometimes she wasn't. Just now she wasn't.

"I bet you're going to give Patricia a real run for her money," Julian mused and then added lightly, *"Lucky me, two beautiful women in one house."*

"I'm only a girl," Ariane replied.

"You look like a woman to me. And believe me I know a woman when I see one." Julian winked at her as he stroked his jaw.

Ariane could feel herself blush as she lowered her gaze to her book, wishing with all her heart that Uncle Julian would just go away and leave her and her family alone.

Ariane couldn't believe it. She had gotten an A+ on her science project. She had worked on her model City of the Future for months, without any help from anyone. Not only that, Mrs. Horton said the local newspaper wanted to do a story on her and take her picture. The newspaper! This was the best!

School had ended early because of a fire in a chemistry class and Ariane practically ran all the way home, bursting to tell her mother the good news. Her mother would be so proud of her.

Ariane opened the front door to the house and stood listening for the sounds of her mother. The house was quiet.

"*Mom?*" *Ariane called out as she went into the kitchen.*

Finding the kitchen empty, Ariane walked back to the entrance foyer and heard something that sounded like the upstairs shower. Now why would her mother be taking a shower in the middle of the afternoon?

A bright smile on her face, Ariane raced up the stairs and into her parents' bedroom. She heard her mother giggle, a low throaty sound that Ariane had never heard before.

"Stop it," her mother said in a breathy voice. "You're supposed to be washing my back."

"I know. But I can't keep my hands off your front," a man's voice replied. It wasn't her father's voice.

Ariane knew that voice.

Her mother and Uncle Julian were in the shower together!

In shock, but unable to tear herself away, Ariane stood, listening to her mother and Julian in the shower, listening to their lovemaking.

"God, that's good," Patricia moaned.

"I know what you like, don't I?"

"Yes, yes." Ariane's eyes were fixed on the blue and white flowered bedspread. Her mother and father's bedspread.

"And you know what I like, don't you?"

"Is this what you want, Julian?" Patricia purred.

"Mmm."

All Ariane heard was the running of water and then Julian's voice sounding strained, "Oh, baby, yes. Don't stop."

Her mother didn't answer.

Ariane's hand flew to her mouth and she ran from the bedroom, from the house. She kept running and running. The tears flowed down her face. She didn't know where she was going. She didn't care. She only knew she had to get away, away from the awful sounds, the sounds her mother and Uncle Julian were making, the sounds she would never forget.

Her life had changed. She hated her Uncle Julian. She wanted to hate her mother, but a small part of her couldn't. The part that remembered her mother's smiling face, how her mother had taken care of her when she was sick, how her mother loved her. But her mother had done something awful with Uncle Julian there in that shower, something terrible against her father.

She looked around and realized it had grown dark. She was sitting on the park bench in front of City Hall. She should be getting home. But she didn't ever want to go home.

Home would never be the same again.

Some days later Ariane was setting the table while her mother prepared dinner.

"Here they are," Julian exclaimed as he entered the kitchen. "The two most beautiful women I know."

Patricia laughed. Ariane frowned. She couldn't stand the sight of her Uncle Julian. Every time she saw him she remembered, and every time she remembered, she hated him. Why wouldn't he leave? Why wouldn't he go away and leave them alone?

"I bought you a little present, niece," Julian said, forcing a brightly wrapped box into Ariane's hands.

"Thank you."

"Aren't you going to open it?" he asked.

"I'll open it later."

"I swear, that child has more self-control than anyone I know," Patricia said to Julian and then,

turning to Ariane, she said, "Open it. I'm dying to see it, even if you aren't."

Without any enthusiasm Ariane opened the box and held up the gift—a very brief bikini.

"Julian! That's positively scandalous. I think it's much too mature for Ariane."

"On the contrary," Julian said, studying Ariane thoughtfully. "I think it will suit her just fine."

Later, after dinner, Ariane put the bikini away in the back of her closet along with all the other gifts Julian had given her—gifts she refused to wear, to use, to look at.

"What are you wearing to Leslie's party?" Sloane asked, ignoring the math homework spread out in front of them.

"I'm not going."

"You're not going? Why not? Everybody's going."

"I have too much work to do," Ariane lied. She lied a lot these days, making excuses for not going to parties, for turning down dates.

"What work? You stay home so much you must be two years ahead by now. Don't you ever want to go out? Have some fun?"

"I have fun. At home." How could she tell Sloane she had to stay home to protect her parents' marriage?

"Oh please!" Sloane sighed dramatically. "Gary told Cliff that he thinks you're a snob and no one's going to ask you out anymore. Leslie said everybody was tired of your snottiness and your stuck-up attitude. Please, Kingsley."

"No, I can't." She preferred having no friends, nobody close to her, nobody close enough to learn her family's dirty secret. Besides, she was afraid to *leave her parents alone, to leave her mother and Uncle Julian alone. She was frightened that one day her father wouldn't forgive her mother, that one day Julian wouldn't be alone when he left.*

Ariane finished her first year of college at a university in Connecticut and was home for the summer. Keeping to herself had become a habit and she hadn't made any friends at school aside from a passing acquaintance with her roommate.

She spent the summer days idly at her parents' country club, playing tennis, swimming, and catching up with Sloane.

"Hey, Mom, how about a game of tennis this afternoon?" Ariane asked one morning over breakfast.

"No thanks. After yesterday's game I need a rest."

"Then how about having lunch with me at the club and then we could go for a swim?"

"Not today. I'm having my hair done. What's with you lately? You haven't let me out of your sight for days. Why don't you spend some time with Sloane?"

Julian had arrived several days before and Ariane didn't dare leave her mother alone—not with Julian in town.

Late that afternoon, having finished a grueling game of tennis with Sloane, Ariane was pouring herself a glass of lemonade in the kitchen.

"Hello, anybody home?" a voice called out. Ariane felt her insides twist, recognizing Julian's voice. She didn't answer, hoping he would go away.

"Hey, little niece. Didn't you hear me?" Julian asked from the entrance to the kitchen.

"No."

"How about a kiss hello?"

Ariane finally turned around to face Julian, hating

*his cheerfulness, his good looks, his treachery. "I'm
all sweaty. I don't think so."*

*Julian's eyes swept over her figure in a way that
was definitely not paternal, making her wish she had
changed out of her tight T-shirt and white shorts. For
days he'd been dogging her footsteps, looking at her
in an odd way.*

"I don't mind."

*"Want some lemonade?" Ariane offered, ignoring
him.*

"Sure."

*She handed him a glass. "How much longer will
you be staying?"*

He shrugged. "Couple of weeks."

*"My mother and I are very busy, so she won't be
able to spend much time with you."*

*"That's all right. I'll find something to do." Julian
followed Ariane to the screened porch at the back of
the house. She felt him watching her, felt his leering
gaze on her.*

*"So, how do you like school?" He sat next to her
on the green and white sofa. "Sorry. I take that back.
You must be pretty sick of everyone always asking the
same question. How's your tennis? Maybe we could
get together for a game."*

*"My tennis is okay, but I would probably slow you
down." He was sitting too close to her and she
shifted, moving away toward the corner.*

*"I don't think you could slow me down, even if you
tried. I'll bet the boys swarm all over you at school,
don't they?"*

"I . . . I have a boyfriend."

*"Have you gone all the way yet?" he asked, mov-
ing closer.*

Ariane blushed miserably, unable to answer.

"I didn't think so," he said with an unpleasant smile. *"He's just a boy. What you need is a man."* He slid his arm around her and began massaging her neck. She tried to shrug his hand away but he persisted.

"A man knows what a woman needs, knows how to satisfy her." His fingers slipped below the collar of her shirt. *"Your first time should be with a man."*

"Stop it." He was disgusting and his touch made her skin crawl.

"Don't be afraid, Ariane. I'll be good." He moved closer and pressed his lips to her cheek. His hand held her neck so she couldn't move.

"Don't touch me." She tried to move away but she was trapped in the corner of the sofa.

"Don't fight it. I know you want me. I've been wanting you for a long time," he murmured in her ear and began planting kisses along her jaw.

"Well, I don't want you! I hate you!" She pushed at his chest, trying to move away from his grasp.

"You don't hate me. You're just confused." He kept kissing her neck and jaw.

One minute Julian was kissing her neck and the next he had twisted her head around and brought his mouth down on hers. Ariane's hands flew to his chest to ward him off, spilling the lemonade all over herself. His mouth was soft at first and then more rough as he plunged his tongue into her mouth, making her gag.

"Come on, relax. It's more fun if we do this together. Besides, I'm good. Better than those boys at school."

"You bastard! Get off of me!"

Julian laughed, the sound confident and arrogant.

"Take it easy. Wait until you see what you've been missing."

His mouth captured hers again while his hands roamed freely over the bare flesh of her arms and legs, over her skimpily clad body.

Tears of rage and fear spilled down her face. She twisted furiously beneath him as he pulled her wet, sticky T-shirt up and slipped his hand underneath to fondle her breast.

"What the hell is going on here?"

At the sound of Patricia's voice, Julian froze. He broke off his assault and said shakily, *"Nothing. It's not what you think."*

"Liar!" Ariane struggled out from beneath Julian's body and stood up. *"Mom—"* she began imploringly. She felt her mother's eyes sweep over her. She glanced down and realized she must look a sight with her wet T-shirt stretched out of shape. She was suddenly aware of the tears on her face and the throbbing of her bruised mouth.

"Go to your room," Patricia said tightly.

"But Mom—"

"I said go to your room."

Ariane had never seen her mother so angry, nor had she ever been spoken to like that. She ran from the porch to the sanctity of her bedroom.

Ariane showered for half an hour. She washed away every trace of the sticky lemonade. But she couldn't wash away the dirty feeling of his groping hands on her body. When she walked into her bedroom she found her mother standing in front of her stuffed animal collection holding Snoopy, Ariane's favorite.

"Are you all right?"

"Y-yes." Ariane nervously tightened the sash on her white terry-cloth robe.

"Are you sure? Did he hurt you?" There was still that hard edge to her mother's voice, as if she were angry.

"No."

"He won't be back again. Ever." Patricia's emphasis on the last word was perfectly clear.

"I'm glad." There was a flicker of understanding in Ariane's dark eyes, a look of relief.

"I don't think we should tell your father about this. It would hurt him terribly and I'm afraid of what he might do. Do you think you'll be able to keep it from him, or will it be too difficult for you?"

Patricia was treating her as a mature adult. And while Ariane appreciated being dealt with as an equal, a part of her longed to be held and comforted as a child.

"No, I don't think so."

"Good." Patricia put Snoopy back in his place and started for the door. She stopped in front of Ariane and, as she had done so many times when she was a child, reached out to smooth back a stray strand of hair. The gesture brought a rush of tears to Ariane's eyes and her lower lip began to quiver.

"Oh God, Ariane, I'm sorry. So sorry." Patricia grabbed her, hugging her fiercely.

Ariane let go, great wracking sobs shaking her body as she collapsed against her mother. Holding her, Patricia led her to the bed.

"I thought you were mad at me," Ariane said.

Patricia gazed intently into her daughter's tear-filled eyes.

"Mad at you? My darling, I could never be mad at you." Patricia pulled Ariane to her, clasping her tightly, stroking her hair. "Ariane, you're all a mother could hope for in a child. You've never brought your father or me anything but pride and happiness. I'm the one who should beg for forgiveness for the pain I've caused you and your father." Hot tears of remorse ran down Patricia's cheeks. "I love you, Ariane. If you can find it in your heart to forgive me, I swear I'll make it up to you. But maybe I'm asking too much. I certainly don't deserve it."

Ariane heard the self-hate and dejection in her mother's voice and, suddenly, she saw Patricia not as the perfect wife and mother she wanted her to be, but as a frail human being with all the weaknesses of any mere mortal. And while Ariane didn't condone her mother's behavior, she understood that it had nothing to do with Patricia's love for her.

Ariane pulled back and looked at her mother, the dark eyes so similar to her own. "I love you, Mom."

Patricia searched Ariane's face and hugged her tightly. "Thank God. Things are going to be different from now on, my darling. I promise you."

Everything was perfect for a time. Ariane graduated college and moved to New York City, sharing an apartment with Sloane. She got a job as a paralegal, met Craig, one of her boss's clients, and began to date him exclusively.

Within the year Ariane and Craig were married at a beautiful ceremony at her parents' country club. They had honeymooned in Anguilla for two marvelous weeks and moved into the newly renovated, exquisitely furnished Park Avenue duplex.

They had been married for six months when William broke the news to Ariane. Her mother had cancer. She was dying and had six months, a year at the most, to live.

Needing to be with her parents as much as possible, Ariane stayed with them during the week and returned home on weekends.

Patricia looked and felt healthy for a while, but that ended all too soon as the disease made her life unbearable.

As a doctor, William was able to provide shots of morphine, but soon even the narcotic was no match for the excruciating pain.

Ariane watched her mother succumb, racked with pain, begging for more morphine, and she thought she couldn't stand another minute of it. Somehow she pulled herself together and cared for her mother, feeding her, washing her, soothing her, loving her.

Craig joined Ariane on the weekends when she refused to leave her mother's side. Ariane was worn out physically and emotionally, a drawn and haggard look on her young face.

One morning Ariane woke late, feeling lethargic and groggy. Her father had given her a sleeping pill the night before, insisting she needed a good night's rest.

She immediately went to her mother's room to find her and William asleep in each other's arms.

But they weren't asleep. Unable to watch his wife suffer anymore, William had given Patricia a fatal dose of morphine and, unwilling to go on without her, had taken his own life.

Ariane was devastated, nearly paralyzed with grief. She clung to Craig fiercely, centering her life on him. When she emerged from her haze of pain and loneliness she realized how lucky she was to have him, and dedicated her life to their marriage and his happi-

ness. But then a more terrifying thought hit her—what if Craig died? She was utterly alone. Craig was all she had and she focused her life on him.

Now she was going to have to learn to live without him. She was going to be alone. Completely alone.

But as she snuggled beneath the covers, Ariane had a thought, a realization that brought her comfort. She would make it alone. She had already been alone for years. Now it was reality.

chapter 14

"My poor darling. You look exhausted," Dulci said as she let Craig into her spacious apartment in the Olympic Tower.

"Please, don't remind me. But one look at you and I feel better already." Craig took in Dulci's tall figure, provocatively revealed in her white silk lounging pajamas.

He settled himself on the pale green silk sofa while she made his drink.

"That goddamn Watson is holding me up for more money. And if I don't pay I'll lose all of his business."

"I don't understand. You're buying his business?" she asked, handing him his scotch.

"Yeah. I put him on the payroll a year ago along with assorted others. For $10,000 a month he steers all his firm's business to me. Only now he's upped it to $15,000."

"Sounds illegal. Is it?"

"Yeah, but you can bet I'm not the only one doing it. And the little bastard's got me. If I don't pay he'll take his business to someone who's willing, and Newman Brothers will lose a fortune.''

''Sounds like a cutthroat business. Let's not talk about it anymore. You need to relax. And I know just what you need. Come with me.'' She stood and, taking his hand, led him to her white marble bathroom.

The Jacuzzi was filled, the water bubbling lazily.

Dulci unzipped her jumpsuit, shrugged it from her shoulders, and let it fall to her ankles, standing for his inspection. She smiled and said, ''Get in.''

He grinned and, wasting no time, was soon immersed in the warm, turbulent water.

Sliding alongside him, she handed him a fresh drink and stroked him between the thighs, cooing seductively, ''Now let's see what we can do about relaxing you.''

''I hate to disappoint you but I think I'm even too tired for that,'' Craig admitted, grinning ruefully.

''Nonsense. You just let me do the work. All you have to do is enjoy it,'' she promised.

Expertly fondling him, her fingers worked their magic as Craig grew hard in her hand. His eyes closed as he leaned his head back, giving himself up to her erotic manipulations. A small sigh of satisfaction escaped him as her fingers found his secret spots. His desire mounted as he began to move his hips toward her, straining against her hand.

She moved to straddle him and, still fondling him, caressed her own sensitive flesh.

Craig watched, mesmerized by the erotic sight, watched as her fingers knowingly played their game. Slowly and seductively she began to lower herself, teasing them both as she brought him to her.

His desire throbbed painfully. He grabbed her by the hips and yanked her down on him. With water sloshing wildly he finished what she had so artfully started.

Later, when they rested in the bedroom, she asked, "Whatever happened with those records that were subpoenaed? Mettrac, wasn't it?"

"Who knows. They took the trading ledgers and now they want the trading tickets."

"What does that mean?"

"There was unusual activity in the stock and they want to find out who the buyers were."

"Were you one of them?"

Craig smiled enigmatically. "Could be."

Ariane looked up from her desk when an attractive man with salt and pepper hair entered the workroom. Stopping dead in his tracks, he announced dramatically, "Aren't you going to introduce me to this gorgeous creature?"

"Ariane Wakefield, meet Bennett Townsend," Gordon said.

Bennett came over to her desk and leaned on the raised edge. "Hello, lovely lady. If I had known what a beauty Gordon's new assistant was, I would have come home in a flash. I hope you can forgive me for not being here to welcome you properly." The green eyes raked over her appreciatively.

"That's quite all right." Ariane smiled in spite of herself. Now she understood what Gordon had meant when he said Bennett was different from his father. "Gordon's made me feel right at home."

"Good. But I insist you allow me to welcome you aboard personally. Let me take you to dinner tonight. We'll make it official."

"That's very kind of you to offer, but I'm afraid I can't."

"Then tomorrow night?"

"No, I'm sorry." She had no intention of explaining herself.

"Next week. You pick the night."

"No. I—"

"Bennett, old boy," Gordon interrupted, "I think the lady is so bedazzled by your charm that she's overwhelmed. Why not give her time to get used to you and then you can take us all to dinner? You know Molly will be furious if she doesn't get to see you."

Ariane smiled gratefully at Gordon, appreciating his interruption.

Later, after Bennett had left, Gordon said, "I hope you didn't mind my intrusion, but I had the distinct impression you didn't want to go out with Bennett and I know how persistent he can be."

"You're right on both accounts . . . and thanks. Is he always like that?"

"No. Only when there's a beautiful woman around. I don't mean to preach, but I think I ought to warn you that Bennett isn't as harmless as he appears. He has a reputation for going after something he wants and then discarding it when he's through. What he enjoys is the chase."

"Thanks for the words of advice, but I have no intention of getting involved with anyone."

"When the time is right, you will. Just remember not to expect anything more from Bennett than a good dinner and a lot of arm wrestling, if you know what I mean."

Gordon's words proved to be prophetic when Ariane found a large arrangement of orchids from Marlo Florist on her desk the next morning. She didn't have to read the card to know they were from Bennett. The next day a five-pound box of Parón chocolates was waiting for her, followed by a tin of beluga caviar, a box of chocolate-covered truffles, and an agenda from Hermès with several of the dates filled in with Bennett's name.

The second week went by with no presents and not a

word from Bennett. Ariane began to relax. Apparently, he had taken the hint.

One morning Ariane arrived at work early and was hanging up her coat when she heard the door to the workroom close. She turned around, expecting to see Gordon, only to find Bennett leaning against the closed door.

"Good morning. Thank you for all your gifts, but you really shouldn't have."

Bennett strolled over to stand close to her. Too close. "If you really want to thank me, why don't you have dinner with me?"

"I . . . I'm sorry. But I can't," Ariane stammered, uncomfortable to have him in her space.

"Why not? You have to eat. I have to eat. Why don't we do it together?"

Ariane brushed past Bennett and walked over to her desk, where she tried to busy herself by moving her pens and chalks around. She turned to find herself face to face with him and even closer than before.

"It has nothing to do with you," she offered as an explanation. "I'm just not dating right now."

Bennett leaned onto the desk with one hand, effectively pinning her between the desk and himself while his other hand moved up her arm. "Okay, then how about thanking me anyway. And I promise not to call it a date."

She raised her hand to push against his chest. "Bennett, stop it."

"Aw, come on. One friendly thank you kiss isn't going to hurt." He took hold of her chin and brought his mouth down on hers.

Ariane had time to register that Bennett's mouth felt warm and soft against hers before she was able to twist out of his grip and push him away.

"I said stop it!"

"Okay, okay." He took one step backward. He didn't seem at all put off by her rejection. "No need to get angry."

At the sound of the door opening, Ariane whipped her head around and smiled with relief at Gordon's timely arrival.

"Well, I have to be going. I have a million things to do. Thanks for explaining the collar on that blouse, Ariane," Bennett said breezily as he turned to leave.

Ariane's days flew by, the hours satisfactorily filled with the excitement of her work. But the nights when she was alone, with no diversions, weren't as easy.

She hadn't heard from Craig since she had moved out. Not wanting any of his money, she had been using the inheritance from her parents to supplement her income from LT.

There were times when she found herself unconsciously waiting for Craig to come home until she remembered her circumstances. Or she found herself thinking, *I must tell Craig about that,* surprising herself at how often she thought about him. As the weeks went by, however, she found herself thinking less and less about him.

But it wasn't as simple to forget Alex—Alex and his warm mouth, his caressing knowing hands, his hard-driving body.

She spent her weekends browsing stores, visiting museums, and going to the movies. Occasionally, when Jessica was free, they had lunch or dinner together, each glad for the other's company.

Never having had the opportunity before, she found she enjoyed cooking. She picked up several cookbooks, began testing her skill, and discovered desserts were her favorite. Looking for an unbiased opinion, she found Gordon was more than willing to sample her homemade delights when she brought them to work for his testing.

One evening after work, she was just putting the finishing touches on her veal marengo when the telephone rang.

"Travis! What a surprise," she said, recognizing the slow Texas accent.

"I told you I'd call. How have you been?"

"Fine. Are you in town?"

"Yes. I flew in for business a few days ago." He paused. "How about dinner this week? Say Thursday?"

"Sure. I'd like that," Ariane answered. Then she had a sudden thought. "Travis, how did you know where to find me?"

"Alex was at the Newmans' for a party."

"And Kristen told him?"

"No, not exactly," Travis hesitated, sounding uncomfortable. "Craig was there."

"Alone?" she asked, somehow knowing the answer before she heard his reply.

"No . . . with a date."

Ariane hung up the phone, stared at the bubbling veal dish, turned off the gas, and walked into the living room, her appetite forgotten. Craig on a date. All of them together. Just like the weekend in Texas, only she was missing. Why did it bother her so much?

After an enjoyable dinner at Chanterelle, Ariane invited Travis up for an after-dinner drink.

She had her back to him and was pouring his drink when she asked, trying for a casual tone in her voice, "How's Alex?"

All evening long Alex's presence had hung between them like some haunting spirit that neither one of them wanted to acknowledge. She had waited for Travis to mention him and when he hadn't she had been both disappointed and relieved.

"Fine," Travis answered.

She handed him his drink and walked to the window to look out at the darkness of Central Park. It looked still and serene, the trees silhouetted against the night sky.

"And Consuelo?" asked Ariane.

"Fine. And so is Thunder and Buttercup and Blaze," Travis answered. When his sarcasm was met with silence, he placed his hand gently on her shoulder, and said, "I'm sorry for that. I know what you're asking. I was just hoping that you'd forget Alex for your own good. Alex isn't capable of having a relationship, let alone loving somebody."

"You're his friend. How can you say such things about him?" Her first thought was that everyone was capable of loving. Then she remembered Craig and felt a chill.

"Because I *am* his friend. There's a large part of Alex that's missing. He isn't whole. He doesn't care about people or their feelings."

"If he's that bad, why are you his friend?"

Travis shrugged. "I know what to expect from him or rather what not to expect. I think it would be different for a woman, don't you?"

Ariane glanced away, not answering.

"Look, maybe if I told you something about him you would understand what I'm talking about."

Ariane sat on the sofa by the window, waiting for Travis to return after he refilled his glass.

"Alex's childhood was far from ideal. It started out well enough; his mother and father were in love and worked the Savage S together. But Faith died when Alex was very young and Lute went a little crazy. He withdrew from the world and buried himself in his bottle. He ignored everything, the ranch, Alex."

"Who took care of Alex?" Ariane asked.

"Consuelo. She raised him. She tried to bring him and Lute together but nothing seemed to get through to Lute. Then gradually he came out of it and discovered Alex."

"Then everything was okay?"

"For a while. Until Doreen." The distaste was evident in Travis's voice. "Doreen McAllister. She was a waitress at the local bar. She knew a good thing when she saw it and set her sights on Lute. Within four months she was Mrs. Lute Savage, mistress of the Savage S."

"What happened to Alex and his father?" Ariane asked with a sinking feeling that told her she already knew.

"She hated Alex on sight. She saw his closeness to Lute as a threat and destroyed their relationship."

"Couldn't anybody see what she was doing? Consuelo?"

"They saw. But they couldn't do anything about it. She was Lute's wife and ruled the house with an iron fist. Anyone who questioned her or complained was fired."

"But how could Lute turn against Alex, his son?" She thought of her own family and realized no matter what troubles they had experienced she had always depended on their love for her.

"Lute was weak and foolish and Doreen knew just how to play him. She was a cold, manipulative bitch."

"That doesn't mean all women are like that," Ariane argued, feeling as though she were defending herself.

"Tell that to Alex. To be perfectly blunt, you're not even the type of woman he gets involved with. The others . . . well, they know what they want and they get it with no strings attached."

Ariane turned away and looked out the window, not wanting to hear about Alex and other women.

"Look, I think I've said enough for one evening. It's late and I'd better be going," Travis said as he stood.

Common sense told her that Travis had been telling her

the truth. She had known from the beginning that Alex was different. But her heart disagreed, irrationally maybe, but they were strong feelings all the same.

Why was Travis so adamant about warning her away? Was it for her own good as he said? She remembered the way he had stared at her over dinner, the look in his amber eyes, warm and appraising. His touch had been gentle when he helped her from the taxi, his hold lingering a bit longer than necessary. Maybe Travis had motives of his own.

The employees of LT were in a joyous mood, celebrating the holiday closing at the annual Christmas party. Ariane was in the kitchen, refilling one of the ice buckets, when she felt a hand snake around her waist. Startled, she dropped the bucket on the counter and whirled around to find herself staring into Bennett's handsome face.

"Ah, alone at last," he said as he brought his other hand to wrap around her waist.

"Oh, Bennett, stop it," she ordered, her voice half joking as she tried to fend him off. He had been following her around all day, declaring his undying love, much to her annoyance and embarrassment.

"Look, why not think of me as some new and exciting gourmet dish?" he said. "You should try it once just to see if you like it and if you don't, you don't order it again. But I'm sure I'm just what you're craving."

"I'm on a diet."

"Don't worry, I'm not fattening."

With that he held her head and met her mouth with his in a moist, searching kiss. The edge of the counter bit into her back and she reached behind her for a weapon to ward him off. Her hand closed around an object and, bringing her hand to the back of Bennett's neck in an apparent caress, she slipped the ice cube down his neck.

Bennett jumped and reached behind his neck to retrieve

the cube. "Are you crazy?" he yelled as he threw the ice into the sink.

Ariane smiled innocently. "No, but I had to cool you off somehow. My dish was just too hot."

"Cute. Very cute." Bennett reached for a towel.

"Am I interrupting something?" Molly asked from the doorway.

"No. I was just leaving." He turned to Ariane and said, "I owe you."

"From the looks of things it appears I got here just in time," Molly said as she watched Bennett's retreating back. "Gordon told me Bennett made you number one on his hit list. Annoying, isn't he?"

"You sound as if you speak from personal experience."

"Oh yes, I've had my share of Bennett Townsend. I guess Gordon didn't want to bring it up. When I first started working here as a model, Bennett was after me all the time. My mistake was that I agreed to have dinner with him once. I was taken in by his charm. After I realized what a terribly conceited womanizer he is, I didn't accept any more dates. But he wouldn't give up, in fact it only piqued his interest. He'd manage to be present at my fittings and always had a helpful suggestion about fitting the garment, which he loved to demonstrate on me. One day all his groping really got to me and I finally put him in his place."

"What did you do?" Ariane asked, intrigued.

Molly grinned mischievously. "I got him where he lives."

Travis leaned forward and toyed with a pen on Alex's desk. "I don't understand why they haven't tapped Wakefield's phones. At least then we could stay one step ahead of him."

"Because the little bastard has his office and house

swept almost daily. Besides, he's too smart to say anything incriminating over the phone. Anytime he talks to Hassan it's in public,'' Alex said, his annoyance obvious.

''Could we get someone with a wire into one of those meetings?''

''We could if Wakefield was the only one we were trying to fool. But the Arab's too slick.'' Just mentioning the Arab was enough to set Alex's temper boiling.

''I took Ariane out the other night,'' Travis said, glancing away, apparently uncomfortable.

''What the hell were you doing out with her?''

''We went out for dinner. I like her.''

''Really? And did she show you a good time?'' His tone was bitter, his jealousy all too apparent.

Travis jumped up from his chair. ''If you weren't my best friend and a fool to boot I'd knock your teeth out.''

Alex leaned back in his seat, utterly relaxed. ''Ah, the protector and defender of her honor. As if her kind needed protecting.''

''You know it's too bad you had such a rough start, but if you'd stop hating long enough you'd see the world isn't such a bad place.''

The silver eyes turned hard and cold. ''No? Next you'll be telling me to believe in fairy tales and happy endings.'' Alex glanced away and then bringing his gaze back to Travis, he said, ''Get off my back. You don't know what the hell you're talking about.''

''Look, I'm sorry. I didn't mean to bring that up.''

''Forget it.''

''It's just that Ariane's different. She's not like the others. She doesn't know this is just a game for you. She'll get hurt.''

''She's a grown woman and she can take care of herself,'' Alex said, effectively changing the conversation.

Alex stayed at his desk long after Travis left. He swiveled his chair to face the backyard of his town house. It was winter, bleak and bare, and it suited him. It was how he felt.

Alone. He had been alone since he was a child. He was four years old when his mother went to the hospital to have a baby, promising to come home soon with a new brother or sister. She didn't. She had lied to him. She had left him. She and the baby had died.

Then his father left him. Oh, he was still around, but he might have just as well been gone, considering that he never spoke to his son or even acknowledged his existence.

Then one day Lute had stepped out of his lethargy. Alex still remembered that day . . .

They had ridden out at a slow walk, Lute on his stallion and five-year-old Alex on his pony. Lute kept up a steady stream of conversation, pointing out buildings, cattle, trees, everything. Stopping at a small rise, Lute's eyes looked out into the distance.

"Some day all this is going to be yours, son. Do you know what that means?"

Alex didn't answer, not quite understanding what his father was talking about. But he liked being with his dad and listening to his voice.

"It's a piece of Texas, the best damn state in the best damn country. It was my grandfather's and it'll be yours and your children's and their children's. Don't let anybody ever take it away from you. It's your heritage, it's who you are."

At least he had his father, Alex thought. He would die if anything ever happened to him.

Two years later, Lute had married Doreen McAllister.

"Alex, what are you doing in here?" Consuelo had

asked one morning when she had entered his bedroom and found him sitting on the floor.

"Nothing," he mumbled.

"Why aren't you downstairs having breakfast?"

"I'm not hungry."

"You hardly ate any dinner last night. You must be hungry. Go on down and I'll have Cook make you some pancakes, okay?"

"She's down there." The young features looked thin and drawn.

"So?"

"She hates me. And I hate her." The gray eyes burned with emotion and unshed tears.

"She doesn't hate you," Consuelo said. "Why do you think that?" She sat down on the bed.

He stared hard at her, and she noticed he didn't seem young anymore. "Because she told me to stay out of her sight," he said. And then his eyes filled with pain. "Why doesn't my father like me anymore?"

"Alex, your father loves you very much," Consuelo stated definitely as though trying to make it true.

"No, he doesn't. He won't let me eat dinner with him anymore and he moved my room away and he's always too busy with her."

"Well, that's because they just got married." Consuelo leaned over to push back a lock of Alex's hair. "Alex, what's that bruise on your arm?"

"She did it." The deadly coldness returned.

"What happened?"

"She said I messed up the new sofa. I was only sitting on it." He threw down a toy soldier.

"She didn't mean it," Consuelo said.

"She meant it." His eyes held hers knowingly, daring her to disagree. He knew all about Doreen. He had known from the beginning.

• • •

Alex and his father were in Lute's study, enjoying a rare moment alone.

"Frank says I'm ready for a bigger horse," Alex said proudly.

"Does he now?"

"Yes. Can I?"

Lute looked at his son and grinned. "Well, I don't see why not. Why don't we go down to the stables and pick out a new mount?"

"Lute, look at this," Doreen said as she swept into the room. She thrust a brooch at him, ignoring Alex's presence.

Alex's face lost its animation at Doreen's intrusion.

"What is it?" Lute asked.

"It's the brooch you bought me when we went to Dallas, remember? I didn't want to tell you but it's been missing for months. I was afraid I'd lost it and I knew how upset you'd be."

"So you found it," Lute concluded.

Doreen glanced at Alex, then back at Lute. "Yes. In Alex's room."

Lute stared at Doreen not saying a word then, turning to Alex, he asked, "Did you take it?"

In that instant Alex knew his father would never believe him. He should never have had to ask. Alex hated him for asking. "No."

"Then how did it get there?"

"Ask her." He wasn't going to defend himself. What was the point? His father always sided with her.

"Watch your mouth, boy." He turned to Doreen. "Is it possible you dropped it in his room?"

"No, Lute." She rested her hand on his shoulder. "I'm sorry, darling, really I am." She kissed his

cheek and left, the look of triumph in her eyes un-mistakable.

"You'd better come with me, boy," Lute said, as he rose from his chair.

Lute took Alex out back for a beating.

Alex didn't cry. By now his childish hate had turned to a cold-blooded loathing.

When Alex was twelve, Doreen took off with her old boyfriend. She took her clothes and her jewels. She took the car.

Alex found his father in his study, sitting at his desk, his head bowed.

"Dad," Alex called as he entered the dark room. His father had been in there all day. It was supper time and he hoped his father would come out and maybe have dinner with him now that she was gone.

His father didn't raise his head. "Dad, do you want dinner?"

Lute raised his gaze to Alex but didn't seem able to focus. His eyes were glazed with drink and pain.

Alex moved forward hesitantly. He had never seen his father looking like that. "Are you all right?"

"Go away. Leave me alone." His voice was slurred.

"Maybe you should stop drinking."

"I said go away! Go on, get out of here!"

Alex turned and left, the look of hurt in his eyes unnoticed. Doreen had done this. Doreen and her lying and manipulating. And now she had run off, leaving his father so that she could be with another man. Women were no good. They couldn't be trusted. They lied. Then they left you.

chapter 15

On the day of Sloane and Justin's premiere, Ariane met Sloane for lunch at the Four Seasons. Ariane knew Sloane was nervous and hoped the activity in the Grill Room would distract her.

Ariane watched Sloane as she nervously fidgeted with her silverware while they waited for their food to arrive.

"Everything's going to be fine," Ariane said. "Justin did his best and you know it doesn't get any better than that. Try and relax."

"I know, I know. It's just that this film really means everything to Justin, and I'm so afraid he'll be shattered if it doesn't get the reception he wants. Let's change the subject, shall we? How's single life?" Sloane asked.

"All right, I guess. Actually it's not much different from when I was living with Craig. He was home so seldom and we rarely did anything together, so nothing's much different. Sometimes I think we were just two polite strangers, living at the same address, passing the time from one party to the next. You know I've always belonged to someone, been someone's daughter or someone's wife and never just me. Now I'm alone, on my own. I have no one to answer to. It's kind of scary but I like it.''

"Feels good to be independent, doesn't it?" Sloane asked.

"Yes, it does. You know you're pretty smart for a dumb redhead," Ariane teased. "All your talk about getting a job and doing something with my life was great advice. I probably should have listened to you a long time ago but I guess I just didn't want to hear it then. I'd been living Craig's dream for so long, I thought it was mine," she admitted.

"What do you want?"

"I'm not sure exactly, but I feel I'm on the right track. It's funny, I always thought I had everything. I had nothing.''

Ariane and Carlo followed Sloane and Justin into Regine's, ready to celebrate. Ariane had allowed herself to be persuaded to attend the premiere with Carlo, not having the energy to fight Sloane and not really minding.

As they were checking their coats in the small vestibule, Richard and Emily came in behind them. They greeted each other exuberantly and proceeded to their table, passing the white baby grand piano and the mirrored bar with its displays of pink ostrich feathers. Ariane idly checked her reflection in the mirrored column, satisfied with her black velvet Armani dinner suit. The short tight skirt showed off her legs to their best advantage in sheer black stockings and sexy black silk pumps.

Sitting at the pink linen-covered table, Justin immediately ordered champagne. He raised the crystal flute and toasted, "To my friends, for their love and support, and to my wife, for putting up with me when I must have been impossible, for having faith even when I didn't, and for always being there. This is for you.''

They all lifted their glasses to accolades of, ''Here, here.'' Ariane saw the look of love that passed between Justin and Sloane and for a second her heart ached with envy as she wondered if she would ever find her love.

Carlo made a toast to Justin. Richard toasted his wife for putting up with his nervous anxiety over the movie, Sloane toasted Justin, and Justin ordered another bottle of champagne. Soon they were laughing and enjoying themselves as they toasted the waiter and the smoked trout he brought.

By the time they finished dinner the trompe l'oeil screen in the rear of the restaurant had been folded back, revealing the dimly lit discotheque. The heavy beat of the music surrounded them as they quickly took the last empty booth against the wall.

The combination of the black and gold booths, the mirrored squares on the walls, and the geometric chunks of mirror that made up the ceiling gave the disco a sensual ambience.

Ariane danced with Justin, Richard, and Carlo before she sat down next to Sloane to catch her breath. Sloane hugged her warmly.

''See, you're having fun,'' Sloane said. ''Aren't you glad I talked you into coming?''

''Yes, yes, you were right. You can talk me into having fun anytime.''

''So what do you think about Carlo?''

''Sloane,'' Ariane said, grinning at her friend's attempt at matchmaking. She absently touched the small round glass ball on the rust lacquered table. ''Get that look out of your eye. Carlo is very sweet, but there's nothing between us and he knows it.''

''Just asking.''

As if on cue Carlo approached, the easy smile on his face hard to resist as he asked Ariane to dance. Smiling her agreement, Ariane tossed Sloane a mischievous grin and rose to follow Carlo's lead. The deejay put on a slow record and she went into his arms. They danced comfortably and easily with each other until, feeling Carlo mysteriously stop moving, she saw that he was focusing on something behind her. She turned around to see what had commanded his attention and came face to face with a pair of silver eyes she had thought never to see again.

Her heart jumped as she stared up at Alex. His face was unreadable as he held out his hand toward her. Without thinking she slipped her hand into his, letting him pull her into his arms, against the hard, lean length of him. She was dimly aware of the music floating around them as they swayed together to their own private rhythm.

When the deejay put on a fast record, Alex led her off the dance floor. He guided them through the crush of the crowd and on to the front door, pausing long enough to retrieve their coats from the checkroom.

Once outside, the cold night air was a refreshing change from the warm, smoky atmosphere of the crowded club. Ariane dug her hands into the pockets of her silver fox coat as Alex linked his arm through hers, and turning left, they began walking uptown. She had no idea where he was taking her, and she didn't care as long as she was with him. From the moment she had seen him tonight she knew the evening belonged to them. It was as if she was following some stronger primitive instinct that she was helpless against. They hadn't spoken a word to each other. Maybe it was better that way. Whenever they spoke they wound up fighting.

As they stopped and waited at a red light at Sixty-fourth and Park, Ariane lifted her arms to pull her fur collar up against the cold. Seeing her struggle, Alex offered his as-

sistance and easily completed the task. For a long moment
he stared down into her upturned face. The silver and black
hair of her coat moved in the night wind, framing the
perfect porcelain oval of her face. Her black eyes seemed
enormous, and her lips were slightly parted. Still holding
the edge of her collar, he drew her to him and his mouth
met hers in a warm, passionate kiss full of promise.

It was incredible, Ariane thought as she felt Alex's warm
demanding mouth take possession of her. With one touch
of his sensual lips he drove the chill from her body and
replaced it with a pleasant spreading warmth.

They walked quietly up Park Avenue, the silence thick
with excitement.

Ariane was nearly breathless from trying to keep up
with Alex's long strides when they stopped in front of a
town house. He put his key in the lock of the dark wood
door and turned on a light switch as he let them in. Without a word between then he took her hand and led her
through an entryway up a carpeted staircase.

On the second floor landing he left her briefly as he
entered the large darkened room to her right. Seconds later
he emerged, carrying a decanter and a brandy glass, then
led her up to the third floor. He entered the room ahead
of her, set the decanter and snifter down on a round walnut
table, and turned on a small black candlestick lamp. While
he lit a fire in the fireplace, Ariane glanced around the
spacious room. She noticed only the large bed covered in
black silk.

It was a room of contrasts that worked effectively. Black
silk-covered walls were distinct against the high white
ceiling. The polished oak floor was covered with a magnificent Tabriz carpet of gold and black. Antique English
and Italian pieces added to the luxury.

His task completed, Alex helped her out of her coat,
tossed it on a nearby sofa, and then did the same with his.

He picked up the decanter and snifter and poured a generous amount of brandy.

When Ariane took the proffered glass, her fingers brushed his and she nearly jumped from the contact. She took a sip of the brandy and stifled an urge to cough as the liquid fire burned the back of her throat. She took another larger swallow, liking the way the brandy worked its magic as it drove the chill from her body.

Alex turned off the lamp and led her by the arm toward the fireplace. Taking the empty snifter from her, he refilled it, his silver eyes never leaving her face as he took a deep swallow.

Her smooth white skin glowed from the effects of the brandy and the warmth of the fire. His eyes traveled down her long, elegant neck to the deep V of her jacket and then to the outline of the proud thrust of her breasts. Large black pearls gleamed seductively on her white throat. The firelight danced like so many flickering flames on the thousands of sequins, accentuating the rise and fall of her chest with each breath she took.

With a quick toss of his wrist, he finished off the rest of his brandy and set the empty glass on the mantel.

Ariane was startled by the look of passion that turned his eyes a smoky pitch. His eyes never left her face as his hand raised her head and he brought his mouth to hers, barely touching her lips. His mouth whispered across hers, tasting and nuzzling. Her apprehension was replaced by a spreading heat that fired her desire.

She returned his gentle kisses, learning the contours of his mouth, tasting the brandy. There was a tightening deep inside her that turned into a pleasant ache. He teased her with the promise of a kiss before his mouth claimed hers in a deep lingering kiss that sent the blood pounding in her veins. Her arms went around his neck, her hands moving over his jacket. He hugged her to him, molding her to him. She could feel his desire hard against her, the proof of his passion exciting her and fanning her own wanting.

Her head whirled dizzily as his mouth moved down her neck and further. He unbuttoned her jacket and slipped it from her shoulders. She buried her fingers in his thick black hair and gasped at the pleasure his mouth caused as it circled and tasted a swollen bud. His mouth sent shock waves of delight through her body, his expert hands sliding tantalizingly over her heated flesh.

Gently he lowered her skirt as she held on to his shoulders for support. The room was a blur as he led her to the bed and undressed in front of her.

She watched intently, her black eyes glowing like burning coals, as Alex revealed his broad, muscled chest with its mat of fine black hair. The need was thick in her throat as her eyes followed its narrow trail to his flat belly and lower still to where it fanned out thickly. She took in the proud naked splendor of him and quivered with excitement, feeling his irresistible force fill the room.

His silver eyes roamed over her, branding her, torches that marked her with heat. She held out her arms to him, whether in supplication or surrender: it didn't matter.

Neither of them spoke. Words didn't matter. They could never explain what was between them.

Alex pulled her against him, wrapping her in his embrace as his mouth sought hers. She could feel the hunger in his hands as they roamed over her, caressing and fondling, making her burn. His mouth began trailing down her flesh, each touch making her writhe seductively. She ached for him. If she couldn't feel the hard strong length of his body next to her she'd go mad.

She urged him to her but he wouldn't comply. Instead, he tortured her sweetly, turning her to liquid fire. Every nerve in her body throbbed, her pulse pounding so loudly in her ears she was sure he could hear it. And then his mouth followed his hands and she couldn't stop the sounds of delight she made.

Ariane was lost in her own world, and that world was Alex. She explored and discovered the different textures and tastes of him, the hard muscles of his chest, the soft mat of hair, the rippling muscles of his flat belly, the narrow trail of hair that branched out into thick curls. As her hand closed around him she heard him groan and felt her own passion burn, knowing she was the cause of his pleasure.

Grabbing her by her upper arms he brought her alongside him and muttered thickly, "You witch. Do you know what you do to me? You're driving me mad." His eyes were dark, glazed and for a moment she thought she saw something other than passion, but it was gone too quickly.

He parted her thighs and slipped easily into her velvet hotness, her gasp of pleasure muffled against his mouth. For a long, wonderful moment he didn't move and she relished the feel of him, her hands clasping him tightly. He started to thrust, his motions leisurely and languid, prolonging their pleasure, tormenting them both with his flirting movements.

Ariane writhed beneath him, urging him on, wanting, needing.

With a deep growl Alex plunged deeply, clutching her to him, filling her completely. He pressed her to him, not moving, as his manhood throbbed against her.

They moved together perfectly, each sensing the other's needs and wants, each taking and giving. Deep inside, Ariane could feel a tight knot of intense pleasure grow and expand, until she became one with the sensation.

Poised on the brink of a wonderful explosion, she matched his driving rhythm with her own. She was shooting up into a black sky, into the unknown. When the first wave of ecstasy burst through her like a meteor, she cried out his name and clasped him to her, feeling him shudder against her. Finally, he relaxed on her, their bodies slick with perspiration, their ragged breathing loud in the silent bedroom. But all she noticed was the wonderful feel of his masculine body covering her.

Alex shifted his weight off her and, propping himself on one arm, looked down into her face. Her eyes opened and tears shone on her black lashes. Alex gently reached out a finger and caught a tear as it rolled down her cheek.

She looked up into his face; the sardonic mask he wore so often was gone, as though he had dropped his guard and she was seeing a side of him that was unknown, even to himself. She reached up and gently caressed his cheek as she murmured huskily, "Alex . . ."

Alex put his finger across her lips, silencing her, then touched his lips gently to hers.

Later, when the fire had died, Ariane shivered and sought the warmth of Alex's body as she turned toward him, wrapping her slender body around the lean hard length of him.

He lifted his arm and wrapped it around her, giving her easier access and pulled her to him as he absently stroked her back. Hearing her murmur contentedly and feeling her lips on the side of his neck roused a feeling in him that he had never experienced. A strange feeling of peacefulness came over him and, pressing a kiss to her forehead, he whispered "Ari" before drifting off to sleep.

The next morning Ariane packed her bags quickly. Alex was sitting in his car downstairs and she didn't want to keep him waiting. They were going away for the weekend—at his request. And she was elated.

They had been driving for some time and were deep in the hills of the Berkshires when she began to have second thoughts. When Alex had prepared them a delicious breakfast of fruit, scrambled eggs and muffins that morning, he had asked her to go away with him. Without thinking she had said yes. But he had become so cold and distant in the car that she was beginning to become concerned. He was so mysterious, he wouldn't even tell her where they were going.

They approached the top of a rise and Ariane saw their destination. She marveled at the sight before her, an enchanting French castle that looked as if it had been magically transported from ancient France. There were leaded glass windows, gray stone turrets, and parapets.

"It's incredible," Ariane said, her soft voice filled with awe. "Is it a hotel?"

"No. It's a small, rather exclusive inn. The owner only takes in guests that he knows personally or referrals made by close friends."

"How did you find out about it?"

"The owner is a friend of mine." Alex pulled the car to a stop on the gravel drive in front of the massive door.

As though awaiting their arrival, a middle-aged man, dressed in country clothes, came out to meet them. He opened Ariane's door and silently assisted her, a curt nod his only greeting. Alex spoke to the man briefly, accepted something from him, and led Ariane inside.

"Friendly sort," she commented dryly.

"Simon? He's okay. Just doesn't take quickly to strangers, that's all."

Greeting people at an inn is a strange job for a man who doesn't like strangers, she thought.

Once inside she looked around her, taking in the stone walls, polished wood floors scattered with Savonniere rugs, and Louis XV furniture. The walls held an impressive display of fine French art.

"Simon told me he laid out a tea for our arrival. Why

don't we eat something and then you can take the tour?'' Alex suggested as he led them into a cozy salon.

There was a blazing fire in the large fireplace, and a linen-draped table set with an elaborate tea in front of it. Ariane sat on one of the love seats, shrugged out of her mink coat, and began pouring from the porcelain pot. ''Tea?''

''No thanks. I have mine,'' Alex answered as he reached for the crystal decanter and poured brandy into a glass.

''How do you know the owner?'' she asked, choosing one of the sweetcakes.

''Business.''

''Oh? I didn't realize Massachusetts had cattle and oil.''

''He's retired.'' Alex's expression was closed, shutting her out. Changing the subject, he gestured to the empty plate that had held the sweetcakes. ''If you're still hungry, I'm sure we can get you some more of those.''

''No, that's all right. I guess I didn't realize how hungry I was.''

They decided to go for a walk outside to stretch their legs after the long ride. Alex stopped to take his sheepskin coat from the car before he led Ariane across the frozen ground and around to the rear of the castle.

The sky had become overcast and looked heavy with the threat of snow. The landscape was bleak, the gray twilight washing the color from everything. The evergreens were still green, though frozen, the fruit trees stripped bare, their brown empty branches stretching ghostlike against the somber sky.

''Down there are the stables, an old tool shed, and some smaller buildings not in use anymore,'' he said, pointing down the slope.

''Who built this place? It's incredibly authentic.''

''It was built by Jean Raphael, a famous smuggler in the early part of the nineteenth century. Pirates used to stop in the area, bringing in their goods from France to divide up before selling to different local merchants. Jean Raphael became quite rich with his ill-gotten gains and, taking a liking to the area, decided to settle here permanently. His partner in France continued to supply him with brandy, lace, silk, and whatever else he could sell at a profit. He was French through and through and unwilling to give up his heritage, so he built an exact replica of his chateau in France.''

They had entered a grove of towering pine trees. The ground was covered with needles, the air fragrant and moist. There was something primeval about the forest in its unearthly silence, as if it were untouched by man.

"Just think," she said, "Jean Raphael could have walked through this very forest. How romantic."

"Romantic?"

"Yes. The chances he took supplying ladies with lace and silk for their gowns and men with their brandy and then deciding to live here. It must have been a terribly exciting time."

"And do you live in an exciting time?" he asked. Suddenly, he reached out in front of her and leaned against a tree, his arm halting her. Ariane looked at him as his other arm reached around her, trapping her against the tree.

He moved closer to her, pushing her back against the tree, studying the slanted black eyes that regarded him. *What a naive romantic,* he thought cynically, *but so desirable,* as he bent his head to claim that tempting mouth which he knew tasted so sweet. Her lips were cold beneath his, but they soon warmed as he searched the inner recesses of her mouth in a slow, lingering kiss. She was fire and ice in his arms, like some mythical wood nymph brought to life by his magic touch.

Had it not been the middle of winter and freezing cold, nothing would have stopped him from taking her right then. He locked his arms behind her back and pulled her against him. His silver eyes burning brightly, he asked, "Still think those were exciting times?"

"Not as exciting as these," she answered huskily.

Her frank and honest reply unnerved him, the open look of passion on her face giving credence to her words. He had been half-teasing when he had asked her, but her totally guileless answer troubled him. Annoyed with himself for letting her get to him, he quickly released her and turned to walk through the forest.

"Hey, slow down," she called as she tagged after him. Then she exclaimed, "Ooh, look, it's snowing."

Alex stopped in his tracks and turned to look at her, amazement on his face. "Haven't you ever seen snow before?" he asked sarcastically.

"Oh, don't be ridiculous." She laughed. "I just love snow. Did you know that every flake has six points and no two are ever alike?"

"You're just a wealth of information, aren't you?"

"Look." She held out her arm. "See?"

In spite of himself Alex couldn't help but look at Ariane's outstretched arm, the delicate snowflakes clearly visible against the black fur. She pointed to first one flake and then another, exclaiming over them.

Alex's surprise at seeing the beauty in a snowflake was no greater than realizing that this narrow slip of a young woman had made him capable of seeing it. An odd feeling that he couldn't identify came over him. He grabbed her and kissed her soundly, drawing the breath from her body, some unknown force driving him to possess her.

He put her from him and searched her face. Her features were softly flushed, as he looked for answers to unformed questions.

"If that's what a few snowflakes do to you," she said in a low voice, "I can't wait for a snowstorm."

He gave her a lazy smile. "I think we're in for one tonight."

They entered the chateau to find Simon stoking the fire. He nodded to them, told them their room was ready, and turned his back, going about his business.

As they walked up the wide staircase Ariane whispered, "Simon is so gothic. He reminds me of something right out of *Wuthering Heights*. I can't help thinking I'll hear Heathcliff's name being called any minute."

They entered a magnificent room that rendered Ariane speechless with its opulence and authentic detail. The deep rose and gold room was divided into two areas: sleeping and sitting. The sitting area consisted of two love seats and a lounge that flanked a marble fireplace. The sleeping area was dominated by a four-poster bed swagged in heavy folds of rose damask and covered with a satin quilt. Fine antique French furniture accented the room, muted Aubusson rugs covering the floor.

"It's beautiful," she said. "Your friend has an incredible eye for detail."

"Speaking of which, I'd like to talk to him. Why don't you get settled and I'll be back soon. There's brandy on the table over there. If there's something you want, I'll have Simon bring it up."

A half hour later Ariane stepped out of the shower, and it occurred to her that not only had she forgotten to pack a nightgown but a robe as well. Wrapping herself in the large plush bath sheet, she felt a shiver run along her spine as she realized there'd be no need for a nightgown. She couldn't help but remember that during her married life she had worn a nightgown every night.

Later, when she was taking a nap, she felt the bed move. Opening her eyes she saw Alex peering at her.

"Mmm . . . You're back." Her voice was husky with sleep as she snuggled under the thick comforter. She came fully alert when she realized Alex was wearing nothing but a towel wrapped about his trim waist.

"If we don't leave for dinner soon we may have to go hungry," he said as he picked up a lock of her hair and let it fall through his fingers.

"Now that you mention it, I am hungry." She sat up and the comforter fell, leaving her barely covered in the towel she had wrapped around herself.

Alex's gaze fell to her skimpily covered form and his silver eyes took on a bright glitter. "I'm hungry," he said. "For you."

chapter 16

Alex had gone downstairs to check on their dinner while Ariane dressed, and now he stood leaning against the doorjamb. He studied her through half-lowered lids, thinking the stark blackness of her sweater was a perfect foil against her flawless alabaster skin. The sweater was cut invitingly low, skimming across her chest.

He had brought her up here for one reason and one reason only—to get her out of his system. But she had a way of disarming him, and he had to force himself to remember.

He formally gestured toward the doorway and led her downstairs and into a small dining room. The room was paneled in dark chestnut and dimly lit by a fireplace. An antique crystal chandelier displayed burning candles. There were three tables in the room but only one was set with white linen, crystal, and silver that sparkled in the flickering light.

Alex helped her into her seat. Simon, changed into a

black suit, appeared as if on cue, bringing a silver bucket that held a bottle of champagne. He uncorked it, poured some into a crystal flute, placed it in front of Ariane, and left. He returned immediately and set a crystal glass containing a generous amount of bourbon in front of Alex and left again.

Lifting his glass in a silent toast to her, Alex took a deep swallow from his glass. She returned his salute and took a sip of the chilled champagne.

"There's no menu here," he explained, his voice sounding too polite, somehow removed. "Jake does all the cooking and waits for an inspiration to help him decide what to prepare. Don't worry, he's an excellent chef."

"I'm glad to hear that." She seemed relieved and took another sip of her champagne. "I suppose the ever friendly Simon is to be our waiter this evening?"

When he nodded, she asked, "What did you think of Justin's movie?"

"I didn't see it."

"Oh? As an investor I'm surprised you didn't want to see the finished product."

Alex gave her a long, lazy look. "I got what I came for."

Ariane blushed hotly. "Are we the only guests here?"

"Yes. Does that bother you?"

"N-no. It just seems strange for your friend to go to all this trouble just for us."

"Like I said, Jake and I are good friends." Alex finished off his drink. "Wouldn't you do anything for Sloane?" The silver eyes glittered coldly, seeming to pin her to the spot.

"Yes, I suppose so."

"What about Craig?" Alex asked, his bland expression matching his voice.

"What about him?" She toyed with her glass.

"Wouldn't you do anything for him?" *She had once,* Alex thought, the memory bringing a bitter taste to his mouth. *What else had she done for him?*

"We're separated," she said.

"What about before?"

"I suppose." She gave a noncommittal shrug of her bare shoulders.

They both fell silent as Simon brought Alex another drink and placed their appetizers of goose pâté in front of them.

"I just assumed a wife would do anything for her husband—lie, cheat, or steal if need be." Alex watched her closely, looking for a flicker of guilt in her eyes. Was there anyone who could be that loyal? He doubted it.

She glanced away, staring into the fire. When she turned her gaze back to him, a fervid gleam burned in her black eyes. "I like to think that a man and woman in love would do anything for each other."

Dinner progressed smoothly and as Simon brought course after course of delicious food, Alex kept refilling her champagne glass. He watched her succumb to the effects of the wine and took the opportunity to casually question her about Craig's business. It appeared she knew very little, hardly any more than what a stranger might from reading the newspaper. It was just as well because he was having a hard time keeping his mind on business.

She was so guileless, so beautiful, that he was hard-pressed to recall why he had originally wanted to get close to her. It didn't seem to matter now. For some strange reason he no longer cared.

The moment the door closed behind them Alex grabbed her and pulled her against him. "Christ, Ari, I think you've bewitched me." His voice was thick with emotion.

"Have I?" she purred, her voice a taunt. She tilted her

head back to gaze into Alex's eyes and felt momentarily off balance by the look of anguish. But it was gone so quickly she couldn't focus on it.

"You know damn well you have. If you had taken one minute more to finish your dessert, I swear, I would have taken you then and there on the table and the hell with Simon."

A wave of desire rippled through her at the vision evoked by Alex's provocative threat, and she felt her pulse quicken. She wanted to tell him that she was under *his* spell. But it didn't matter. Nothing mattered as he lowered his mouth to hers and she closed her eyes, surrendering herself to the heat of the passion he aroused in her.

The effects of the champagne were nothing compared with the intoxicating effect Alex had on her. She molded herself against the hard length of him, her arms entwining themselves around his neck, seeking the heat of his body.

She felt drunk, weak with desire. She ached for him, a terrible, wonderful ache that possessed her. Her desire was a beating in her brain and it was one word—Alex.

Quickly he shed his clothing and helped Ariane with hers before he lowered her onto the carpet in front of the fireplace. His movements were fierce and urgent as he plunged deeply into her, his driving thrusts commanding her body. The exquisite ache of desire in her grew, filling her, demanding release as she strove to meet his driving onslaught. She was breathless, mindless, her fingers digging into his shoulders as the wild fury in him drove her senseless. Her mind went blank as she felt herself spiraling upward, higher and higher until the ecstasy burst free in her and she was a star shooting across a blackened sky as wave after wave of rapture ripped through her.

Alex stood at the French door in a fierce turmoil, at war with himself, with no possible winner in sight. He had thought all he had to do was have her once, and once the mystery was over he'd be through with her just like a mystery novel when one learns the ending. All women were the same. The names changed, the faces changed, but in the end they were only good for one thing.

But Ariane. Against his will he grudgingly admitted that there was something different about her. For one thing, he couldn't seem to get enough of her. He couldn't remember how many times he'd taken her, but each time was better than the last. Even now, just thinking about the way they had made love after dinner, he could feel the desire coiling hotly inside him. He had never experienced this overpowering urge and it baffled him, leaving him annoyed and irritated at something he couldn't understand and control.

The way she gave herself to him and welcomed his touch was so different from the others who coldly took from him, every move calculated. There was a sensual innocence about her as she returned his passion, her movements seeming natural and unpracticed as if this were all new to her. But it wasn't; she'd been Craig's wife for years. The thought brought a sour taste to his mouth.

And looming over it all was the reality of his assignment. Once she found out about him, about his investigation of her husband, it would all be over.

The room had grown cold, the burning fire barely smoldering as Ariane turned in her sleep, seeking Alex's warmth. Scanning the dark room, she spied him standing at the French doors, staring out moodily at the garden. She watched as he ran a hand through his thick black hair and took a long swallow of brandy from his glass, his movements abrupt and angry.

He was in one of his black moods. She studied him, the moonlight illuminating his tall form, the hard muscles rippling across his broad back as he moved. He raised one arm to lean against the window frame, the well-developed muscles in his arm tensing. She took pleasure in the perfect symmetry of his body, so virile and vital.

She slipped from the bed, walked to where he stood, and molded her naked body against his back, wrapping her arms around his waist. He straightened his back as she rested her cheek there.

"Go back to bed," he said, his voice emotionless.

She flinched and dropped her arms. "Can't you sleep?"

"No. Please, just go back to bed," he said roughly.

Dejected, she turned to walk away just as he reached out his arm and grabbed her, turning her toward him.

"Look, I . . ." Alex began, as though unable to find the words.

She looked up at him, waiting. "Never mind," she said tiredly, wrenching her arm free. In the process she knocked his other arm, sending the brandy spilling down his chest. They stared at each other, frozen, as the amber liquid ran down his torso.

Suddenly, a bemused smile lit his eyes, softening his harsh look. "I guess that makes us even," he said.

"Alex, it was an accident. I . . . I didn't mean . . ." Ariane stuttered, as surprised by his reaction or rather lack of it, as by what had happened. She had expected his volatile temper to flare.

"I think you did that on purpose," he said. "And there's only one suitable punishment." A devilish light glittered in his silver eyes.

Before she knew what he was doing, he grabbed her, picked her up in his arms, and rubbed his damp body against her.

"No, stop! You're all wet," she cried, laughing as she tried to push away from him.

Laughter caught in her throat and she felt her pulse quicken at the look of heated lust in his silver eyes. Still holding her in his arms, he lifted her slightly higher and began licking the brandy from her breasts. The touch of his warm mouth sent her head spinning. She threw her head back and clasped his dark head to her.

He unceremoniously dropped her on the bed, walked away, then came back holding the brandy decanter. Thinking he meant to finish his drink, she was surprised to see him poise the angled bottle directly above her. Before she could utter a word he tipped the decanter and directed a slow stream at her belly. She shrieked and tried to scramble out of the path, only to feel him firmly grip her ankle and straddle her thighs.

She was pinned to the bed, trapped beneath his powerful thighs, with one hard muscular arm leaning against her shoulder.

"I thought you said we were even," she argued.

"I changed my mind." He held the decanter over her again.

"You can't. That's not fair!"

"Ah, Ari. Life's not fair." He let two drops of the amber-colored liquid spill between her breasts. The brandy slowly trickled across her chest. He licked at the fiery liquid, pausing to take a taut pink bud in his mouth. Lifting his head and looking at her, he said, "That wasn't so bad, was it?"

"No," she managed, her voice a whisper.

He continued his unique form of punishment, and she was no longer an unwilling prisoner but an eager participant. Her shrieks of protest were replaced by giggling and then low moans of pleasure.

Finally, satisfied and glowing from Alex's lovemaking, she pushed him on his back and, straddling his waist, reached for the brandy bottle.

"Now it's my turn." Her black eyes sparkled mischievously.

"Oh no, you don't," he protested, reaching for the bottle.

"Too late." She jerked the bottle out of his reach, splashing a little too much on his chest. "Whoops!" she giggled, watching the brandy run down his sides, realizing he was quite wet. "Oh well," she said as she splashed even more on his belly and groin.

"You little witch." He grabbed the now empty decanter from her and pulled her down on top of him, kissing her mouth fervently.

"I should make you dry me," he threatened against her mouth.

"Why don't you?" Her mouth had gone dry at the tempting prospect.

His silver eyes met hers, dark and hot. Then he muttered thickly, "Do it."

She took her time, leisurely exploring the hard, muscled length of him, her mouth and tongue tasting the brandy, the smoothness of his neck, the hard muscles of his chest, his flat belly and lean hips. Her mouth teased, licked, and nibbled at him, seeking his sensitive spots, taking satisfaction in his low groans of pleasure. She heard his sharp intake of breath, as she pleasured him, delighting in his heated response.

He pulled her toward him, and kissed her as he slipped between her thighs, burying himself in her tightness.

They moved together, seeking their own pleasure and taking satisfaction from the joy they gave. Their rhythm increased as they each felt that heavenly promise of ecstasy draw closer until their movements became mindless, and they froze in rapturous delight as they attained their goal.

The sun reflected glaringly off the fresh snow, causing Ariane and Alex to shield their eyes momentarily against the brilliance as they stepped outside. The sky was a perfectly clear dazzling blue, the air crisp and clean.

Alex walked beside Ariane, their steps crunching cleanly on the perfect whiteness. He walked fast, angry at her, angry with himself. Wanting her body in bed was one thing, but that was all he wanted from her. At least that was what he kept telling himself.

This morning when he had held her sleep-warm form in his arms, a strong feeling of something he couldn't identify had come over him. He knew he wanted to make love to her again—not in that hungry, insatiable way he had the night before, but slowly, tenderly. He had to force himself out of bed in order not to give in to the temptation.

And his mood had degenerated even further as he had sat across the table from her over breakfast. He was accustomed to hearing empty-headed chatter from his bedmates as they flattered his prowess and sought compliments on their own accomplishments. They seemed to demand constant reassurance as they clung possessively to him, jealous of his past and anything that drew his attention. Yet Ariane enjoyed her breakfast quietly, only occasionally remarking on the food or the inn, as if she sensed his temperament. Her easy quietness and consideration bothered him more than if she had babbled on like the others.

Alex led her through an open field that was surrounded by a pine forest. It was colder and getting late, the afternoon sun casting long, golden shadows across their path. The once brisk winter day had turned bitter, giving Alex cause to turn up the collar of his sheepskin coat.

Abruptly, Ariane reached out a black gloved hand and grabbed at his arm, stopping him. He looked down at her, her black eyes wide with wonder, and followed her gaze. There ahead of them was a young deer poking its nose in the snow, looking for something to eat.

Not finding anything particularly remarkable about a

deer in the woods, Alex opened his mouth to speak when she shushed him. The young deer raised its head and stared at them. Then the animal turned and bolted into the safety of the woods.

"Wasn't he beautiful?" Ariane asked, her voice filled with awe as she turned to him.

He looked down into her face, her open expression of exhilaration making her appear more like a young girl. Without thinking, he grabbed her and kissed her cold lips, finding the mouth inside warm and receptive.

She shivered in his arms. In a ragged voice, he said, "You're cold. Why don't we go back and finish what we started?"

She grinned impishly and ran ahead, racing him to the inn.

He caught up with her at the front door and pulled her body roughly to him. With a hint of menace in his deep voice, he said, "Don't ever think you can run away from me."

Afterward, Ariane wrapped her slender form against him, resting her head on his chest, one leg thrown casually across his thighs as his warm fingers stroked the length of her back. This calm, seemingly peaceful Alex was certainly different from the forceful man who had seemed almost violent only a short time ago.

There was an underlying truth to his warning that frightened her and thrilled her at the same time.

Ariane played absently with his hair as she snuggled closer to him. Maybe there was an undercurrent of danger in him, but she didn't care. All she knew was that no man ever made her feel the way he did—so desired, so wanted, so wonderful.

• • •

The afternoon traffic was light, enabling the stretch limousine to make good time traveling down the FDR Drive. It reached the tip of Manhattan and pulled into Battery Park City.

Less than ten years ago there had been nothing there. After years of litigation and hundreds of millions of dollars, an entire city now covered the vacant landfill.

"Have you got it?" Hassan asked.

From his position in the front seat Khazi turned and patted the front of his coat before leaving the car.

The dark tinted windows hid Hassan's identity as he watched Khazi's progress through the park. The cold wind whipped at Khazi's coat, slapping it around his legs as he walked to the water. He met his contact, a short man with a pale, thin face. The short man appeared nervous, his gaze darting around.

Hassan squinted through the haze of blue smoke in the car as Khazi handed the bulging white envelope to the customs agent. The agent quickly pocketed the money.

There was a rush of cold air as Khazi slid into the front seat.

"It's done," he said as he slammed the door.

"Let's go, Sayed." Hassan turned to stare out the window and caught a glimpse of the Statue of Liberty guarding the harbor, her torch a beacon across the river, inviting the immigrants to her shores.

His mouth twitched. He felt welcomed. Indeed, he did.

"We'd better get going. We're meeting Jake for dinner," Alex said as he stepped into the shower with Ariane.

"What are you doing in here?"

An amused smile lit his face as he replied smoothly, "Being that we're running late, I thought we could save time by showering together."

She returned his smile. "Hand me the soap."

"It'll be faster if I do it," he replied as he reached for the soap and began to lather her body.

But it wasn't faster. It was deliciously slow.

Ariane barely had time to make up her eyes and apply a dab of pink lipstick before Alex whisked her downstairs. Dressed in a black velvet halter dress that bared her arms and clung seductively to her curves, she hastily knotted her hair.

Alex led her to the back of the inn and entered a cheerful room decorated in yellow, blue, and white. The lace curtains on the windows and baskets of dried flowers and bowls of fruit gave the room a cozy country feeling.

Jake was already seated at the table and rose at their entrance.

Alex made the introductions, skipping last names. Ariane felt at ease with Jake immediately. His soft brown eyes crinkled as he smiled at her and welcomed her to his home. He appeared to be in his mid-fifties. He wasn't as tall as Alex but was thick-set with a muscular build.

The conversation, led by Jake, was pleasant and innocuous, but Ariane couldn't help noticing the way he looked at her. She supposed it had to do with their wet hair and the obvious conclusion to be made from it. But that wouldn't explain the pointed looks Alex gave Jake.

"So, how do you know each other?" she asked as she swallowed the last bite of her squab.

"Jake and I own some oil wells," Alex answered quickly.

She looked at Jake for verification but he was looking down at his plate.

Ariane decided not to ask any more personal questions for the rest of the meal.

"Why don't you go upstairs? I'll be along later," Alex said after dinner, taking a sip of espresso. "I'd like to talk to Jake."

"Sure." She was being put aside and it annoyed her. All through dinner she'd felt as though she were intruding. There was something mysterious about Alex and Jake that had nothing to do with business. Now she was being sent to her room so that the grownups could talk.

"That's quite a woman you've got there. If I had someone who looked like that to go upstairs with, I wouldn't be sitting here drinking cognac with an old friend," Jake said, purposely ignoring Alex's black mood. Jake had observed Alex during dinner and watched as his friend's pleasant mood had darkened. Jake didn't know what to make of it but knew Alex well enough not to question him.

"She's just a woman."

"The last time we talked you said she was in on Wakefield's scam. But she seems honest. I can't imagine her being involved."

"No woman's that honest."

"Really?" Jake regarded Alex carefully. He was too detached, too unconcerned, as if it were a deliberate effort. "Then what are you doing with her?"

Alex stared at him, his expression bland and unreadable. "Nothing."

He was lying, Jake thought, but he probably didn't even know it. The mere fact of Ariane's presence told Jake plenty. Alex had never brought a woman to the inn before. He would show up unannounced, from time to time, to be alone. Sometimes he sought Jake out, but mostly he came for the solitude. This place was special to Alex. And if he had brought a woman here, she was special too. "How's the investigation coming?"

"Great." The sarcasm was thick in Alex's voice. "Wakefield's so dirty we could haul him in right now and he'd be doing time until he was old and gray. Anatech alone is enough to put him away."

"Do you think Wakefield has any idea just how dangerous Hassan is?"

"I don't know," Alex answered slowly. "Wakefield's so damn greedy I'm not sure he'd be smart enough to stay away from Hassan even if he knew. The temptation's too great. Only this time he's in way over his head."

"I'll say. I hope for his sake he doesn't do anything to antagonize the Arab. The slightest disagreement and Hassan will settle it his way—permanently. Good thing we have Wakefield. He's the perfect patsy."

"Tell me something I don't know." Alex swirled the brandy in his snifter. "It looks like Wakefield's started laundering Hassan's money. He's been buying up worthless companies and selling stock. He also started a paper trail of transactions through Central America and Europe. We've got his bank in Switzerland under surveillance."

"Good. Let them get confident. They'll get sloppy and we'll have both of them." Jake paused and, changing the subject asked, "Why did you come back to work? I thought you were through with the agency."

"I was. But they showed me Hassan's file and they made sense. With my holdings and business credentials I was the perfect candidate. Besides, after they told me about his penchant for murdering young women, I wanted him." His jaw grew rigid. "I saw the pictures. That was all the convincing I needed."

"Has it occurred to you that Ariane fits the profile?"

There was a flicker in the silver eyes. "Yes."

Jake was suddenly apprehensive. This wasn't business for Alex. It was personal. There were too many factors influencing him, too many wild cards. Wakefield, Hassan, Ariane. From the beginning Alex had had a natural instinct for his work that had saved him from many a difficult and dangerous situation. He had never become emotionally involved but had handled his assignments coldly and professionally. In their business, any kind of involvement was deadly.

"Are you all right on this one?" Jake asked.

"Of course. Why wouldn't I be?"

"Look, I've known you since you came to the agency twenty years ago and I've never seen you so determined."

"Determination's what kept me alive."

Jake couldn't argue with him on that. Alex had come to the agency hot-headed and full of hate. The agency had channeled his anger for their own nefarious purposes, playing on Alex's barely suppressed rage and turning him into a cold, hard, unforgiving man.

After he quickly mastered the intelligence training, he had moved on to weapons instruction. It was unfortunate, Jake realized now, that Alex was good at it—too good. He was taught how to use every available weapon known to man and how to turn ordinary objects into lethal weapons. He learned to kill swiftly and silently with his bare hands or merely render a victim helpless with one easy stroke. His trainer channeled the cold-bloodedness in Alex, turning him into his star pupil.

"After this assignment, I think you ought to stay away from the agency," Jake said quietly.

"Why?"

"It's not good for you. It never was. If you go on like this, you're going to die a bitter old man, all alone."

"What about you? You're alone," Alex argued.

"Yes, but I've had my love. I don't need anything else or want anything else. But you, Alex, you have nothing, don't you see that? You're consumed with hate and bitterness and it's eating you alive. You've lived in the dark for so long you can't see anything else."

Alex stared into his brandy and then raised his gaze to Jake, a look of torment on his harsh features. "Don't you think I know that?'' His voice carried a frightening sound of despair, of hopelessness, of fear.

"You've got to let it go, let go of the hate. Trust someone, let yourself feel."

"I can't."

Jake heard the fearful anguish in Alex's voice and was suddenly afraid for him, afraid that maybe he was right.

Alex sat in the dining room long after Jake had gone to bed. Restless, he rose to stare out the window. But his gaze was unseeing. He remembered the first time he had had to kill. It had been in self-defense and the agency easily accepted his explanation.

That was how it began, subtly, so he never noticed until it was too late. He began traveling more, the assignments becoming more dangerous with a higher element of risk involved. He was forced to protect himself more frequently, and more often than not, extreme violence was the only answer. Eventually, the assignments began to resemble execution orders more than intelligence work.

He went about his work efficiently, never noticing the gradual change taking place in him. If it had not been for one particular assignment he might still be with the agency carrying out their dirty work.

He had been trailing a foreign agent, hoping to relieve him of a roll of microfilm. Having searched his room, he concluded the agent obviously had it on his person. There seemed to be no way to avoid a personal confrontation. He was going through the agent's personal effects while he slept. Suddenly, the agent woke up, much to both of their surprise. Alex had drugged the man's brandy, intending to render him unconscious so that he could go about his work uninterrupted. Unfortunately for both of them, the agent had only drunk half the brandy.

The agent was older than Alex, having been in the busi-

ness many years. At the time, he was only doing occasional courier work. Alex froze, tensed and poised, ready
to strike should he make a move. The agent quickly told
him where to find the microfilm.

Having achieved his goal, Alex looked down into the
older man's face, wondering what he should do. He had
never been identified; if the agent were allowed to live, he
could expose Alex and jeopardize his career and his life.

Alex looked at the old man and was startled by the look
of fear in his knowing, aged eyes. Alex had come face to
face with his victims before, but this was the first time his
victim had had the time or the inclination to plead for his
life.

For the first time he saw himself as the old man must
have seen him—a merciless killer. The realization shook
him more than he thought possible.

He stared down at the old man, the cold gray eyes sending a clearly understood message of warning before he
turned and left, anxious to escape what he had seen in that
room.

Alex had fled to the mountains after that, living off the
land, not seeing another human being for six months.
When he had returned and tendered his resignation, he
offered no explanation.

Alex walked back to the table to refill his glass and, spill-
ing the brandy, realized he was drunk. It didn't matter.
He didn't want any more brandy. What he wanted was
Ariane, wanted to hold her, needed to feel her warmth.

chapter 17

She was asleep when he entered their room, the dying fire in the fireplace casting a dim golden glow in the darkness. He shed his clothes quickly, letting them drop in his path, anxious to hold the familiar form.

He needed to forget that small room in Europe. Needed to forget the look of fear, of recognition, in the old man's eyes.

He slid naked between the sheets and gathered her to him. Surprise turned to annoyance when he didn't feel her bare body and, flinging back the covers, he saw she was wearing his shirt.

She opened her eyes as he leaned over her, his hand grasping the front of the shirt. Her voice was a husky whisper. "I was cold."

"I'll keep you warm," Alex promised, his voice thick with desire and cognac.

Her fingers moved too slowly for his satisfaction. Fumbling with impatience, Alex ripped the shirt off, and with a muttered curse, tossed it out of reach. He wanted to make love to her until she cried out his name in surrender. He longed for the feel of her, her warmth against him, as though it had been years and not hours since he last held her.

Drawing her into his arms, he ran his hands along the satiny smoothness of her skin. He needed her to make him forget what he had been, what he had done. "Ari, so sweet," he mumbled, his hands touching her everywhere as he buried his face in her neck, inhaling her haunting scent. She would make him forget. She would drive away the ghosts. His fingers sought the fine silkiness of her hair, delighting in its glossy texture.

He pressed her against the long length of him, their bodies a contrast of hardness and softness, chest to chest, thigh against thigh.

Hazily, he thought that he never knew anyone could feel so perfect in his arms. Unaware that he did he murmured thickly, "Christ, Ari, you're incredible." His mouth was hot and passionate, drawing the very breath from her. She was supple and yielding in his arms, returning his passion, and he felt the flames of desire burning within him like a wildfire out of control.

He moved down her neck, tasting the sweet flesh, feeling her pulse beating wildly beneath his lips. Her breast felt heavy with desire as his hand held it, fondling it before his mouth captured the pink tip. He dimly heard her small moan of pleasure, but the lust thundering through his body drowned out everything.

Ariane writhed seductively beneath his fingers as he found her sensitive flesh and caressed her. His mouth followed the path of his fingers, tasting and licking, reveling in her passionate response. His desire raged as her delicate hands wandered over him, down his side, over his thigh, her touch igniting fires in him he couldn't control. Then her mouth began to move over his jaw, down his neck, planting light feathery kisses that felt like little flames of heat.

She moved over his chest, taking a nipple in her mouth, the action sending a jolt through him. He buried his fingers in her hair as she moved lower, her mouth teasing, flirting, full of promise. He would be lost if he let her continue. He would die if she stopped. He didn't hear the low groan he made deep in his throat, as his passion turned white-hot.

He grabbed her arms and brought her to him. Her long hair fell around them like a curtain blocking out the world. He had to have her, wanted to possess her so completely that she would never want another. He murmured against her mouth, "I want you now."

Flipping her over, he brought them together, causing her to gasp against his mouth. He held her to him tightly, not moving, filling her completely with his passion. He opened his eyes to look at her and the sight of her passionate mouth, slightly bruised from his kissing, her glossy black hair fanned out wildly against the white sheet, reminded him of a wild pagan goddess. With a soft growl of pleasure he claimed that mouth with an intensity that startled both of them as he began to move his hips slowly and seductively. He teased them both, promising, fulfilling, empathizing with her moans of discontent when he held back. His lust throbbed painfully as she moved lasciviously, urging him on, demanding, threatening his self-control.

Her wanton abandonment, with legs wrapped around his hips, matched his passion and sent his restraint reeling out of control. He wanted to possess her and leave his mark on her, and he thrust into her deeply with a savagery that was unlike him.

As the first wave of her pleasure rippled through her,

he lost himself and let go as violent spasms of ecstasy convulsed him.

Later, when the blood stopped pounding in his head and his breathing returned to normal, he shifted his weight to look down at her face. Her porcelain skin glowed damp with perspiration and he reached out to gently smooth back a strand of hair from her face. Her eyes fluttered open, unnerving him with the revealing look shining in those depths. She reached up and ran a finger along his jaw.

He studied her face, wondering at his fascination. She looked so innocent and something pulled at him. He turned away, pulling her with him as he rolled onto his back.

She entwined herself around him, nestling, cuddling trustingly. He stared at the ceiling. What more did the agency want from him? It had cost him everything. Was there no end to what he had to pay? He glanced down at Ariane and closed his eyes against the truth. There would be one more price to pay.

In the middle of the night Ariane woke, a feeling of dread and anxiety filling her. She was confused, disoriented. She looked around, frantic. When she saw Alex and heard his deep breathing, some of the panic left her. She lay on her back, taking deep breaths, trying to calm her racing heart.

It had been the dream again and worse than ever before. Each episode grew more intensely frightful than the last. This time the quicksand had been up to her thighs, pulling at her, sucking her down until she knew it meant to kill her.

Her agitation churned. She broke out into a cold sweat, the fear rippling along her spine, choking off her air. Her hands gripped the covers tensely as she tried to catch her breath.

"Ari, what is it?"

The sound of Alex's voice made her jump. "Nothing."

Alex reached out and gently pulled her into his arms. With his hand on her head, he smoothed the errant strands of hair back from her face.

Ariane let herself be pulled into his arms, the heat from his body a welcoming warmth against her chilled flesh. Inexplicably, her eyes filled with tears and she struggled to keep from crying. His hands stroked her back as he held her, asking no questions. The relaxing, hypnotic rhythm calmed her and she sagged against him, her tension and fear draining away. Her eyelids grew heavy and she was aware of him pressing his lips to her forehead. It was odd, she thought, but now the dream didn't seem so real as she lay in the safe comforting embrace of Alex's arms.

Ariane finished dressing and was standing at the French doors, staring at the white covered landscape. She was nervous and apprehensive, residue from her nightmare and Alex's absence. He had left her after breakfast with the excuse of having things to take care of as they would be leaving soon. He always seemed to be angry and fighting something, and she couldn't tell if it was himself or her. Suddenly, she could no longer stand being in the room with all its pleasant memories.

She walked down the wide maroon-carpeted hallway, complete with suits of armor and antique tapestries hanging on the paneled walls. She didn't notice the magnificent Louis XV ormolu in the entrance gallery as she opened the carved door.

The air had a decided snap to it, causing her to turn up her collar and huddle into the warmth of her coat. The blue sky was streaked with clusters of thick white clouds that blocked the morning sun.

All she could think about was Alex; all she wanted to think about was Alex. He filled her mind completely. He had come into her life with the force of a tornado, grabbing her, turning her world upside down.

There were times when she could feel him pull back from her and retreat behind the barrier he erected between them. But there were times when nothing came between them. When they laughed, when they made love—those were the times.

She had walked down to the lake and, noticing how far she had come, decided to go back. Turning, she saw Jake waving and walking toward her.

"Out for some fresh mountain air, I see," Jake said. "Mind if I join you?"

"No, of course not."

They walked quietly for a while and then Jake asked, "How long have you known Alex?"

"I met him in April." Such a short time, she realized. How had he become so important to her so quickly?

"And been together ever since?" Jake asked.

"No, I was married then."

"Excuse me," he said. "I didn't mean to pry. I hope you enjoyed your visit."

"Yes, I did very much." For such a strong, muscular man there was a kindness, a softness about Jake that endeared him to her.

"I've known Alex for a number of years," he said. "And I can tell you that he's a very complex man. But I guess you know that already."

Ariane gave him a knowing grin as she answered, "That's putting it mildly."

"That bad, huh? It's probably hard to believe at times but he is a special man and worth getting to know. He doesn't have many friends, but the few he has would go to hell and back for him as he would for us. Once you have his loyalty there's no one more loyal than Alex. The trick is finding the key to unlock him."

"He's such a private person." They passed a hedge and Ariane ran her hand along the top of an evergreen, knocking the snow off.

"He's been alone his whole life and by choice, I might add. He was hurt badly and more than once. Unfortunately, he's never learned to let it go. He thinks he doesn't need anyone and can go it alone, but that's only because he's never found anyone worth needing. Until now, that is."

Ariane looked sharply at Jake and felt a sudden nervousness in the pit of her stomach. "Me?"

Jake didn't answer but continued, "I had always hoped that the right woman would come along who could soften Alex's heart and make him let go of his anger. It's only a shield he uses to protect himself from any more hurt."

"What makes you think this is different from . . . just different?" Ariane asked, unable to think of the other women.

"I can see that you care for Alex and I know Alex feels something for you, at least as much as he's capable of feeling right now. I don't even think he realizes it himself. He's had that wall around him for so long and nobody's ever cracked it or even come close, until now . . . until you."

"I wish you were right." Ariane sighed, a note of sadness in her voice.

"He does care for you, believe me, even more than you can imagine." The certainty in his voice lifted her spirits slightly. "But I'm afraid he's going to make this very hard and fight you every step of the way. Just hang in there. It'll be worth it, for both of you. I think that the two of you could be good for each other, if the stubborn hardheaded fool ever lowers his guard long enough to realize it. You know, the love of a good woman and all that."

Seeing the softness on Jake's rugged features, she said, "You care for him very much, don't you?"

"Yes, I do." His soft brown eyes peered intently at her. "Almost as much as you do."

On the ride back to the city, Ariane's mind raced as she wondered what would happen when Alex dropped her off. She turned on the radio to distract her thoughts, determined to act the part of the cool sophisticate and not make any demands or ask any questions.

A chill swept over her when the news announcer reported another murder of a wealthy young woman. This woman, like the other victims of the Rapunzel Strangler, had been choked to death, her own long hair wrapped around her throat.

Ariane glanced at Alex, who seemed to be listening very closely. His jaw grew rigid, a muscle clenching, as he quickly changed the station.

The Aston Martin made its way down the FDR Drive, and her nerves jumped as the dreaded destination drew closer. Alex exited on Seventy-first Street, but instead of going to Fifth Avenue, he turned to Park. She thought he had forgotten where she lived and was going to correct him when, to her elated surprise, they pulled into the driveway of his town house.

He took their bags from the car and led her inside. She followed him up the stairs.

Once they reached his bedroom he set the bags on the floor and turned around to catch her yawning.

"Tired?" he asked.

"Mmm . . . a little."

"Then why don't we take a nap?" he suggested, his sensual tone belying the innocent words.

Her heart began to race at the look in his eyes. She should be used to it by now, she reasoned. Yet every time he looked at her with that burning light, she felt her insides melt and her will dissolve. It was as if he owned her.

"I didn't know you were tired," she said, disappointed at her response. She wanted to sound worldly and clever, yet she always felt so unsophisticated in his presence.

"I didn't say I was," Alex replied, his arms encircling her. He looked into her upturned face, and added, "But maybe afterwards I will be."

He gathered her to him as his mouth claimed hers in a kiss that set the fires of her passion burning brightly. Her head began to swim in that wonderful way as a delicious languor filled her body and she wrapped her arms around his neck. The moment he touched her she felt the quickening deep inside her, that wonderful tightening that was only the beginning.

She never knew a man's mouth could be so erotic, so perfect. She returned his kiss, lingering over his lips, tasting their smoothness, feeling the hint of his beard.

His kiss deepened, intoxicating her, and she made a small moan of pleasure deep in her throat. The breathless yearning that only Alex could fire in her turned into a pleasurably inviting ache that only he could gratify.

He stopped long enough to pull her cashmere sweater off, the cool air chilling her before he clasped her to him, reclaiming her mouth. She molded herself to him, longing for the feel of him.

The desire pulsed within her, commanding her, ruling her. She tugged at his sweater, raising it so she could feel his body against hers, rubbing herself on his nakedness, delighting in the feel of his hard muscled chest, aching for more.

The pleasant warmth turned to a familiar heat that radiated from her very core. She was warm, hot, the cool air not cool enough on her fevered body.

He raised his head and she stared at him with passion-heavy lids. She was taken aback by the look of lust darkening his features. There was something almost frightening in his intensity, but she forgot it all in the fierce possession of his mouth.

He led her to the bed, quickly did away with their clothes, and pulled her on top of him as he fell on the spread. He clasped her to him tightly, rolling them around the bed, his mouth never leaving hers.

She reveled in the feel of his body against hers and moved against him sensuously, luxuriating in the beauty of textures that was Alex. He was rough and smooth, hard and soft, as they explored each other greedily on the silk spread.

His lips trailed burning, searching kisses down her neck and over her breast, making her mind reel drunkenly. Her breath came faster as his warm mouth closed over one tight peak, and she dug her fingers into the black straight hair, holding him to her as waves of pleasure washed over her.

The small knot of pleasure that had started with his first kiss began to fill her as the pleasant ache spread to take hold of her. There was nothing now except Alex—his hands, his mouth were everywhere. Gently, he caressed her until she thought she would go mad with wanting him. When she thought she couldn't stand the pleasurable pain any longer, his lips began their magic and she knew she would go crazy.

Wild with desire, her hands moved over his broad chest, feeling the muscles ripple beneath her touch. She followed the curve of his ribs to the hard flat belly, the narrow waist, and lower to the thick thatch of curls. She heard his groan and took pleasure from it as her fingers brushed him.

Her touch teased and seduced but it wasn't enough. She

wanted, needed him. Drunk with desire, her lips trailed over his body, pleasuring him, pleasuring herself.

His hands pulled her to him and she let him, her heart pounding wildly, uncontrollably. She was sure he could hear it beating. He entered her slowly, moving exquisitely, perfectly, knowing what she wanted, what she needed. She clutched him to her, delighting in the heaviness of his body, rejoicing in their sexuality, relishing the joining of their bodies.

She was flying. He was taking her to that place she had never known before him. The ache inside of her tightened, coiling hotly, controlling her. No, not yet. Yes, now, now. He took her to the sky and beyond, climbing higher and higher. There was nothing. Nothing except Alex. Alex. Alex.

"Make sure our man in Switzerland is discreet and doesn't tip our hand," Alex said. "If Wakefield even suspects something and mentions it to the Arab, we'll lose him."

"I told him once but I'll remind him." Travis had obviously surprised Alex with his unannounced visit. And from Alex's brief attire of jeans and the condition of his hair, it was apparent he wasn't alone.

"Oh, hi, Travis," Ariane said, entering the living room clad only in a white shirt of Alex's. She seemed as surprised by his presence as he was by hers.

"Hello." He tried to hide his shock at her appearance as well as by her choice of clothes. Glancing at Alex, he was met with an utterly bland expression that told him not to make a big deal of it. But it was. And Travis knew it.

He watched Ariane settle herself on the sofa beside Alex. She sat close to him, tucking her legs beneath her, her body pressed against his bare arm, her thigh against his jean-clad thigh.

There was a radiant glow about her. Her dark eyes were

luminous, sultry, the long black hair hanging down her back in glossy waves. He couldn't help but notice how Alex's shirt rode up, revealing a smooth, white thigh as she sat next to him. There was something terribly sexy about her wearing Alex's shirt, and Travis wondered, not for the first time, what would have happened had he met her first.

The three of them chatted comfortably, Ariane mentioning that it had snowed where they had spent the weekend.

"Oh? Where were you?" Travis asked.

"At Jake's," Alex said curtly as he shot Travis a look that told him to leave it alone.

At Jake's? Now there was an interesting turn of events, Travis thought. What was even odder, perhaps more telling, was the way Alex allowed Ariane to sit so close to him. There was an unspoken intimacy in the way their bodies pressed together that made Travis feel as if he were intruding. He had never known Alex to permit any woman such liberties "after."

If he didn't know better, Travis thought, he'd think Alex enjoyed having Ariane nestle against him.

"Why don't you run upstairs and get dressed and we'll go out for dinner?" Alex asked Ariane. Turning his attention back to Travis, he asked, "Care to join us?"

"Sure," Travis agreed, his eyes following Ariane as she left the room.

Ariane was in Alex's bedroom taking off his shirt when she realized she didn't know where they were going and didn't know how to dress. Rebuttoning Alex's shirt, she walked with bare feet down the steps. At the foot of the stairs she froze, hearing Travis mention her name. Warning bells went off in her head. She shouldn't eavesdrop, but she couldn't help herself. Maybe Alex would tell Travis what he thought of her.

"You know she's in love with you. You can see it in her eyes," Travis said.

"It doesn't matter." Alex's voice sounded indifferent, detached. "The day we arrest Wakefield it'll be all over. I can't wait to see that guy behind bars."

Her knees buckled and she sagged against the wall.

"It's too bad she's going to be hurt. She's the only innocent one in this," Travis said.

"Yeah, well, when it's something as big as this we all have to make sacrifices." Alex's voice was cold and dispassionate.

Afraid she would cry out, her hand flew to her mouth. She felt sick, battered.

"Have you thought about what this is going to do to her?"

There was silence, long and heavy. Ariane waited, holding her breath. Then Alex said, his voice oddly husky, "There's no point in thinking."

She let her breath out and stood there dazed, too stunned by Alex's words to move. But she had to move. She had to get out of there, away from Alex.

She didn't know how, but she managed to find her way back upstairs. She was so numbed by Alex's words that she couldn't begin to assimilate their meaning as she stood dumbly in his bedroom. Suddenly, she realized she had to leave before he came up after her. Her shaking fingers tried to unbutton his shirt and, failing miserably, she angrily ripped it from her, showering buttons all over the floor.

"So, where do you want to go for dinner?" Alex asked as he entered the bedroom.

Ariane whirled around to face him, but she said nothing.

"Ari, what is it?" Something was wrong. Her face was deathly white, her black eyes enormous.

She turned back to her bag, zipping it closed with a finality. A tremor went through her body and she leaned heavily on her tote.

"Answer me," he ordered, his voice harsher than he intended.

When she didn't reply he went to her and, grabbing her upper arm, turned her around.

She yanked her arm free and stood glaring at him, her eyes black and hot. "What *is* it?" There was a catch in her voice. She studied his face as if searching for something and then said, her voice bitter with disappointment, "Nothing." The slanted eyes were glazed with pain.

"You're leaving?" His voice turned cold.

"Yes. I'm leaving. Only not soon enough . . ." Her voice was taut with rage and then she exploded, "You lying, rotten bastard! When were you going to tell me? Before you sent my husband to jail or after?" She was shaking.

Jesus, she heard us. How much had she heard? His voice turned clipped, professional. "You don't understand."

"What don't I understand? How you used me to get to my husband? How you only slept with me because I was Craig's wife? Everything's been a lie. *You're* a lie." A rush of tears filled her eyes, but she quickly suppressed them. She was controlled, utterly and tightly controlled. It would have been easier if she had broken down and cried. He could have dealt with that. But this, her seething hatred, her accusing eyes. The truth.

He wanted to tell her everything, to make her understand somehow. But he couldn't. First and foremost there was the matter of her safety. "Exactly what did you hear?"

"Enough to know I can never trust you again." Her

voice quivered. He could tell she was holding on by a thread.

He ignored her pain, her loyalty to Craig. He didn't have time for it now. "Don't repeat anything you heard to anyone, is that clear?"

"Or what? You'll send me to jail too?"

"No, you little fool . . ." he said between clenched teeth, then drawing a long breath to calm himself, finished, "just trust me on this."

"Trust? You don't know the meaning of the word."

"I don't care what you think of me. Swear to me you won't mention this to anyone." He grabbed her arm forcefully. "For your sake."

"Don't touch me! Don't ever touch me again!" She yanked her arm free and ran from the room, from him. He'd never seen such hurt, such pain.

He couldn't let her go like this. She was too upset to be alone. He was afraid for her.

He ran down the stairs and stopped at the front door. What could he do? What could he say? She would never believe him now. Why should she?

chapter 18

Standing outside, Ariane breathed greedily of the cold night air. She had been suffocating in Alex's bedroom, smothered by his treachery. She turned and walked quickly down Seventy-first Street, wanting to put as much distance between them as possible. It was bitter cold, but she took no notice as the first shock began to wear off and a deep-seated pain took its place.

Belatedly, she realized she much preferred the feeling of dazed shock, preferring its numbness to the wretched anguish that was tearing at her insides. Alex had used her. He had never cared anything about her. He had coldly taken her to bed to get close to Craig, to spy on him. She was nothing more than a means to an end.

The blast of a taxi's horn made her jump as the car swerved in front of her, barely missing her. As if coming out of a fog, she looked around and realized she had long since passed her apartment building and was standing in front of the Pierre Hotel. Turning around, she began to walk up Fifth Avenue, heedless of the light snow that had begun to fall.

Ten minutes later she let herself into the apartment and sagged against the closed door, not having the strength to go on. The pain twisted in her, a raw bleeding wound that forced hot scalding tears to run down her face. She heard his voice, so cold and deadly, saying it didn't matter. She felt as though she were bleeding, dying, but she couldn't find the wound. She began sobbing and slumped to the floor, crying out her broken heart. She cried until she thought she couldn't cry anymore.

Later she began to shiver with cold and dimly realized her coat and clothes were wet, the melting snow forming a puddle around her. She rose unsteadily, took off her coat, and tossed it onto a nearby chair. The coat slid to the floor but she didn't notice or care. She left the lights off, preferring the darkness. She didn't want to see anything; she just wanted to curl up and die.

Great wracking sobs tore at her as she collapsed on a sofa, devastated. She hated him! How could he have done this to her? How could he have lied so well? Used her so coldly? He must be inhuman to do this to her. And what a fool she was to believe him.

Somewhere in the distance she heard bells. It was the telephone. Alex! She froze, unable to move, poised like a frightened deer caught in the headlights of an oncoming car. Each ring was a knife going through her, a knife painfully twisted by Alex.

She let it ring. *I'm not going to answer. I never want to speak to him again.* But it kept ringing and ringing. It wouldn't stop.

She ran to it and picked up the receiver. "Hello." There was no answer but she could tell the line was open.

"Leave me alone!" she screamed and slammed it down.

Hassan replaced the receiver. Covering his body with

the now damp satin sheet, he leaned back with a sigh of satisfaction. It was enough. For now.

Alex sat in a club chair in his bedroom. He had asked Travis to leave and now he sat in the dark, brooding. The rumpled bed was a sore reminder and he rose to straighten his room, to put everything back to normal. He picked his shirt up and noticed the buttons had been ripped off as though she had been in a great hurry. Catching her haunting sensual scent on the shirt, he bunched it up and threw it on the floor. It would fade soon enough, just like the memory of her.

Ariane had been working at her desk for an hour when Gordon arrived. He greeted her warmly, coming over to her after he'd hung up his coat.

"And how was your vacation, love? Enjoy yourself?" he asked, holding her at arm's length.

"Yes, it was very nice." Her voice was empty and hollow, her skin unusually pale, making the dark shadows under her eyes more noticeable.

"So where have you been this last week? When you left here you said you didn't have any definite plans."

"Visited with friends."

"Sounds like fun."

"Mmm." Why didn't he stop talking? She didn't want to remember her last week, the last weekend. She didn't want to remember anything about Alex.

"Well, Molly and I had a fabulous vacation. We went to visit her family in Wisconsin. All the relatives meet there for an annual get-together and . . ."

Ariane heard Gordon's voice drone on but she found it difficult to pay attention. She nodded her head occasionally as if she were listening, but the truth was she couldn't have cared less. She didn't want to hear about Gordon's great time or anything else, for that matter. She just wanted to be left alone, alone with her misery and pain. She had learned her lesson the hard way. Never would she trust or believe a man again. Never.

Gordon grew alarmed as the weeks wore on and Ariane seemed to fade away. She grew thinner, an air of despondency about her, her once bright eyes dull and vacant, her usually mobile mouth stiff and grim. She reminded Gordon of a delicate porcelain doll, so fragile that the slightest breeze would send it crashing, splintering into a million pieces.

No matter how early Gordon arrived, she was always at work ahead of him. At the end of the day she would lag behind, claiming some unfinished work, but he knew better.

One day while Ariane was out for lunch, Gordon approached Logan in his office. "Have you got a few minutes? There's something I'd like to talk to you about."

"Sure, come in. I was just going over the projection for summer. What's up?" Logan moved his papers aside.

"It's Ariane. There's something wrong with her. She seems so depressed. I was wondering if maybe she mentioned anything to you."

"No. I noticed a change in her, but I thought maybe the two of you were having one of your disagreements."

"Unfortunately no. It's more serious than that. It's as if the life's gone out of her. I just feel like I should help her, but I don't know how and she won't let me. Maybe you ought to try talking to her. Sort of father to daughter."

"You know, Gordon, you're no kid anymore. You qualify for that 'father-daughter' talk yourself."

"Maybe. But I think the white hair is more convincing. And it wouldn't hurt to find out exactly what frame of mind she's in before you spring your little surprise on her. Don't you agree?"

"Yes. Most definitely. She'll probably tell me to butt out, but I'll give it a try."

The daylight hours were bad enough, but it was the long quiet nights that took their toll. All day Ariane held a tight rein on her emotions but at night, alone in the darkened bedroom, her brittle facade shattered. Her heart ached and she vowed to hate Alex forever. But then the ache would become unbearable, turning to despair when she remembered their time together, the odd eager light in his eyes, his whispered words. The words of a traitor, a liar, a man to be avoided at all costs.

She couldn't stand it any longer. Remembering tore her apart, and she began taking Valium every night in hopes of finding peaceful oblivion.

She was never tired but never quite awake either, passing each day in a haze of pain. She preferred the fuzziness, the blurred edges around her world. She didn't have to think, to feel, to remember. Anything was better than remembering.

Why did Logan want to talk to her? Ariane was a nervous wreck all day. She needed another Valium, so she popped her second one of the day.

They were seated at Logan's usual table at Lutece when Ariane thought, panic-stricken, *Oh God, he's going to fire me.*

"Ariane, this may be none of my business," he said. "But believe me I have nothing but your best interest at heart. I know something's troubling you." At her sign of protest he interrupted, "Please, you don't have to explain. I only want to offer my services as a friend. If you want to talk about it, fine. If you want to tell me to mind my own business, I'll understand."

Touched by his offer, her eyes filled with tears. Everything made her cry these days. She stared at her wine glass, unable to meet his gaze.

Logan reached out his hand, patted hers, and held it saying, "Why don't we forget it for now and enjoy our dinner? Just remember, I'm here, if you need me."

Ariane squeezed his hand. "Thank you, Logan. I'll remember that."

They ordered dinner and were having a friendly disagreement over whether women dress for other women or for men when Logan said, "There's something I've wanted to do for quite a while now, only I've been waiting for the proper time and this is it. I think it's time I went into women's evening wear. What do you think?"

"It sounds fabulous. People are spending again and there seems to be a return to elegance that was missing. I know when I was married . . ." she paused, "when I was married, we got enough invitations to benefits and balls and testimonials that we could have gone out every night of the week during the charity season."

"My sentiments exactly. I'd like to do something elegant, feminine, and expensive. The best fabrics and workmanship. The problem is, I'd like to show it by the end of May, and that doesn't give us much time. Do you think you could be ready by then?"

"What?" Ariane asked, not understanding his question. What did she have to do with his new line?

"Do you think you could be ready by then?" he repeated, his blue eyes twinkling mischievously. "I couldn't very well show my new line if my designer wasn't ready, now could I?" He sat back and watched as her look of confusion changed from disbelief to amazement.

"You want me to design your new line?" Ariane asked, afraid she had misunderstood.

"That's right."

"With Gordon."

"No."

"Just me?"

"That's right."

She leaned back, speechless. Her own line. What she had always dreamed of.

"Logan, I'm flattered more than I can say that you thought of me, but I don't know if I'm ready for such an undertaking."

"Flattered? You think I offered you my new line to flatter you? Believe me, I do what's best for my business, and I'm sure you're right for the job. Now do you think you could be ready by the deadline I mentioned?"

As Ariane sat at her desk, staring into space, a kaleidoscope of dazzling colors and sumptuous fabrics swirled through her mind as she imagined elaborate ballgowns, simple sheaths of sensually clinging fabrics and combinations of colors and styles that left her dizzy. Logan's offer was too good to be true.

But suppose she took his offer and couldn't produce the line on time? Or suppose she completed the line on time and the press panned it and none of the stores bought it? The scenarios she painted got blacker and blacker as she let her mind imagine the worst.

"Well?" a patient voice asked. Ariane looked up to see Logan standing beside her desk. She hadn't even noticed that he had walked into her office.

"Could I have a little more time?" she asked. "Just until after the weekend?"

"On one condition."

"What's that?"

"That you accompany me to a party this evening." When she began to protest, he continued, his voice gentle, "Ariane, you have to get out. There's a life outside this office. Please, trust me."

• • •

Ariane chose her Givenchy, the black lace dress shot with occasional rhinestones. It was a trim little dress with long narrow sleeves, the bodice and skirt lined with fuchsia silk. A black satin sash accented the fitted waist. She pulled her hair into a chignon at the nape of her neck and slipped on diamond and platinum earrings.

Logan's Rolls-Royce drove through the entrance of the gray stone wall of the River House and dropped them off in front. Upstairs, they were greeted by a uniformed maid who took Ariane's sable before they entered the spacious living room. The room was crowded with guests, their conversations and music filling the air. Logan smiled and greeted several people he knew as he steered her through the gathering, looking for their host.

"Oh Jonathan, there you are," Logan called as they approached his friend.

Logan made the introductions and Ariane was greeted warmly by Jonathan Sawyer, his weather-beaten face breaking into a crooked grin.

A butler brought their drinks, handing Ariane her white wine. She sipped her drink while she half-listened to Logan and Jonathan's conversation. Jonathan didn't work but dabbled in a variety of investments, doing quite well with his family's money. He had a wide range of interests, from breeding horses to collecting great works of art, but his real love was sailing.

Her attention drifted when they started discussing boat engines, her eyes scanning the crowded room. Suddenly she froze, unable to move or think, her breath caught in her throat. *Oh God! Alex!* The piercing silver eyes held her trapped with their gaze, their hostile look holding her like a helpless butterfly pinned to a board. With a great effort she tore her eyes from him but not before she noticed the voluptuous redhead leaning against him, boldly ogling him.

Just seeing him again brought all the pain flooding back.

What she needed was a drink. She began to raise her wine glass to her mouth and lowered it just as quickly when she saw her hand shaking.

"Ariane, are you all right?"

The sound of Logan's voice made her flinch. "Yes . . . No. I mean, I have this terrible headache and I think I'd better go home." In truth her head had begun to pound.

"Oh, my dear. I'm so sorry. Perhaps you'd like to lie down in one of the bedrooms for a while?" Jonathan suggested.

"No!" Ariane returned adamantly. She had to control herself. "No, thank you. That's very kind of you, but I think it's best if I just go home."

"Why don't you get your coat and I'll see you home," Logan offered.

"No, please don't leave on my account. I can take a taxi." Against her will her eyes were drawn back to Alex, his dark presence impossible to ignore. He was watching her like a falcon eyeing his prey.

"Are you sure?" asked Logan, taking one of her hands. It was like ice.

"Yes, really. I'll be fine."

"All right. But my driver will take you home. I'll call him and tell him you're on your way."

"All right. That will be fine," Ariane answered quickly, willing to agree to anything that would get her out of there as soon as possible. The air felt thick with Alex's presence, coiling itself insidiously around her so that she felt as if she were choking.

"Good. I'll go call. Feel better and rest this weekend. You're going to need it," Logan said, alluding to his new line and, bending forward, he brushed his lips against her pale cheek.

"I will." Ariane tried to smile and failed miserably. She thanked Jonathan for his invitation and left the room, searching for the maid to retrieve her coat.

Alex's date—Stacy, Tracy, Lacy, or something like that—was apparently feeling neglected. She had begun massaging the back of his neck while she rubbed her breast against his arm. She whined in his ear that he wasn't paying attention to her, favoring him with what she thought was an attractive pout. Only she was too big to pout and the heavily glossed red mouth looked more like a caricature to him. He whispered what he intended to do to her later when they were alone, and she settled down.

He had noticed Ariane's presence the moment she had arrived. His temper began to burn at the possessive way the white-haired stranger held her arm. Willing her to look in his direction, he was pleased to see her look of shock. But she looked paler than usual, her cheekbones sharper. And her eyes: they looked haunted.

The party was in full swing now and the maid was nowhere to be found. In a hurry to leave and not wanting to wait for the maid to turn up, Ariane went in search of her coat. She walked down a long corridor and looked into several rooms before she came to the last bedroom, which was lined with standing coat racks. The racks were crammed full with assorted fur coats, and she sifted through them looking for her sable.

She found her coat, checked the monogram to be sure and turned to leave, only to find Alex leaning indolently against the closed door.

There was a predatory quality about him as he stood there watching her. He was dressed in a black shirt, black slacks, and gray cashmere jacket, his seemingly casual stance belying the tension on his face. She stared at him with empty eyes. In a dead voice she said, "Get out of my way."

His penetrating gaze slid over her figure, his expression harsh in the dim light. She shivered inwardly at the ice in his eyes.

"What's the matter? Anxious to run away?" he said, his voice laced with contempt.

"I'm not running away." Wasn't she? She remembered his deadly words, *It doesn't matter.* She didn't matter. She was tired. Tired of his games. Right now, all she wanted to do was get away from him and go home.

She could feel the waves of anger emanating from him, and she didn't feel at all safe being alone with him.

"Ah, the innocent act. Very good. But then you're very good at pretending, aren't you?" When she didn't answer, he repeated, "Well, aren't you?"

"Just leave me alone." Her voice was void of emotion. She had nothing left.

"Which role is it tonight, Mrs. Wakefield?" Alex said derisively as though he hadn't heard her plea. "The loyal devoted wife defending her home, or the poor neglected wife luring men into her bed?"

Ariane heard the click of the lock in the door and took a step backward as Alex advanced toward her.

"I didn't know you were looking for a sugar daddy. Guess it's easier to keep the old ones satisfied. They're so grateful for anything," he taunted.

"You're disgusting," she retorted, coming out of her lethargy.

"Oh? Then perhaps you'd like to explain what you're doing with a man old enough to be your father."

"I don't owe you an explanation. I don't owe you anything."

Without realizing it, Ariane had backed herself against the wall. Alex stood dangerously close, close enough that she could smell the liquor on his breath as he reached out an arm and leaned his palm against the wall, on a spot next to her head.

"Have you told anyone what you heard?" The silver eyes were intent.

That's all he cared about, she thought. "No." She paused. "Not yet."

"Don't, for your own sake. You don't understand what's involved."

"I don't care. Now get out of my way and leave me alone."

"Not just yet, I'm not through with you."

"Well I'm through with you and thankful for it. I can't even imagine what I ever thought I saw in you. But that was part of the trap, wasn't it? You're not going to use me anymore!" Her black eyes flashed.

"Use you? Who are you kidding? You're nothing but a lying little whore!"

"You bastard!" Without thinking, she brought her hand back to slap him but he grabbed her wrist.

"Bitch!" he returned as he applied pressure to her wrist.

Ariane refused to cry out, even though he was hurting her wrist. It suddenly became a battle of wills, each refusing to give any quarter. Hot tears filled her eyes and she bit her lower lip as Alex's grip threatened to break her wrist. Finally, unable to stand the pain any longer, she said with as much defiance as she could muster, "Okay. You can stop now. You've made your point."

Alex relaxed his pressure but didn't release her. "I said let go." She tried to jerk her wrist free and, failing that, exploded with rage, "I hate you!" She began pounding on his chest, trying to wrestle her wrist free.

She caught Alex off guard and he released her wrist,

trying to fend off her blows. She flailed at him wildly, her body twisting away from his as he attempted to subdue her. His arms went around her and he hugged her to him, trapping her.

She twisted in vain but his arms were like steel bands. Frustrated, she sagged against him and wept. His grip dissolved into an embrace and she was dimly aware of him stroking her back. She became conscious of the press of his body, of the very maleness of him, of his sensuality.

"You want me and you know it." His voice was deeper, heavier.

"I don't want you!" She wrenched her body as though to prove her point.

"Don't you?" He bent his head to her mouth but she jerked away, offering him the smooth white column of her throat.

When his lips touched the side of her neck she twisted her head, pushing him away. "I *hate* you!"

His voice was velvet smooth. "Then hate me."

She saw his intent and tried to shift her head, but he anticipated her move and grabbed her head, holding her still before she could move. His mouth was gentle yet insistent, evoking an alarming response in her as it moved sensuously over her mouth.

No, her mind cried even as her body responded. But she could no more stop her reaction than she could stop breathing.

He was far more dangerous now as he plundered the inner recesses of her mouth, sending flames of desire rippling through her. Fresh tears filled her eyes at her body's betrayal, as his mouth hungrily demanded a response she sought hard to deny. If only he were cruel and brutal, she could fight him and hate him. But this . . . this she had no defense against.

His mouth scorched her skin as it moved down her

throat, making her go weak as a warm, languorous feeling invaded her body. No, she mustn't let this happen. It was wrong. She hated him.

"Please," she whimpered softly, only she no longer knew if it was a plea for him to stop or to continue.

He lifted his head and looked down at her. "You really want me to stop?"

"Y—yes."

As though he hadn't heard her, he bent his head and pressed his lips to her throat. "Are you sure?" His voice was filled with emotion, fairly caressing her as he continued scorching a path up her neck. Reaching his destination, he muttered heavily into her ear, "I want you, Ari, more than I've ever wanted any woman."

There was an odd selfishness to his kiss, as though he were trying to take something from her.

"Open your eyes," he demanded, his voice ragged.

She did as he said. Her eyes were black with passion.

"Do you still want me to stop?"

"No," she whispered, feeling drugged.

"Then tell me. Tell me that you want me," he said hoarsely, a strange light in his eyes, as though some dark alien force were driving him.

She stared into his face. From his expression she knew she could deny him nothing any more than she could deny the feelings aroused in her. "I want you, Alex."

He led her to the bed, pulling her down with him. Rolling onto his side, he fitted her supple curves against him. Her slender arms wrapped around him, one hand buried in his hair. Deftly, he unzipped the back of her dress and ran his hands hungrily down her bare back.

Her dress had been pushed up to her hips and his hand moved unimpeded along her supple thigh to the top of her stocking. He stroked her soft bare flesh, eliciting a moan of pleasure from her as his fingers moved over her silk panties.

She was lost, caught up in the madness he unleashed in her. She was past thinking or caring. She only knew she ached terribly and only Alex could satisfy her. She clutched him to her frantically, wanting to get closer and feel him against her. Frustrated at the barrier between them, she unbuttoned his shirt and helped him out of it while he pulled her dress down to her waist. She reveled in the feel of his chest against her and moved lasciviously against him.

Somewhere in the back of her mind she knew this was insanity, but when his fingers teased at the point between her thighs she knew that nothing mattered, nothing except Alex and the almost unbearably intense pleasure he gave her.

He removed the delicate black silk panties barring his intrusion and she eagerly accepted him, her warm tightness welcoming him.

She was out of control, her body straining against him as he drove her senseless. As the first wave of ecstasy exploded in her she clutched him to her, her body trembling. She was unaware that she was crying or that she had called out his name.

"Jesus, Ari," he whispered hoarsely as his body shuddered against her. He moved inside her as he claimed her mouth in a deep, drugging kiss.

As if coming out of a trance, Ariane slowly became aware of the sound of their heavy breathing in the silent room. She could feel the perspiration between their bodies and the dampness on his broad back. She couldn't breathe beneath his heavy weight and tried to shift her body to a more comfortable position, causing him to lift his head and look at her. She drew back at the look she saw. His eyes were glazed, staring at her intently, their look a mixture of triumph and disgust.

Silently he got up, dressed, and without so much as a backward glance let himself out of the bedroom.

Hearing the bedroom door close after him, she felt the stiffness leave her body. She had watched him dress through lowered lashes, not missing the deep red welts her nails had caused on his back. The sight of those marks sent shame and humiliation coursing through her. My God, she cried inwardly, how could she do this? There must be something wrong with her. He only had to hold her and with a little coaxing, very little, she surrendered her pride, her honor, to become a quivering, panting thing eager for his touch.

Maybe he was right. She was a whore. How else could she explain her behavior toward a man who betrayed her, a man she vowed to hate for all eternity?

Ariane spent the day at the beach. She resolved that it was time she got her life in order, put the past behind her. Her mind made up, she got in the car and left for the city.

Entering Montauk Highway for the ride home, she turned on the radio and pushed in a cassette. Strains of Craig's favorite opera filled the car. She hated opera. With a mischievous grin on her lips she opened her window, popped the cassette, and threw it out. Still grinning, she reached into the console, found a cassette of the Doors, and slid it in. Craig hated her taste for rock and roll. Turning up the volume, she listened to Jim Morrison's sensuous voice fill the car, ordering her to touch him. So much for opera.

chapter 19

Dulci examined her nude body in the bathroom mirror, scrutinizing the bruises on her thighs. They could be covered with make-up. She had warned him to be careful this time, but as usual he had lost control.

She returned to the bedroom to find him sitting up in bed, his naked body half covered with the sheet while he idly smoked a cigarette.

"So are you keeping our friend happy?" Hassan asked.

"What do you think?" Dulci returned, grinning as she slipped between the red silk sheets.

"As long as he doesn't know. You're our little secret, aren't you?"

"Yes, of course." Dulci knew Hassan well enough to recognize a threat when she heard it.

"What have you learned?"

Dulci breathed easier, relieved the moment had passed. "He's been trading in nondiscretionary accounts." She referred to Craig's trading of Mettrac, using his customers' money without their permission, allowing him to rack up untold commissions with no risk to his own money or the firm's.

"Anything else?"

"I met Russ. You're right. I don't think he's going to be any trouble. Although his wife is a pain in the neck."

"Don't start trouble. Just stick to Craig as I told you."

"What's his wife like?"

"Quite attractive," Hassan paused. "Beautiful, in fact."

"Oh?" Dulci didn't like the interested note in Hassan's voice.

"Yes." He squinted at her. "There's something unspoiled about her. And of course, she's younger than you."

Dulci winced and wondered, not for the first time, why she was with this man whose words often left deeper wounds than the bruises on her thighs.

The first thing Ariane did Monday morning was to march into Logan's office and accept his offer.

With her spirit restored, an effusion of enthusiasm filled her, the days quickly stretching into weeks as she threw herself wholeheartedly into her project.

Work filled the void in her life. It didn't heal the pain, but it helped.

She was sitting in bed, her sketches spread out in front of her, when the telephone rang.

"Besides work, how are you?" Sloane asked after they had been talking for a while.

"Fine," Ariane replied. "I have everything now, a job, a career, my own life. What could be bad?"

"I don't know. Suppose you tell me." Ariane's voice was too bright.

"I don't know, Sloane. Sometimes I just feel as if

something's missing. I thought that once I had everything I wanted I'd be happy but . . .'' Ariane's voice trailed off.

"What do you want?'' asked Sloane.

"That's just it. I don't even know exactly. I just know I haven't got it.''

"Well, to quote one of the great women of our time, my mother, 'Believe me, you'll know.' ''

Alex sat at his desk in his town house reading the latest dossier on the Arab. He read the same sentence twice and pushed the report away, disgusted with himself. He couldn't concentrate, hadn't been able to concentrate for some time. Reluctantly, he pulled Ariane's photo from her file and stared at it.

His temper had begun to boil the minute he saw her enter Sawyer's apartment. He had sent his date home with the excuse about an emergency.

What did it matter? He couldn't even seem to recall her features now anyway. That's the way it had been since Ariane walked out on him. There had been a steady string of ready, willing women all too anxious to please his every whim. And when he tired of one, which he did almost immediately, there was always another to take her place. Maybe if he hadn't been drinking so heavily he could have recalled a face or a name.

Maybe Travis was right, he admitted ruefully. They had had a heated argument when Travis told him he should take it easy. Alex was going out every night, not returning until the wee hours of the morning, and then he was usually drunk. He had begun drinking earlier than usual, and Travis had warned him he'd better stop drinking and whoring or he'd blow the assignment. Alex's temper had flared and he had told Travis to mind his own damn business.

Unfortunately, Alex was not as unaffected by Ariane as he wanted to believe. There was something about her. She seemed to have invaded him, her very essence filling his mind like a drug. How else could he explain her face flashing before his eyes when he was with another woman, making him lose interest in the body beneath him? But it was more than that. He remembered her undisguised innocent joy, so pure and simple, at the beauty of a single snowflake. He was finding it harder to believe in her duplicity, and his conjured hate for her was no longer the talisman capable of protecting him from the magic spell she wove around him.

He wondered at the attraction. True, she was beautiful—but so were many of the women he slept with. It was more than that. She got under his skin. He had images of her, the way she laughed in the bright sunshine when she threw a snowball at him or in their moonlit room when she splashed brandy over him. Ariane, fighting so hard to deny her passion and then surrendering so completely. And in the end he no longer knew who the victor was.

It had occurred to Ariane that she should warn Craig that Alex was investigating him. Only something had prevented her from making the call, some insane thought that she'd be betraying Alex. But how could she when he'd already deceived her? Hadn't he? Why couldn't she stop remembering what it was like to lie in his arms, to be held by him?

She wondered why she should care about either one of them. They had both used her. But she had been married to Craig for seven years and maybe she did owe him something.

"Craig," she said when he answered the telephone. "I have to talk to you."

"Go ahead." His voice sounded distracted, as if he were busy.

"No, not on the phone. Can I see you?"

"Sure." She could sense his interest as though he had

pushed his work aside. "The Wall Street Charity Association is this week. Why don't you come with me?"

Maybe that would be the best place to warn him, surrounded by people. "Okay."

"Ariane knows about the investigation," Alex said into the telephone.

"Jesus, Alex, how the hell did that happen?" Jake sounded accusatory.

"It was an accident."

"An accident? You can't afford any accidents, not with this one. How much does she know?"

"I don't know." *Enough to hurt her,* he thought.

"Have you thought about what will happen if she tells Wakefield?"

That's all he'd been thinking about. That and Hassan. "Yeah."

"You've got to tell her. Everything. She's got to be protected."

"I know."

While dressing in her Bill Blass gown for her date with Craig, Ariane felt nervous apprehension fluttering in the pit of her stomach. Maybe this wasn't such a good idea after all, she mused belatedly as she realized she wasn't looking forward to seeing him. But she wanted to warn him about the investigation and decided this was the best way.

The minute she and Craig entered the Grand Ballroom of the Pierre Hotel, Ariane knew with a gnawing certainty that this date was a mistake. It wasn't Craig exactly. He had been pleasant enough in the limousine, even complimenting her appearance when he arrived, something he had never done in their marriage. But seeing the crowd of familiar faces unsettled her. All their friends were there. All their friends who had witnessed their separation and probably knew the reason for it. Their friends who had supported Craig and stood by him. And now she had to face them. Squaring her bare shoulders, she determined not to let them get the best of her.

In a perverse way she enjoyed watching their reactions to her presence. When she and Craig had separated she had become persona non grata. Without her position as Craig's wife, it was as though she had ceased to exist. Such was true for any woman in their social and political sphere. Men who lived and breathed business couldn't afford to antagonize Craig by remaining Ariane's friend. The choice was simple: ignore her and stay in Craig's good graces or befriend her and have Craig cut them off. There was no choice.

There was no one as unwelcome by other women as a single, unattached female in their midst. First, they didn't want their husbands getting any ideas. Second, her single status reminded them of their own vulnerability and dependency on their husbands. Without their husbands there would be no invitations, no position for them in society, and most of all no money.

The Cotillion Room was crowded, the guests nudging each other as they got in the party spirit.

"Craig, we have to talk," Ariane said.

Craig's gaze was darting about, searching. "Not now," he said absently. "I see Brad."

With that he cupped her elbow and led her toward Brad.

Ariane and Craig spent the rest of the time before dinner circulating around the room. It was business as usual, the men huddling together while the women feigned interest in each other to pass the time.

Oh hell, Ariane thought as they approached their table. It was already occupied with Russ, Kristen, Hassan and a tall anorexic looking brunette, not to mention Alex and a flashy redhead. What a nightmare! And worst of all, she realized she would be seated next to Alex while Craig took the empty seat next to Hassan's date. Everyone murmured polite greetings. Alex looked at her and offered her a wry smile as she sat down.

"Ariane, darling, what a surprise. I had no idea that you and Craig were dating," Kristen declared loudly.

"I didn't know we needed your permission," Ariane tossed back, determined not to let Kristen have the advantage no matter how small.

She could feel Alex's gaze on her, feel herself growing warm at his nearness. She turned to see a look of amusement in his eyes and glared at him, annoyed that he should find Kristen's sniping at her amusing. But she was relieved that he gave her a ready excuse to be angry at him. It was infinitely safer for her to stay angry than to let down her guard. If he even suspected the power he had over her and her susceptibility to him, she would be lost.

The appetizers were served and it was impossible not to notice the tension at the table. Everyone seemed just a little preoccupied and anxious—everyone except Alex. He seemed perfectly at ease and unaware of the undercurrents going on around him. Ariane had enough to do with trying to avoid Hassan's flat stare. Unaccountably, a wave of dread swept over her, chilling her. She pushed it aside, concentrating on returning Kristen's barbs which flew regularly across the table. She noticed Russ's discomfort at Kristen's behavior and decided that she no longer sympathized with him. He was a fool if he believed she really loved him.

Craig was entertaining Hassan, the woman in between them practically disappearing for their purposes. Alex's date was chatting away, hoping to catch everyone's attention about some acting audition she'd been on. It was going to be a very long evening.

At the sound of Alex's voice mentioning her name, Ariane turned to him. "What did you say?"

"I was just telling Cara that if she gets the part she ought to have you design her wardrobe," Alex explained, his expression inscrutable.

"Thank you for offering my services. But I'm afraid that would be impossible."

"Oh really? Why is that?" Alex persisted.

"Because I have no experience designing for a movie," Ariane replied, trying hard to control her temper. She'd like to scratch that smug smile off his face. Instead she added, "And I'm busy working on my own line right now."

"Oh you are? What fun that must be. I guess you just think of something you want to wear and that's it," Cara gushed.

"Something like that." Ariane cast a glance in Alex's direction. What was he doing with this bubblehead? As though reading her mind, he shrugged.

"Don't tell me you're still drudging away in that factory," Kristen cut in loudly. "What a bore!"

"No, I never worked in a factory. I'm designing under my own label right now."

"How divine. I presume it will be something simple and modest then."

"On the contrary. It will be very elegant and very expensive. But don't despair, Kristen, I'm sure Frederick's of Hollywood can continue to accommodate you," Ariane answered, a sweet smile on her mouth.

"I think I'd like to dance," Craig announced abruptly as he helped Ariane out of her chair.

Out on the dance floor Ariane asked, "Who were you rescuing, Kristen or me?"

Craig laughed. "Kristen, I suppose. I think you're a little more than she bargained for."

Mollified by his answer, she relaxed.

"Of course you didn't have to be that rough on her. After all, Russ and I are still partners."

All of her old resentments rushed to the surface. He was still trying to control her and manipulate the situation to his satisfaction. Nothing had changed. Nothing and everything. In that instant she knew there was no future for them, never had been. It was odd. In a way she felt a great sense of relief. All these months she had wondered if she were making a mistake by leaving Craig. Now she realized with a certainty that her instincts had been right. All she felt now was a lingering sadness for something they never had.

When they returned to their table, Craig immediately began a conversation with Hassan and ignored Ariane.

"Enjoying the party, Mrs. Wakefield?"

The mere sound of the deep voice at her shoulder sent a tremor through Ariane. Alex's very closeness rattled her nerves.

"Yes, I'm having a wonderful time." She strained to keep her voice even.

"That's surprising, because I know how boring parties can be. I remember the last one I attended didn't really get exciting until after it was over," Alex said blandly.

She had been staring straight ahead, trying to avoid him. But she turned sharply toward him, sucking in her breath, ready to make a scathing reply. The breath caught in her throat at the cool, long look he gave her, a knowing smile playing about his sensuous mouth.

Alex continued in the same infuriatingly smooth voice, "Of course, it was well worth the wait."

A hot blush flooded her cheeks at the uncontrollable shiver of excitement his words had caused. Her eyes blazing with anger, she whispered tightly, "Will you stop it!"

"You'd better smile when you say that. After all, you

wouldn't want to make a scene in front of all your friends, would you?'' Alex mocked, his tone daring her.

She smiled coldly. ''How's this? Leave me alone.''

''Oh! Much better. By the way, I see congratulations are in order.''

''For what?''

''Why, your reconciliation with your husband.''

''We haven't . . .'' she began and then thinking better of it, replied, ''It's none of your business.''

''But that's where you're wrong, love. You are my business.''

Flustered, she reached for her wine glass and nearly knocked it over. Alex's hand reached out quickly to steady the tipping glass and held her hand. His palm was warm and she felt the familiar thrill at his touch. She looked at him and recognized the look of desire in his silver eyes as his thumb moved lightly across her palm and up to the pulse at her wrist. She was mesmerized by his look, his touch, her heart beating furiously at the message in his eyes. At the sound of her name she jerked her hand free and turned away.

''Excuse me, Ariane. Would you give me the pleasure of dancing with me?'' Hassan asked, his flat eyes peering intently at her. Anxious to get away from Alex, she rose without thinking. She realized her error too late.

Hassan slipped his arm around her waist and moved them smoothly across the floor. She felt her skin crawl as if something loathsome had touched her, and she had to fight down the urge to jerk out of his grasp. She felt the sharpness of his shoulder through his jacket and his hand felt bony as his long, spindly fingers closed around hers. He wore a heavy, sweet-smelling cologne that overwhelmed her. She tried to put more space between them only to feel his arm tighten around her. A tremor of dread rushed through her, surprising her with its intensity.

"You are a beautiful woman."

"Thank you," she muttered.

"Most beautiful women are so enthralled with their own beauty they have little interest in anything else. You are not like them. Tell me, what interests you?"

"Oh, lots of things," Ariane answered, trying to sound casual. He repulsed her, the nearness of him making her shake.

Hassan's black eyes bored into her as he pressed his point. "Like what?"

She grew more and more miserably uncomfortable every minute. His eyes were so black and flat they looked lifeless. If the eyes were the mirrors to the soul, this man had no soul.

"Like world affairs," she tossed smartly for want of something else.

"You joke. But I could show you things you never dreamed existed." His fingers picked up a lock of her hair and wound it in his hand. "Things that would take your breath away," Hassan said in a voice as lifeless as his eyes.

"Excuse me." Alex stood behind Hassan. "May I?"

Hassan shot him a look of annoyance and left the dance floor.

Relieved at Alex's timely arrival, she was confused by the tenseness in him as he took her in his arms. He seemed almost angry and held her tightly, his hand hurting hers. Then the tautness faded and he was holding her in an all too familiar way.

There was a strangled feeling in her throat as she fought against the riotous emotions he was causing within her. She felt indecent beneath his knowing look and glanced away, unable to meet his heated gaze. The caress of his fingers moving across the bare skin at her waist caused a warmth to rise in her. His fingers found a space between the straps and dipped lower below her waist, teasing sensually at the small of her back. She wanted to melt into his arms, forget her anger and give herself up to him. But she knew she meant nothing to him, no more than a night's pleasant diversion.

"Stop it! Please," she said in a choked voice.

Alex ignored her plea, one hand holding hers firmly while the other slipped beneath the edge of her dress. She could smell the scent of her own perfume as the warmth of her body caused waves of it to rise, surrounding them. He pulled her closer and she let him, wanting him. He held her hand against his chest and she could feel the heavy thudding of his heart.

The crowd receded and it was as though they were alone on the dance floor. Oblivious to the people around them, they were caught up in a world of their own. Ariane felt her throat tighten as the evidence of Alex's desire for her brushed against her, telling her that he wanted her as much as she wanted him. The temptation to reach up and touch her lips to the soft vulnerable side of his neck was nearly overpowering and she had to restrain herself. Instead, her fingers found the thick black hair that fell carelessly over the black tuxedo collar. She brushed it with her fingertips, playing with its silken texture.

The orchestra picked up the tempo to a current rock beat and Ariane felt a stab of disappointment as Alex led her back to the table. It had been bad enough just sitting next to him, but dancing with him and feeling his strong arms around her, his hand on her flesh, was nearly her undoing. She had to force herself to remember that he had only wanted to use her. And now he thought she and Craig were back together.

She was distracted on the ride home in Craig's limousine. They had left the party soon after dessert was served,

Craig's role as co-host forcing them to make many good-byes. Most of them were easy. All she had to do was smile and agree what a successful and enjoyable party it had been. Until they had to say good-bye to Alex, that is. Then the smile froze on her lips and the words caught in her throat as she stared into his dark, unreadable features.

Craig invited himself into her apartment, claiming he wanted to talk.

As soon as they sat on the sofa Craig startled her by putting his hand at the back of her neck.

"How long are you going to keep this up?"

"Keep what up?" She didn't like the feel of his hand on her.

"The independence. The job. You've made your point. Why don't you give it up now?"

"I'm not giving it up, and I didn't do this to prove any point. You still don't understand, do you?" She was tired of trying to explain the important aspects of her life to Craig. "Maybe you'd better leave."

Once she had wanted to tell him she hated him. For making her afraid, for manipulating her, for demeaning her. Now it didn't matter. She no longer cared.

"Come on, just pretend I'm one of your dates," he said.

With that Craig pressed his mouth firmly on hers, his hand holding her neck so she couldn't escape. She felt a cold detachment and realized that she had never loved Craig, not even in the beginning. And now, the only response he evoked from her was distaste. She twisted her head sharply, her hands pushing hard against his chest to break his hold.

"Craig, stop it!"

"Why? You're my wife. You belong to me. I have every right."

"I don't belong to you or anybody! And you gave up any rights a long time ago. I want you to leave now."

"Oh, come off that holier-than-thou attitude. For Christ's sake, you even carried it to our bed. Lying there as if nothing could touch you. Maybe all you need is some coaxing." Grabbing her roughly by the shoulders, he tried to kiss her.

"You're disgusting," she said, struggling against him. "We're finished. It's over. Can't you see that?"

"All I see is you've been holding out on me. Spreading it around all over town while you played the ice maiden in my bed. And if we are finished, so be it. But let's see if you can respond at all. Maybe you need a little convincing."

Ariane pushed him away and leapt up from the sofa. But before she could move further his hand grabbed one of the straps of her dress and tugged hard, pulling her back. The strap tore away from the neckline of her dress as she stumbled backward and fell onto the sofa.

Half the front of her dress fell away, revealing the creamy globe of her breast. Craig slipped his hand beneath the fabric and grabbed her breast while he threw himself on top of her. In a reflex action she brought her hand back and slapped him in the face. The crack sounded like a gun exploding.

Stunned, Craig stared at her for a moment, his face cold and angry. He returned the slap full force.

The impact snapped her head back, dazing her momentarily. Tears rushed to her eyes, but pride prevented her from putting a hand to her burning cheek. "Get out of here before I call the police," she said with icy control.

Craig stood, adjusted his jacket, and looked down at her with contempt. "You're not even worth the effort." With that he left, slamming the door behind him.

She sat motionless on the sofa. It took her a few moments to realize the sound intruding in on her was the doorbell. The ringing persisted and somewhat unsteadily she got to her feet and walked to the door.

Without thinking, she opened the door to find Alex.

"What the hell are you doing here?"

Alex quickly took in her appearance, shocked by what he saw, although only a slight flicker in his eyes gave anything away. The front of her dress was torn and she was obviously unaware that most of her breast was exposed. Her shiny black hair was mussed, her mouth looked bruised, and there was the unmistakable red mark of a palm print on her smooth, pale cheek. But it was the bruise mark on the creamy white flesh of her breast that hit him like a blow to his stomach.

He stepped inside quickly and closed the door behind him before she had time to react. "Are you all right?" His voice sounded cold and hard in his effort to suppress his rage at what Craig had done.

She replied just as coldly, matching his anger, "Of course I'm all right. But I'd like to know what you're doing here."

It was a good question and he really had no answer. He had sat outside in his car waiting for Craig to leave, telling himself he had to find out if she told Craig about the investigation. Now, seeing what that bastard had done, he was sorry he had waited in the car and not burst in on them and the hell with the investigation.

"I was in the neighborhood and thought I'd stop in for a drink," he answered casually as he stepped past her and walked into the living room.

She followed him into the living room, where he began filling two brandy snifters. He held out one of the glasses to her.

"I don't want any," she mumbled.

"Take it." He fairly pushed the glass into her hand.

She walked over to the sofa, sat down, and took a sip

of the amber-colored liquid. Her hands began to shake as she put the snifter down and hugged her arms to herself.

Alex went to her immediately, slipping off his tuxedo jacket and putting it around her bare shoulders. Sitting next to her, he hugged her to him, feeling the slender body shivering against him.

"Here. Take some." He held his snifter to her lips.

Dutifully, she parted her lips and let him tip some of the cognac into her mouth.

"Finish it," he ordered, not removing the glass.

"I don't want any more," she argued.

"Must you fight with me about everything? Just finish the goddamn drink so you will stop shaking."

His deep voice held a note of exasperation as a father's would when addressing a recalcitrant child who refused to take some medicine. Obediently, she finished the rest of the cognac.

He settled back, an agreeable Ariane trustingly curled up against him, and he wondered what he was doing playing nursemaid. One glimpse of her—the torn dress, the glazed look in her eyes—was enough for him. He had only meant to ascertain that she was all right and then leave. But she hadn't been all right and now that he had her in his arms he was loathe to give her up. Oddly enough, and much to his surprise, he found a previously unknown contentment in merely comforting her, knowing his presence helped her.

They sat like that for some time, quietly, at peace. Alex heard her sigh deeply, an easy relaxed sigh, that told him she was feeling better.

"I think I'd better be going," his deep voice rumbled in his chest as he made an attempt at removing his arm from around her.

She sat upright and at her movement his jacket fell from her shoulders. His gaze went to her breast and returned to her face, the look of desire filling his eyes. She returned his unrelenting gaze, the blush of passion on her pale skin unmistakable. Her eyes fluttered closed as he slowly bent his head to touch her mouth. His lips were gentle as they nuzzled and played with hers, enjoying their softness, their sensuality.

Then his gentle kisses weren't enough and his mouth took hers hungrily, demanding and receiving a response which she gave freely. He stood, scooped her up in his arms, and carried her into the bedroom.

She must have dozed off afterward, she realized, because she woke up feeling famished and then remembered she hadn't eaten her dinner. It was a shame to have to move because she was warm and content under the covers, her head resting on Alex's shoulder. She thought he might be sleeping and lifted her head to find him staring at her.

"I'm starved," she announced.

"Pushy little thing, aren't you? Well, if you insist," he agreed, his eyes alight as he turned toward her.

She laughed at his mistake and at how quickly he was ready to comply and, putting a restraining hand against his chest, laughter tickled her voice as she explained, "No, no, I mean food. I'm hungry." Seeing him freeze in mid-motion she added, seductively, "Why don't you hold that thought for dessert?"

"You always wake up in the middle of the night and eat?"

"No. Only when I'm really happy," she blurted without thinking.

"And you're happy now?" His penetrating gaze held her tightly for a motionless moment.

She returned his intent look, hesitated briefly, and then knew. "Yes."

He slid his eyes away as though uncomfortable.

• • •

Back in bed after their snack, Alex cradled her head on his shoulder as her hand gently caressed the side of his neck. She made small sounds of contentment and snuggled against him.

"Alex?" she whispered.

"Mmm."

"What's your middle name?"

"I don't have one. Why?"

"Just wondering."

"I was four when my mother died. . . ." he began, his voice sounding cold and emotionless in the darkened bedroom.

There was a controlled hardness to his voice, the long suppressed pain creeping through as if he were reliving the whole horrible past. One hand absently stroked her hair, the gentle gesture incongruous with the harsh, ugly pictures his words were painting.

He stopped talking, feeling drained and exhausted, yet oddly cleansed as if he had let out some loathsome thing that had been buried deep inside him all these years. He didn't know what had prompted him to tell Ari or even why he had, but somehow he felt good about it and was glad he had. Abruptly, he had deep misgivings about his disclosure and the good feeling fled, replaced by a gnawing dread. He had exposed himself to her and for what? Her pity? He couldn't stand to have her pity.

He shifted his arm around her, pulling her up so he could see her face. Her face was wet with tears, but there was no pity there. Only a look of mutual pain in her dark, expressive eyes. Reaching out a finger, he wiped a tear from her smooth pale cheek.

"Don't cry for me, Ari," he said softly, oddly touched by her emotion.

"Oh Alex, I would do anything to take away your hurt," she whispered as fresh tears filled her eyes.

"You have, Ari love." He hugged her tightly to him, burying his face in her hair as he murmured, "You have."

"That's all you're having?" Ariane asked after Alex ordered coffee from the waiter. They were having breakfast in the Regency Hotel. She had offered to fix him breakfast in her apartment but he had insisted on going out. All morning he had seemed preoccupied, distant, and she wondered at his sudden mood swing.

"I'm not hungry." He gazed about the room, his seat in the corner affording him a clear view of the wood-paneled room. At this early hour the restaurant was filled with businessmen having their power breakfasts.

The waiter placed a bowl of fresh fruit in front of Ariane and she spooned a piece of cantaloupe.

"I want to talk to you about what you heard," he said. "It's time you knew the whole story."

His eyes were intent on her, and suddenly she was afraid, afraid to hear the truth. She put down her spoon. "Go ahead." Her voice was as detached as his.

"I work for an agency that's after Hassan. Craig wasn't the target, only the conduit to Hassan. You weren't expected to be involved at all. What happened between us wasn't part of the plan. It wasn't supposed to have happened." His expression was blank, unreadable, but there was something in his voice that told her it was an effort.

She couldn't discuss their relationship yet. She had to know more. "Why are you after Hassan?"

"He's the Rapunzel Strangler." His eyes held hers steadily, unwavering.

The color drained from her face. Unconsciously, her hand went to the ponytail hanging down her back. Cold fear rippled along her flesh. Hassan had touched it, touched her. Hassan was a murderer. She had always disliked him, had hated his eyes on her, his hands on her. She shook at the memory of his touch, a murderer's touch.

"Does Craig know about him?" A terrifying chill settled over her.

"I doubt it. There'd be no way for him to know. Theirs is strictly a business arrangement."

"What's going to happen?" She was amazed at herself that she was able to remain so calm. But Alex was so controlled, so cool, he left her no alternative.

"Craig will probably be arrested for security violations and we'll get Hassan."

"Why are you telling me all this? Isn't it top secret or something?"

"That's exactly why I'm telling you. Now do you understand why I told you not to mention this to anyone?"

She immediately thought how close she had been to telling Craig last night. The thought sent a shiver down her spine, but it was nothing compared to the tremor of fear that went through her at how close she had been to Hassan.

"Are you all right?" For the first time his voice didn't sound so professional, so removed. And she knew the investigation wasn't the only reason Alex had told her.

The innocent sounds of the men in their business suits discussing mergers and acquisitions returned, replacing the darkness his deadly words had caused. But strangely enough she realized she was relieved. The barrier that Alex had hid behind was gone. There was nothing between them now. No lies, no evasions, no misunderstandings. Just the truth. She was more than all right.

"What about you? What happens after?" *What about us?* she wanted to ask.

Something flickered in his eyes. "I go home."

• • •

"A steak, blood rare, and a bottle of champagne." Hassan replaced the receiver. The bedroom's heavily lined drapes had been drawn against the night but the soft glow of the lamps clearly illuminated the bed's offering. The beautiful blonde lay naked, spread eagle, her ankles and wrists tied to the brass bars of the headboard. Her smooth, white flesh contrasted alluringly with the red satin sheets. The scent of sex hung heavily in the air.

"Hassan, untie me," Dulci asked.

"Not yet. We've hardly begun." Hassan sat on the edge of the bed and absently fondled the creamy globe of her breast.

"Are you kidding? We've been at it for hours. I'm exhausted. I need a rest." Dulci strove to keep her voice light. She'd been seeing Hassan for some time. When he first began tying her up it had just been fun and games. But lately he'd been tying the ropes tighter and keeping her bound longer. It wasn't fun anymore.

"Shh. Just lie there. Just be beautiful. I'll do everything." His finger gently touched her lips and trailed down her chin to her neck. He continued his path, pointing his finger, digging his nail deeply into the white flesh, raising a deep red welt tinged with blood down the length of her body.

"Stop it! You're hurting me," she cried.

"But look how beautiful you are." He lowered his head and slowly made his way along the swollen wound, his mouth licking and sucking at it.

When he moved to her breast, nipping and gnawing at the taut peak, she groaned deep in her throat. *So he's a little kinky,* she thought. *It's not all that bad.* But then his mouth moved across her breast, biting the tender flesh, his teeth sharp and vicious.

"Ow," she protested.

Hassan bit harder but at the same time thrust his hand

between her thighs, finding her sensitive spot. Her protest died on a moan.

Abruptly he straightened up, shrugged out of his robe, and released her ankles. He moved over her, straddling her. His body was slick with perspiration as he leaned over her to untie her wrists. Dulci could smell the odor emanating from him; it filled her nostrils, pungent and rank.

She rubbed her freed wrists, massaging the circulation back into them.

"Turn over," he ordered, his voice flat.

She froze, her eyes searching his face, his eyes, but they were empty. "No, Hassan."

"Come now, Dulci. You don't want to disappoint me." He lowered his voice, and added, "Or make me angry."

The game was over. At that moment she realized how vulnerable she was, how helpless. No one even knew where she was. Fear filled her eyes. "Hassan, please," she begged, knowing it was pointless. A peculiar light shone in his black eyes. For the first time they didn't look lifeless, dead, but alive. Horribly alive. He knew she was afraid and was enjoying her fear.

When she didn't move fast enough he pulled her arm and twisted it so that she fell face down on the bed. The sheets, damp with perspiration, chilled her body. Her hair fell over her face, but before she could brush it aside he pinned her arms to the bed.

When the jolt of searing pain ripped through her, threatening to tear her apart, she screamed. *Oh God, he had to stop.* She lifted her head but his hand clutched her neck, pushing her down, smashing her face into the bed.

Hassan was in a frenzy, his movements frantic. There was nothing for Dulci to do but cry and pray that she survived the night.

chapter 20

"Look, I don't give a goddamn about the investigation and your damn timing," Alex fairly shouted into the telephone. "I want Wakefield and I want him now. I'm tired of your excuses and your stalling. What the hell are you people doing over there anyway?"

"Alex, has something happened you're not telling me about?" the voice on the telephone asked quietly.

"No."

"Then I really don't understand the urgency. We're right on schedule. Everything is going as planned. To move now would be precipitous on our part and it could cost us our goal. Maybe you ought to step back a bit and we'll take it from here."

"That won't be necessary." His voice was quieter as he heard the implied threat in his contact's voice. "Wakefield trusts me and if I were to back off now he'd become suspicious. We'll play it your way."

"Good. The subpoenas are ready to go. The indictments should be handed up any day and we'll serve them as soon as they are. Believe me, we want Wakefield and Hassan.''

Dulci closed her antique store on Madison Avenue eager to sort out her new shipment. She specialized in English, French, and Italian antiques from the eighteenth and nineteenth centuries, with an occasional oddity from another century, another country.

With space at a premium on Madison Avenue, the back room was small and jammed with her newly arrived delivery. She sidestepped an English cricket table to admire a large Italian rococo mirror. She caught her reflection in the glass and absently pushed back a stray lock of blond hair.

That's odd, she thought. The mirror seemed to be of fine quality with no distortions. She moved to the side of the frame and peered at it closely, her trained eye expecting to see the waves of imperfections that declared it authentic nineteenth-century. There were none. The mirror was perfect. She could have sworn the antique frame had held the original mirror when she bought it.

She heard a sound and looked up to see Hassan standing in the doorway.

''Hassan.''

''Dulci, my dear, did I frighten you? I didn't mean to. I just wanted to make sure your shipment arrived intact.'' Hassan walked into the storeroom, taking in the new furniture with a glance.

''I was just going over it.'' This was the first time she had seen Hassan since that horrible night in his hotel room, the night he had abused her. Fear knotted in her stomach at the memory.

Hassan picked up a Moroccan dagger and weighed its heavy, hammered gold handle in his hand. Putting it down, he moved toward Dulci. ''Why don't you do this tomorrow and come join me in my suite for dinner?''

"No." The word rushed out before she could temper her tone. "I . . . I should really check everything in case something's missing."

When she had woken up the morning after and seen the ugly purple bruises left by his teeth, she knew the man was crazy. The last thing in the world she wanted was to be alone with him again.

"The shipment can wait. I can't." Hassan reached out and stroked her arm. She cringed at the touch.

She stepped away quickly. "No, Hassan. No more. That's finished."

"Finished? Don't be a fool. We've only just begun."

Dulci tried to control her fear, knowing that Hassan fed on it, reveled in it. But just the thought of him touching her again terrified her. The memory of that night would haunt her forever.

"I think it's best if we keep our relationship strictly business from now on," she said. "What with Craig and all, I don't think we should be seen together."

"You have a point." Hassan took a step closer. "But I hardly expect to see Craig in my hotel suite this evening. Get your things."

"No. I won't."

Hassan moved closer still, standing directly in front of her. "Yes. You will."

Dulci could smell the cigarettes on his breath, the stale odor sickening her. The fear twisted inside her, and she began to shake. "Leave me alone." Without thinking, driven by a primitive instinct for survival, she grabbed the Moroccan dagger and pointed it at Hassan.

Hassan made a short disparaging sound. "Put that down."

Her eyes were wide with fear. "No. Don't come near me."

Hassan lunged for her, grabbing her wrist and painfully twisting it.

She tried to hold on to the dagger, her other hand pushing against his shoulder. Her wrist felt as if it were breaking, the hot pain shooting up her arm. She dropped the dagger. Still pushing against Hassan, trying to break his grip, she tripped on a rolled carpet and slammed into the Italian mirror.

They both froze as the mirror shattered around them, shards of glass falling to the floor.

Dulci didn't notice the blood streaming from her cut arm, staining her white silk blouse. On the floor at their feet lay twenty or more packets of white powder.

The silence was thick, ominous, in the cramped windowless room.

"What is that?" Dulci asked, her breathing heavy from their struggle.

"You know exactly what it is."

"I won't have you using my store for drugs. You know how I feel about drugs. I want no part of it."

"I'm afraid you have no choice in the matter." Hassan was utterly calm.

"I'll stop you. I'll go to the police." The minute the words were out of her mouth she knew she had made a mistake.

"Will you now?" The black eyes barely flickered.

"No," she said quickly. "I won't. I didn't mean it."

"But you thought it. And that means I can never trust you again." Hassan moved toward her.

Dulci stepped back, hardly aware of the broken mirror that crackled beneath her feet. She was trapped. "Hassan, please. I won't say anything. I swear."

"I know you won't."

Hassan's hands went around her throat. He began to squeeze. Her fingers clawed at his hands, her cry of protest abruptly cut off. She recognized the peculiar glow shining in his dead eyes. That horrible sickening light. She fought furiously, frantically.

He strangled her slowly, his choking hold measured, his killing grip controlled. He moved against her, rubbing himself on her, making her repulsively aware of his hardness. And then his fingers began to tighten.

The last thing Dulci saw was Hassan's cadaverous smile before permanent darkness claimed her.

Craig was uneasy. They were getting close, too close. He couldn't be sure what they knew, but the fact that Brad was subpoenaed behind closed doors was enough to set his teeth on edge. Of course, they could be questioning Brad about some other business not related to him, but if they were out to get him, this was just how they would go about it. Craig had learned long ago the SEC went after the smaller fish first, offering them deals to get the big catches they were really after. Craig knew human nature all too well, and he knew that once someone was caught and offered a way out, nothing would stand in his way of cutting the best deal. Nobody was brave enough or stupid enough to go down for a friend. There was no loyalty among thieves. At least not on the Street.

There was a knock on his door and Russ entered.

"Did you hear?" Russ asked.

"No, what happened?" Craig asked, not liking the look on Russ's face.

"Stuart Conway's been subpoenaed. He thinks Clayton's next. What the hell's going on?"

"Beats me. Probably just a witch hunt, as usual. You know the SEC boys like to have everyone jumping to their tune. Bunch of frustrated cops who couldn't make the grade," Craig answered, sounding more confident than he felt.

"I hope you're right. Still, it makes me a little nervous. First Brad's subpoenaed and now Stuart. If Clayton is next we're sure to be called, since we do so much of our business with those three. I just hope our books hold up to their scrutiny."

"They will. Don't worry about it," Craig said. If not, there was always Switzerland.

Craig passed quickly through the Pierre's lobby and took the elevator up to Hassan's elegant suite. As usual he was met by one of Hassan's associates, bodyguard was more like it, and ushered into the living room. Hassan was sitting in a wing chair, a silver coffee service placed in front of him on a small antique walnut table.

"Would you care for some coffee?" Hassan offered.

"No thanks." Craig was anxious to get down to business.

"You don't mind if I do." Hassan made elaborate work of pouring the thick, dark coffee.

Craig stood and began pacing the length of the Persian rug. "No, no, go ahead."

"You have something to tell me?"

"Yes. Brad and Stuart have been subpoenaed, and the word is out that Clayton's next."

"So?" His thin face revealed nothing.

"So . . ." Craig sat in a chair next to Hassan and lowered his voice, "It's only a matter of time before I'm called."

"Yes."

"Damnit, Hassan. Don't pull that Middle East tranquility crap with me. If I go, you go." Craig pointed his finger at Hassan. "I've covered our tracks pretty well, and if it's just a minor SEC investigation they won't dig that deep. If we're lucky. Even so, it could wind up costing me a pretty penny in fines, and possibly a suspension. Of course, if they go further, it could mean everything.''

''And that is why you have come here today, to tell me of the SEC investigation?'' He replaced the delicate Limoge cup and saucer on the table.

''Yes. And to tell you I want twenty million dollars deposited in my Swiss bank account.'' When Hassan didn't answer Craig continued, ''I'll need it for lawyers' fees, fines and let's say compensation for taking the heat.''

''I see. Twenty million dollars.'' Hassan sat quietly, seeming to mull it over as he fingered his ruby pinky ring. ''What of the payments I have already made to your bank account? Were they not generous enough?''

''For their purposes, yes. They covered my fee nicely for laundering your money. But that's past business. What I'm talking about is payment to protect your future.''

Hassan absently stroked his cheek. ''Oh? And how can twenty million dollars protect my future?''

''Well, you see, Hassan, I kept a little diary of our business transactions.'' Craig noticed that Hassan didn't move so much as an eyebrow. The man was cool. He had to give him that. ''Now of course, I have no intention of using the information. I just thought I might need some protection. But if they were to come down hard on me and I was running short of funds . . . well, you see my point, don't you? It's nothing personal, you realize, just good business.''

''Yes. I see.''

''I don't think your associates, let alone your uncle, would be pleased to have their names bandied about in an investigation.''

''No. I see your point.'' Hassan nodded carefully.

''Good. Then you'll take care of the transaction?''

''Immediately,'' Hassan answered, his black eyes flat.

Craig watched as he picked up a nearby phone and spoke a few short sentences of Arabic.

Replacing the receiver he said, "The arrangements have been made."

Craig breathed a small sigh of relief, amazed that everything had gone so smoothly. Trust old Hassan not to quibble over a mere twenty million dollars. Maybe he should have asked for more.

The blustery spring storm finally ended and Ariane decided to take advantage of it by going for a walk. She'd been cooped up in the apartment all day and needed an escape.

There was an unusual freshness in the air that only a prolonged driving rain could bring to the city. The streets were relatively empty, the combination of the severe weather and late afternoon hour keeping shoppers home and dry.

Valentino's windows, starkly framed in black lacquer, beckoned and Ariane stopped to peer at the summer fashions. But the printed dresses were nearly overpowered by the unusual mannequins made of perfectly formed topiary. As she turned, the plate glass caught the light and reflected the other side of the street. In that instant she noticed a man across the avenue. There was nothing unusual about him except that he seemed to be looking in her direction. He was tall, wearing a dark suit and mirrored sunglasses. He turned away and Ariane strolled down the block, forgetting him.

She passed Armani's small window front, its unique setback from the street making it appear even more exclusive. Ungaro's large window trimmed in shiny silver displayed a variety of suits and Ariane entered, taken with the look of the trim black and white stripes.

Having tried on several suits, Ariane made her selection and waited while the saleswoman wrapped it.

She exited Ungaro, shifting her package to a more comfortable position, and came up sharply at the sight of the man across the street. It was the man with the mirrored sunglasses who had been watching her at Valentino's.

A prickling feeling ran along her spine. She turned toward home, her steps brisk. She came to the corner and glanced behind her, trying to appear casual. He was there. She jaywalked, not daring to wait for the light. Her steps were hurried, urgent. Her heart was pounding. She pretended to look in Charles Jourdan's window and saw the man again. She wanted to run, but she knew he could catch her easily. She had to get home.

No! She couldn't go home. Then he'd know where she lived. Where could she go? Sixty-first was a busy street, with the hotel's garage and service entrance. Ariane turned down Sixty-first, her steps racing. The block was long, endless.

She turned the corner onto Park Avenue. The entrance to the Regency Hotel was only steps away. Dashing around the planted flower boxes, she leaned against the limestone wall, breathing heavily.

A young, muscular doorman in a gray uniform approached her. "Excuse me, may I help you?"

"A man's been following me. A man in a dark suit with mirrored sunglasses." Ariane pointed in the direction.

The doorman followed Ariane's gesture and looked down the block. "I don't see anyone."

Ariane didn't believe him. She looked but no one was there. The man was gone.

Sitting on a black molded plastic chair in the atrium of IBM's midtown tower, Hassan impatiently drummed his fingers on the low round table. Tucked between soaring office buildings, the four-story indoor park was in shadow and offered no view of the street.

An exuberant young child tore loose from his mother and approached Hassan with a striped ball in his out-stretched hand. Hassan stared at the happy child. The smile on the four-year-old's mouth vanished and he ran away.

Hassan lit a cigarette and, letting the smoke out slowly, gazed up at the towering bamboo trees that dotted the area. The three hundred soaring columns of trees accen-tuated the starkness of the sanctuary.

Hassan saw Khazi enter and extended his hand, eager to accept the package his assistant was carrying.

While Khazi settled himself, Hassan opened the manila envelope and flipped through the photographs of the beau-tiful woman caught unaware by the zoom lens. There were slices of her life, walking down Madison Avenue, exiting Le Cirque, entering Chanel.

"Did she spot you?" Hassan asked.

"No." Khazi nervously stroked his cheek.

"Good. You know what you have to do next."

"Yes."

"Do it. I'll be waiting."

Ariane stood in the center of the Crystal Room in Tavern on the Green and looked around her at the amazing trans-formation. The room was ready for the show, with an hour to spare.

The carpenters and electricians had worked their magic and the room looked like something out of a fairy tale.

The large floor-to-ceiling windows were draped with layers of sheer white gauze, obscuring the garden outside, making it look hazy and dreamlike with thousands of tiny lights sparkling in the trees. Ivory curtains draped the car-peted stage. Tall palm trees dotted the periphery, providing a lush background for the exquisite arrangements of white peonies, tulips, and freesia.

Ariane ran backstage when the first guests began to arrive. Logan had invited the executives of the top department stores and their buyers, his business and personal friends, the media, and anyone else he deemed necessary to make Ariane's debut a success.

Backstage was a madhouse. Near-naked models searched the racks that held their costume changes and rummaged through their cartons, making sure they had the proper accessories. Glad for the diversion, Ariane was too busy helping the models dress to notice Logan standing in the doorway.

"Okay, everybody. It's showtime," he announced.

Ariane spun around, a bracelet in her hand, her expression a mixture of surprise and fear.

"It is?" she whispered, her black eyes wide with anticipation. She self-consciously smoothed the skirt of her black Moroccan silk dinner suit as though preparing to walk down the runway.

"Relax," Logan said softly as he wrapped his arm around her shoulders and hugged her briefly. "You're going to be a hit."

"Oh, Logan, I hope you're right. But how can you be so sure?"

"Shh. Because I'm always right. Now don't argue with the boss," he said before he left to get the models lined up for their entrance.

The music began to play and Ariane could see the stage lights shining through the curtain. She stood in the wings, her heart in her throat, as the first model made her entrance. Suddenly, she didn't feel anxious anymore. A welcoming calm overcame her, soothing her rattled nerves. She had done her best. It was out of her hands now. The powerful people seated out in front would decide if she was a success.

All too soon, Ariane heard the oohs and ahs as her last creation walked down the runway. As tradition dictated, it was a wedding dress and one of the designs she had created from her heart. The old-fashioned, traditional gown was made of layers upon layers of delicate white silk chiffon with a long, flowing train that gave the bride the illusion of fairly floating down the aisle. The fitted bodice had an overlay of delicate antique lace covered with thousands of hand-sewn seed pearls. Long lace sleeves ended in points below the wrist. The headpiece was an intricate ring of white babies' breath with seed pearls woven through, crowning the gauzy veil that blurred the model's face and trailed softly behind her. A bouquet of white tea roses and orange blossom completed the picture.

The show was over and as Ariane listened to the applause, she realized dazedly it was for her. One of the models came to get her and led her out onto the runway where the other models had gathered. Smiling shyly, her cheeks flushed, she nodded in acceptance and held out her hand toward Logan, who was standing in the wings. Even though they were her designs, it was Logan's production, and after letting the crowd appreciate Ariane alone, Logan joined her on stage. He smiled broadly at the crowd and, hugging Ariane to him, bent his white head and kissed her cheek.

"See, I told you," he whispered for her ears alone.

She looked up into his twinkling blue eyes and said simply, "Thank you."

Lost in the triumph of the moment, Ariane didn't see the tall, dark figure in the back of the room. Nor did she notice when he detached himself from the shadows and left.

Anticipating a success, Logan had arranged for champagne to be served after the show. Most of the guests remained, enjoying the debut of a new designer and the free champagne. Ariane mingled among the crowd, graciously accepting the proffered congratulations. She quickly found Gordon and Molly and was fairly crushed in Gordon's embrace listening to his, "I told you." Searching the crowd, Ariane found Jessica, who raved enthusiastically about her designs.

Ariane was recounting some near disasters to Jessica when she felt a pair of warm lips press to the side of her neck. Whirling about quickly in surprise, she saw Bennett's laughing face.

"Congratulations, my pet. You are a success. I always knew you'd make me proud," Bennett teased good-naturedly.

"Thank you, Bennett. I'm glad I didn't disappoint you."

"You never could," Bennett said a little too seriously, his green eyes too intent.

Sloane interrupted, fairly attacking Ariane, hugging her fiercely. "It was the greatest! I loved everything."

"Am I glad you're here," Ariane said and then looking in Bennett's direction, added quietly, "And just in time too."

"I know. The man has the hots for you." Sloane pulled back and said thoughtfully, "You seem different. I can't put my finger on it exactly, but I guess calmer or more relaxed would be it. I sensed an undercurrent of restlessness or nervousness in you the past couple of years, but it seems to have disappeared."

"It's work. I like how I feel."

"I don't buy it," Sloane said, shaking her head.

"Buy what?"

"That work and work alone can leave you looking this

good. There's a satisfied air about you I never noticed before. Christ, you're practically glowing.''

Ariane smiled mysteriously. "Let's just say I finally found out what I want and nothing is going to stop me from having it. Tell your mother she's brilliant.'' Ariane didn't want to tell Sloane about her feelings for Alex—not yet. They were too special and too intense. They were too good to share.

Ariane was dressed and ready to leave, but she decided to wait another half hour just to be on the safe side. Craig always left for work before eight, but she wanted to be sure she wouldn't run into him at the apartment, especially after their last encounter. Nine o'clock would do just fine.

Hilda was off on Mondays, and Ariane was relieved she wouldn't have to face the housekeeper's kind looks and sympathetic eyes. She didn't want sympathy, didn't need any. All she wanted was her grandmother's brooch that she had somehow left behind.

Thirty minutes later, when Ariane let herself into the apartment, she was assailed by a terrible overpowering smell. It was thick and cloying. Like bad meat. Hilda must have forgotten to empty the trash. She went to the kitchen, looking for the offensive garbage and, not finding it, proceeded to the library and its safe.

She froze in the doorway. The room was a shambles. Every book was pulled down from the mahogany bookshelves. One-of-a-kind first editions and priceless antique books lay in a heap like worthless trash. The gold, green, and blue leatherbound copies were ripped apart, their covers scattered.

She turned to leave and stopped in her tracks. Oh God! Craig. He lay face down on the forest green carpet. Her hand flew to her mouth, stifling a scream. A large black circle stained the carpet beneath him. Blood. Too much blood. He had to be dead.

She gagged, the bitter taste of bile filling her mouth. She ran from the room. From the sickly sweet stench that was suffocating her. The smell of death.

chapter 21

Ariane paced the lobby, waiting for the police to answer the 911 call she had placed at the doorman's console. Finally, two men in plain clothes arrived. The large, burly man with sandy brown hair, mustache, and sharp blue eyes approached her. He introduced himself as Detective Lyons and his partner as Detective Murphy, a man of slighter proportions with dark hair and soft brown eyes.

The doorman looked on curiously as Ariane led the two detectives upstairs. At the door to the apartment Detective Lyons stopped and took out a small notebook and a pen.

"What did you touch, exactly?" he asked.

Ariane paused, trying to gather her thoughts. "The front door."

"What else?"

"Nothing." She was in a movie. A very bad movie.

"You're sure?" But the blue eyes were too sharp and too professional.

"Yes."

"Would you show us where you found him, ma'am?" Detective Lyons pushed open the door with his pen and motioned Ariane inside.

"Do I really have to go back in there?"

"I'm afraid so."

The smell nauseated her, but she steeled herself and walked through the marble foyer, her steps sure and definite. When she turned down the hallway, however, she faltered. Turning her back to the doorway she said, "In there."

Detective Murphy looked at her and said kindly, "Why don't you wait outside, Mrs. Wakefield? And thank you."

Ariane stood in the hallway outside the apartment trying not to think, trying not to feel. She turned her mind off, not wanting to deal with it, unable to.

Later. She would deal with it later.

She didn't know how long she had been standing there when a man carrying a black suitcase arrived. Soon two other men appeared, wheeling a stretcher.

"Ma'am," Detective Murphy said, holding open the door. "Would you mind coming back inside? We'd like to ask you a few questions. From the condition of the room it looks like your husband surprised a burglary in process. The burglar panicked and . . ."

Ariane followed him back to the library and hesitated briefly at the doorway. A sound caught her attention and she automatically turned in the direction of the noise.

The two men were zipping up a large, dark green plastic bag. It was a body bag. Craig's body bag.

They lifted the bag onto the stretcher and rolled it out. A corner was hanging off the stretcher and it brushed her leg as they passed.

The smell. Craig. The blood. The bag. The room was receding, sounds fading. A thick gray fog enveloped her, suffocated her. She welcomed its soothing, blanketing cold. Her vision was fuzzy and obscured. She barely heard her name being called as though from a great distance. It was far easier to sink into the coldness than try and answer.

Someone was pushing something between her lips and pouring a liquid into her mouth. She swallowed reflexively and choked, coughing as the fiery liquid burned her throat. She shook her head against the unwanted intrusion only to feel more of the liquid forced into her mouth.

"Mrs. Wakefield? Can you hear me?"

Ariane tried to focus and saw Detective Murphy peering at her closely.

"Are you all right?" He seemed concerned.

"Yes, I'm fine." She looked around, surprised to discover herself sitting on the library sofa.

"Take a deep breath. You'll be all right."

"Ma'am, do you feel up to answering a few questions?" Detective Lyons asked.

The brandy had driven the chill from her body, and she determinedly pulled herself together. "Yes."

"From what you already told us I gather you haven't been back to the apartment since you left in November. Is that correct?"

"Yes." Had it only been seven months? It seemed like a lifetime ago.

"And as far as you know no one has keys except your husband, the housekeeper, and yourself?"

"Yes." What was all this nonsense about keys? They said Craig had surprised a burglar in the act and the burglar had panicked.

"Would you mind taking a look around and seeing if anything is missing?"

Ariane rose somewhat unsteadily and glanced around at the disarray. "I can't tell about this room. I had already taken all my jewelry when I left."

"What about the rest of the apartment?"

The detectives followed Ariane as she passed down the hallway and entered the living room.

She stood at the entrance to the grand room, her gaze drifting about the space. Everything was there. The paintings were hanging in their places, the Giacometti and Brancusi sculptures were present, the several silver pieces from Buccellati were there. Her eyes stopped. Something was wrong.

Everything was there. But it had all been moved, very slightly, but enough for her to notice. A chill went down her spine.

"Everything's been moved," Ariane said.

"You sure?" Detective Lyons asked.

"Yes."

This time when she walked through the apartment inspecting the other rooms, her steps were quick and sure. The detectives followed closely.

"Everything's a little off," Ariane said after her inventory. Every room had been carefully scoured. Something was horribly wrong. Why was the apartment so thoroughly searched? And why so neatly, as though the burglar didn't want it known that he had gone through the apartment?

Fear shivered inside her and she couldn't wait to leave the apartment.

The moment Khazi let himself into the suite at the Pierre, Hassan's voice called, "Did you get it?"

Khazi entered the living room, took the object from his pocket, and handed it to Hassan. He watched, his expression blank as Hassan fingered the delicate shimmering black silk and then held the woman's camisole up to his face and, closing his eyes, inhaled her scent.

We're in trouble, Khazi thought, *again.* He recognized the familiar signs. Only this time Khazi was truly worried.

He'd never seen Hassan so consumed. He was obsessed with this woman, making him follow her, making him break into her apartment and steal her lingerie. And Khazi knew exactly where all this was leading.

"Did you have any trouble?" Hassan asked, breaking into Khazi's thoughts.

"No. I waited until she left for work."

"Anybody see you?"

"No. The security in that building is a joke."

Hassan sat on the blue and yellow sofa, idly rubbing the silk against his thin cheek. "You can go now," he said absently.

Khazi left, glad for the dismissal.

Why couldn't Hassan stick to prostitutes, unimportant women? Khazi wondered. Women who could disappear with no one caring or even noticing. Hassan's fetish for wealthy, long-haired beauties had already caused them to flee their homeland. If he did this one, they'd have to leave New York and possibly the country. And Khazi didn't want to have to make a fresh start . . . again. Hassan was entitled to his fun. Every man was. But this game was getting old—fast.

The day of the funeral dawned a dark, dismal gray, the threat of rain heavy in the chilled air. *How perfectly appropriate,* Ariane thought as she laid out her clothes. Opening her lingerie drawer, she took out her sheer black stockings and reached for her black silk camisole. It wasn't there.

She looked for it everywhere and couldn't find it. Assuming she had missed it the first time around, she pulled the peach lacquer drawers open all the way and began removing all her lingerie. Clouds of silk from the palest ivory to the richest black decorated the pale bedroom, the drawers to the custom-designed dresser yawning open, adding to the unusual disarray.

It wasn't like her to lose something; she never did. It'll probably turn up eventually, Ariane decided, not really believing it.

Something told her it was gone for good. And she didn't like it.

She sat at the window and waited for Russ and Kristen to pick her up. Russ had been a godsend to her during these past few days as they had prepared for the funeral. He had been at her side when she had gone to the funeral parlor to make the arrangements and had volunteered to identify Craig's body at the morgue.

She had tried to reach Sloane and Justin but they were on a safari. She would just have to go it alone.

But she wasn't alone, Ariane thought as she looked around at the people crowding the cemetery. It seemed as if all of Wall Street was there. Brad and Maggie, Stuart and Joanna, Eric and Melissa, Clayton and Lydia, Kit and Ellie were in the first line, and there were scores of other familiar faces behind them. Logan, Gordon, and Molly had quietly greeted Ariane and then stood off to the side. Jessica hugged her briefly before moving away to stand with Logan and Gordon.

Ariane kept her dark sunglasses on throughout the service despite the sunless day, but nobody seemed to think it peculiar. They assumed it only natural that she would want to hide her tear-filled eyes. She was hiding behind the safety of her dark glasses, but her eyes were dry. *I wonder what they'd all think of that,* she mused, blocking out the words of the service. The truth was, she hadn't shed a tear since Craig had died. The only emotion she had felt in days was guilt—guilt that she wasn't overcome with grief and loss. Her husband was dead, murdered, and she couldn't cry. What was wrong with her?

Shaking the upsetting thought from her mind, she covertly glanced around the crowd. Her eyes quickly slipped from one face to another as if she was searching for something. A light drizzle had begun to fall, wetting her glasses, blurring her vision. Quickly, the drizzle turned to a soft, steady rain, causing a handful of black umbrellas to spring open. How odd, she thought, that she and Kristen should be sharing an umbrella together in the rain at Craig's funeral. Then she realized she felt none of the old animosity toward her. Kristen had been unusually subdued during the ride to the cemetery after she had stiltedly offered her sympathies. She seemed truly upset over Craig's death, and Ariane couldn't help wondering if maybe Kristen had loved Craig and he had used her. In a strange, detached way she felt sorry for her.

The onset of a heavy downpour effectively ended the service, sending the mourners scurrying for the dry comfort of their limousines. Russ led Ariane and Kristen, their heads bowed against the rain, toward the car. Kristen ducked quickly into the car and Ariane was about to follow when she heard a familiar voice that made her heart race. She turned to see Alex talking to Russ.

"My condolences," Alex offered, turning his attention to her.

"Thank you." She felt a lump rise in her throat and suddenly she did feel like crying, crying against Alex's broad shoulder. She stood, oblivious to the rain that was soaking her, as she drew comfort from the fact that he was standing beside her, looking so strong, so safe.

"I won't keep you. I just wanted to pay my respects." He reached out to cup her elbow to help her into the car.

But Ariane didn't move. She stared into Alex's dark face, conscious of the gentleness of his touch and well aware that he didn't let her go.

"Thank you. We appreciate it. I'll be in touch," Russ said.

They shook hands and with a polite nod to her, Alex turned and was gone, disappearing into the crowd.

The ache of sadness that had begun when she saw Alex spread to engulf her painfully, choking her with despair. Just as the emotion of seeing Alex had released her feelings, she knew only Alex could help her now. But he was gone. He was always leaving her.

Hassan stood on Fifth Avenue, the street dappled with shade. He didn't take his eyes off the building across the way while his foot impatiently ground out a cigarette on the gray cobblestones.

When the doorman went inside to answer a ringing telephone, Hassan glanced at his watch. Right on time.

Hassan waited for the green light and crossed the street.

By the time he got to the front door of the building the doorman was in the mailroom, checking the tenant's question, allowing Hassan to enter unnoticed.

Ariane left her attorney's office in midtown and turned up Park Avenue, her mind in a daze. The rush-hour traffic was barely moving, horns blaring, drivers impatient. But Ariane was unaware of the commotion around her. She had been to a reading of Craig's will. He had left her everything, the apartment, the art collection, his portfolio, a life insurance policy worth millions—everything. She shouldn't have been surprised at his worth, but the fact that it was all hers and hers alone came as a shock.

Their attorney, Todd Caswell, had been solicitous of Ariane, inquiring after her well-being and offering his sympathies and services. But Todd's kindness combined with the largeness of the estate had left Ariane feeling ill at ease and guilty. They had been separated and she knew it had only been a matter of time before she filed for divorce. Why should she benefit from his death? She decided to walk home, needing the time to absorb the news.

By the time she reached her block, her long walk in the late afternoon sun had left her feeling hot and tired. As she entered the coolness of her apartment building's lobby, all she could think of was slipping out of her pumps, undressing, and finding something cold to drink.

Ariane closed the door behind her and dropped her purse on the marble console. On the way to her bedroom, she began removing the pins from her hair, shaking it loose, letting it fall down her back.

She reached her bedroom and froze. Shock and fear rushed at her. Her eyes quickly took in the open drawers, the spilled lingerie, the dark figure of a man. "Hassan."

chapter 22

With Hassan not appearing at Craig's funeral, Alex was afraid he might disappear now that his contact was gone. Alex also had a distinct feeling that Hassan had something to do with Craig's death. Things were moving too quickly and too violently for Alex's taste. But it wasn't his own safety that concerned him.

There were too many unanswered questions, and it was time he got some answers. He was tired of sitting around and waiting, tired of taking orders. After making a phone call that went unanswered, he left his town house. He knew what he had to do.

The lobby of the Pierre offered no security to speak of and Alex made his way directly to the bank of elevators.

He stood in front of Hassan's suite, removed a small black leather case from the inside pocket of his jacket, and extracted a thin metal rod. In seconds he had picked the door's lock.

Alex closed the door behind him, his expert gaze quickly

evaluating the room. Systematically, he searched the reproduction Chippendale desk, knowing he would find nothing.

In the bedroom his eyes briefly registered the brass headboard before turning to the mahogany dresser. He pulled open the drawers, looking for something, anything.

He rifled the contents of the drawer quickly, not bothering to be careful, not caring. His fingers brushed an envelope and he pulled it out. He opened it up, sliding the contents into his hand.

His blood ran cold. They were photographs. Photographs of Ariane. Entering a store. Leaving a restaurant. Walking down the street. She had been followed all over the city.

A hard knot of fear formed in the pit of his stomach. He continued searching, his movements hurried but thorough, not daring to miss a thing.

The delicate black bit of silk took Alex by surprise and he pulled out the fabric. A camisole. And judging by the size, a petite woman. He buried his face in the silk and breathed in the unmistakable scent of Ariane's perfume. Sickening dread flooded his body, leaving his knees weak.

He grabbed the phone and dialed.

"Get over to Ariane's right away. Don't ask questions. Just do it. I'm on my way."

"Ariane." Hassan seemed perfectly at ease as he lounged against her dresser.

"What the hell are you doing here?" She forced her voice to sound strong but she unconsciously took a step backward. If she ran he could catch her. She mustn't panic.

"I didn't think you'd return so quickly," he said. "But never mind. It doesn't matter." There was a suggestion of a grin on Hassan's thin face as he ignored her question and moved forward.

"You'd better leave," Ariane ordered. Her mouth went dry; she couldn't swallow. She couldn't let Hassan know how afraid she was. Turning toward the living room, she prayed he would follow.

"Where is it?" Hassan's voice was flat.

Ariane turned around. Hassan hadn't moved. "Where's what?" she asked automatically.

"The diary."

"I don't keep a diary." Her heart pounded. She couldn't stand being alone with him. In her bedroom.

"Not your diary. Craig's." Hassan stepped forward, the black eyes hard and icy. "I want it."

"I don't have it. Now would you please leave?" Ariane turned but Hassan grabbed her arm, spinning her around. She tried to wrest her arm free, but his bony fingers dug painfully into her flesh.

"Let go of me!"

"I want the diary. Do you understand?" The black eyes looked dead.

"I don't have it! I don't even know what you're talking about!" He was dangerous. She could feel it. She could smell it. As she kicked out blindly, the heel of her pump caught him on the shin.

With a howl of pain, Hassan released her. She raced for the front door. She saw the knob and stretched out her hand, reaching, straining for it. But before she could touch it, her head jerked back as Hassan grabbed her hair and yanked her to her knees.

Alex saw the cab coming up Fifth Avenue and ran to it, cutting ahead of the couple who had flagged it down. The man cursed at him, but Alex was already inside ordering his destination to the driver.

The cab turned up Madison Avenue and became ensnarled in the traffic. It only moved inches and stopped.

The light turned red, then green, but still they didn't move. Fear pumped in Alex, a fear he had never known.

Frantic, he jumped out of the cab and began running.

Ariane scrambled to her feet, twisted around, and clamped her teeth down on Hassan's hand. He let go of her hair. She tried to fight her way around him, but he blocked her path. She whirled and bolted for the service entrance. She lost her footing on the slick marble floor, giving Hassan the advantage. Grabbing her, he threw her into the wall. His hands went around her throat and he squeezed, almost gently.

"I want it. And I'm not leaving without it." His hot breath was stale, reeking of cigarettes.

"I told you I don't have it." She clawed at his hands, desperate, trying to pry his fingers loose.

Hassan made a horrible sound, like a sickening laugh as he slammed her head against the wall. Things went black for an instant, but she came out of the daze kicking and fighting. Her hands tore at Hassan's grip. The deadly gleam in his black eyes terrified her. She clutched at his face, raking her nails down his cheek.

Hassan grabbed at his bleeding face and Ariane ducked beneath his arm and ran. She sprinted around the sofa to avoid his reach and collided with the glass coffee table. A Gallé vase fell, shattering on the marble floor. She staggered momentarily, pain shooting up her leg.

Hassan tackled her from behind and hurled her face down onto the burled wood desk. He threw himself on top of her, reaching for her arms. An inkwell cut into her chest.

Ariane thrashed and bucked wildly beneath him. Frantic, she groped for a weapon. The Tiffany lamp went flying, crashing to the floor. Priceless art objects became projectiles shattering on the floor.

Her hand closed around the letter opener and she stabbed blindly behind her, catching him in the arm. He snatched the opener from her and threw it across the floor. Distracted by his wound, Ariane was able to flip herself over.

She panted heavily, her throat raw. She went for his face again but he grabbed her wrists and pinned them to the desk. She tried to kick him, but he anticipated her move and blocked it. And then she saw the look in his eye. The maniacal gleam. He was insane.

Hassan leaned forward, rubbing himself against her, his blood-crazed lust obvious.

Oh, God. He's going to rape me and kill me, she thought. More than anything else the deadly look of pleasure in the dead black eyes petrified her. He was enjoying this. She bucked, fighting for her life. She never saw the fist coming that made her world go black.

Pain. She was in terrible pain. All over. The blackness was lifting. The more it lifted, the more she hurt. Her leg stung. Her jaw throbbed, the pain shooting into her ear. She wanted to go back to sleep, back to the darkness. There was no pain there. Nothing.

No! She couldn't go back to sleep. If she slept, he would kill her. She had to escape.

Her eyes fluttered open, her vision blurred at first. Her eyesight cleared and she saw him. Hassan sat in front of her, watching her.

She tried to get up, but she couldn't move. She was tied to the desk chair. Looking down, fear knotted in her throat at the sight of her legs stretched apart and tied to the legs of the chair. Tied with her stockings. The stockings she had been wearing. Her narrow skirt was hiked up around her thighs. Each arm was tied to an arm of the chair. The jacket to her suit had been removed, revealing her white silk blouse.

"You're crazy! You won't get away with this." She didn't notice the pain that shot up her jaw when she spoke.

Hassan's mouth twitched. "I already have." He rose and came toward her. He grabbed the thick mass of her hair and entwined it around his arm, the movement almost sensual.

Ariane tried to turn her head away only to have him jerk her hair. He fingered the silken strands.

"See? I can do whatever I want. Nobody can stop me." Suddenly, he let go of her hair, and reaching into his pocket, he withdrew a silver metal object. He held it in front of Ariane's face and pushed a button to release the deadly blade of the stiletto.

Ariane's eyes went wide with fear. "Don't! Please! I won't say anything to anybody. Just let me go."

Hassan ignored her pleas and reached for her. Ariane watched in horror as the blade came toward her and cut through her blouse, separating it at the shoulder. He tugged the sleeve down, exposing her arm.

Hassan dropped the knife to the coffee table, the sound of metal striking glass loud in the silent apartment. He reached into his pocket again and withdrew two small objects. She couldn't see what he was doing as he fumbled with them. Then he held the objects up in the air and she saw the syringe and small ampule.

He was going to kill her with drugs. "Let me go. Please. You can get away before someone comes."

Hassan filled the syringe and tapped it, releasing any air bubbles. "No one's coming. No one can save you."

He moved toward her, holding the syringe upright. She thrashed and twisted in the chair, wrenching her body away from him.

Hassan retreated and then the stiletto was at her throat.

"Don't make this any more unpleasant than it has to be."
His black eyes bored into her, flat and indifferent.

The point of the blade pressed into the base of her
throat. She could feel its razor-sharp tip pricking her skin.
She froze.

"That's better." As Hassan spoke she could feel him
dragging the tip down her chest. It hurt and she wondered
briefly if she were bleeding. But she didn't dare take her
eyes off him.

Hassan threw the blade aside and picked up the syringe.
This time she didn't move. His odor was rancid, repug-
nant as he leaned over her. She flinched when he jabbed
the needle into her.

She watched as he tossed the syringe onto the carpet
and sat down on the sofa across from her. She waited to
die. But she didn't feel as if she were dying. She was
fainting. Very slowly. She had fainted with the detectives
and she remembered the faraway feeling. Hassan looked
fuzzy, as if he were moving away from her. The room
grew blurry around the edges, the haziness moving closer
and closer. A thick fog was wrapping around her.

She was falling down a deep, dark hole. There was
nothing to stop her fall. She tried to fight, to catch herself,
but she kept falling. Faster and farther until there was
nothing. Nothing but a void.

Hassan glanced at his watch. It was time. She should be
under.

"Ariane," his voice was sharp. "Can you hear me?"
She didn't answer. "Answer me," he ordered.
"Yes."
"Did Craig keep a diary?"
"I don't know."
"Where is Craig's diary?"

"I don't know."

Hassan was getting annoyed. "Did you ever see Craig write in a diary or journal, anything?"

"No."

Hassan believed her. Or rather he believed the drug. He'd questioned her long enough. He'd had enough business. It was time for fun.

He picked up the knife and, holding Ariane's blouse in his grip, sliced the front open. The white silk fell away, revealing a delicate ivory camisole. He pushed the tip of the blade between the spaces of the fragile lace trim, playing with the fine netting. He made the hole bigger and bigger.

Hassan had waited a long time for this, for this woman. He was going to enjoy it, every minute of it.

The sidewalks of Madison Avenue were jammed with people on their way home. Alex raced along the gutter, dodging cars. He ignored the changing light, not seeing the cab coming at him. The taxi screeched to a halt only inches from him.

Alex slammed his fist on the hood and ran on.

Oh God, the apartment was turning to quicksand again. The walls, the floor, the furniture. There was nothing but a thick, sludgy mass sucking at her. She had to get out. But she couldn't escape. It held her trapped. It was pulling her down, further and further. Scream. *Scream,* her mind ordered. But her voice was no more than a whisper. No one could hear her. No one could save her.

It was alive. Horribly alive. It felt like hands reaching for her, pulling at her. It grabbed at her legs, her thighs. It was moving up her body, dragging her down. The thickness crushed her midriff. She couldn't breathe. It was up to her chest, pressing, crushing the air from her. She was smothering, choking. Dying.

Hands were pulling at her. But these hands were different. They didn't hurt. They were pulling her up, freeing her. The quicksand was below her chest. She could breathe easier. The gentle hands lifted her and the quicksand was at her waist, her legs. She could move. The sand was receding, disappearing.

Someone was talking, calling to her. It was hard to hear. The voice was familiar. She liked the voice.

"You're all right, baby. You're safe. I've got you."

Instinctively, her arms went around his neck. She gazed up at him, her eyes clear for a moment. Then she closed them and whispered, "Alex."

The front door was open and Travis rushed into Ariane's apartment. He was momentarily stunned by the destruction. Vases were smashed, accessories lay shattered. The red, blue, and green glass fragments of a priceless Tiffany lamp formed a prism, the sun sending streaks of color into the room.

And then Travis saw Alex and Ariane. Alex was holding her closely, protectively. She was barely dressed in what was left of a silk camisole. She appeared to be sleeping.

"What the hell happened?" Travis asked. His eyes went to Ariane and he noticed the beginning of a bruise on her jaw, the ugly contusion startling against her white skin.

"Hassan." The name sounded like poison on Alex's tongue.

"Is she all right?"

"She will be."

Travis saw the concern in Alex's eyes, heard the emotion he'd never witnessed before, and he knew. Alex loved Ariane. For a fleeting moment Travis was jealous, but he quickly forgot his own feelings in the face of reality. It was inevitable. It had been from the beginning.

"What'd he give her?"

Alex gestured to the ampule and syringe on the carpet. "Pentothal."

"Did you call it in?"

"No." The silver eyes were hard. "I'll take care of it." There was a flicker of something in Alex's eyes that made him nervous.

"Maybe you should let someone else take over," Travis suggested.

"No. This is personal." Alex gently laid Ariane back against the sofa. She reached for him in her sleep and he tenderly folded her arms together. Then he took off his charcoal linen jacket and slipped it over her near nakedness. The sensitivity of his actions was completely at odds with the rigid set of his jaw, with the suppressed rage that made his hands shake.

"Alex, don't." Travis grabbed Alex's arm as he passed him.

Alex shook it off. "Stay with her." There was a murderous rage in his eyes and then he was gone.

Alex kicked open the door to Hassan's suite, sending it crashing into the wall. He stormed toward the bedroom, his blood boiling.

Hassan came through the door and Alex's fist smashed into his face. Reeling from the blow, Hassan staggered into the bedroom and tripped on an open suitcase. Before he could recover, Alex was on him. He grabbed him by the collar and hauled him to his feet.

Hassan came up fighting. A side hook caught Alex by surprise. Alex shook his head and punched Hassan in the stomach. Hassan doubled over. Alex slammed his fist into Hassan's jaw, snapping his head up.

Alex was larger, but Hassan was fighting for his life. He punched and kicked, managing to hurt Alex with several well-placed blows. But visions of Ariane filled Alex's head, the ampule, the syringe. She had been that close to becoming another morgue shot. Deadly rage made Alex forget his professional training, his cool detachment. He was out for blood—Hassan's blood.

Hassan fell back and Alex went for his throat. But he froze at the sound of the deadly click. Hassan held the stiletto in his hand, flaunting it at Alex.

"I believe the advantage is mine. Game. Set. Match." Hassan wheezed heavily.

The silver eyes didn't even flicker. Alex looked cool and relaxed. "Your game is up. You're finished."

"Not quite. I was interrupted this afternoon."

Alex lunged at him, going for Hassan's wrist. The Arab cut him, slicing open his forearm before Alex could grab his arm. They grappled for the knife, twisting and turning in a deadly dance of mortal combat.

Their breath was hot in each other's faces. The smell of fear filled the room.

Hassan's arm faltered for a split second and that was all Alex needed to drive the stiletto home. The razor-sharp blade pierced flesh and muscle.

Silver eyes locked with black eyes as Alex waited for the Arab to fall.

Moments later, he stood over the body, watching as the pool of Hassan's blood spread on his white shirt. His dead eyes stared up at the ceiling, their unfeeling gaze no different in death than they had been in life.

It was over. She was safe.

Alex turned and left, the grisly scene behind him already forgotten.

He had more important things on his mind. Ariane needed him and he had to be there.

• • •

"Are you all right?" Travis asked, staring at Alex's blood-stained arm.

"Yeah." Alex went directly to the bar and poured a large amount of brandy into a crystal highball.

"Hassan?"

Alex took a deep swallow of the brandy. "It's over. How is she?" Alex glanced at Ariane, still on the sofa.

"She hasn't moved."

"You can go. I'll stay." Then, as an afterthought, he added, "You might want to have someone take care of the mess at the Pierre."

Travis nodded and left the apartment. Alex fell into a club chair and watched Ariane sleeping on the sofa. The room was darkening, long fingers of golden sunlight giving it a warm peach glow. But the warmth didn't touch him. He had come that close . . . Suddenly, he jumped up, unable to sit still.

Alex looked out the window at the orange sun that was dipping low over the green trees of Central Park. He stared, oblivious to the bucolic scene, seeing only Ari as she was when he rescued her, her eyes unfocused, wild with fear. His insides twisted.

And then he remembered those black eyes, so vibrant, so revealing. They sparkled with gaiety, twinkled mischievously. He had seen them pained and troubled, confused and frightened. They blazed with the fire of anger. But the glow in Ari's eyes when she made love was the best.

Christ, how he wanted her, more than he had ever wanted anyone, more than he thought possible. Wanted that perfect body, hot and passionate, writhing with desire in his arms. Wanted her warm and cuddly as she nestled against him so trusting. He longed to hear her laughter as it rippled through him, making him feel . . .

He went to the bar to refill his glass. His fingers slipped and he dropped the crystal stopper on the glass bar, the sound sharp in the quiet room. He quickly glanced over at Ariane. Her eyes snapped open.

"Alex?" Ariane looked at him, confused, a hint of fear in her voice.

He put down his glass and went to her. "I'm here." He crouched in front of her. Her eyes were still dilated, the drug still in her system.

She searched his face and then her gaze fell to his arm. "You're hurt."

He had forgotten all about it. "It's nothing."

Her eyes filled with tears. "No. You're hurt. You're bleeding." She began to cry.

Alex sat beside her on the sofa and gathered her in his arms, holding her to him. "Shh. Don't cry, Ari love." He rubbed her back. The sound of her crying tore at him, hurting him more than any wound.

Her face was buried in the side of his neck and he could feel the wetness of her tears on his skin.

"Where . . . where is . . . ?" Ariane asked between sobs.

"He's gone. Gone for good. It's over," Alex murmured. "It's all over." His voice was tender, caressing, as gentle as his hands that stroked her body.

Ariane's sobs quieted but she didn't move. Her face rubbed against the crook in his shoulder, her lips brushing his neck, her action reminding him of a contented kitten.

"I love you," she said with a sigh.

Alex peered intently into her face as though trying to see into her soul. Her face was streaked with the evidence of her tears, the thick black lashes wet, looking like star points. He searched her face hungrily, questioningly, looking for something he couldn't name. Her dark eyes stared back at him, honestly and openly, their look painfully revealing, inviting his inspection.

The emotion in those eyes alarmed and frightened him, yet oddly excited him.

His gaze fell to her generous mouth and, without thinking, he leaned forward and gently touched her lips. But Ariane's mouth held his, demanding more.

Alex scooped her up into his arms and she held onto him tightly, burying her face in his neck.

He carried her to the bedroom and made love to her long into the night. Their lovemaking was a celebration of her having survived, an exaltation of being alive. There was no beginning, no end, just the two of them . . . together . . . and the night.

She didn't want to wake up but something tugged at her consciousness, pushing her awake. Her eyes felt heavy and it was an effort to open them. The room was flooded with sunlight and she squinted against the brightness. And then she saw him. He was sitting on the bed, watching her. She smiled slowly, a warm contented smile.

"How do you feel?" Alex asked, his eyes searching her face. He was dressed in fresh clothes.

"Okay."

"Travis is in the living room. He's going to take you out to the beach. I think it's best if you leave the city."

"Where are you going?"

"I have things I have to take care of. Business." Ariane's gaze fell to Alex's wound and she understood.

"Will you be back?" She wasn't about to let him off the hook so easily. She was tired of him breezing in and out of her life. She wanted more.

He gently smoothed back a lock of her hair. His eyes looked troubled. "I don't know."

He was leaving her. Again. Would he ever stop running from her?

"Really, Travis, you can go. I'm fine," Ariane said as she persuaded Travis to leave the beach house. They had been there for three days and she wanted to be alone. There had been no word from Alex.

"Okay, but call me if you need anything," he said as he got into his car.

What I need you can't give me, Ariane thought.

Changed into a bikini, Ariane stood outside on the patio to enjoy the early quiet of the morning. Dew shimmered on the grass like specks of diamonds. Her garden was in bloom, the cool whiteness of the clematis, lilacs, and impatiens in full bloom. The sparkling pool beckoned in the sun; a bob-white called out his name.

Entering the pool quickly, Ariane swam long, easy strokes back and forth. She swam slowly, enjoying the warm water against her skin in contrast to the cool morning air under the shining sun. She swam enough to make her tired, climbed from the pool, and quickly donned her terry-cloth robe. Peering about to make sure no one was around, she deftly slipped off her wet bikini from beneath the robe.

She settled herself comfortably on a double-sized lounge. Wrapped cozily in her robe, she felt herself growing pleasantly languorous under the warming sun. She felt as if she could doze off right now. Giving in to the languid feeling, she let her mind wander dreamily, thinking how wonderful it would be if Alex was here just before she fell asleep. He'd kiss her and hold her and love her. Her dream seemed so real she didn't want to wake up and tried hard to capture the feeling in her sleep. *If only this was real,* she thought dreamily.

In her dream she lifted her arms and wrapped them around Alex, holding him, feeling his strength, never wanting to let go. Alex's mouth was soft and tender as it took hers, gently, and then hungrily. She returned his kiss, his mouth so passionate and sensuous against her own. She felt him untying the sash on her robe and when he parted the robe she could feel the cool air on her nakedness. It seemed so real that in surprise and against her will, Ariane opened her eyes.

"You're real," Ariane blurted in shock as she stared up into Alex's clear silver eyes, only to be met by a raised black brow.

"I . . . I mean, I was dreaming. I thought I was dreaming."

"Oh?" Alex asked, studying her features closely, his own expression guarded.

"Yes. I was dreaming of you," Ariane answered candidly, her emotions plain to see.

Alex bent his head then and captured her mouth in a deep, intense kiss that touched her very soul. He gathered her slender form to him and pressed her body against him as she wound her arms around him. Her head was spinning with the passion of his kiss, a thousand questions tumbling through her mind. Her bare breasts pressed against his chambray shirt and she struggled to get closer. There was a fire burning in her that had nothing to do with the heat of the sun.

Suddenly, he pushed away from her only to quickly remove his shirt and slide her robe from her shoulders before embracing her again.

She ran her hands over his strong back, feeling his muscles tense as he settled them down on the chaise. Then he lay down beside her, and they melted together. Their arms and legs wrapped around each other so completely that she couldn't tell where one started and the other stopped.

They made love outside in the clear light of day and it was as if it was the first time. The past and all its troubles melted away in the clean burning flame of their love. She opened her heart to him, offering herself completely, letting her love speak for her as she muttered his name over and over. This was different from all the times before. She felt herself consumed by his insatiable passion as he took them to a shining place of ecstasy that left them breathless.

Afterward she gently touched the perspiration on his forehead, only to have him capture her hand and tenderly kiss her palm. His black hair was tousled, his features relaxed.

"I love you, Alex," she stated plainly, needing to say it in the daylight, after their passion had been quenched.

"I know," he said as he gently touched his lips to hers.

"But how much?"

"Enough." There was a tightness in her chest.

"Enough to give up everything and spend the rest of your life with me?"

"Are you asking me to?" A constriction in her throat made breathing impossible.

"Yes, damnit!" he almost exploded.

"Well you don't have to shout," she shot back, annoyed at his inability to give her what she needed so desperately.

"Jesus, Ari, I almost lost you. When I think how close . . ." His voice was pained. "I love you. I want to marry you. What more do you want?" he asked exasperated. His features softened, making him look boyish.

"Nothing, my love," she said, her answer clear as she stroked his cheek.

"Ari, I love you. I need you for my life. I have nothing without you," he whispered, softly this time, with his heart, before he kissed her with a yearning tenderness that made her heart ache with love.

He wrapped her in his warm embrace and she thought

it was as if she had been lost and being in Alex's arms was coming home. As she tilted her head back to better look at her beloved's face, Ariane thought how bright the sun was but not as bright as the love shining in Alex's eyes.